Walt Disney's

UNCLE SCROOGE

Himalayan Hideout

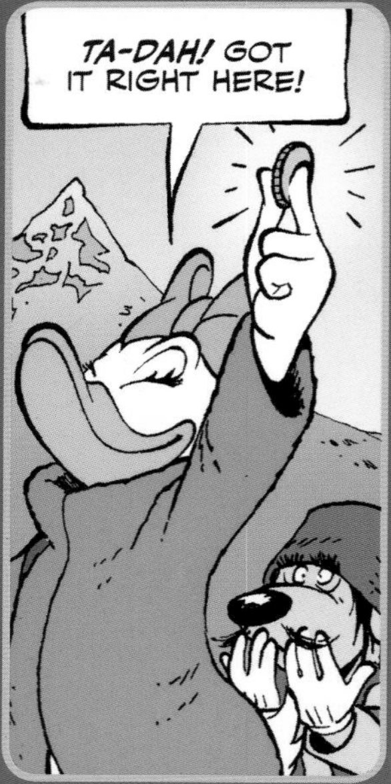
TA-DAH! GOT IT RIGHT HERE!

Himalayan Hideout

From Swedish *Kalle Anka & C:o* #26-28/2013
Writer: Jens Hansegård
Artist: Francisco Rodriguez Peinado
Colorists: Digikore Studios with Nicole and Travis Seitler
Letterers: Nicole and Travis Seitler
Dialogue: Gary Leach

Gum Disease

From Italian *Topolino* #2511, 2004
Writer and Artist: Enrico Faccini
Colorists: Disney Italia with David Gerstein
Letterers: Nicole and Travis Seitler
Translation and Dialogue: David Gerstein

The Glomgold Heritage

From Norwegian *Donald Duck & Co.* #24/2015
Writer: Lars Jensen
Artist: Marco Rota
Colorists: Digikore Studios with David Gerstein
Letterers: Nicole and Travis Seitler
Dialogue: Lars Jensen and David Gerstein

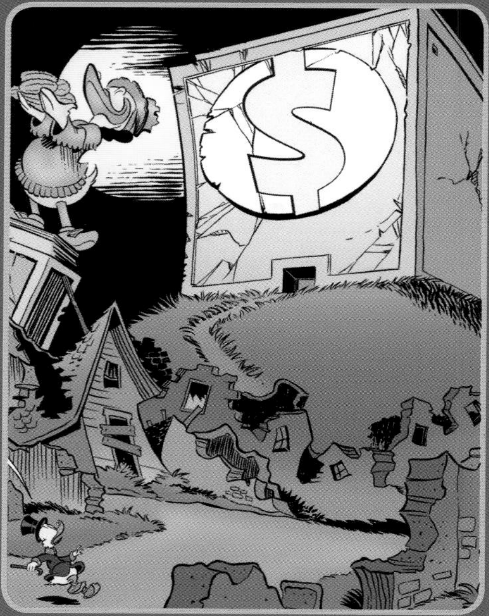

When Magica Won

From Swedish *Kalle Anka & C:o* #39/2014
Writer: Olaf Solstrand
Artist: Noel Van Horn
Colorist: Digikore Studios
Letterers: Nicole and Travis Seitler
Dialogue: Byron Erickson

Special thanks to Daniel Saeva, Julie Dorris, Manny Mederos, Roberto Santillo, Chris Troise, Camilla Vedove, Stefano Ambrosio, and Carlotta Quattrocolo.

For international rights, contact **licensing@idwpublishing.com**

ISBN: 978-1-63140-822-9

20 19 18 17 1 2 3 4

IDW®
www.IDWPUBLISHING.com

Facebook: facebook.com/idwpublishing • Twitter: @idwpublishing • YouTube: youtube.com/idwpublishing
Tumblr: tumblr.idwpublishing.com • Instagram: instagram.com/idwpublishing

Originally published as UNCLE SCROOGE issues #17–19 (Legacy #421–423).

The Miner's Granddaughter

From Italian *Topolino* #577, 1966
Writer and Artist: Romano Scarpa
Inker: Giorgio Cavazzano
Colorists: Disney Italia with Digikore Studios
Letterers: Nicole and Travis Seitler
Translation and Dialogue: Thad Komorowski

HOWDY-HO, GRAN'PA SCROOGE!

"GRAN'PA"!? WHUH—

Scrooge Vs. Scrooge

From Polish *Kaczor Donald* #36/2009
Writer: Olaf Solstrand
Artist: Arild Midthun
Colorist: Digikore Studios
Letterers: Nicole and Travis Seitler
Dialogue: Byron Erickson and David Gerstein

QUITE *REFRESHING!* IN FACT, I FEEL *GREAT!* AND *LIGHT AS A FEATHER!*

Hiccup to No Good

From Italian *Topolino* #2527, 2004
Writer: Nino Russo
Artist: Alessio Coppola
Colorists: Disney Italia with Nicole and Travis Seitler
Letterers: Nicole and Travis Seitler
Translation and Dialogue: David Gerstein

Gyro's Manager

From Swedish *Kalle Anka & C:o* #50/2014
Writers: Carl Barks and John Lustig
Artist: Daan Jippes
Colorist: Digikore Studios
Letterers: Nicole and Travis Seitler

The Biggest Fleet in the World!

From Italian *Topolino* #734, 1969
Writer: Dick Kinney
Artist: Al Hubbard
Colorist: Digikore Studios
Letterers: Nicole and Travis Seitler

Series Editor: Sarah Gaydos
Archival Editor: David Gerstein

Cover Artist: Andrea Freccero
Cover Colorist: Mario Perrotta
Collection Editors: Justin Eisinger
and Alonzo Simon
Collection Designer: Clyde Grapa
Publisher: Ted Adams

DISNEY COMICS

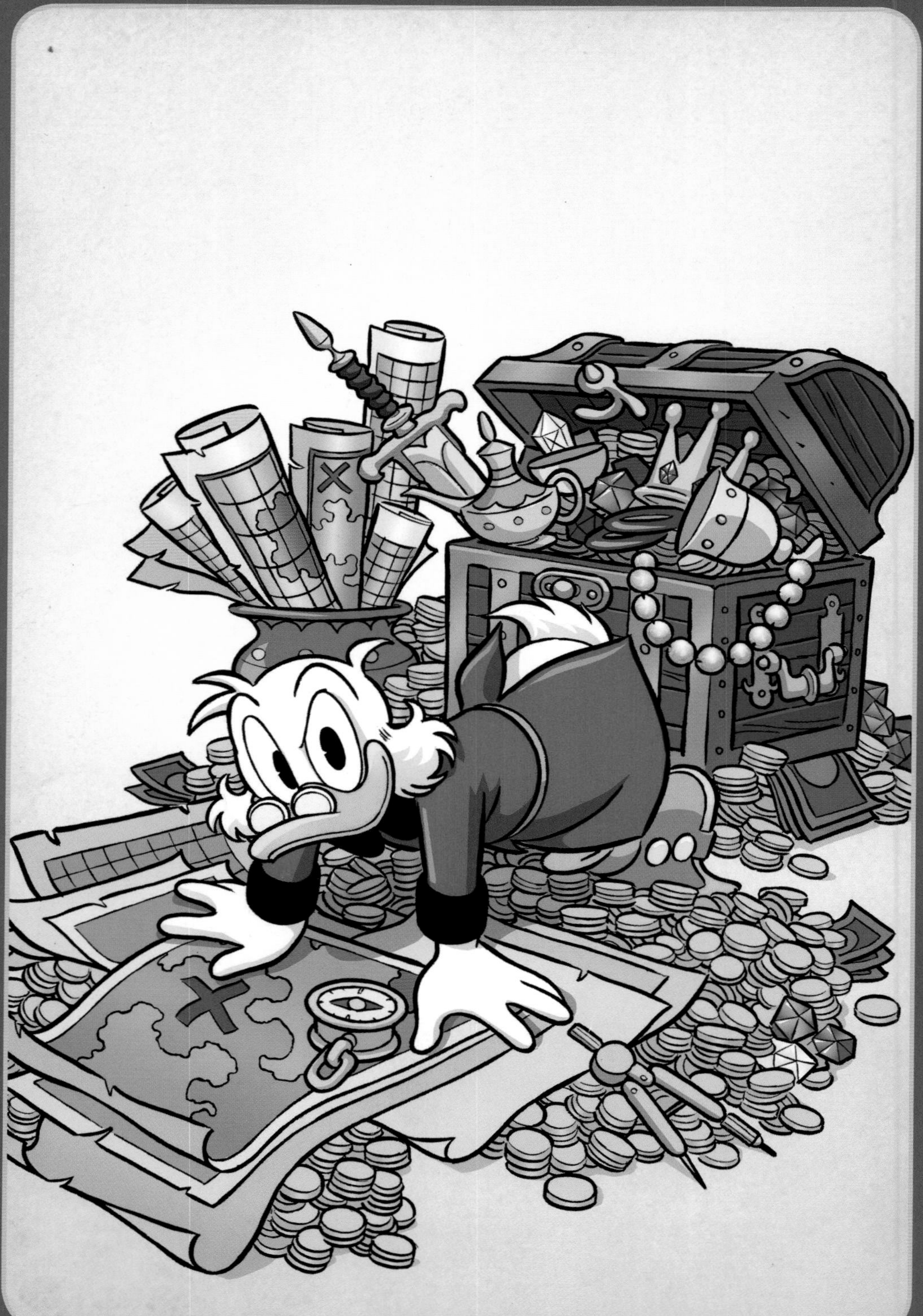

Art by Andrea Freccero, Colors by Ronda Pattison

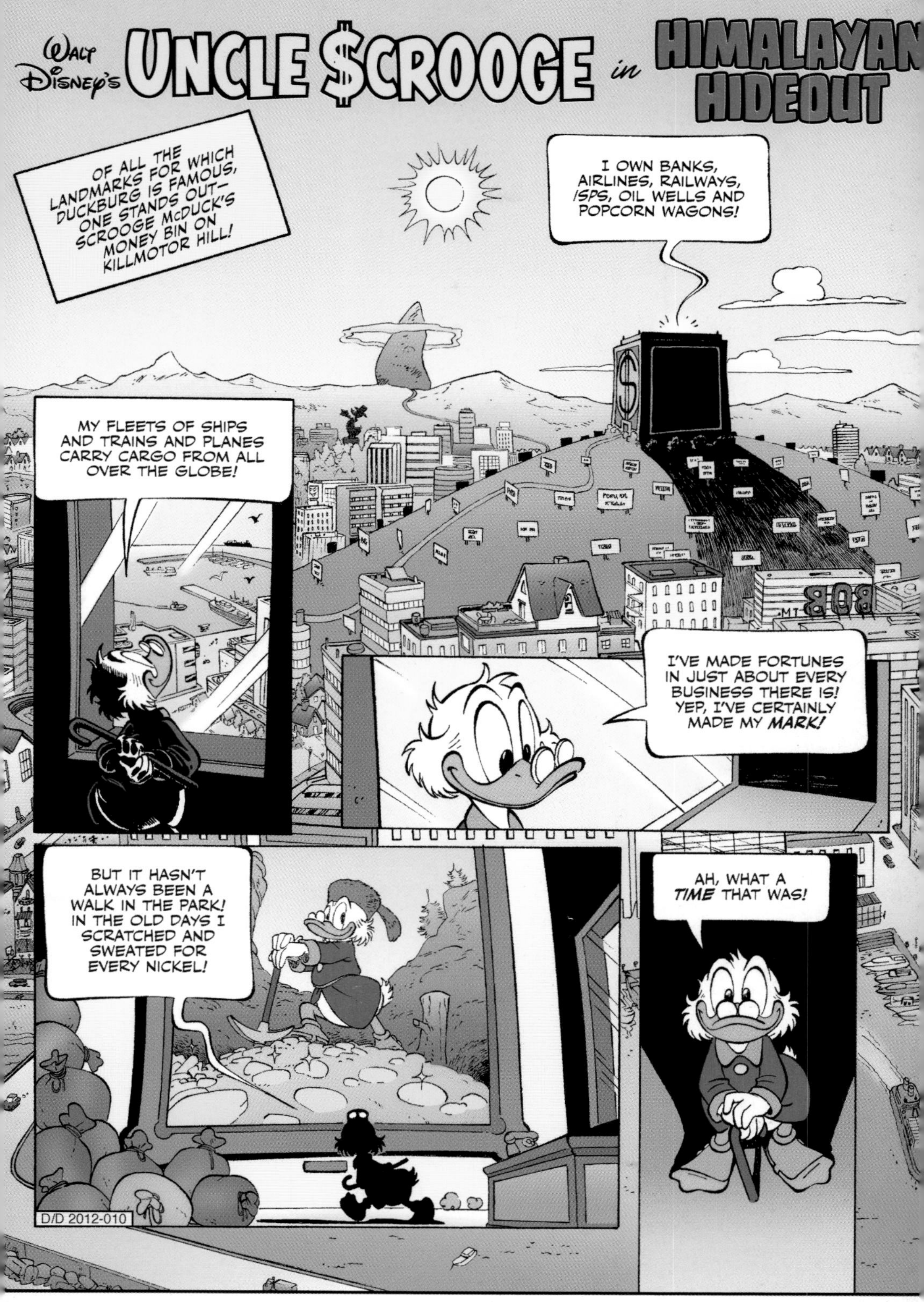
Walt Disney's UNCLE $CROOGE in HIMALAYAN HIDEOUT
OF ALL THE LANDMARKS FOR WHICH DUCKBURG IS FAMOUS, ONE STANDS OUT— SCROOGE McDUCK'S MONEY BIN ON KILLMOTOR HILL!
I OWN BANKS, AIRLINES, RAILWAYS, ISPS, OIL WELLS AND POPCORN WAGONS!
MY FLEETS OF SHIPS AND TRAINS AND PLANES CARRY CARGO FROM ALL OVER THE GLOBE!
I'VE MADE FORTUNES IN JUST ABOUT EVERY BUSINESS THERE IS! YEP, I'VE CERTAINLY MADE MY MARK!
BUT IT HASN'T ALWAYS BEEN A WALK IN THE PARK! IN THE OLD DAYS I SCRATCHED AND SWEATED FOR EVERY NICKEL!
AH, WHAT A TIME THAT WAS!
D/D 2012-010

Originally published in *Kalle Anka & C:o* #26-28/2013 (Sweden, 2013)

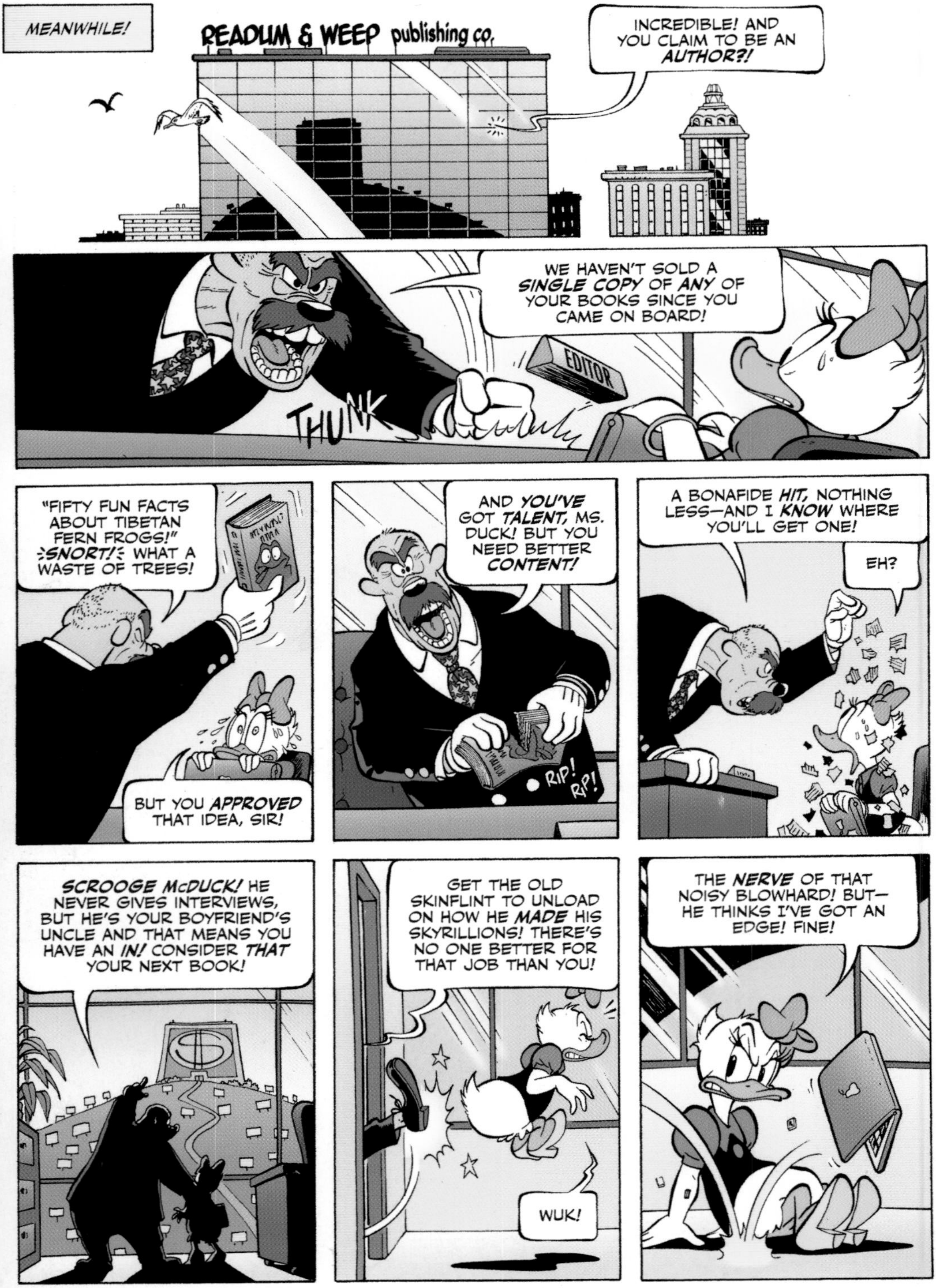
MEANWHILE!
READUM & WEEP publishing co.
INCREDIBLE! AND YOU CLAIM TO BE AN AUTHOR?!
WE HAVEN'T SOLD A SINGLE COPY OF ANY OF YOUR BOOKS SINCE YOU CAME ON BOARD!
EDITOR
THUNK
"FIFTY FUN FACTS ABOUT TIBETAN FERN FROGS!" SNORT! WHAT A WASTE OF TREES!
BUT YOU APPROVED THAT IDEA, SIR!
AND YOU'VE GOT TALENT, MS. DUCK! BUT YOU NEED BETTER CONTENT!
RIP! RIP!
A BONAFIDE HIT, NOTHING LESS—AND I KNOW WHERE YOU'LL GET ONE!
EH?
SCROOGE McDUCK! HE NEVER GIVES INTERVIEWS, BUT HE'S YOUR BOYFRIEND'S UNCLE AND THAT MEANS YOU HAVE AN IN! CONSIDER THAT YOUR NEXT BOOK!
GET THE OLD SKINFLINT TO UNLOAD ON HOW HE MADE HIS SKYRILLIONS! THERE'S NO ONE BETTER FOR THAT JOB THAN YOU!
WUK!
THE NERVE OF THAT NOISY BLOWHARD! BUT— HE THINKS I'VE GOT AN EDGE! FINE!

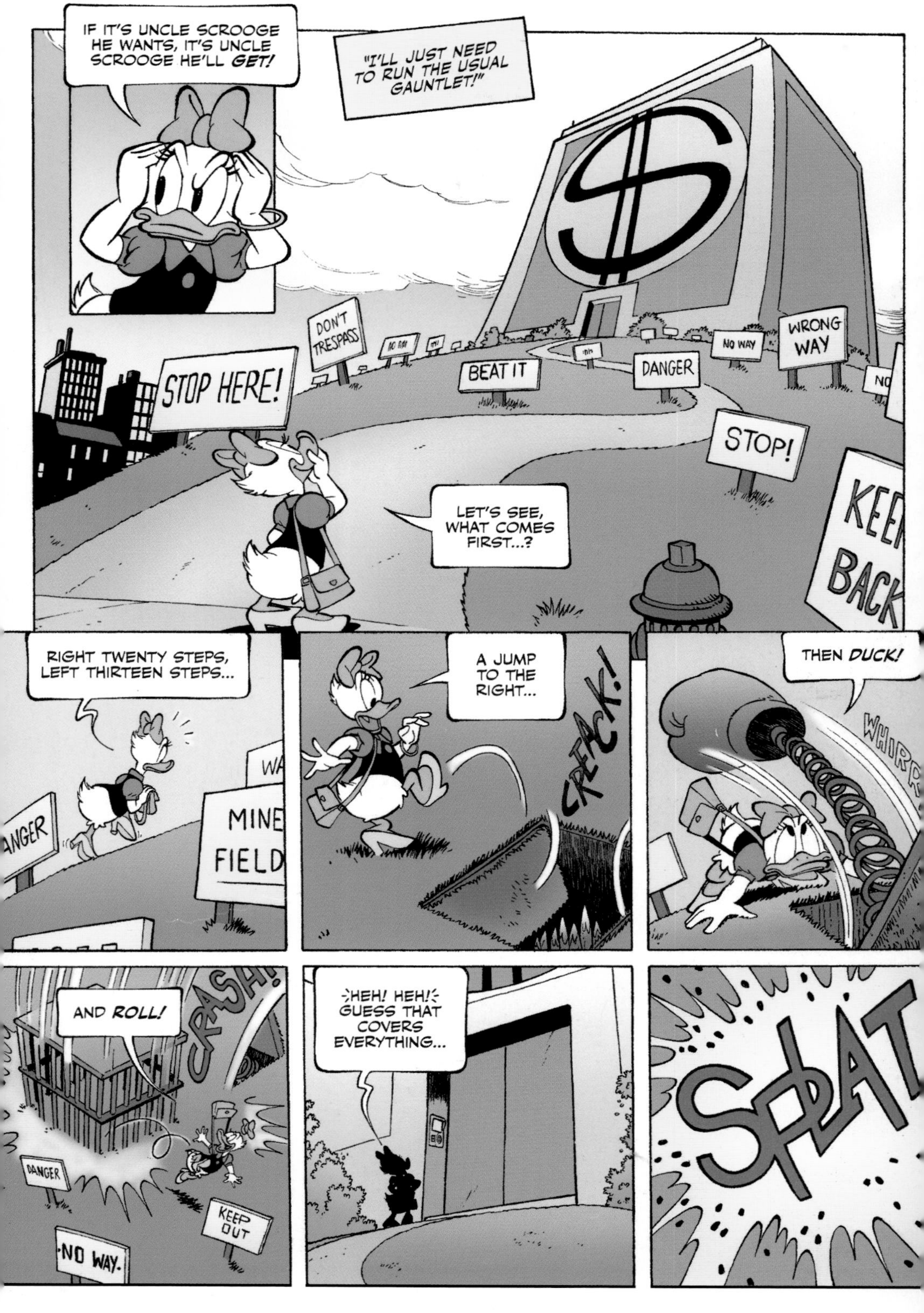

IF IT'S UNCLE SCROOGE HE WANTS, IT'S UNCLE SCROOGE HE'LL *GET!*
"I'LL JUST NEED TO RUN THE USUAL GAUNTLET!"
DON'T TRESPASS
STOP HERE!
BEAT IT
DANGER
NO WAY
WRONG WAY
STOP!
LET'S SEE, WHAT COMES FIRST...?
RIGHT TWENTY STEPS, LEFT THIRTEEN STEPS...
MINE FIELD
A JUMP TO THE RIGHT...
CREACK!
THEN *DUCK!*
AND *ROLL!*
CRASH!
DANGER
KEEP OUT
NO WAY.
HEH! HEH! GUESS THAT COVERS EVERYTHING...
SPLAT

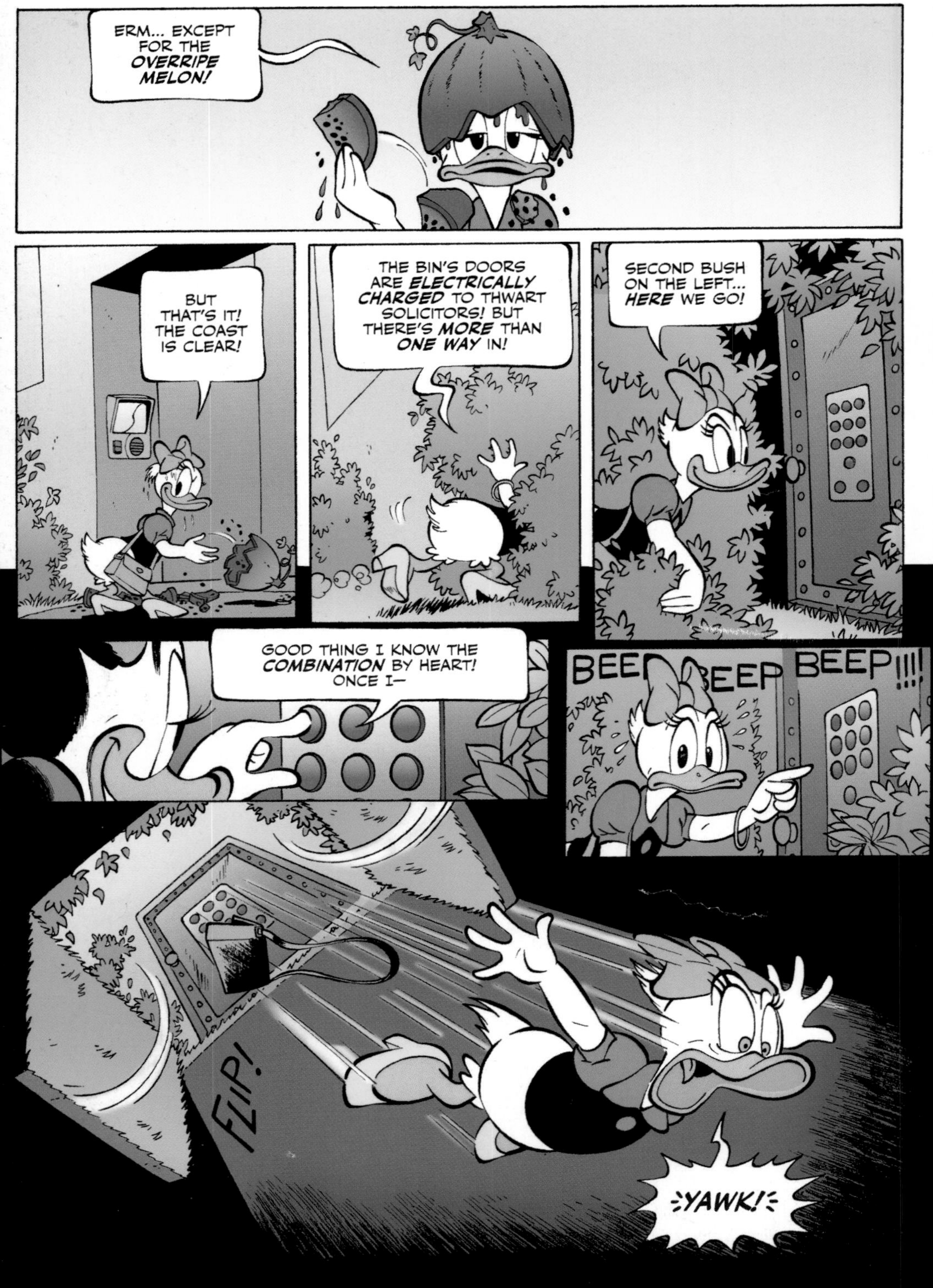
ERM... EXCEPT FOR THE OVERRIPE MELON!
BUT THAT'S IT! THE COAST IS CLEAR!
THE BIN'S DOORS ARE ELECTRICALLY CHARGED TO THWART SOLICITORS! BUT THERE'S MORE THAN ONE WAY IN!
SECOND BUSH ON THE LEFT... HERE WE GO!
GOOD THING I KNOW THE COMBINATION BY HEART! ONCE I—
BEEP BEEP BEEP!!!!
FLIP!
YAWK!

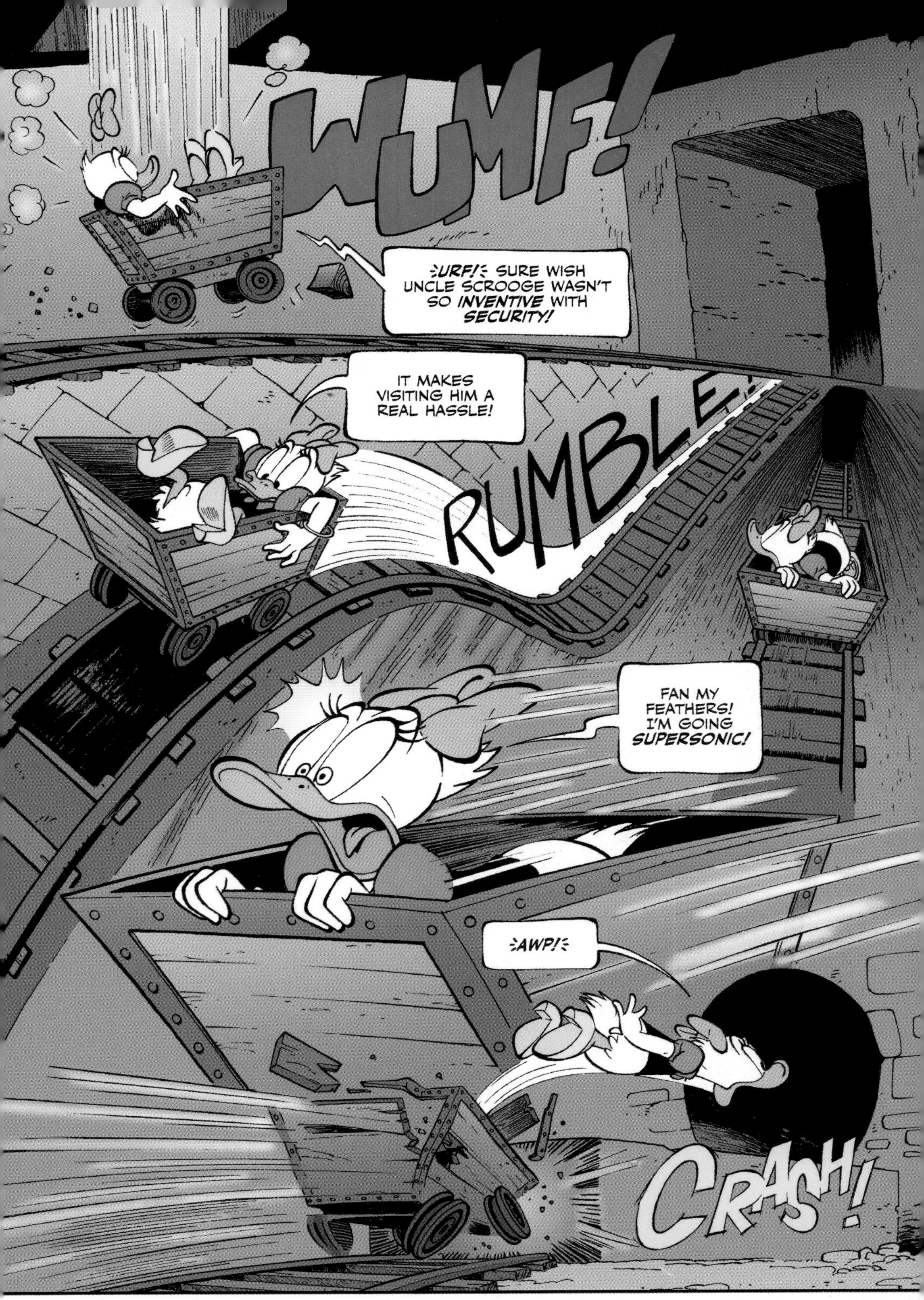
WUMF!
¡URF!¡ SURE WISH UNCLE SCROOGE WASN'T SO INVENTIVE WITH SECURITY!
IT MAKES VISITING HIM A REAL HASSLE!
RUMBLE!
FAN MY FEATHERS! I'M GOING SUPERSONIC!
AWP!
CRASH!

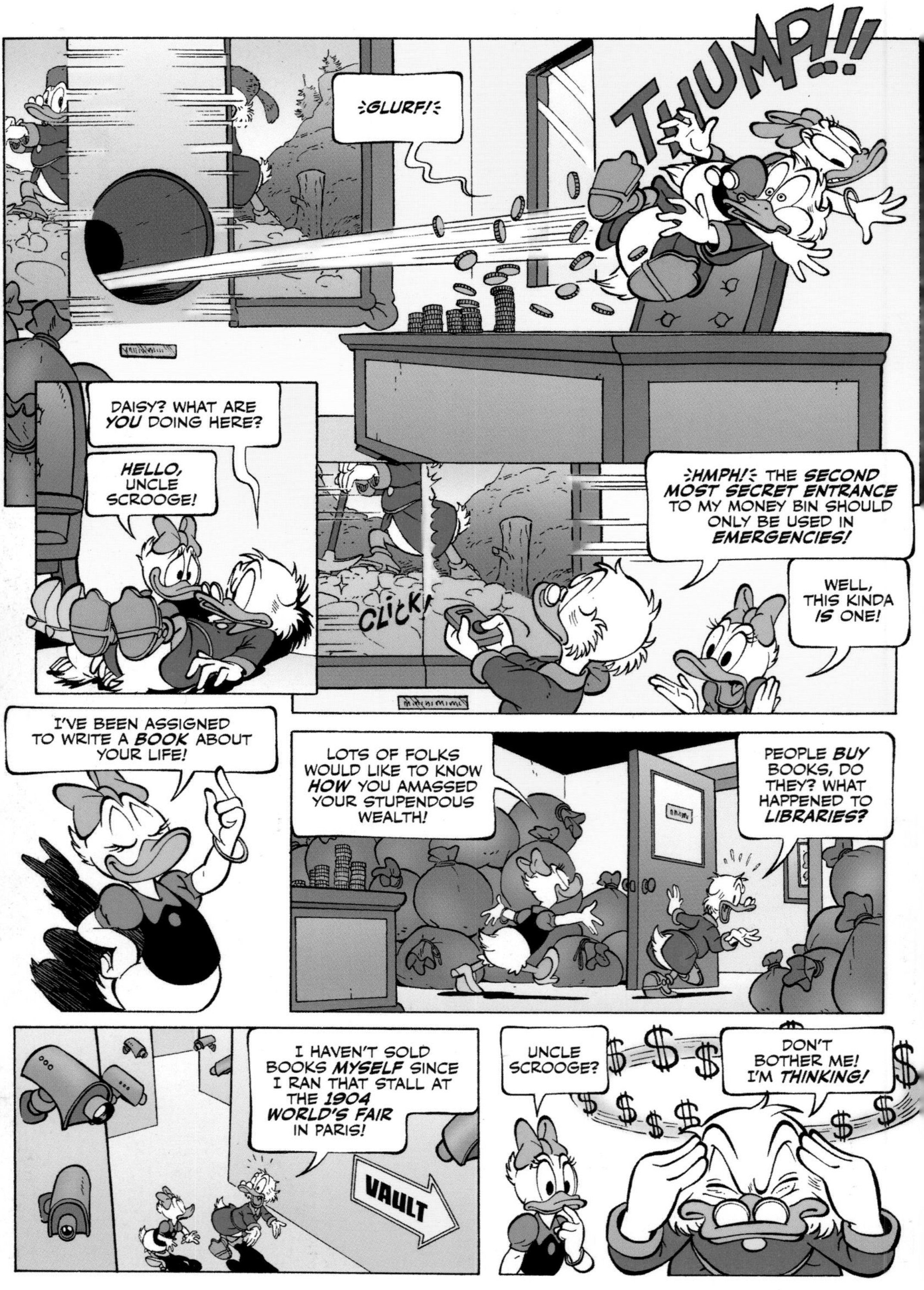

¡GLURF!¡
THUMP!!!
DAISY? WHAT ARE YOU DOING HERE?
HELLO, UNCLE SCROOGE!
¡HMPH!¡ THE SECOND MOST SECRET ENTRANCE TO MY MONEY BIN SHOULD ONLY BE USED IN EMERGENCIES!
CLICK!
WELL, THIS KINDA IS ONE!
I'VE BEEN ASSIGNED TO WRITE A BOOK ABOUT YOUR LIFE!
LOTS OF FOLKS WOULD LIKE TO KNOW HOW YOU AMASSED YOUR STUPENDOUS WEALTH!
PEOPLE BUY BOOKS, DO THEY? WHAT HAPPENED TO LIBRARIES?
I HAVEN'T SOLD BOOKS MYSELF SINCE I RAN THAT STALL AT THE 1904 WORLD'S FAIR IN PARIS!
VAULT
UNCLE SCROOGE?
DON'T BOTHER ME! I'M THINKING!

ALL RIGHT! TELL YOUR PUBLISHER I GET *75 CENTS* ON *EVERY DOLLAR IN SALES! THAT'S* THE DEAL!

YOU ARE ONE OF THE FEW DUCKS I'D *TRUST* TO PEN *MY BIOGRAPHY!* IN FACT, YOU MAY BE THE *ONLY* DUCK!

AND I HAVE A *STORY* FOR *EVERY COIN* IN MY VAULT! THE NICKEL I MADE HERDING HIGHLAND CATTLE ON THE OUTER HEBRIDES, FOR INSTANCE!

BUT THE READERS ONLY WANT TO READ ABOUT *EXCITING* STUFF! ABOUT *SHOOTOUTS* IN THE WILD WEST AND SUCH!

PHOOEY ON THAT! I'M ALL ABOUT THE JOYS ONLY *COLD CASH* CAN BRING AND WHAT IT TAKES TO...

OH, MY BUGGING EYEBALLS! THE BIN'S EMPTY! *SOMEONE'S STOLEN ALL MY MONEY!*

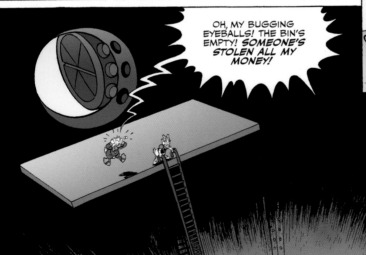

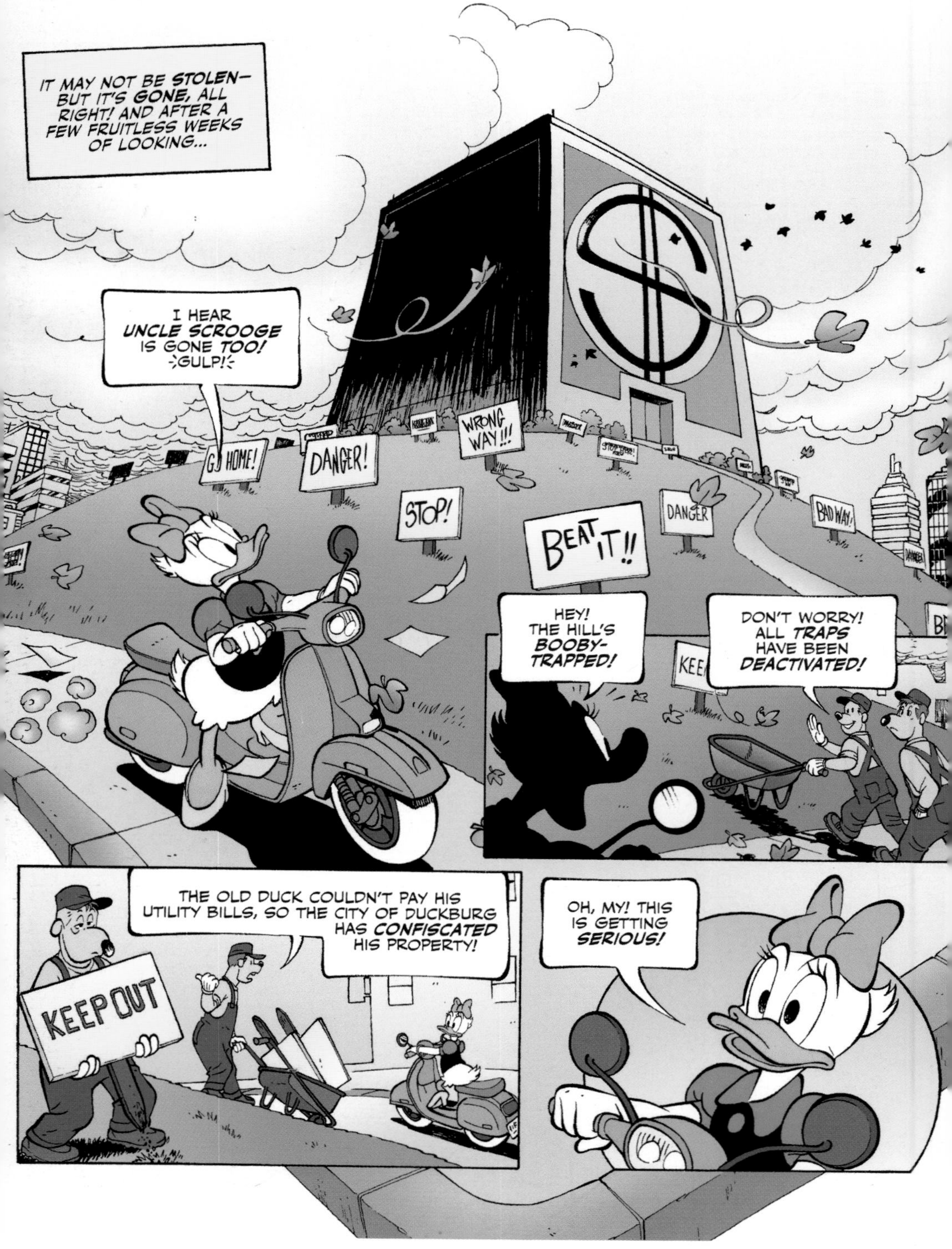

IT MAY NOT BE STOLEN— BUT IT'S GONE, ALL RIGHT! AND AFTER A FEW FRUITLESS WEEKS OF LOOKING...
I HEAR UNCLE SCROOGE IS GONE TOO! GULP!
GO HOME!
DANGER!
WRONG WAY!!!
STOP!
DANGER
BEAT IT!!
BAD WAY!
HEY! THE HILL'S BOOBY-TRAPPED!
DON'T WORRY! ALL TRAPS HAVE BEEN DEACTIVATED!
THE OLD DUCK COULDN'T PAY HIS UTILITY BILLS, SO THE CITY OF DUCKBURG HAS CONFISCATED HIS PROPERTY!
KEEP OUT
OH, MY! THIS IS GETTING SERIOUS!

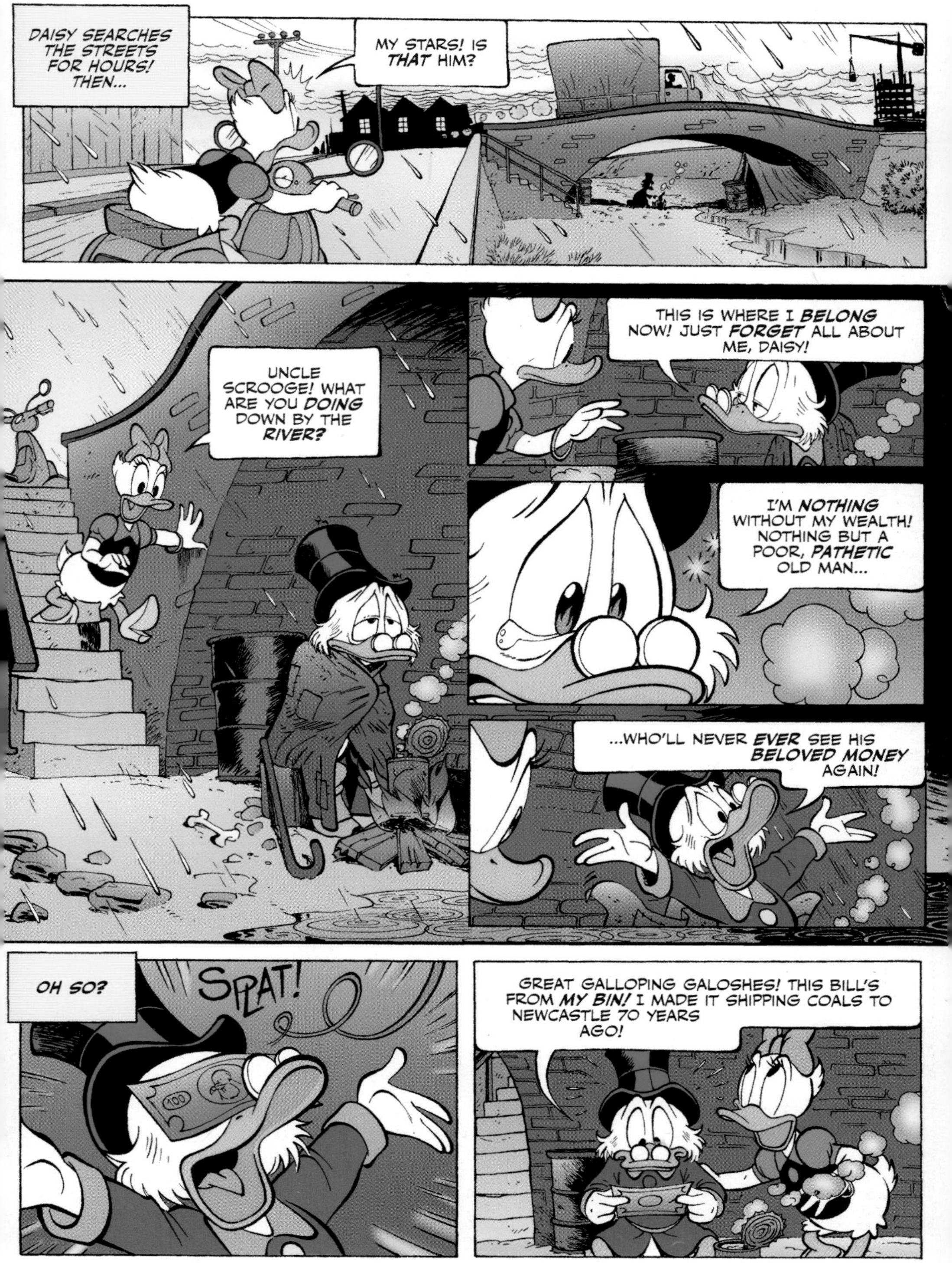
DAISY SEARCHES THE STREETS FOR HOURS! THEN...
MY STARS! IS *THAT* HIM?
UNCLE SCROOGE! WHAT ARE YOU *DOING* DOWN BY THE *RIVER?*
THIS IS WHERE I *BELONG* NOW! JUST *FORGET* ALL ABOUT ME, DAISY!
I'M *NOTHING* WITHOUT MY WEALTH! NOTHING BUT A POOR, *PATHETIC* OLD MAN...
...WHO'LL NEVER *EVER* SEE HIS *BELOVED MONEY* AGAIN!
OH SO?
SPLAT!
GREAT GALLOPING GALOSHES! THIS BILL'S FROM *MY BIN!* I MADE IT SHIPPING COALS TO NEWCASTLE 70 YEARS AGO!

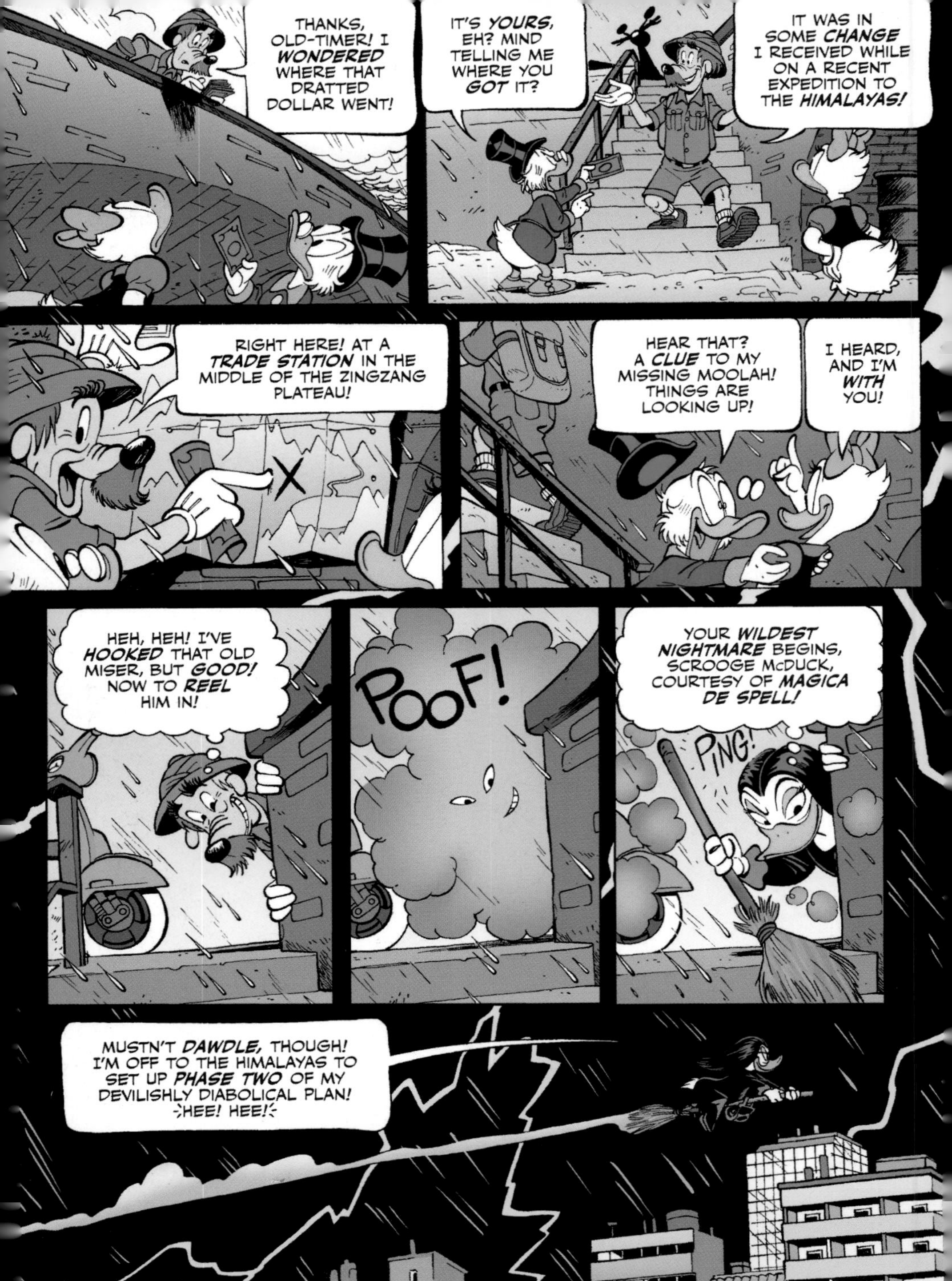
THANKS, OLD-TIMER! I WONDERED WHERE THAT DRATTED DOLLAR WENT!
IT'S YOURS, EH? MIND TELLING ME WHERE YOU GOT IT?
IT WAS IN SOME CHANGE I RECEIVED WHILE ON A RECENT EXPEDITION TO THE HIMALAYAS!
RIGHT HERE! AT A TRADE STATION IN THE MIDDLE OF THE ZINGZANG PLATEAU!
HEAR THAT? A CLUE TO MY MISSING MOOLAH! THINGS ARE LOOKING UP!
I HEARD, AND I'M WITH YOU!
HEH, HEH! I'VE HOOKED THAT OLD MISER, BUT GOOD! NOW TO REEL HIM IN!
POOF!
YOUR WILDEST NIGHTMARE BEGINS, SCROOGE McDUCK, COURTESY OF MAGICA DE SPELL!
PING!
MUSTN'T DAWDLE, THOUGH! I'M OFF TO THE HIMALAYAS TO SET UP PHASE TWO OF MY DEVILISHLY DIABOLICAL PLAN! HEE! HEE!

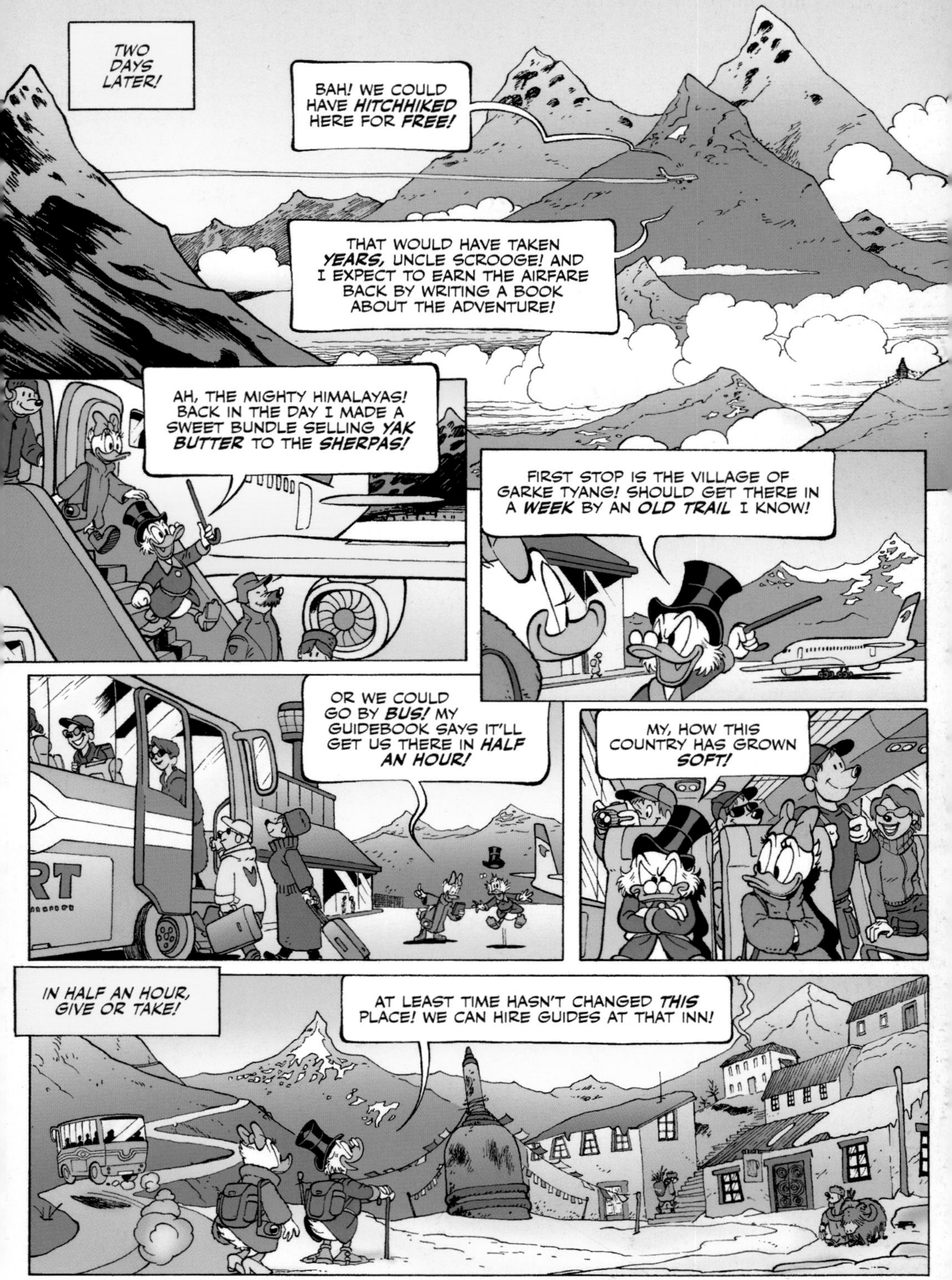
TWO DAYS LATER!
BAH! WE COULD HAVE HITCHHIKED HERE FOR FREE!
THAT WOULD HAVE TAKEN YEARS, UNCLE SCROOGE! AND I EXPECT TO EARN THE AIRFARE BACK BY WRITING A BOOK ABOUT THE ADVENTURE!
AH, THE MIGHTY HIMALAYAS! BACK IN THE DAY I MADE A SWEET BUNDLE SELLING YAK BUTTER TO THE SHERPAS!
FIRST STOP IS THE VILLAGE OF GARKE TYANG! SHOULD GET THERE IN A WEEK BY AN OLD TRAIL I KNOW!
OR WE COULD GO BY BUS! MY GUIDEBOOK SAYS IT'LL GET US THERE IN HALF AN HOUR!
RT
MY, HOW THIS COUNTRY HAS GROWN SOFT!
IN HALF AN HOUR, GIVE OR TAKE!
AT LEAST TIME HASN'T CHANGED THIS PLACE! WE CAN HIRE GUIDES AT THAT INN!

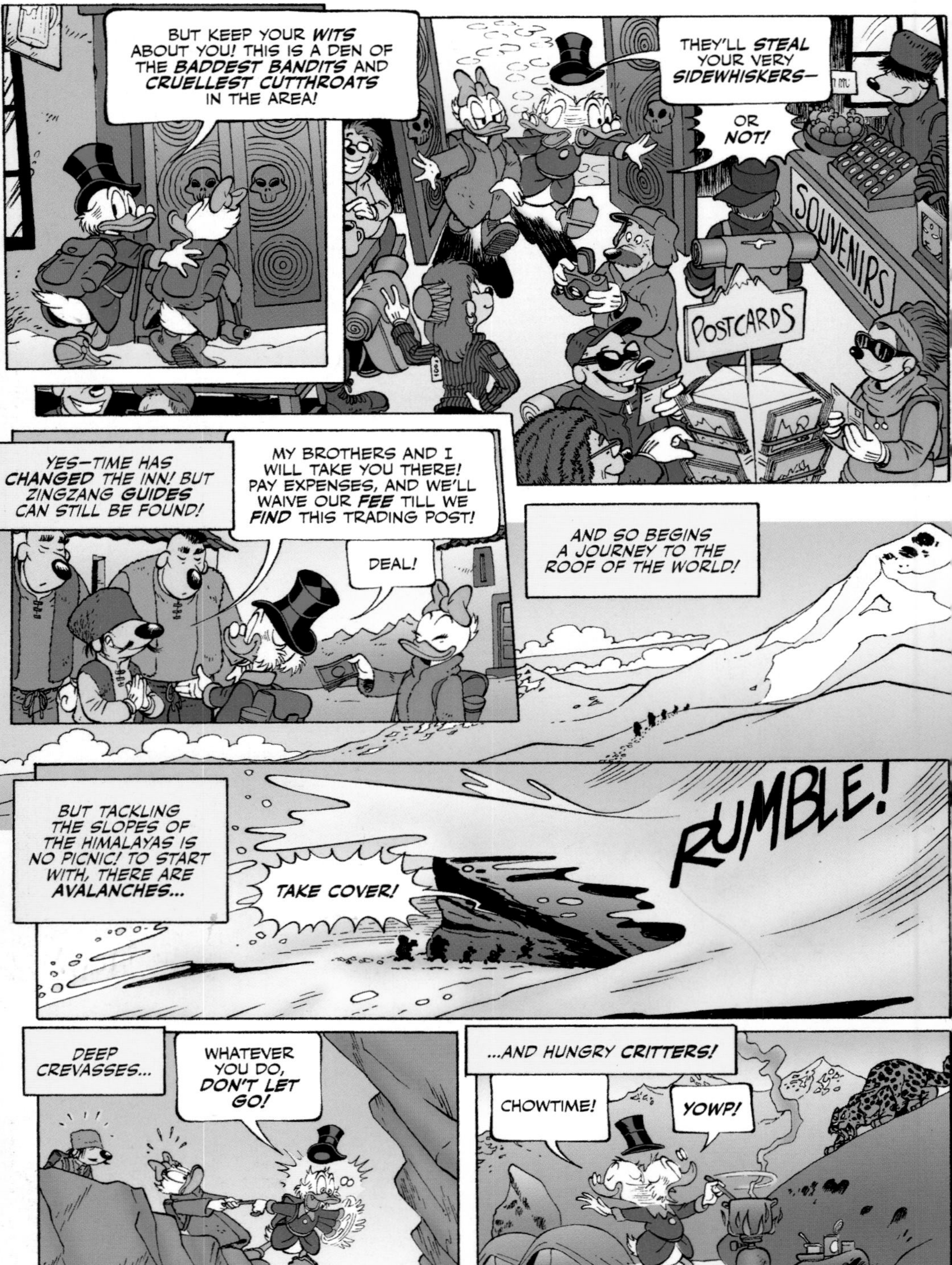

BUT KEEP YOUR WITS ABOUT YOU! THIS IS A DEN OF THE BADDEST BANDITS AND CRUELLEST CUTTHROATS IN THE AREA!
THEY'LL STEAL YOUR VERY SIDEWHISKERS—
OR NOT!
SOUVENIRS
POSTCARDS
YES—TIME HAS CHANGED THE INN! BUT ZINGZANG GUIDES CAN STILL BE FOUND!
MY BROTHERS AND I WILL TAKE YOU THERE! PAY EXPENSES, AND WE'LL WAIVE OUR FEE TILL WE FIND THIS TRADING POST!
DEAL!
AND SO BEGINS A JOURNEY TO THE ROOF OF THE WORLD!
BUT TACKLING THE SLOPES OF THE HIMALAYAS IS NO PICNIC! TO START WITH, THERE ARE AVALANCHES...
RUMBLE!
TAKE COVER!
DEEP CREVASSES...
WHATEVER YOU DO, DON'T LET GO!
...AND HUNGRY CRITTERS!
CHOWTIME!
YOWP!

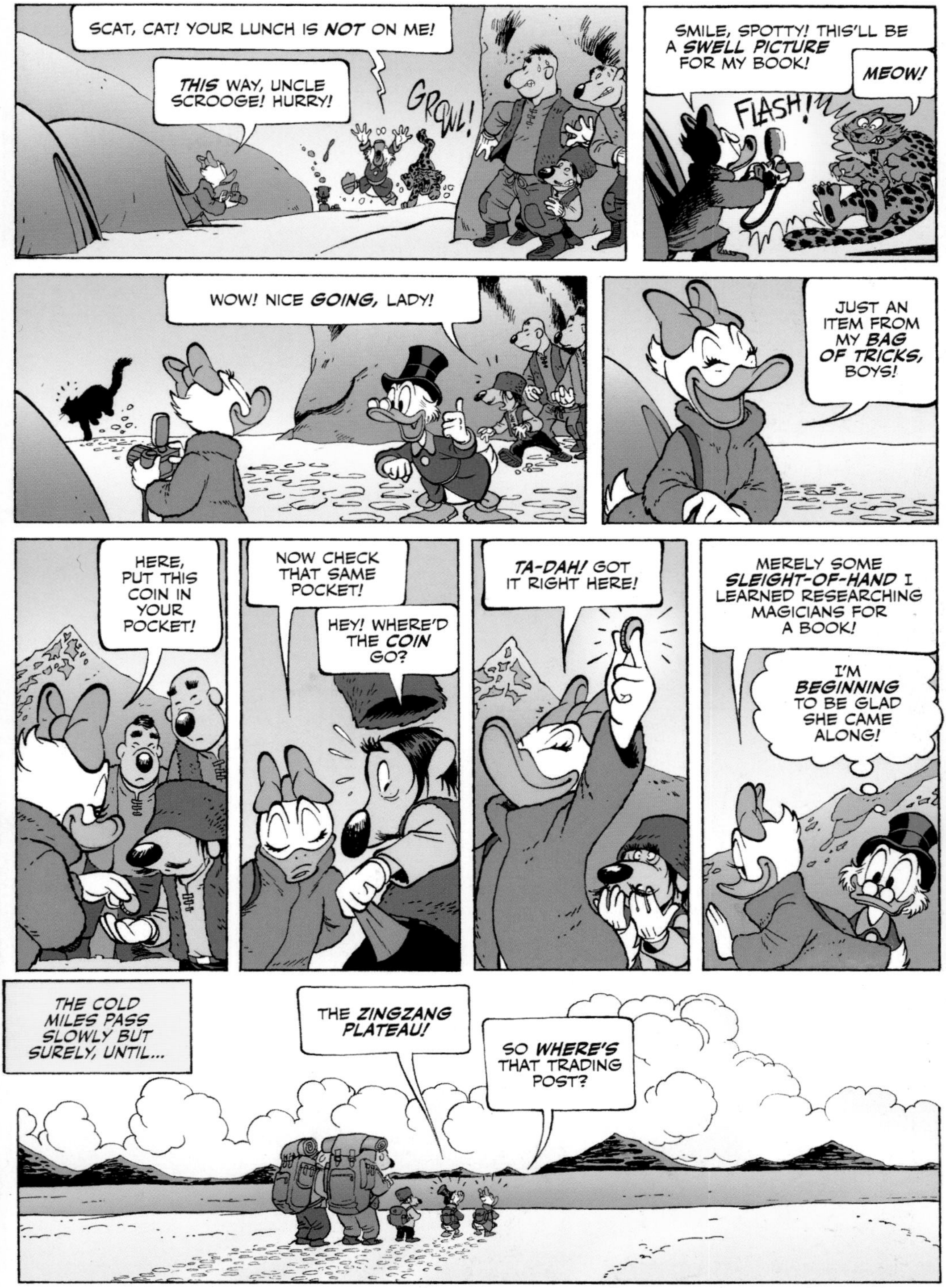

SCAT, CAT! YOUR LUNCH IS NOT ON ME!
THIS WAY, UNCLE SCROOGE! HURRY!
GROWL!
SMILE, SPOTTY! THIS'LL BE A SWELL PICTURE FOR MY BOOK!
MEOW!
FLASH!
WOW! NICE GOING, LADY!
JUST AN ITEM FROM MY BAG OF TRICKS, BOYS!
HERE, PUT THIS COIN IN YOUR POCKET!
NOW CHECK THAT SAME POCKET!
HEY! WHERE'D THE COIN GO?
TA-DAH! GOT IT RIGHT HERE!
MERELY SOME SLEIGHT-OF-HAND I LEARNED RESEARCHING MAGICIANS FOR A BOOK!
I'M BEGINNING TO BE GLAD SHE CAME ALONG!
THE COLD MILES PASS SLOWLY BUT SURELY, UNTIL...
THE ZINGZANG PLATEAU!
SO WHERE'S THAT TRADING POST?

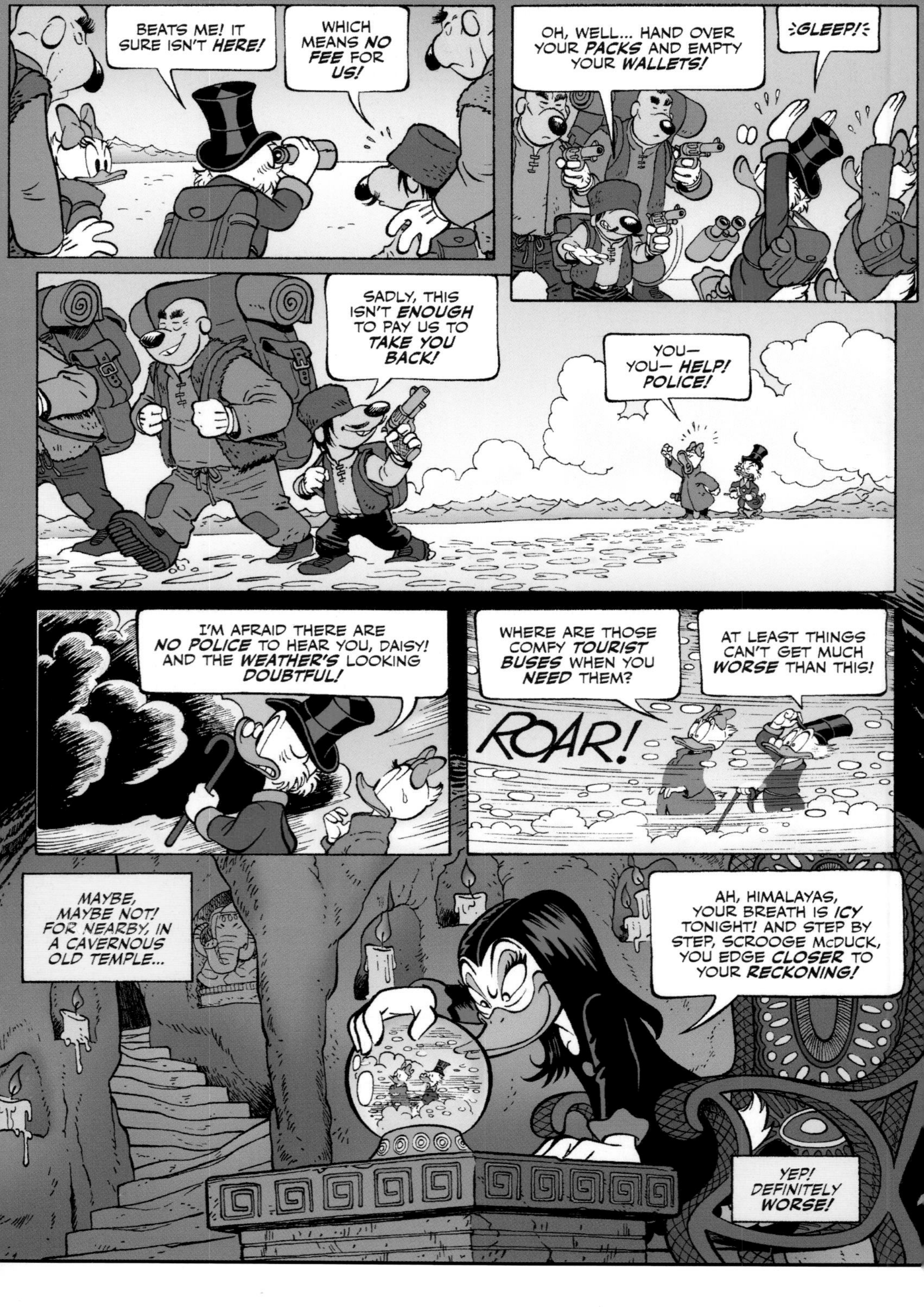
BEATS ME! IT SURE ISN'T HERE!
WHICH MEANS NO FEE FOR US!
OH, WELL... HAND OVER YOUR PACKS AND EMPTY YOUR WALLETS!
GLEEP!
SADLY, THIS ISN'T ENOUGH TO PAY US TO TAKE YOU BACK!
YOU— YOU— HELP! POLICE!
I'M AFRAID THERE ARE NO POLICE TO HEAR YOU, DAISY! AND THE WEATHER'S LOOKING DOUBTFUL!
WHERE ARE THOSE COMFY TOURIST BUSES WHEN YOU NEED THEM?
AT LEAST THINGS CAN'T GET MUCH WORSE THAN THIS!
ROAR!
MAYBE, MAYBE NOT! FOR NEARBY, IN A CAVERNOUS OLD TEMPLE...
AH, HIMALAYAS, YOUR BREATH IS ICY TONIGHT! AND STEP BY STEP, SCROOGE McDUCK, YOU EDGE CLOSER TO YOUR RECKONING!
YEP! DEFINITELY WORSE!

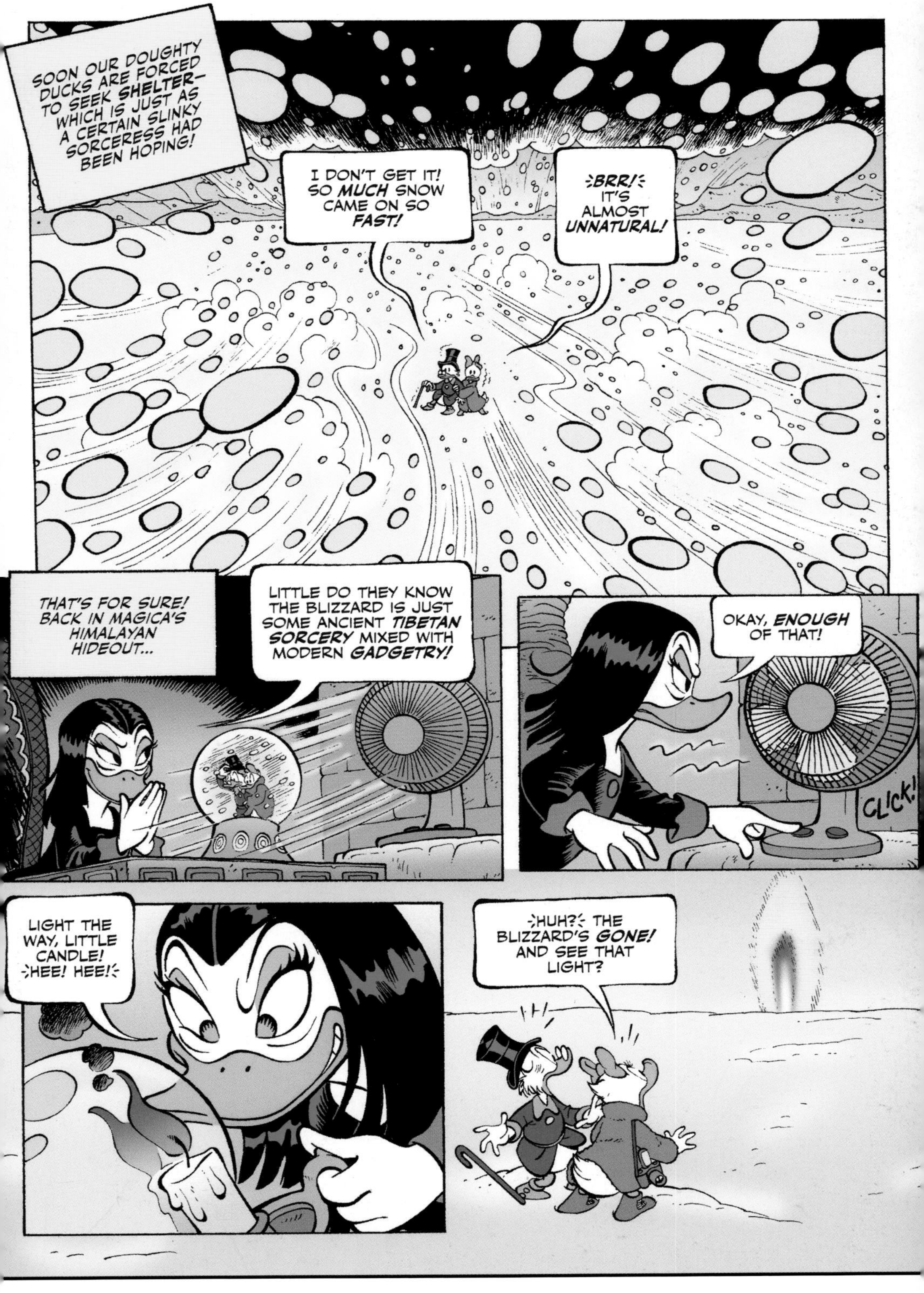
SOON OUR DOUGHTY DUCKS ARE FORCED TO SEEK SHELTER— WHICH IS JUST AS A CERTAIN SLINKY SORCERESS HAD BEEN HOPING!
I DON'T GET IT! SO MUCH SNOW CAME ON SO FAST!
BRR! IT'S ALMOST UNNATURAL!
THAT'S FOR SURE! BACK IN MAGICA'S HIMALAYAN HIDEOUT...
LITTLE DO THEY KNOW THE BLIZZARD IS JUST SOME ANCIENT TIBETAN SORCERY MIXED WITH MODERN GADGETRY!
OKAY, ENOUGH OF THAT!
CLICK!
LIGHT THE WAY, LITTLE CANDLE! HEE! HEE!
HUH? THE BLIZZARD'S GONE! AND SEE THAT LIGHT?

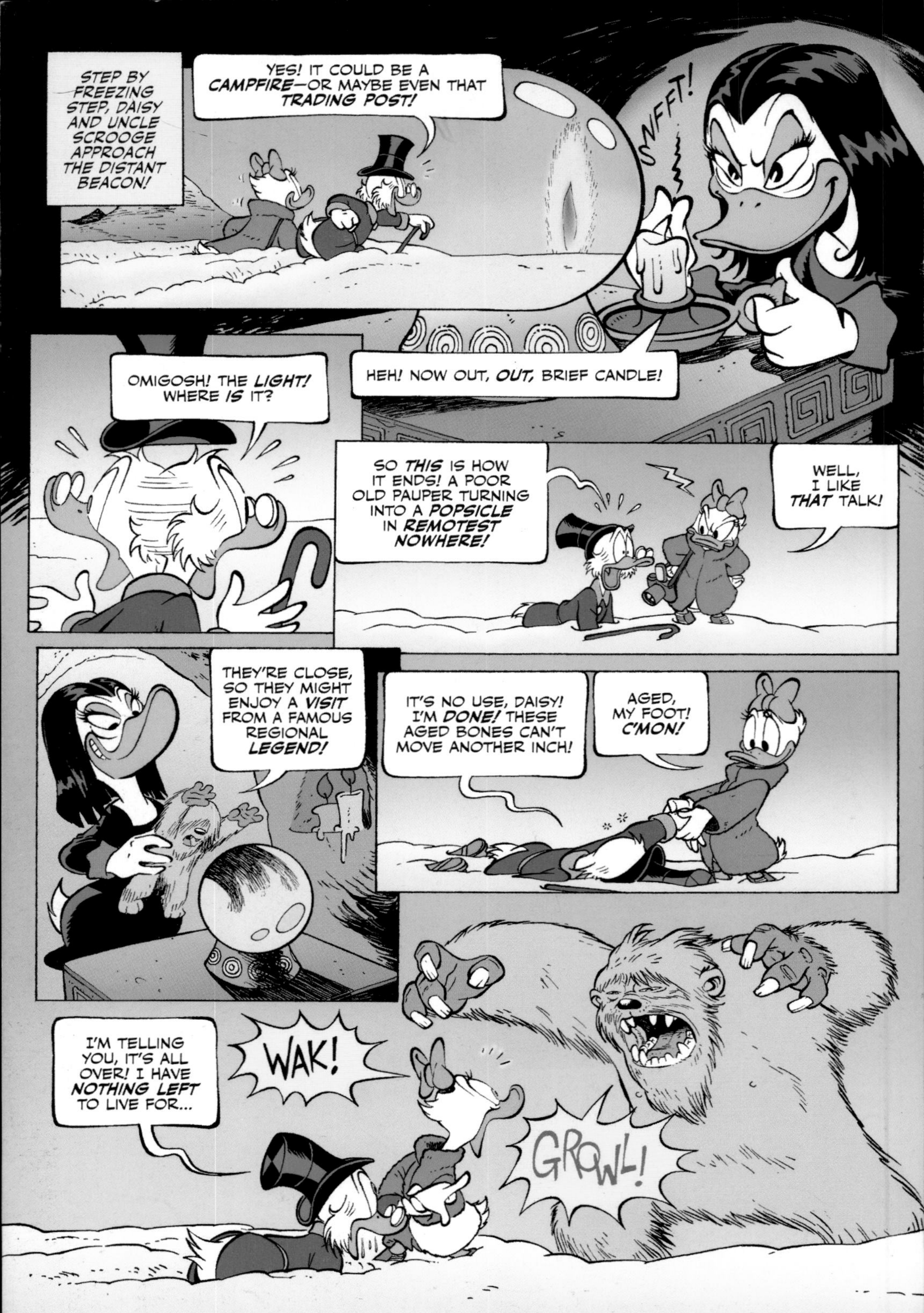
STEP BY FREEZING STEP, DAISY AND UNCLE SCROOGE APPROACH THE DISTANT BEACON!
YES! IT COULD BE A CAMPFIRE—OR MAYBE EVEN THAT TRADING POST!
SNFFT!
HEH! NOW OUT, OUT, BRIEF CANDLE!
OMIGOSH! THE LIGHT! WHERE IS IT?
SO THIS IS HOW IT ENDS! A POOR OLD PAUPER TURNING INTO A POPSICLE IN REMOTEST NOWHERE!
WELL, I LIKE THAT TALK!
THEY'RE CLOSE, SO THEY MIGHT ENJOY A VISIT FROM A FAMOUS REGIONAL LEGEND!
IT'S NO USE, DAISY! I'M DONE! THESE AGED BONES CAN'T MOVE ANOTHER INCH!
AGED, MY FOOT! C'MON!
I'M TELLING YOU, IT'S ALL OVER! I HAVE NOTHING LEFT TO LIVE FOR...
WAK!
GROWL!

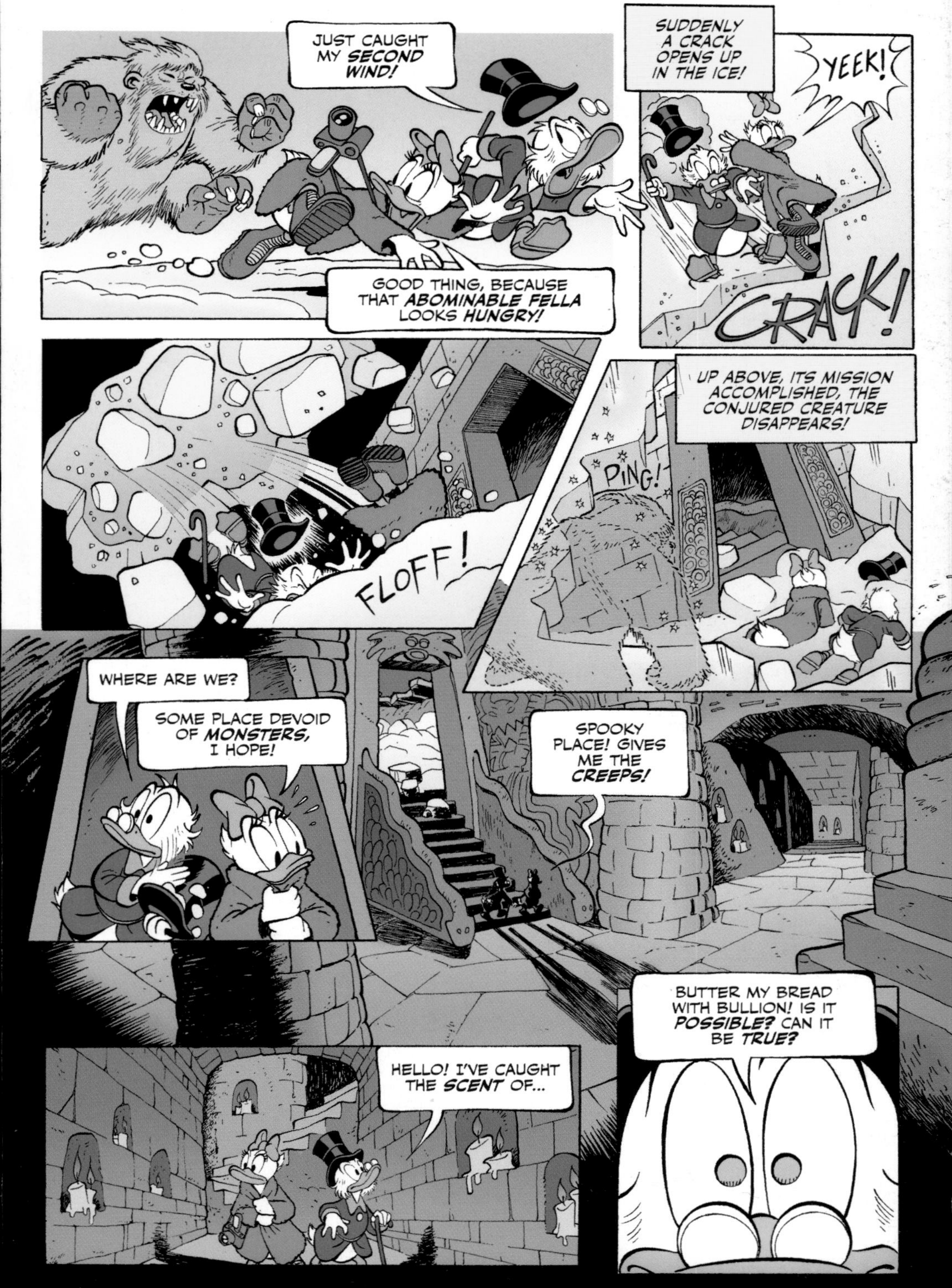
JUST CAUGHT MY SECOND WIND!
GOOD THING, BECAUSE THAT ABOMINABLE FELLA LOOKS HUNGRY!
SUDDENLY A CRACK OPENS UP IN THE ICE!
YEEK!
CRACK!
FLOFF!
UP ABOVE, ITS MISSION ACCOMPLISHED, THE CONJURED CREATURE DISAPPEARS!
PING!
WHERE ARE WE?
SOME PLACE DEVOID OF MONSTERS, I HOPE!
SPOOKY PLACE! GIVES ME THE CREEPS!
HELLO! I'VE CAUGHT THE SCENT OF...
BUTTER MY BREAD WITH BULLION! IS IT POSSIBLE? CAN IT BE TRUE?

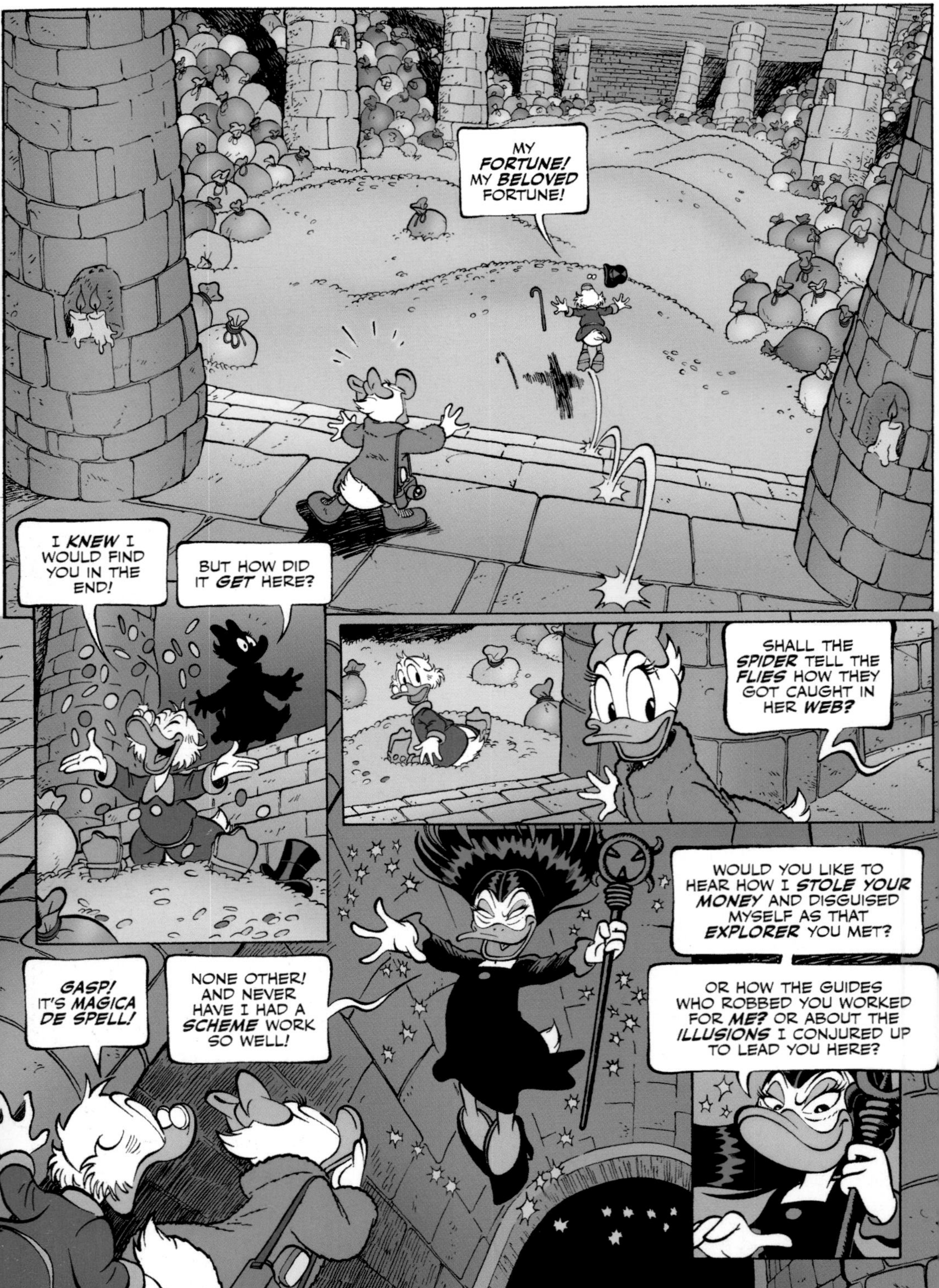
MY FORTUNE! MY BELOVED FORTUNE!
I KNEW I WOULD FIND YOU IN THE END!
BUT HOW DID IT GET HERE?
SHALL THE SPIDER TELL THE FLIES HOW THEY GOT CAUGHT IN HER WEB?
GASP! IT'S MAGICA DE SPELL!
NONE OTHER! AND NEVER HAVE I HAD A SCHEME WORK SO WELL!
WOULD YOU LIKE TO HEAR HOW I STOLE YOUR MONEY AND DISGUISED MYSELF AS THAT EXPLORER YOU MET?
OR HOW THE GUIDES WHO ROBBED YOU WORKED FOR ME? OR ABOUT THE ILLUSIONS I CONJURED UP TO LEAD YOU HERE?

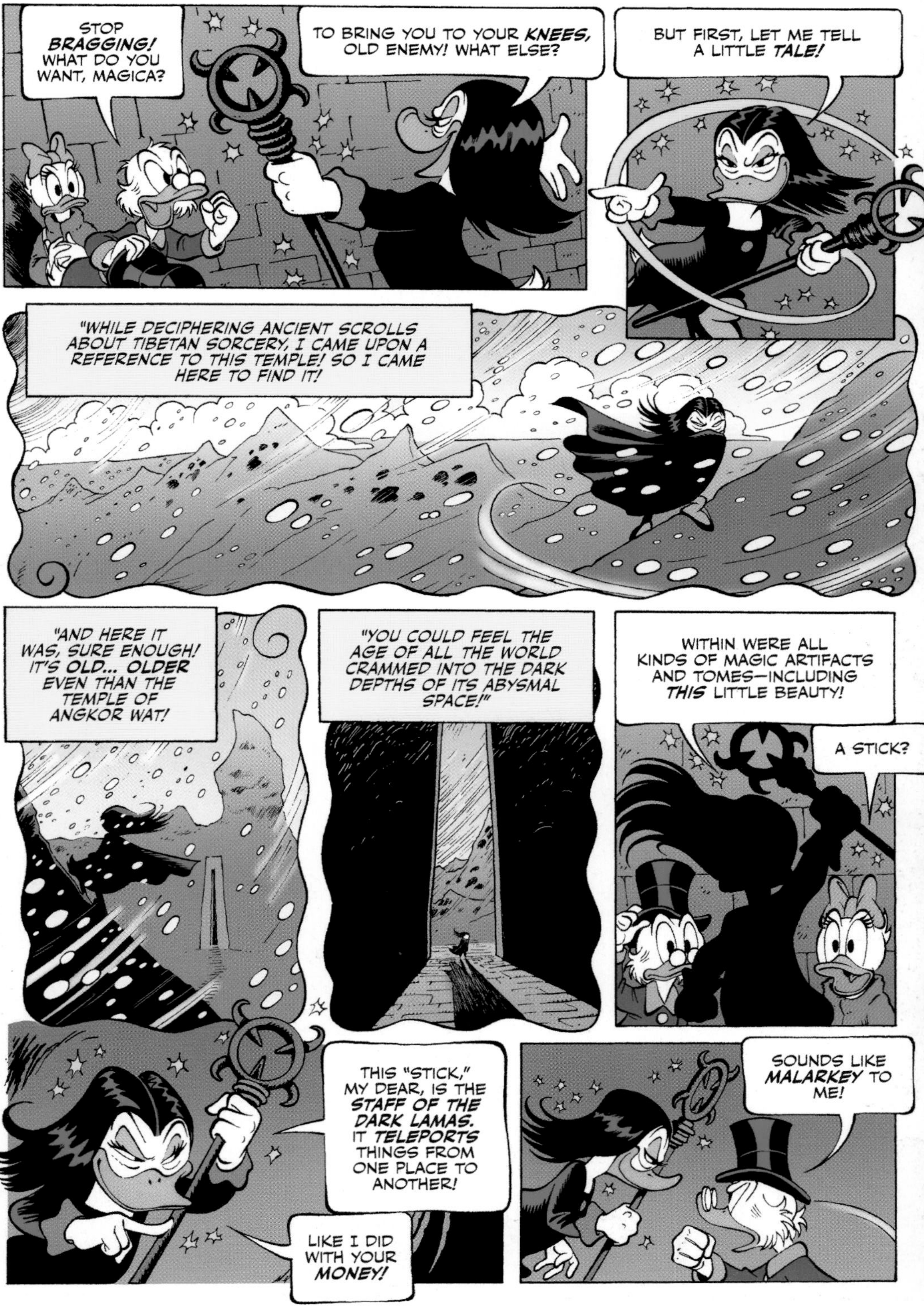
STOP BRAGGING! WHAT DO YOU WANT, MAGICA?
TO BRING YOU TO YOUR KNEES, OLD ENEMY! WHAT ELSE?
BUT FIRST, LET ME TELL A LITTLE TALE!
"WHILE DECIPHERING ANCIENT SCROLLS ABOUT TIBETAN SORCERY, I CAME UPON A REFERENCE TO THIS TEMPLE! SO I CAME HERE TO FIND IT!
"AND HERE IT WAS, SURE ENOUGH! IT'S OLD... OLDER EVEN THAN THE TEMPLE OF ANGKOR WAT!
"YOU COULD FEEL THE AGE OF ALL THE WORLD CRAMMED INTO THE DARK DEPTHS OF ITS ABYSMAL SPACE!"
WITHIN WERE ALL KINDS OF MAGIC ARTIFACTS AND TOMES—INCLUDING THIS LITTLE BEAUTY!
A STICK?
THIS "STICK," MY DEAR, IS THE STAFF OF THE DARK LAMAS. IT TELEPORTS THINGS FROM ONE PLACE TO ANOTHER!
LIKE I DID WITH YOUR MONEY!
SOUNDS LIKE MALARKEY TO ME!

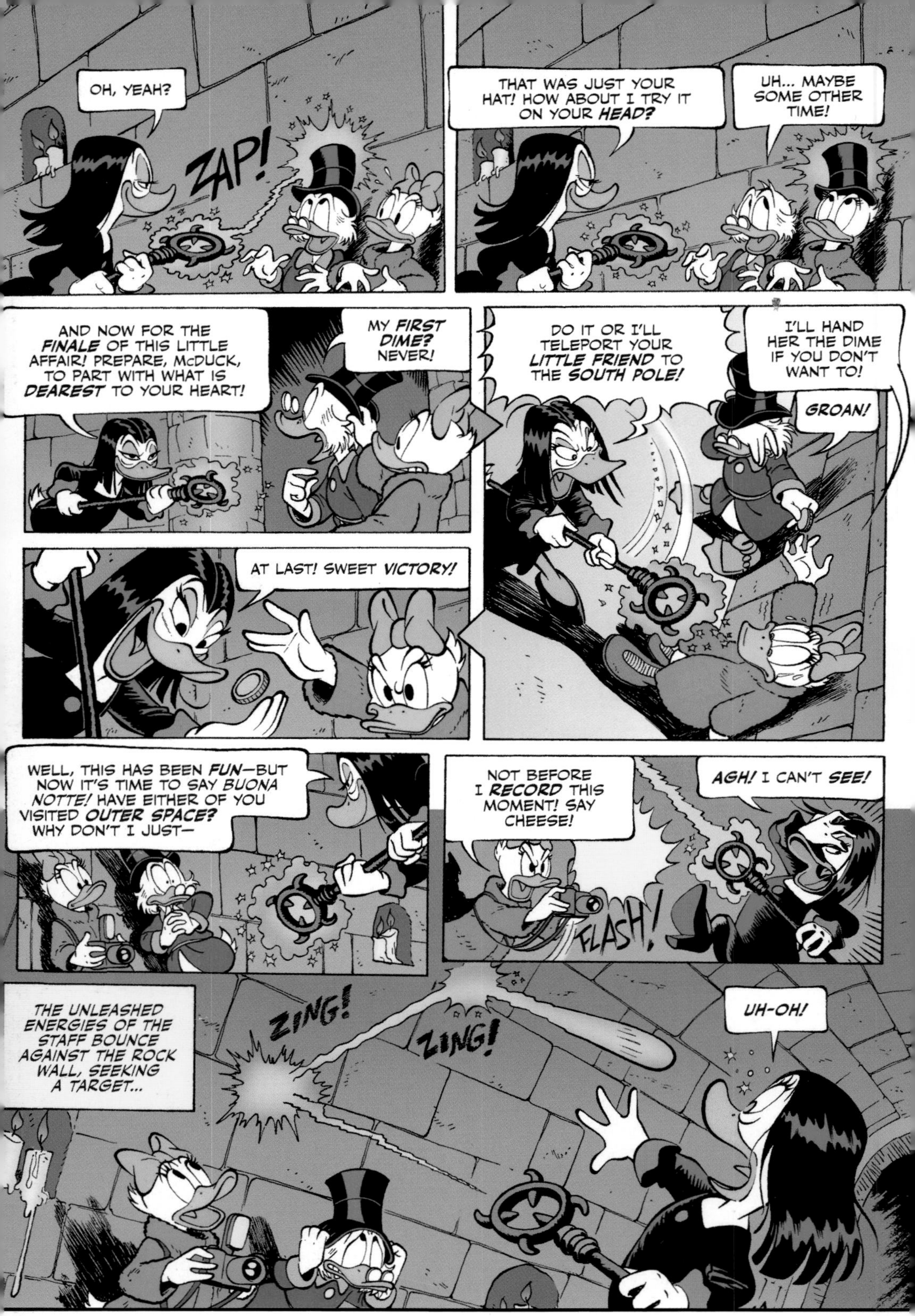
OH, YEAH?
ZAP!
THAT WAS JUST YOUR HAT! HOW ABOUT I TRY IT ON YOUR HEAD?
UH... MAYBE SOME OTHER TIME!
AND NOW FOR THE FINALE OF THIS LITTLE AFFAIR! PREPARE, McDUCK, TO PART WITH WHAT IS DEAREST TO YOUR HEART!
MY FIRST DIME? NEVER!
DO IT OR I'LL TELEPORT YOUR LITTLE FRIEND TO THE SOUTH POLE!
I'LL HAND HER THE DIME IF YOU DON'T WANT TO!
GROAN!
AT LAST! SWEET VICTORY!
WELL, THIS HAS BEEN FUN—BUT NOW IT'S TIME TO SAY BUONA NOTTE! HAVE EITHER OF YOU VISITED OUTER SPACE? WHY DON'T I JUST—
NOT BEFORE I RECORD THIS MOMENT! SAY CHEESE!
AGH! I CAN'T SEE!
FLASH!
THE UNLEASHED ENERGIES OF THE STAFF BOUNCE AGAINST THE ROCK WALL, SEEKING A TARGET...
ZING!
ZING!
UH-OH!

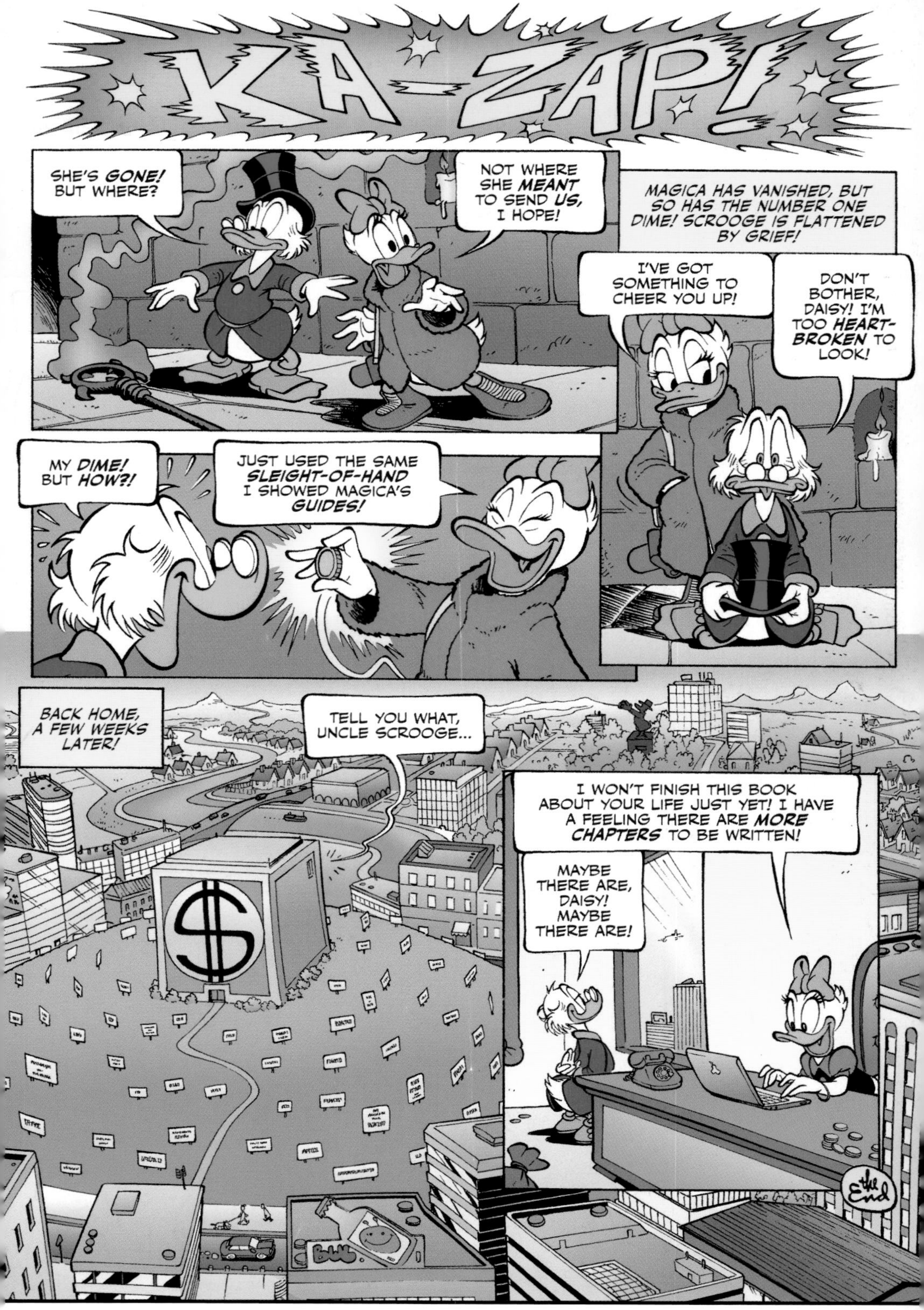
KA-ZAP!
SHE'S GONE! BUT WHERE?
NOT WHERE SHE MEANT TO SEND US, I HOPE!
MAGICA HAS VANISHED, BUT SO HAS THE NUMBER ONE DIME! SCROOGE IS FLATTENED BY GRIEF!
I'VE GOT SOMETHING TO CHEER YOU UP!
DON'T BOTHER, DAISY! I'M TOO HEART-BROKEN TO LOOK!
MY DIME! BUT HOW?!
JUST USED THE SAME SLEIGHT-OF-HAND I SHOWED MAGICA'S GUIDES!
BACK HOME, A FEW WEEKS LATER!
TELL YOU WHAT, UNCLE SCROOGE...
I WON'T FINISH THIS BOOK ABOUT YOUR LIFE JUST YET! I HAVE A FEELING THERE ARE MORE CHAPTERS TO BE WRITTEN!
MAYBE THERE ARE, DAISY! MAYBE THERE ARE!
the End

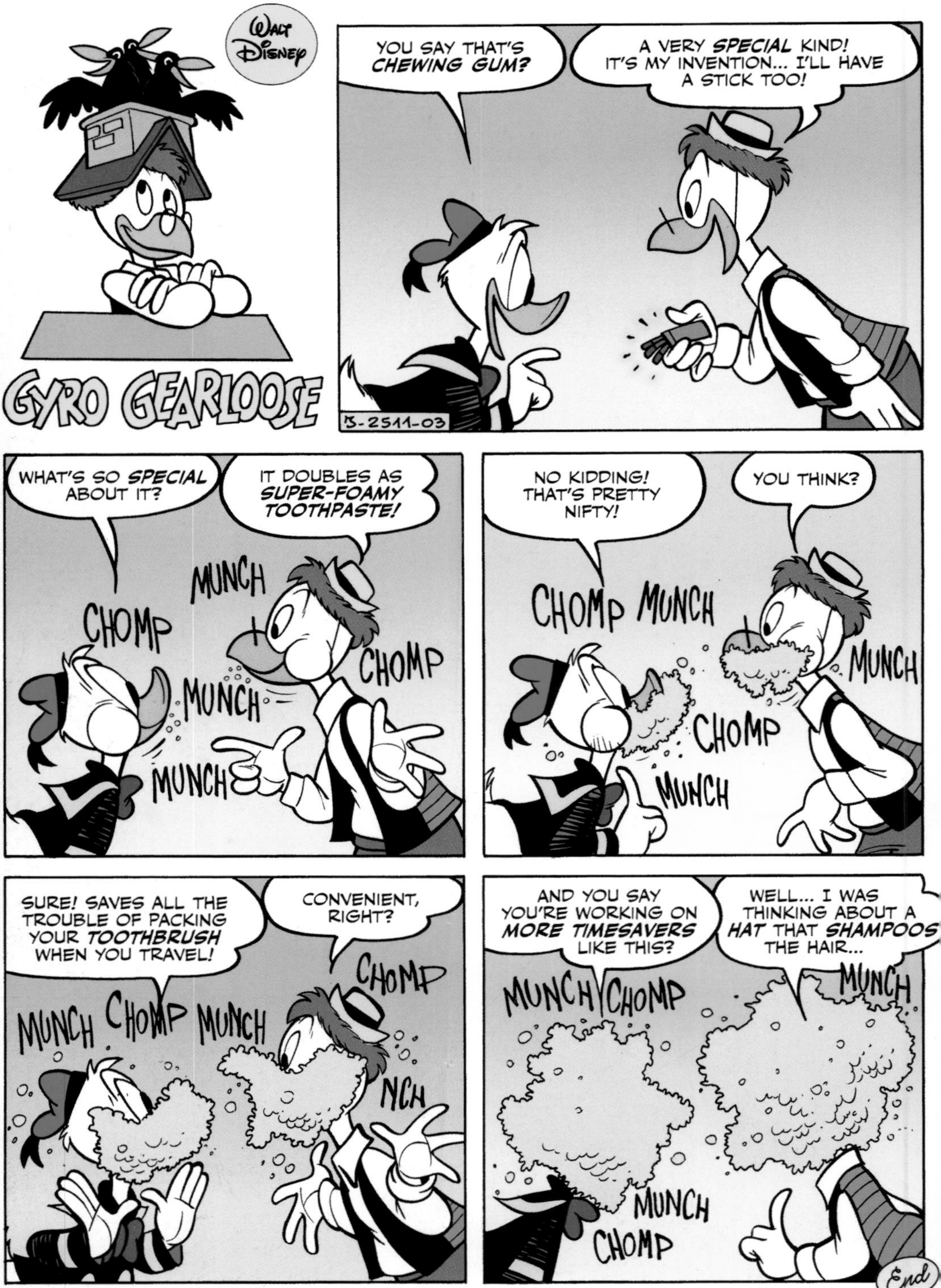
WALT DISNEY
GYRO GEARLOOSE
YOU SAY THAT'S *CHEWING GUM?*
A VERY *SPECIAL* KIND! IT'S MY INVENTION... I'LL HAVE A STICK TOO!
B-2511-03
WHAT'S SO *SPECIAL* ABOUT IT?
IT DOUBLES AS *SUPER-FOAMY TOOTHPASTE!*
MUNCH
CHOMP
CHOMP
MUNCH
MUNCH
NO KIDDING! THAT'S PRETTY *NIFTY!*
YOU THINK?
CHOMP MUNCH
MUNCH
CHOMP
MUNCH
SURE! SAVES ALL THE TROUBLE OF PACKING YOUR *TOOTHBRUSH* WHEN YOU TRAVEL!
CONVENIENT, RIGHT?
CHOMP
MUNCH CHOMP MUNCH
NCH
AND YOU SAY YOU'RE WORKING ON *MORE TIMESAVERS* LIKE THIS?
WELL... I WAS THINKING ABOUT A *HAT* THAT *SHAMPOOS* THE HAIR...
MUNCH CHOMP
MUNCH
MUNCH
CHOMP
End

Originally published in *Topolino* #2511 (Italy, 2004)

Walt Disney's FLINTHEART GLOMGOLD in THE GLOMGOLD HERITAGE

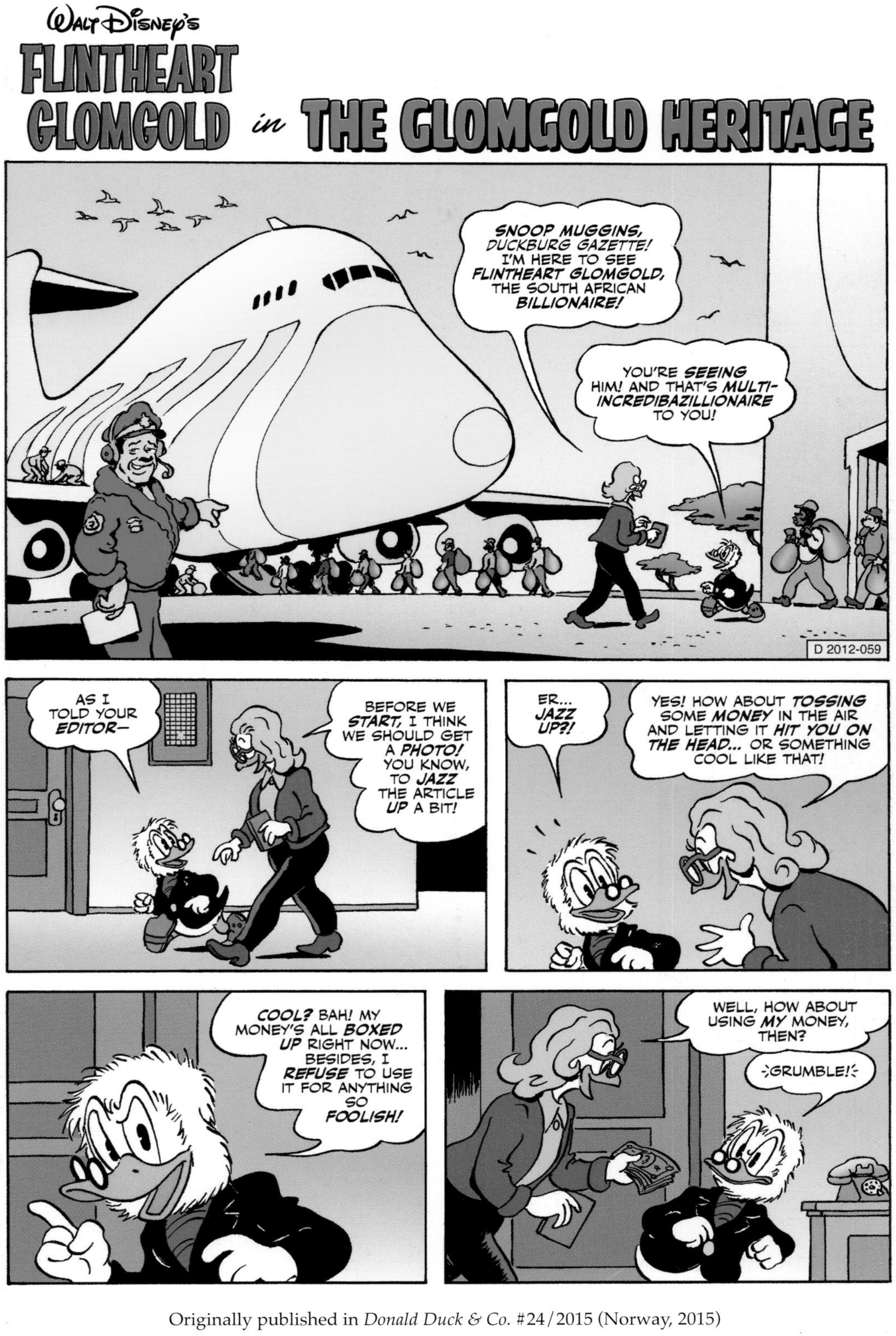
SNOOP MUGGINS, DUCKBURG GAZETTE! I'M HERE TO SEE FLINTHEART GLOMGOLD, THE SOUTH AFRICAN BILLIONAIRE!
YOU'RE SEEING HIM! AND THAT'S MULTI-INCREDIBAZILLIONAIRE TO YOU!
D 2012-059
AS I TOLD YOUR EDITOR—
BEFORE WE START, I THINK WE SHOULD GET A PHOTO! YOU KNOW, TO JAZZ THE ARTICLE UP A BIT!
ER... JAZZ UP?!
YES! HOW ABOUT TOSSING SOME MONEY IN THE AIR AND LETTING IT HIT YOU ON THE HEAD... OR SOMETHING COOL LIKE THAT!
COOL? BAH! MY MONEY'S ALL BOXED UP RIGHT NOW... BESIDES, I REFUSE TO USE IT FOR ANYTHING SO FOOLISH!
WELL, HOW ABOUT USING MY MONEY, THEN?
-GRUMBLE!-

Originally published in *Donald Duck & Co.* #24/2015 (Norway, 2015)

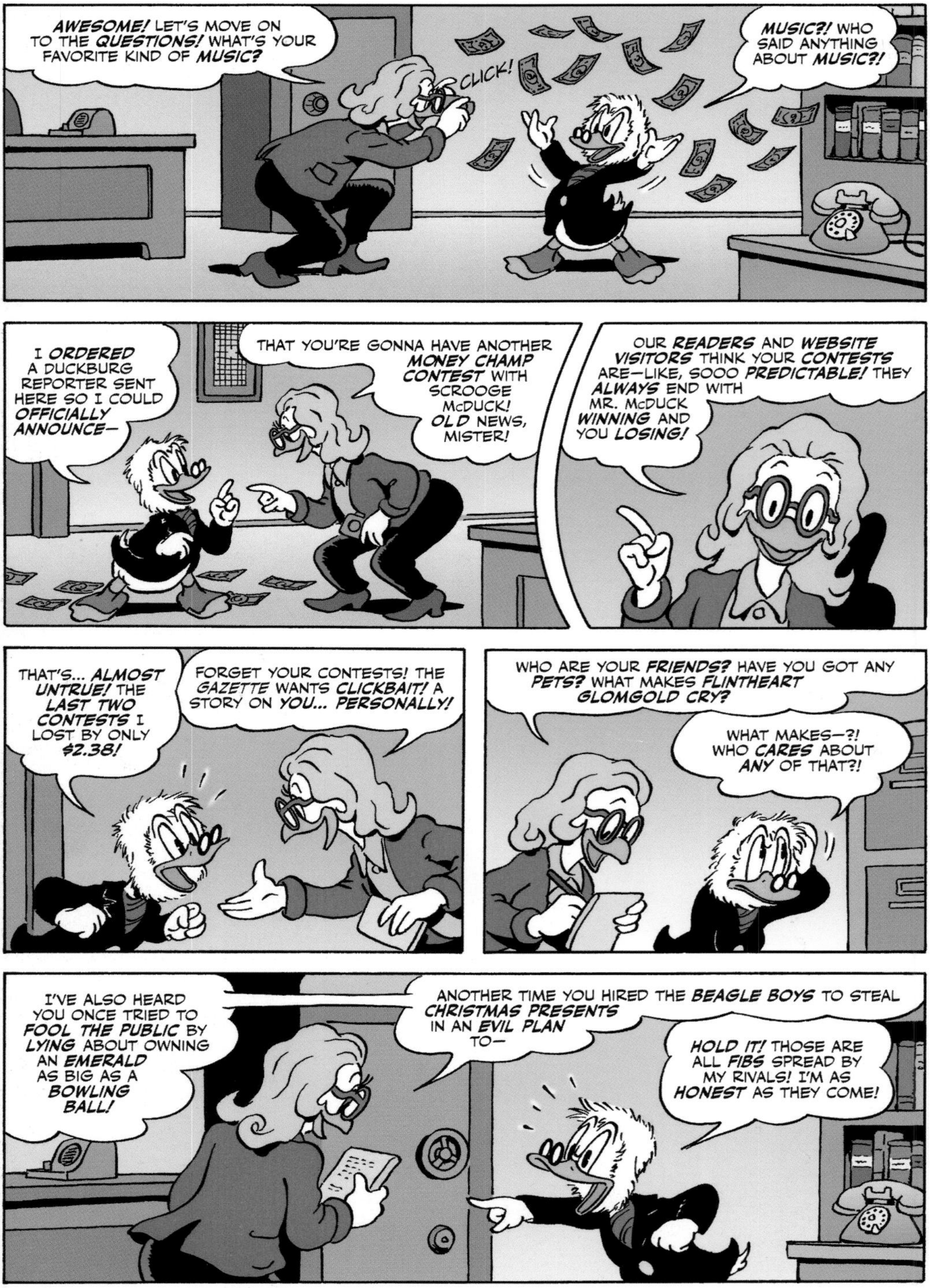
AWESOME! LET'S MOVE ON TO THE QUESTIONS! WHAT'S YOUR FAVORITE KIND OF MUSIC?
CLICK!
MUSIC?! WHO SAID ANYTHING ABOUT MUSIC?!
I ORDERED A DUCKBURG REPORTER SENT HERE SO I COULD OFFICIALLY ANNOUNCE—
THAT YOU'RE GONNA HAVE ANOTHER MONEY CHAMP CONTEST WITH SCROOGE McDUCK! OLD NEWS, MISTER!
OUR READERS AND WEBSITE VISITORS THINK YOUR CONTESTS ARE—LIKE, SOOO PREDICTABLE! THEY ALWAYS END WITH MR. McDUCK WINNING AND YOU LOSING!
THAT'S... ALMOST UNTRUE! THE LAST TWO CONTESTS I LOST BY ONLY $2.38!
FORGET YOUR CONTESTS! THE GAZETTE WANTS CLICKBAIT! A STORY ON YOU... PERSONALLY!
WHO ARE YOUR FRIENDS? HAVE YOU GOT ANY PETS? WHAT MAKES FLINTHEART GLOMGOLD CRY?
WHAT MAKES—?! WHO CARES ABOUT ANY OF THAT?!
I'VE ALSO HEARD YOU ONCE TRIED TO FOOL THE PUBLIC BY LYING ABOUT OWNING AN EMERALD AS BIG AS A BOWLING BALL!
ANOTHER TIME YOU HIRED THE BEAGLE BOYS TO STEAL CHRISTMAS PRESENTS IN AN EVIL PLAN TO—
HOLD IT! THOSE ARE ALL FIBS SPREAD BY MY RIVALS! I'M AS HONEST AS THEY COME!

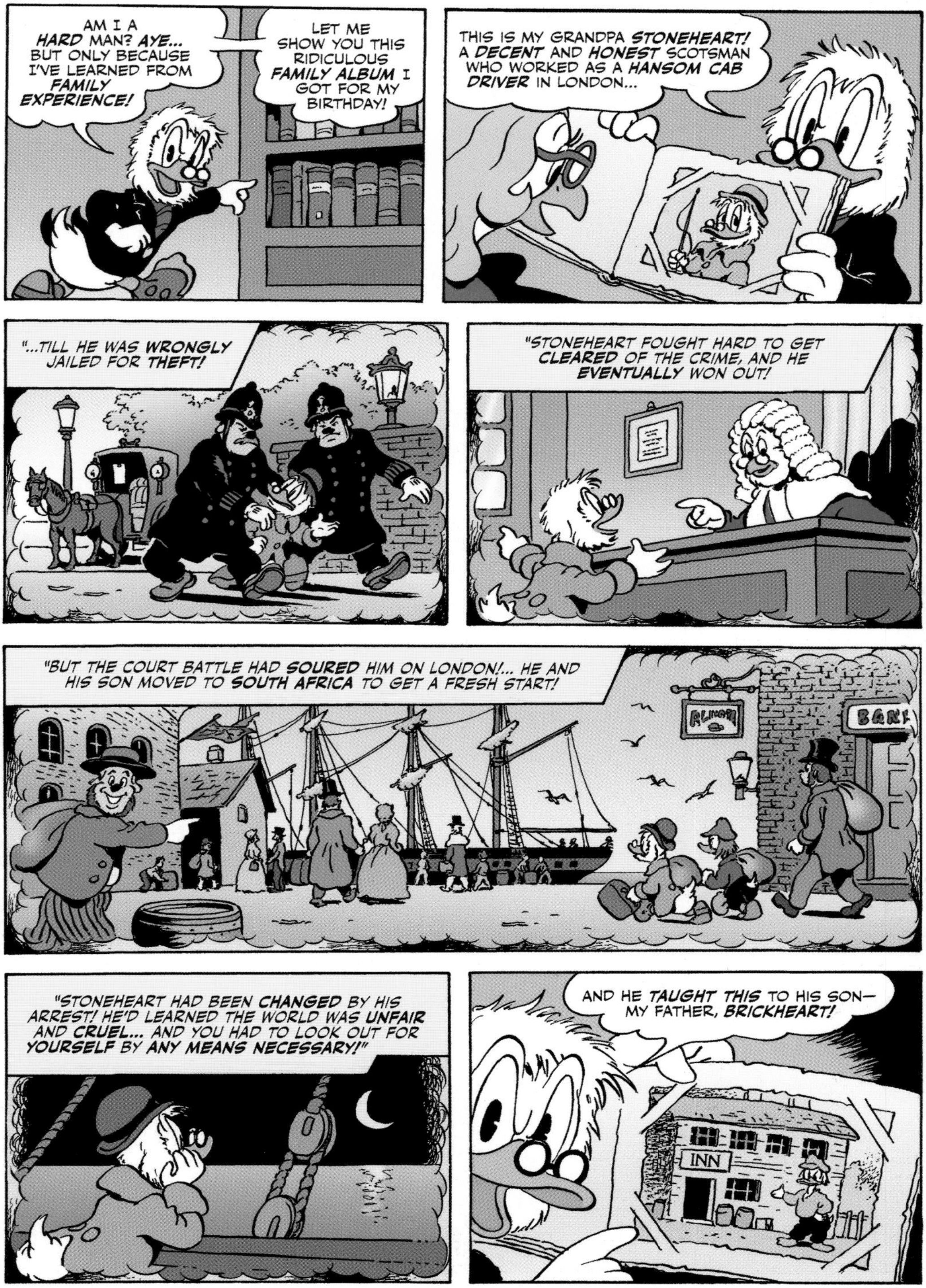
AM I A HARD MAN? AYE... BUT ONLY BECAUSE I'VE LEARNED FROM FAMILY EXPERIENCE!
LET ME SHOW YOU THIS RIDICULOUS FAMILY ALBUM I GOT FOR MY BIRTHDAY!
THIS IS MY GRANDPA STONEHEART! A DECENT AND HONEST SCOTSMAN WHO WORKED AS A HANSOM CAB DRIVER IN LONDON...
"...TILL HE WAS WRONGLY JAILED FOR THEFT!
"STONEHEART FOUGHT HARD TO GET CLEARED OF THE CRIME, AND HE EVENTUALLY WON OUT!
"BUT THE COURT BATTLE HAD SOURED HIM ON LONDON!... HE AND HIS SON MOVED TO SOUTH AFRICA TO GET A FRESH START!
"STONEHEART HAD BEEN CHANGED BY HIS ARREST! HE'D LEARNED THE WORLD WAS UNFAIR AND CRUEL... AND YOU HAD TO LOOK OUT FOR YOURSELF BY ANY MEANS NECESSARY!"
AND HE TAUGHT THIS TO HIS SON— MY FATHER, BRICKHEART!
INN

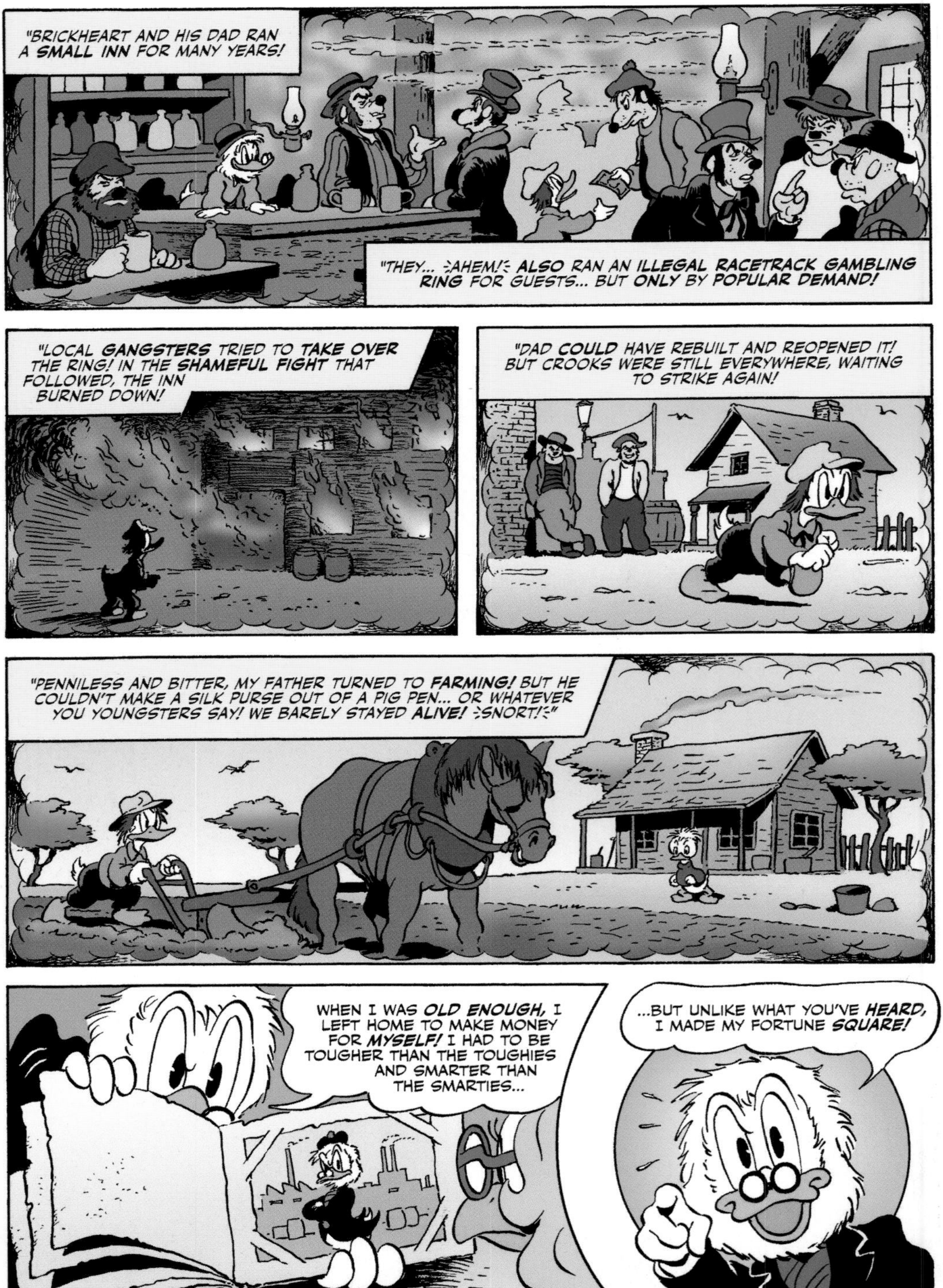
"BRICKHEART AND HIS DAD RAN A SMALL INN FOR MANY YEARS!
"THEY... ⁝AHEM!⁝ ALSO RAN AN ILLEGAL RACETRACK GAMBLING RING FOR GUESTS... BUT ONLY BY POPULAR DEMAND!
"LOCAL GANGSTERS TRIED TO TAKE OVER THE RING! IN THE SHAMEFUL FIGHT THAT FOLLOWED, THE INN BURNED DOWN!
"DAD COULD HAVE REBUILT AND REOPENED IT! BUT CROOKS WERE STILL EVERYWHERE, WAITING TO STRIKE AGAIN!
"PENNILESS AND BITTER, MY FATHER TURNED TO FARMING! BUT HE COULDN'T MAKE A SILK PURSE OUT OF A PIG PEN... OR WHATEVER YOU YOUNGSTERS SAY! WE BARELY STAYED ALIVE! ⁝SNORT!⁝"
WHEN I WAS OLD ENOUGH, I LEFT HOME TO MAKE MONEY FOR MYSELF! I HAD TO BE TOUGHER THAN THE TOUGHIES AND SMARTER THAN THE SMARTIES...
...BUT UNLIKE WHAT YOU'VE HEARD, I MADE MY FORTUNE SQUARE!

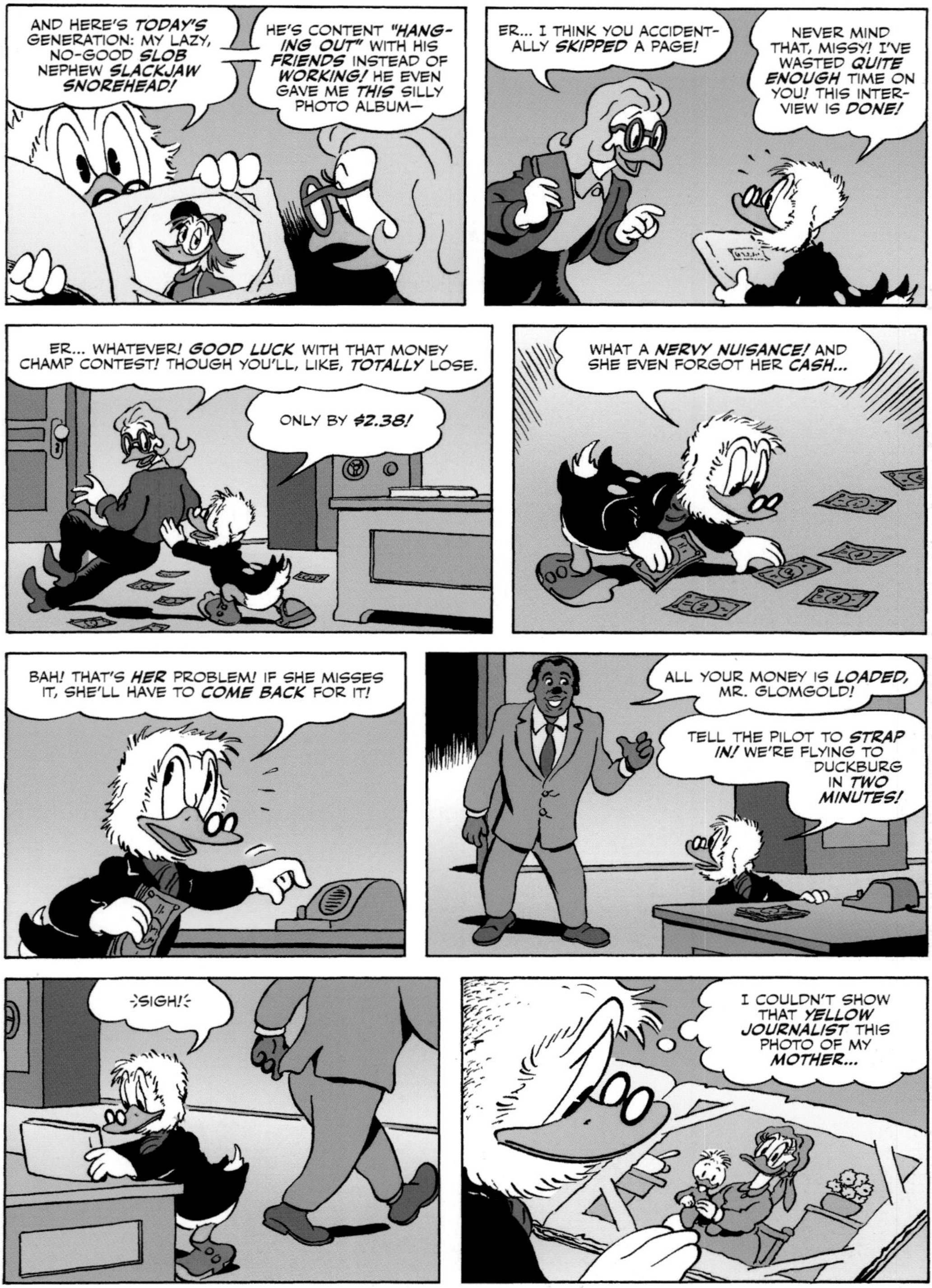
AND HERE'S TODAY'S GENERATION: MY LAZY, NO-GOOD SLOB NEPHEW SLACKJAW SNOREHEAD!
HE'S CONTENT "HANGING OUT" WITH HIS FRIENDS INSTEAD OF WORKING! HE EVEN GAVE ME THIS SILLY PHOTO ALBUM—
ER... I THINK YOU ACCIDENTALLY SKIPPED A PAGE!
NEVER MIND THAT, MISSY! I'VE WASTED QUITE ENOUGH TIME ON YOU! THIS INTERVIEW IS DONE!
ER... WHATEVER! GOOD LUCK WITH THAT MONEY CHAMP CONTEST! THOUGH YOU'LL, LIKE, TOTALLY LOSE.
ONLY BY $2.38!
WHAT A NERVY NUISANCE! AND SHE EVEN FORGOT HER CASH...
BAH! THAT'S HER PROBLEM! IF SHE MISSES IT, SHE'LL HAVE TO COME BACK FOR IT!
ALL YOUR MONEY IS LOADED, MR. GLOMGOLD!
TELL THE PILOT TO STRAP IN! WE'RE FLYING TO DUCKBURG IN TWO MINUTES!
SIGH!
I COULDN'T SHOW THAT YELLOW JOURNALIST THIS PHOTO OF MY MOTHER...

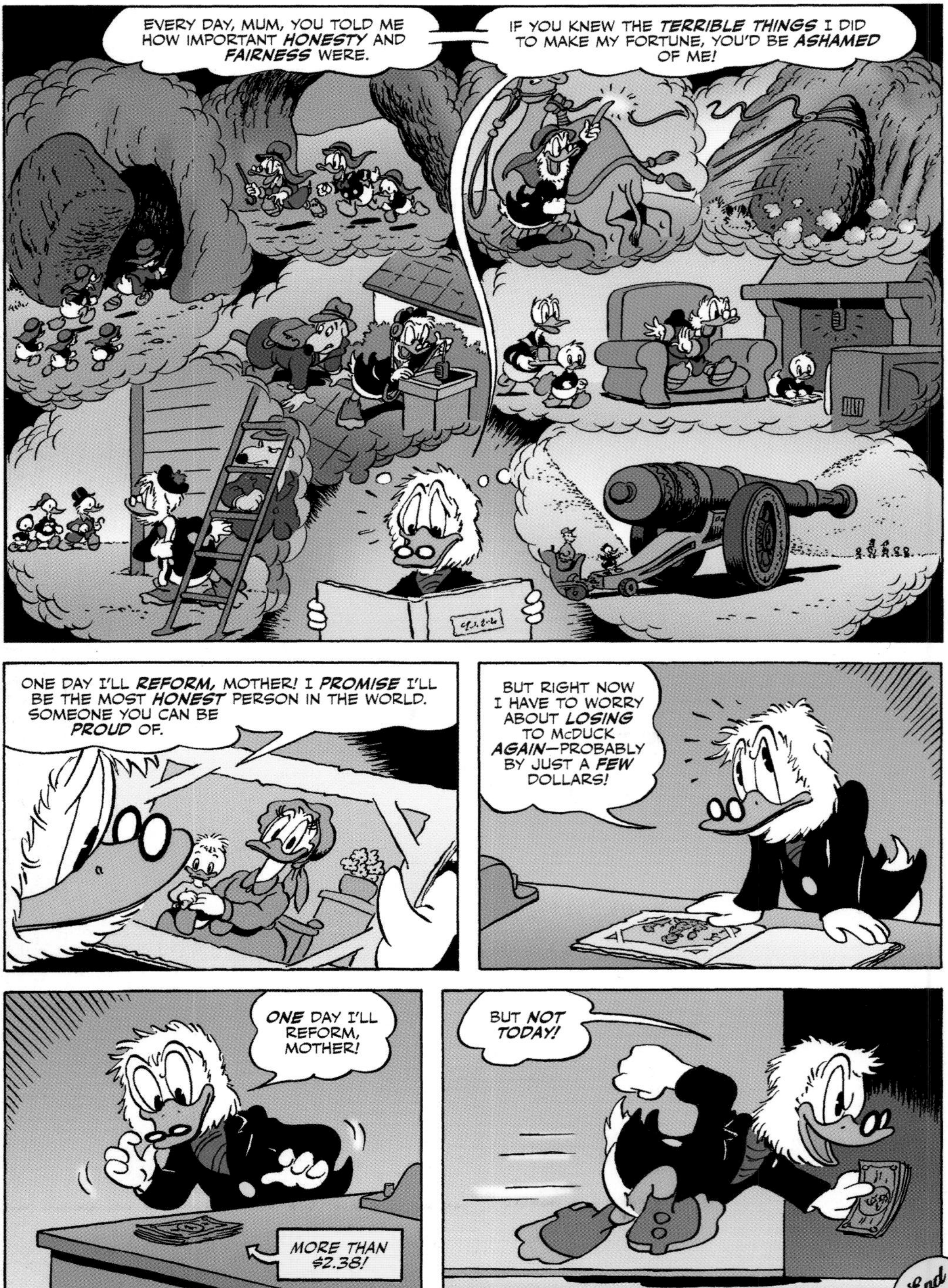
EVERY DAY, MUM, YOU TOLD ME HOW IMPORTANT HONESTY AND FAIRNESS WERE.
IF YOU KNEW THE TERRIBLE THINGS I DID TO MAKE MY FORTUNE, YOU'D BE ASHAMED OF ME!
ONE DAY I'LL REFORM, MOTHER! I PROMISE I'LL BE THE MOST HONEST PERSON IN THE WORLD. SOMEONE YOU CAN BE PROUD OF.
BUT RIGHT NOW I HAVE TO WORRY ABOUT LOSING TO McDUCK AGAIN—PROBABLY BY JUST A FEW DOLLARS!
ONE DAY I'LL REFORM, MOTHER!
MORE THAN $2.38!
BUT NOT TODAY!
End

Walt Disney's Uncle Scrooge

WHEN MAGICA WON

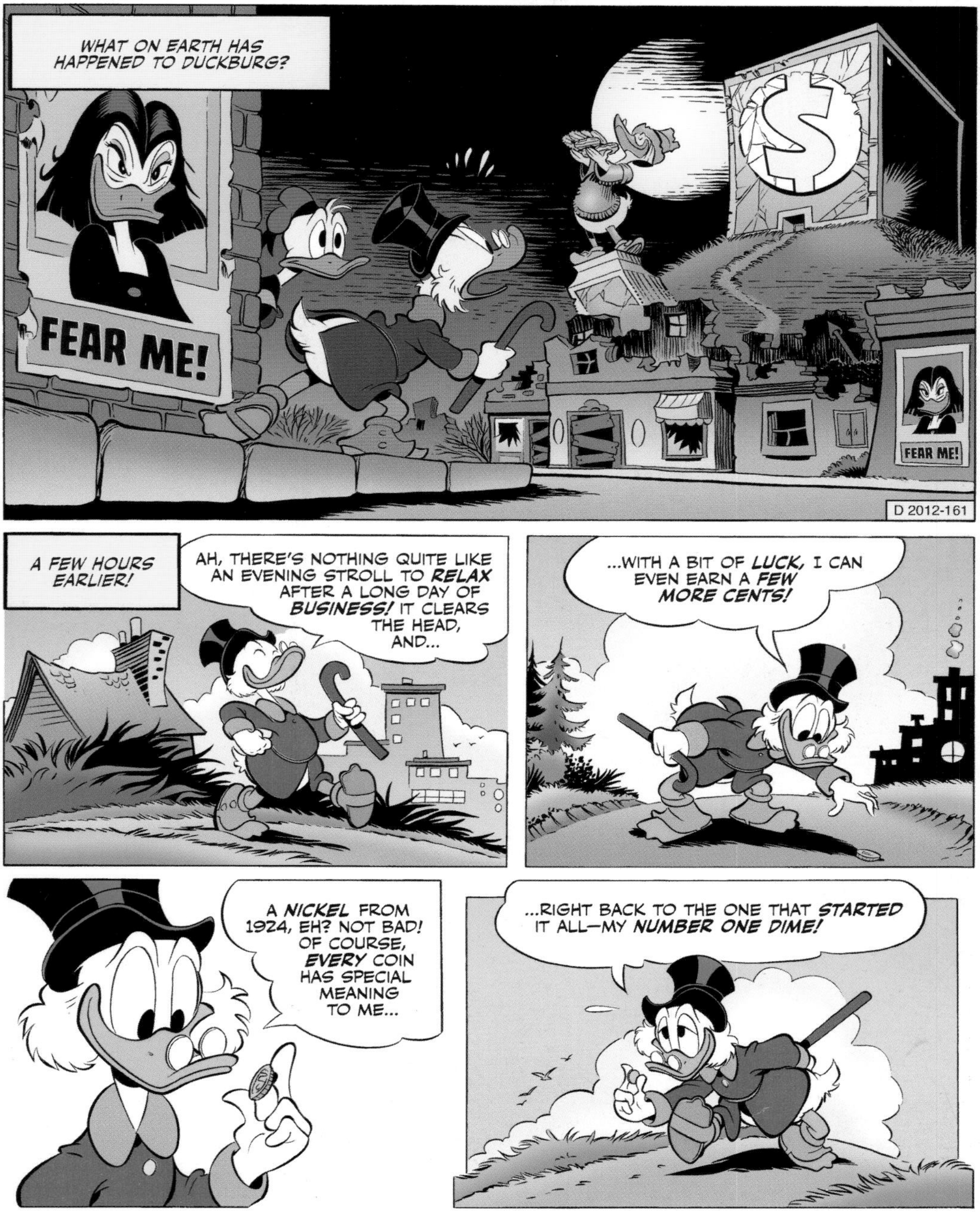
WHAT ON EARTH HAS HAPPENED TO DUCKBURG?
FEAR ME!
FEAR ME!
D 2012-161
A FEW HOURS EARLIER!
AH, THERE'S NOTHING QUITE LIKE AN EVENING STROLL TO RELAX AFTER A LONG DAY OF BUSINESS! IT CLEARS THE HEAD, AND...
...WITH A BIT OF LUCK, I CAN EVEN EARN A FEW MORE CENTS!
A NICKEL FROM 1924, EH? NOT BAD! OF COURSE, EVERY COIN HAS SPECIAL MEANING TO ME...
...RIGHT BACK TO THE ONE THAT STARTED IT ALL—MY NUMBER ONE DIME!

Originally published in *Kalle Anka & C:o* #39/2014 (Sweden, 2014)

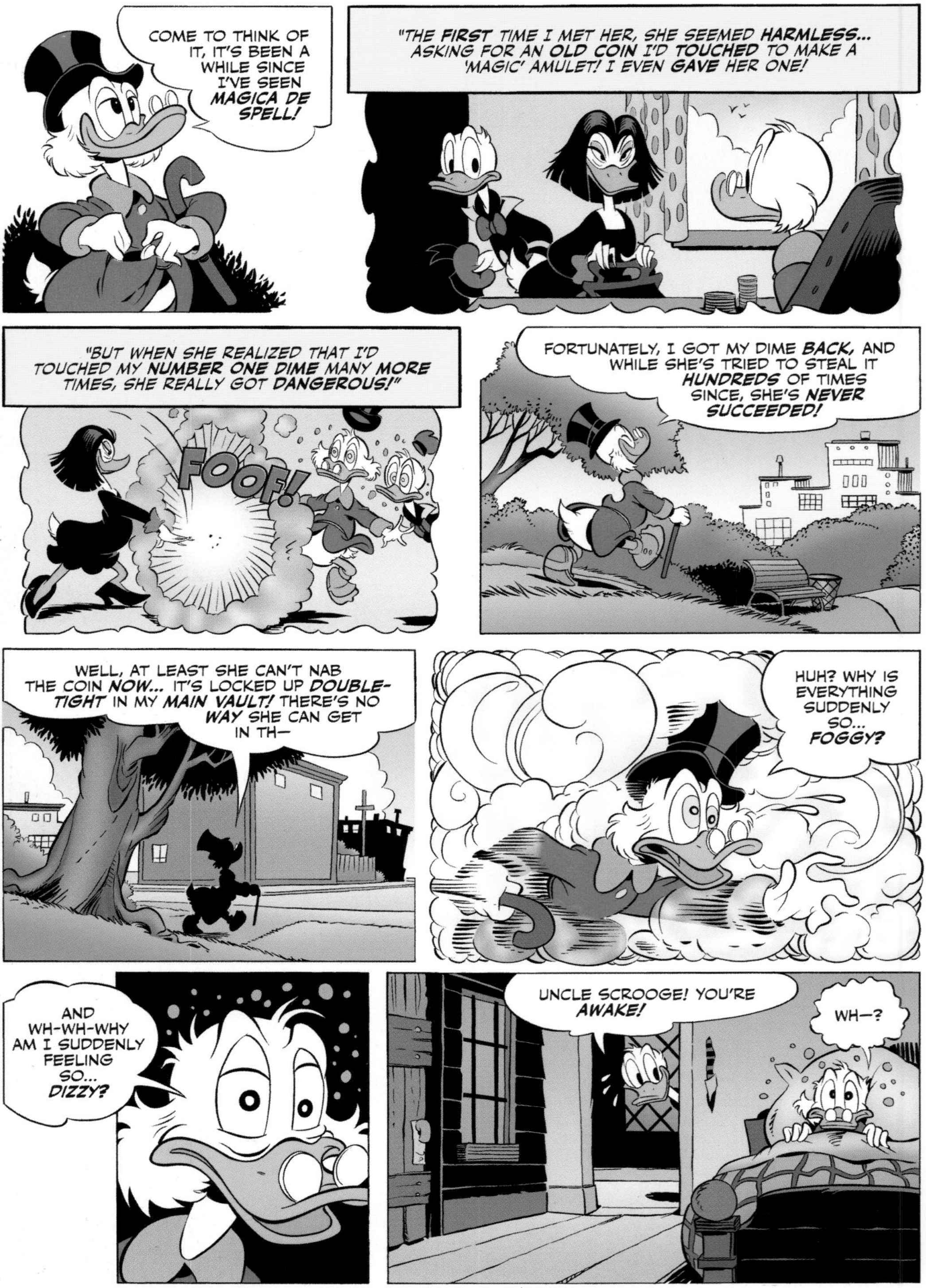
COME TO THINK OF IT, IT'S BEEN A WHILE SINCE I'VE SEEN MAGICA DE SPELL!
"THE FIRST TIME I MET HER, SHE SEEMED HARMLESS... ASKING FOR AN OLD COIN I'D TOUCHED TO MAKE A 'MAGIC' AMULET! I EVEN GAVE HER ONE!
"BUT WHEN SHE REALIZED THAT I'D TOUCHED MY NUMBER ONE DIME MANY MORE TIMES, SHE REALLY GOT DANGEROUS!"
FOOF!
FORTUNATELY, I GOT MY DIME BACK, AND WHILE SHE'S TRIED TO STEAL IT HUNDREDS OF TIMES SINCE, SHE'S NEVER SUCCEEDED!
WELL, AT LEAST SHE CAN'T NAB THE COIN NOW... IT'S LOCKED UP DOUBLE-TIGHT IN MY MAIN VAULT! THERE'S NO WAY SHE CAN GET IN TH—
HUH? WHY IS EVERYTHING SUDDENLY SO... FOGGY?
AND WH-WH-WHY AM I SUDDENLY FEELING SO... DIZZY?
UNCLE SCROOGE! YOU'RE AWAKE!
WH—?

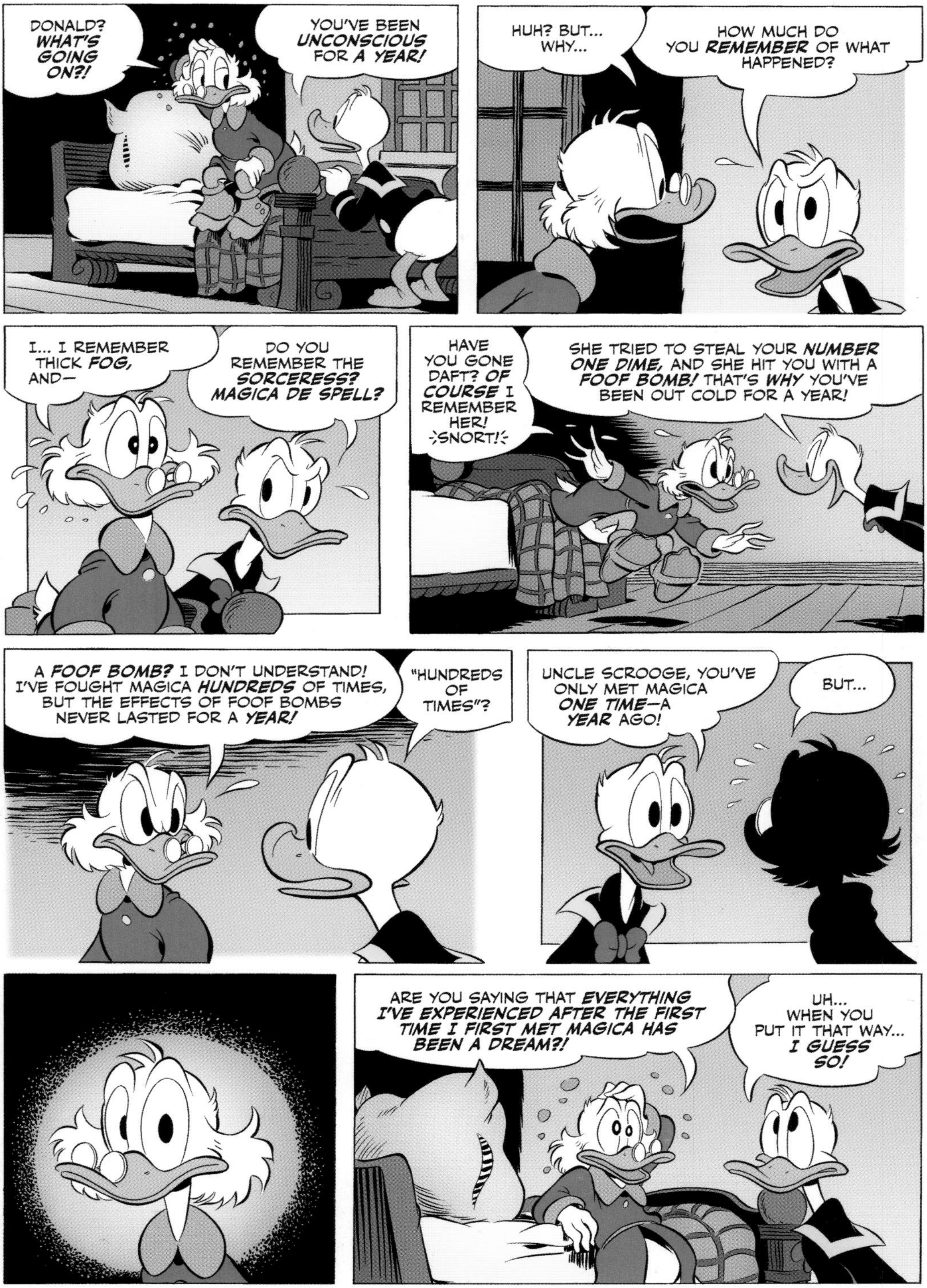

DONALD? WHAT'S GOING ON?!
YOU'VE BEEN UNCONSCIOUS FOR A YEAR!
HUH? BUT... WHY...
HOW MUCH DO YOU REMEMBER OF WHAT HAPPENED?
I... I REMEMBER THICK FOG, AND—
DO YOU REMEMBER THE SORCERESS? MAGICA DE SPELL?
HAVE YOU GONE DAFT? OF COURSE I REMEMBER HER! SNORT!
SHE TRIED TO STEAL YOUR NUMBER ONE DIME, AND SHE HIT YOU WITH A FOOF BOMB! THAT'S WHY YOU'VE BEEN OUT COLD FOR A YEAR!
A FOOF BOMB? I DON'T UNDERSTAND! I'VE FOUGHT MAGICA HUNDREDS OF TIMES, BUT THE EFFECTS OF FOOF BOMBS NEVER LASTED FOR A YEAR!
"HUNDREDS OF TIMES"?
UNCLE SCROOGE, YOU'VE ONLY MET MAGICA ONE TIME—A YEAR AGO!
BUT...
ARE YOU SAYING THAT EVERYTHING I'VE EXPERIENCED AFTER THE FIRST TIME I FIRST MET MAGICA HAS BEEN A DREAM?!
UH... WHEN YOU PUT IT THAT WAY... I GUESS SO!

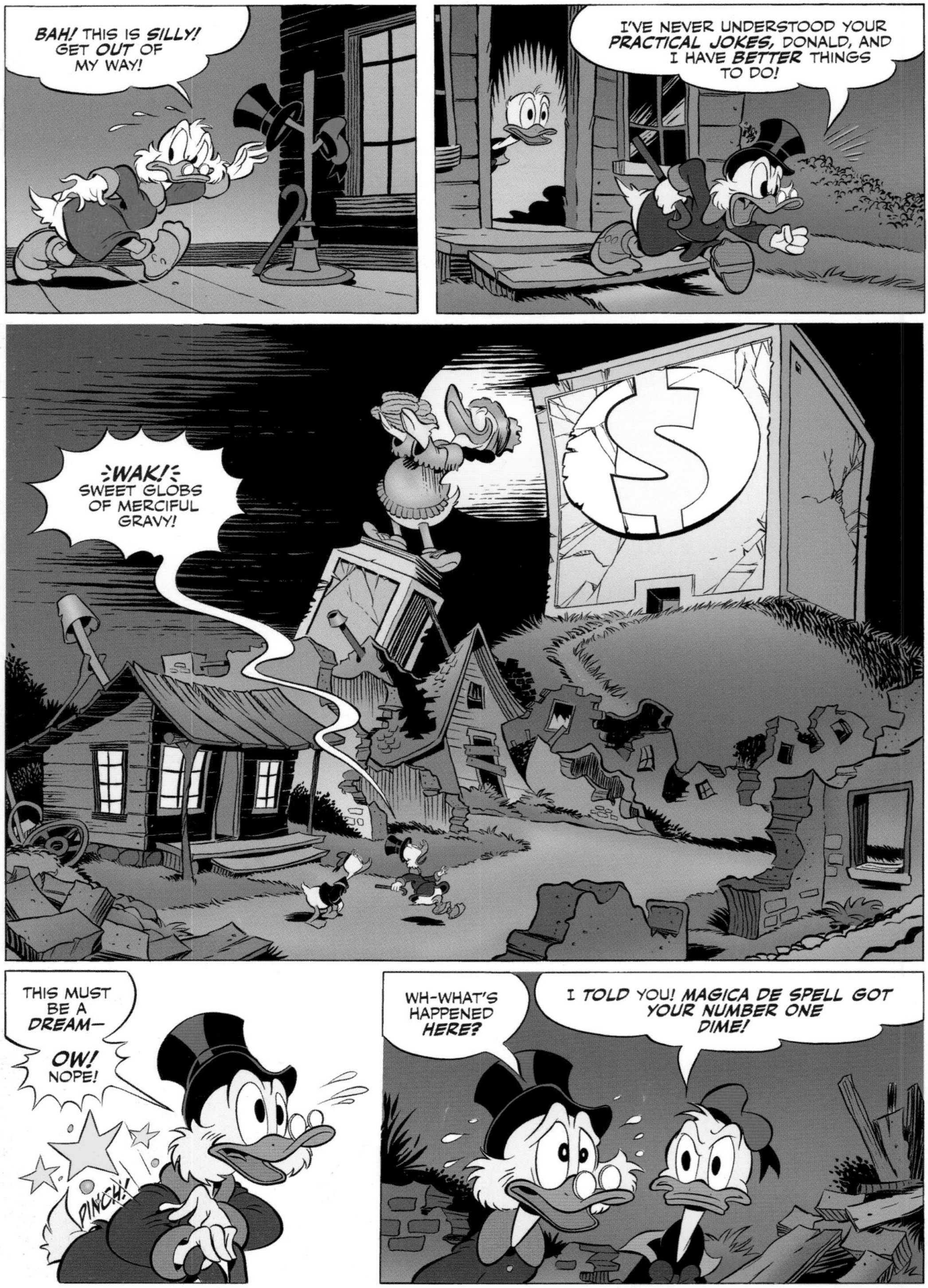
BAH! THIS IS SILLY! GET OUT OF MY WAY!
I'VE NEVER UNDERSTOOD YOUR PRACTICAL JOKES, DONALD, AND I HAVE BETTER THINGS TO DO!
WAK! SWEET GLOBS OF MERCIFUL GRAVY!
THIS MUST BE A DREAM—
OW! NOPE!
PINCH!
WH-WHAT'S HAPPENED HERE?
I TOLD YOU! MAGICA DE SPELL GOT YOUR NUMBER ONE DIME!

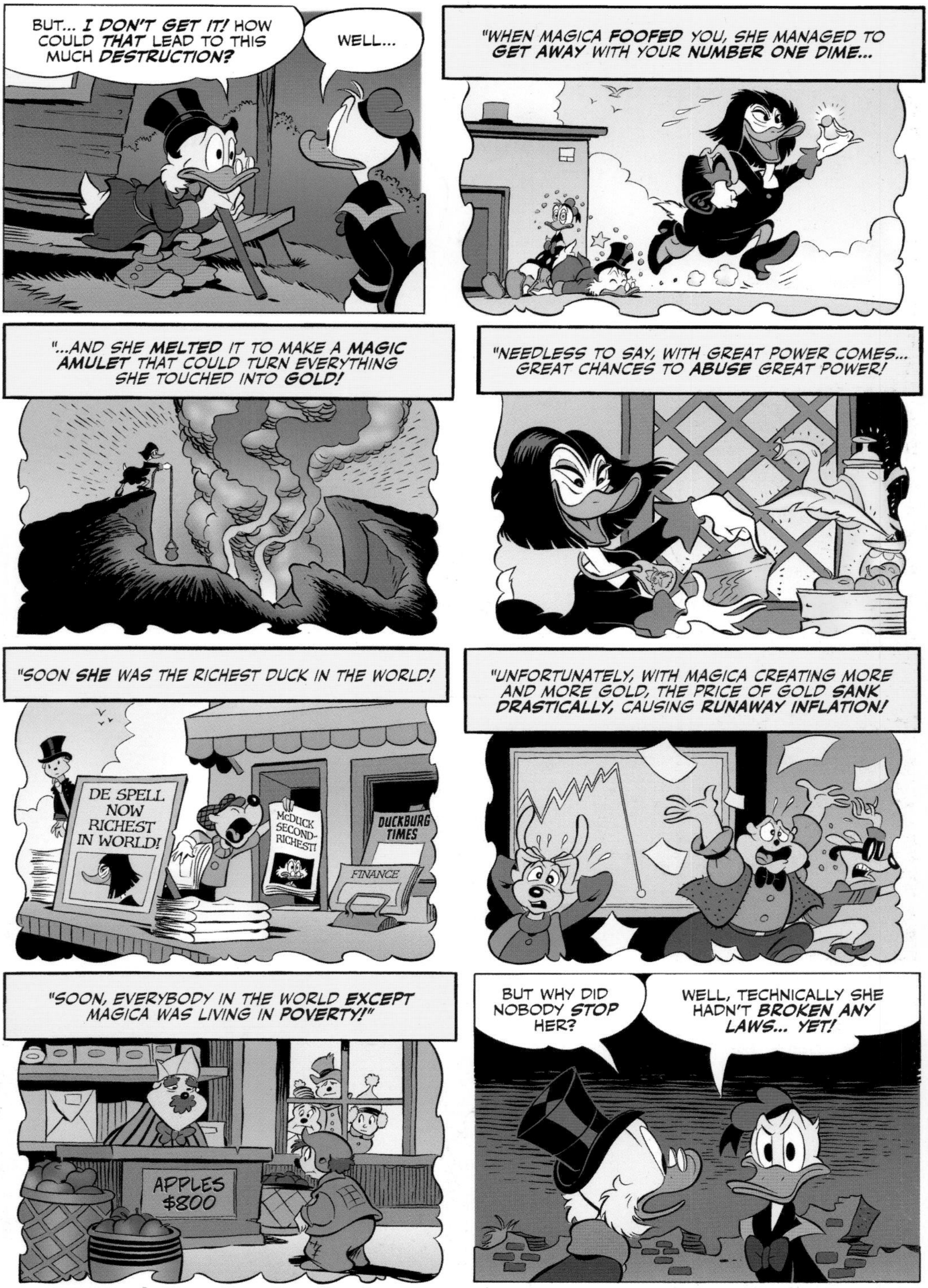
BUT... I DON'T GET IT! HOW COULD THAT LEAD TO THIS MUCH DESTRUCTION?
WELL...
"WHEN MAGICA FOOFED YOU, SHE MANAGED TO GET AWAY WITH YOUR NUMBER ONE DIME...
"...AND SHE MELTED IT TO MAKE A MAGIC AMULET THAT COULD TURN EVERYTHING SHE TOUCHED INTO GOLD!
"NEEDLESS TO SAY, WITH GREAT POWER COMES... GREAT CHANCES TO ABUSE GREAT POWER!
"SOON SHE WAS THE RICHEST DUCK IN THE WORLD!
DE SPELL NOW RICHEST IN WORLD!
McDUCK SECOND-RICHEST!
DUCKBURG TIMES
FINANCE
"UNFORTUNATELY, WITH MAGICA CREATING MORE AND MORE GOLD, THE PRICE OF GOLD SANK DRASTICALLY, CAUSING RUNAWAY INFLATION!
"SOON, EVERYBODY IN THE WORLD EXCEPT MAGICA WAS LIVING IN POVERTY!"
APPLES $800
BUT WHY DID NOBODY STOP HER?
WELL, TECHNICALLY SHE HADN'T BROKEN ANY LAWS... YET!

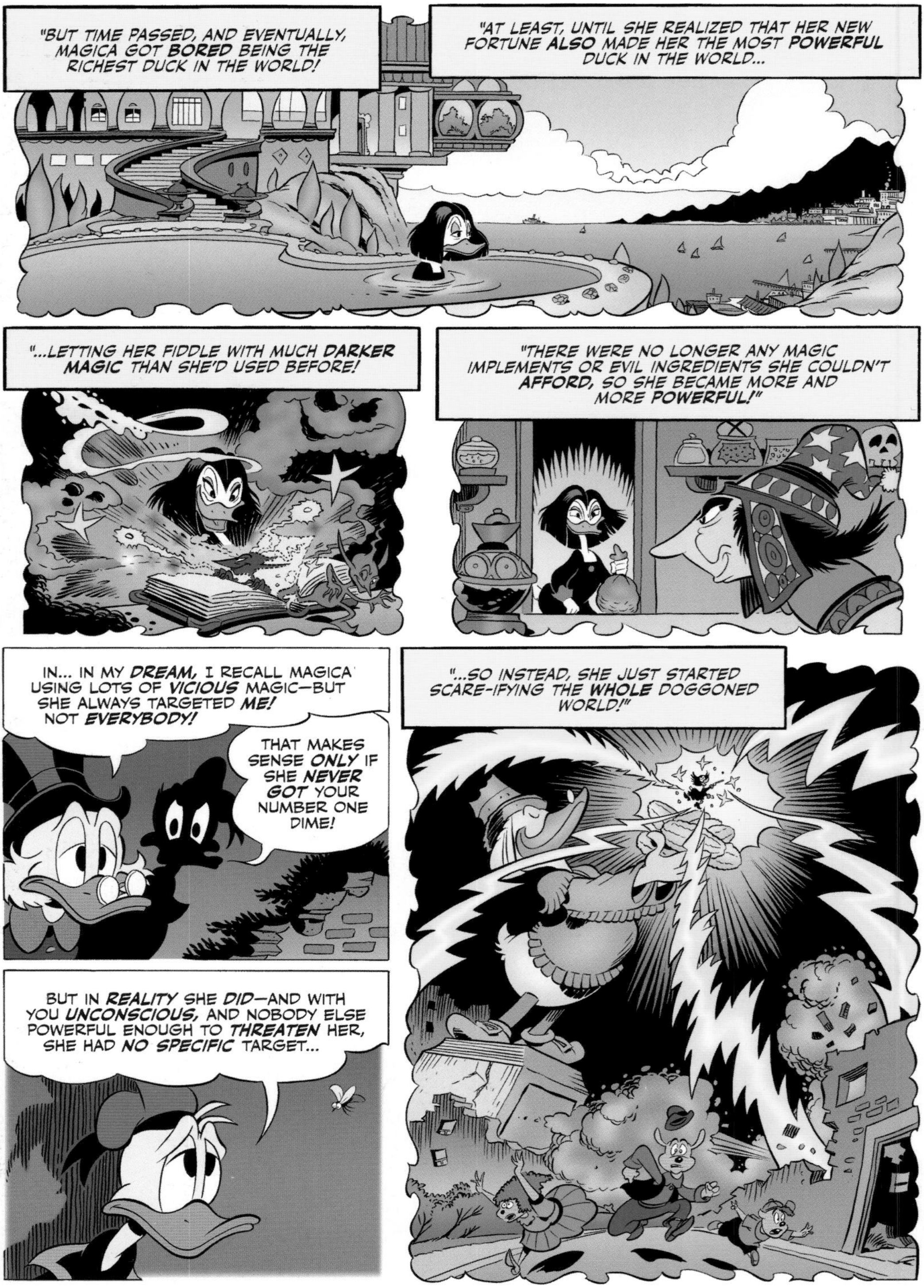
"BUT TIME PASSED, AND EVENTUALLY, MAGICA GOT BORED BEING THE RICHEST DUCK IN THE WORLD!
"AT LEAST, UNTIL SHE REALIZED THAT HER NEW FORTUNE ALSO MADE HER THE MOST POWERFUL DUCK IN THE WORLD...
"...LETTING HER FIDDLE WITH MUCH DARKER MAGIC THAN SHE'D USED BEFORE!
"THERE WERE NO LONGER ANY MAGIC IMPLEMENTS OR EVIL INGREDIENTS SHE COULDN'T AFFORD, SO SHE BECAME MORE AND MORE POWERFUL!"
IN... IN MY DREAM, I RECALL MAGICA USING LOTS OF VICIOUS MAGIC—BUT SHE ALWAYS TARGETED ME! NOT EVERYBODY!
THAT MAKES SENSE ONLY IF SHE NEVER GOT YOUR NUMBER ONE DIME!
BUT IN REALITY SHE DID—AND WITH YOU UNCONSCIOUS, AND NOBODY ELSE POWERFUL ENOUGH TO THREATEN HER, SHE HAD NO SPECIFIC TARGET...
"...SO INSTEAD, SHE JUST STARTED SCARE-IFYING THE WHOLE DOGGONED WORLD!"

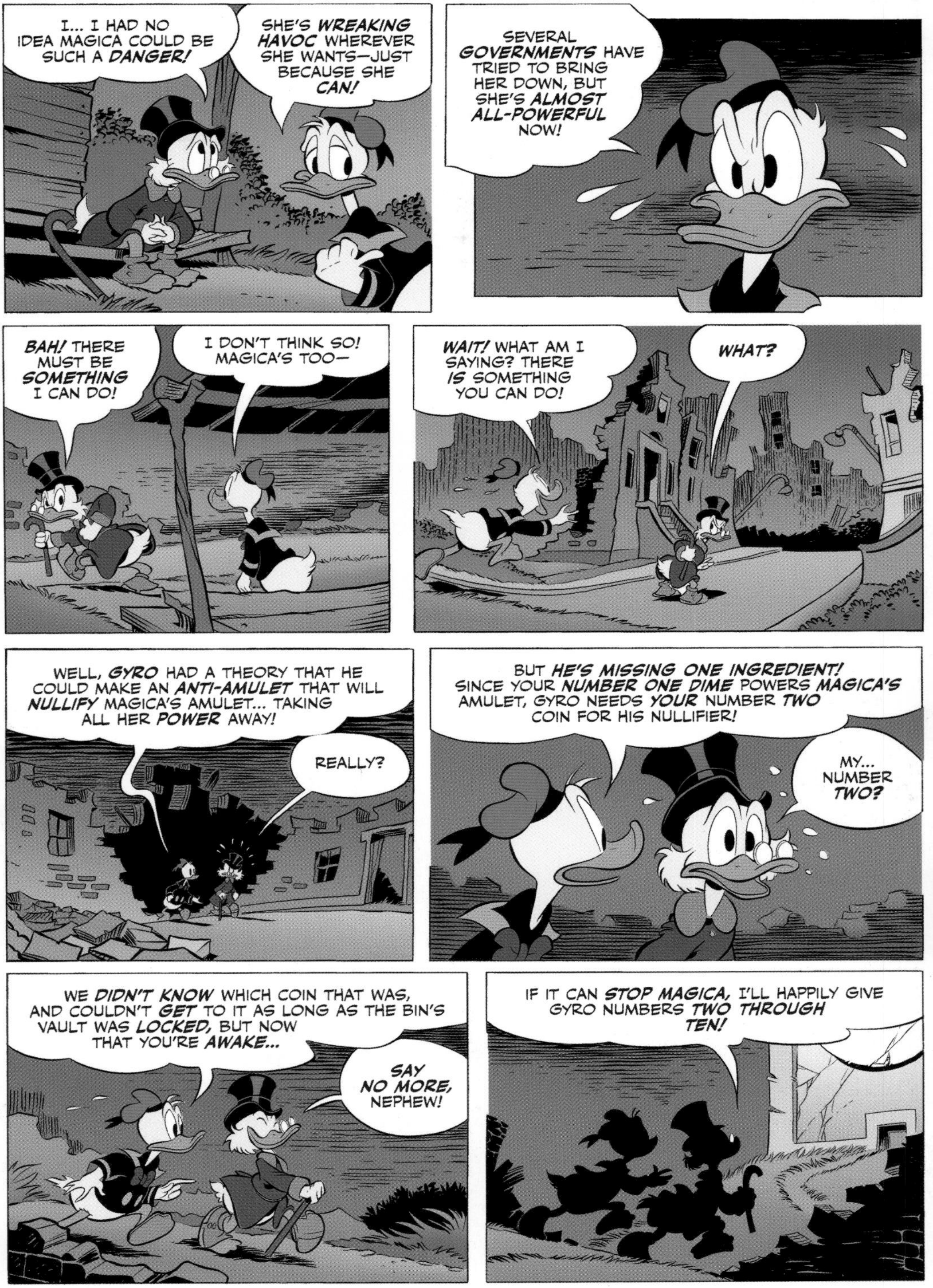
I... I HAD NO IDEA MAGICA COULD BE SUCH A DANGER!
SHE'S WREAKING HAVOC WHEREVER SHE WANTS—JUST BECAUSE SHE CAN!
SEVERAL GOVERNMENTS HAVE TRIED TO BRING HER DOWN, BUT SHE'S ALMOST ALL-POWERFUL NOW!
BAH! THERE MUST BE SOMETHING I CAN DO!
I DON'T THINK SO! MAGICA'S TOO—
WAIT! WHAT AM I SAYING? THERE IS SOMETHING YOU CAN DO!
WHAT?
WELL, GYRO HAD A THEORY THAT HE COULD MAKE AN ANTI-AMULET THAT WILL NULLIFY MAGICA'S AMULET... TAKING ALL HER POWER AWAY!
REALLY?
BUT HE'S MISSING ONE INGREDIENT! SINCE YOUR NUMBER ONE DIME POWERS MAGICA'S AMULET, GYRO NEEDS YOUR NUMBER TWO COIN FOR HIS NULLIFIER!
MY... NUMBER TWO?
WE DIDN'T KNOW WHICH COIN THAT WAS, AND COULDN'T GET TO IT AS LONG AS THE BIN'S VAULT WAS LOCKED, BUT NOW THAT YOU'RE AWAKE...
SAY NO MORE, NEPHEW!
IF IT CAN STOP MAGICA, I'LL HAPPILY GIVE GYRO NUMBERS TWO THROUGH TEN!

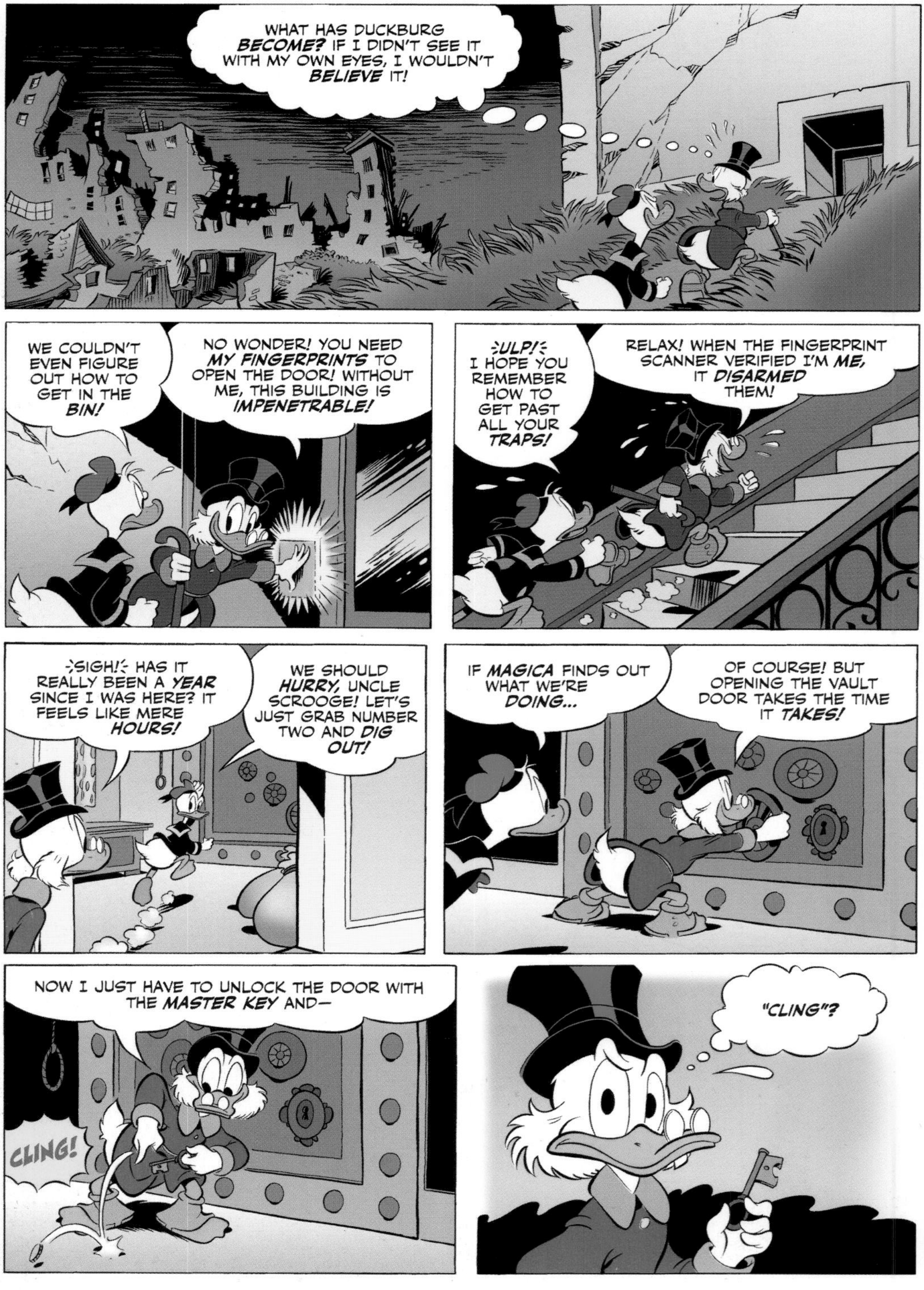

WHAT HAS DUCKBURG BECOME? IF I DIDN'T SEE IT WITH MY OWN EYES, I WOULDN'T BELIEVE IT!
WE COULDN'T EVEN FIGURE OUT HOW TO GET IN THE BIN!
NO WONDER! YOU NEED MY FINGERPRINTS TO OPEN THE DOOR! WITHOUT ME, THIS BUILDING IS IMPENETRABLE!
ULP! I HOPE YOU REMEMBER HOW TO GET PAST ALL YOUR TRAPS!
RELAX! WHEN THE FINGERPRINT SCANNER VERIFIED I'M ME, IT DISARMED THEM!
SIGH! HAS IT REALLY BEEN A YEAR SINCE I WAS HERE? IT FEELS LIKE MERE HOURS!
WE SHOULD HURRY, UNCLE SCROOGE! LET'S JUST GRAB NUMBER TWO AND DIG OUT!
IF MAGICA FINDS OUT WHAT WE'RE DOING...
OF COURSE! BUT OPENING THE VAULT DOOR TAKES THE TIME IT TAKES!
NOW I JUST HAVE TO UNLOCK THE DOOR WITH THE MASTER KEY AND—
CLING!
"CLING"?

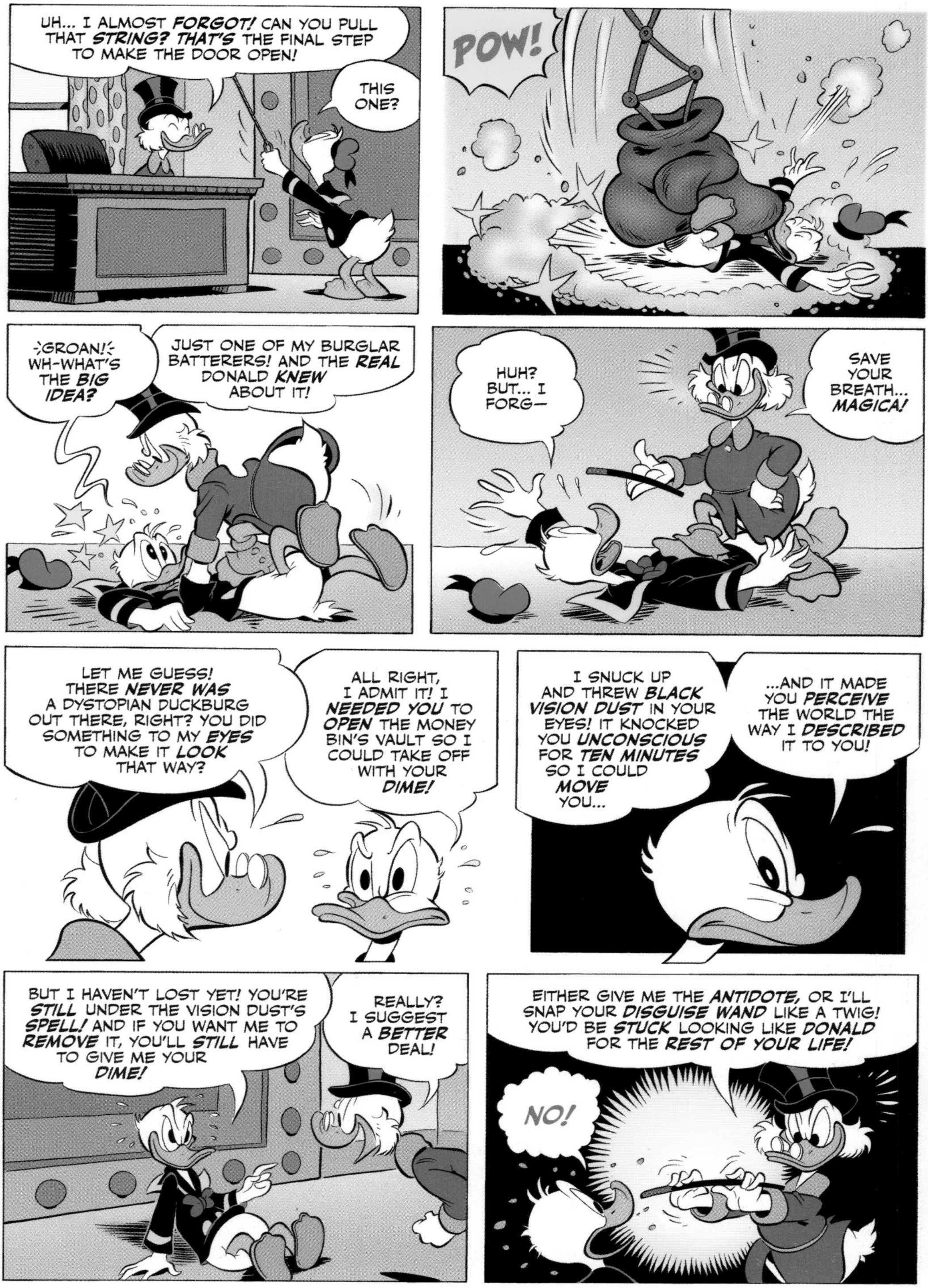
UH... I ALMOST FORGOT! CAN YOU PULL THAT STRING? THAT'S THE FINAL STEP TO MAKE THE DOOR OPEN!
THIS ONE?
POW!
GROAN! WH-WHAT'S THE BIG IDEA?
JUST ONE OF MY BURGLAR BATTERERS! AND THE REAL DONALD KNEW ABOUT IT!
HUH? BUT... I FORG—
SAVE YOUR BREATH... MAGICA!
LET ME GUESS! THERE NEVER WAS A DYSTOPIAN DUCKBURG OUT THERE, RIGHT? YOU DID SOMETHING TO MY EYES TO MAKE IT LOOK THAT WAY?
ALL RIGHT, I ADMIT IT! I NEEDED YOU TO OPEN THE MONEY BIN'S VAULT SO I COULD TAKE OFF WITH YOUR DIME!
I SNUCK UP AND THREW BLACK VISION DUST IN YOUR EYES! IT KNOCKED YOU UNCONSCIOUS FOR TEN MINUTES SO I COULD MOVE YOU...
...AND IT MADE YOU PERCEIVE THE WORLD THE WAY I DESCRIBED IT TO YOU!
BUT I HAVEN'T LOST YET! YOU'RE STILL UNDER THE VISION DUST'S SPELL! AND IF YOU WANT ME TO REMOVE IT, YOU'LL STILL HAVE TO GIVE ME YOUR DIME!
REALLY? I SUGGEST A BETTER DEAL!
EITHER GIVE ME THE ANTIDOTE, OR I'LL SNAP YOUR DISGUISE WAND LIKE A TWIG! YOU'D BE STUCK LOOKING LIKE DONALD FOR THE REST OF YOUR LIFE!
NO!

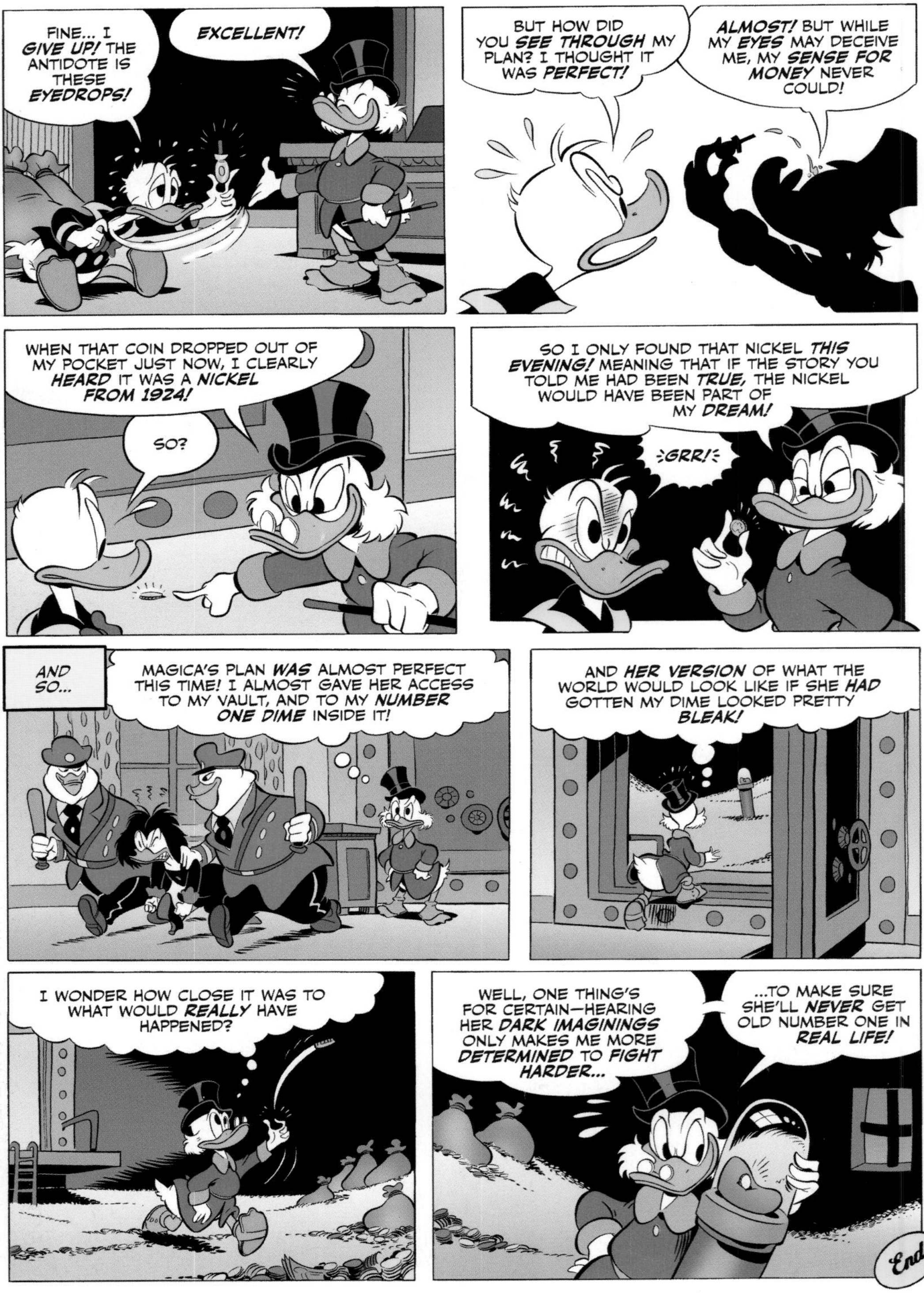
FINE... I GIVE UP! THE ANTIDOTE IS THESE EYEDROPS!
EXCELLENT!
BUT HOW DID YOU SEE THROUGH MY PLAN? I THOUGHT IT WAS PERFECT!
ALMOST! BUT WHILE MY EYES MAY DECEIVE ME, MY SENSE FOR MONEY NEVER COULD!
WHEN THAT COIN DROPPED OUT OF MY POCKET JUST NOW, I CLEARLY HEARD IT WAS A NICKEL FROM 1924!
SO?
SO I ONLY FOUND THAT NICKEL THIS EVENING! MEANING THAT IF THE STORY YOU TOLD ME HAD BEEN TRUE, THE NICKEL WOULD HAVE BEEN PART OF MY DREAM!
GRR!
AND SO...
MAGICA'S PLAN WAS ALMOST PERFECT THIS TIME! I ALMOST GAVE HER ACCESS TO MY VAULT, AND TO MY NUMBER ONE DIME INSIDE IT!
AND HER VERSION OF WHAT THE WORLD WOULD LOOK LIKE IF SHE HAD GOTTEN MY DIME LOOKED PRETTY BLEAK!
I WONDER HOW CLOSE IT WAS TO WHAT WOULD REALLY HAVE HAPPENED?
WELL, ONE THING'S FOR CERTAIN—HEARING HER DARK IMAGININGS ONLY MAKES ME MORE DETERMINED TO FIGHT HARDER...
...TO MAKE SURE SHE'LL NEVER GET OLD NUMBER ONE IN REAL LIFE!
End

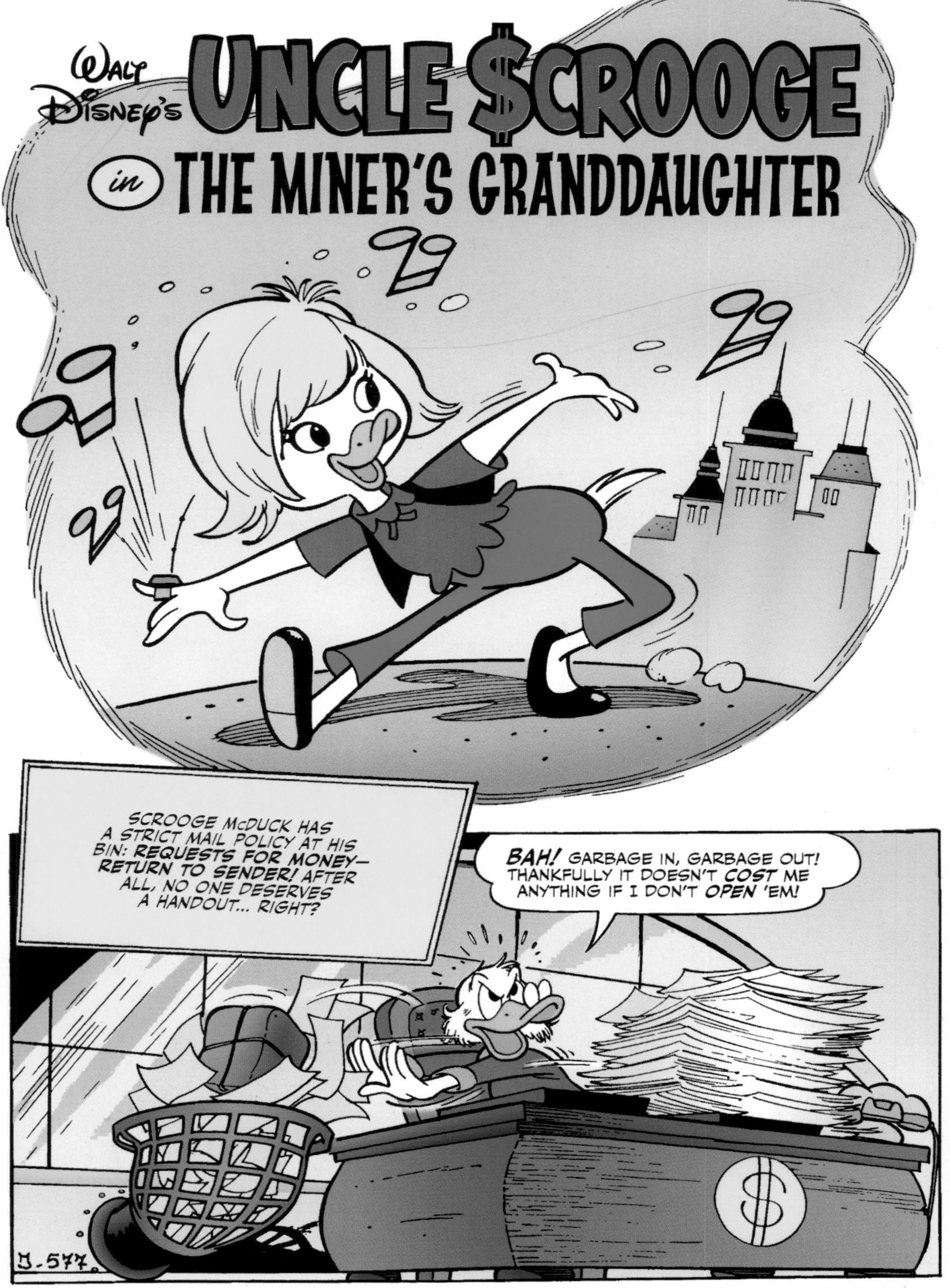
Walt Disney's
UNCLE $CROOGE
in THE MINER'S GRANDDAUGHTER
SCROOGE McDUCK HAS A STRICT MAIL POLICY AT HIS BIN: REQUESTS FOR MONEY—RETURN TO SENDER! AFTER ALL, NO ONE DESERVES A HANDOUT... RIGHT?
BAH! GARBAGE IN, GARBAGE OUT! THANKFULLY IT DOESN'T COST ME ANYTHING IF I DON'T OPEN 'EM!

Originally published in *Topolino* #577 (Italy, 1966)

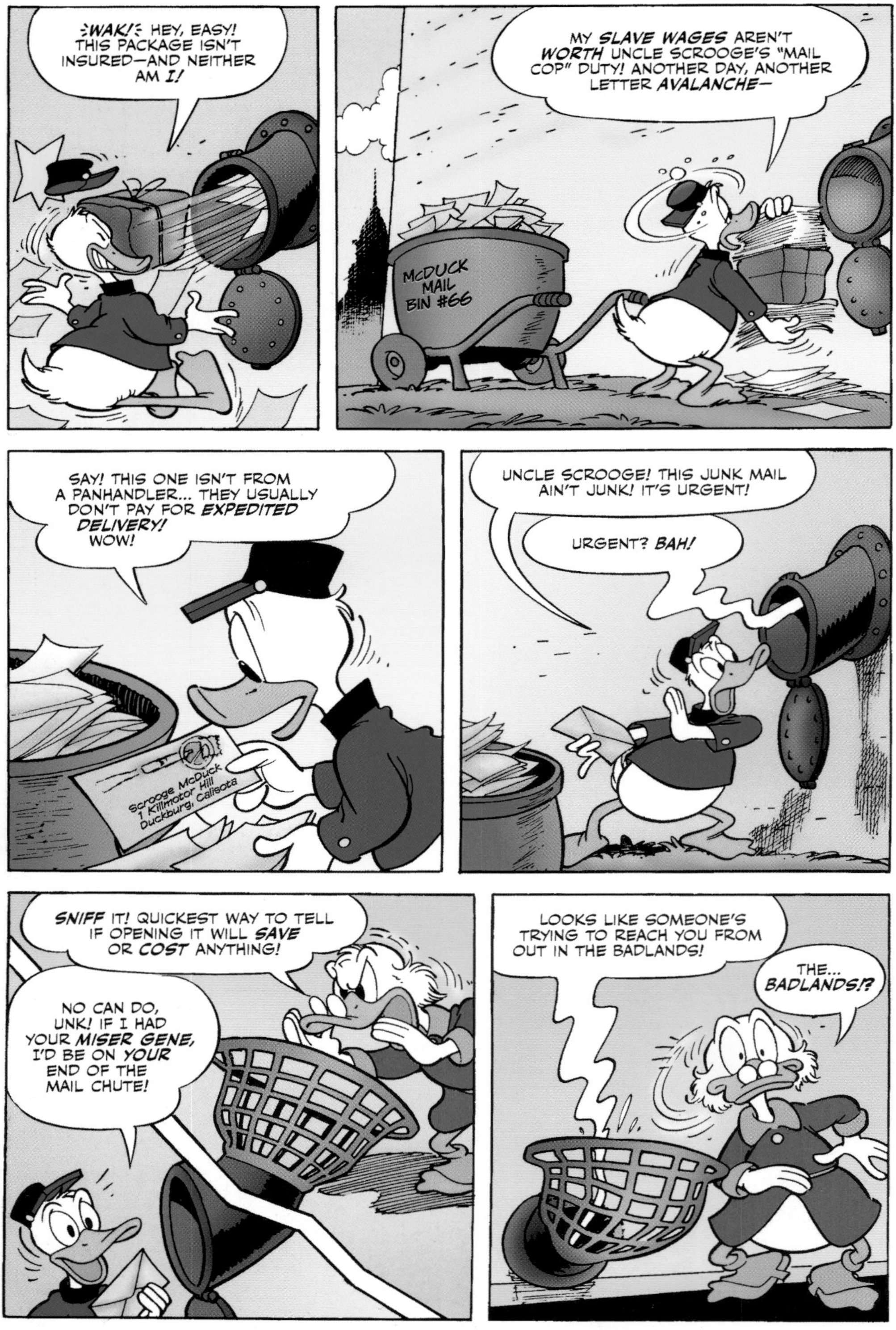

:WAK!: HEY, EASY! THIS PACKAGE ISN'T INSURED—AND NEITHER AM I!
MY SLAVE WAGES AREN'T WORTH UNCLE SCROOGE'S "MAIL COP" DUTY! ANOTHER DAY, ANOTHER LETTER AVALANCHE—
McDUCK MAIL BIN #66
SAY! THIS ONE ISN'T FROM A PANHANDLER... THEY USUALLY DON'T PAY FOR EXPEDITED DELIVERY! WOW!
Scrooge McDuck
1 Killmotor Hill
Duckburg, Calisota
UNCLE SCROOGE! THIS JUNK MAIL AIN'T JUNK! IT'S URGENT!
URGENT? BAH!
SNIFF IT! QUICKEST WAY TO TELL IF OPENING IT WILL SAVE OR COST ANYTHING!
NO CAN DO, UNK! IF I HAD YOUR MISER GENE, I'D BE ON YOUR END OF THE MAIL CHUTE!
LOOKS LIKE SOMEONE'S TRYING TO REACH YOU FROM OUT IN THE BADLANDS!
THE... BADLANDS!?

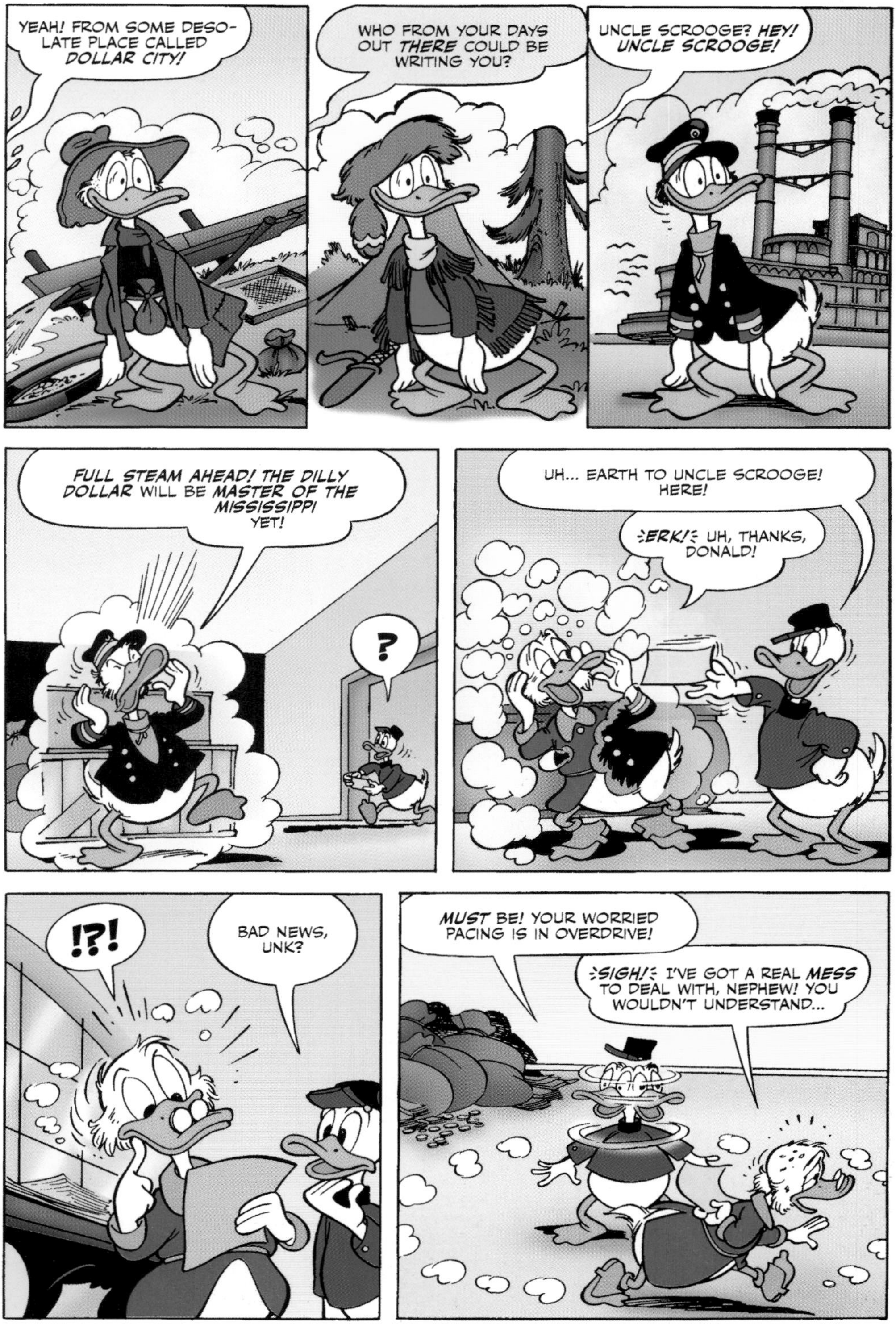
YEAH! FROM SOME DESO-LATE PLACE CALLED DOLLAR CITY!
WHO FROM YOUR DAYS OUT THERE COULD BE WRITING YOU?
UNCLE SCROOGE? HEY! UNCLE SCROOGE!
FULL STEAM AHEAD! THE DILLY DOLLAR WILL BE MASTER OF THE MISSISSIPPI YET!
?
UH... EARTH TO UNCLE SCROOGE! HERE!
ERK! UH, THANKS, DONALD!
!?!
BAD NEWS, UNK?
MUST BE! YOUR WORRIED PACING IS IN OVERDRIVE!
SIGH! I'VE GOT A REAL MESS TO DEAL WITH, NEPHEW! YOU WOULDN'T UNDERSTAND...

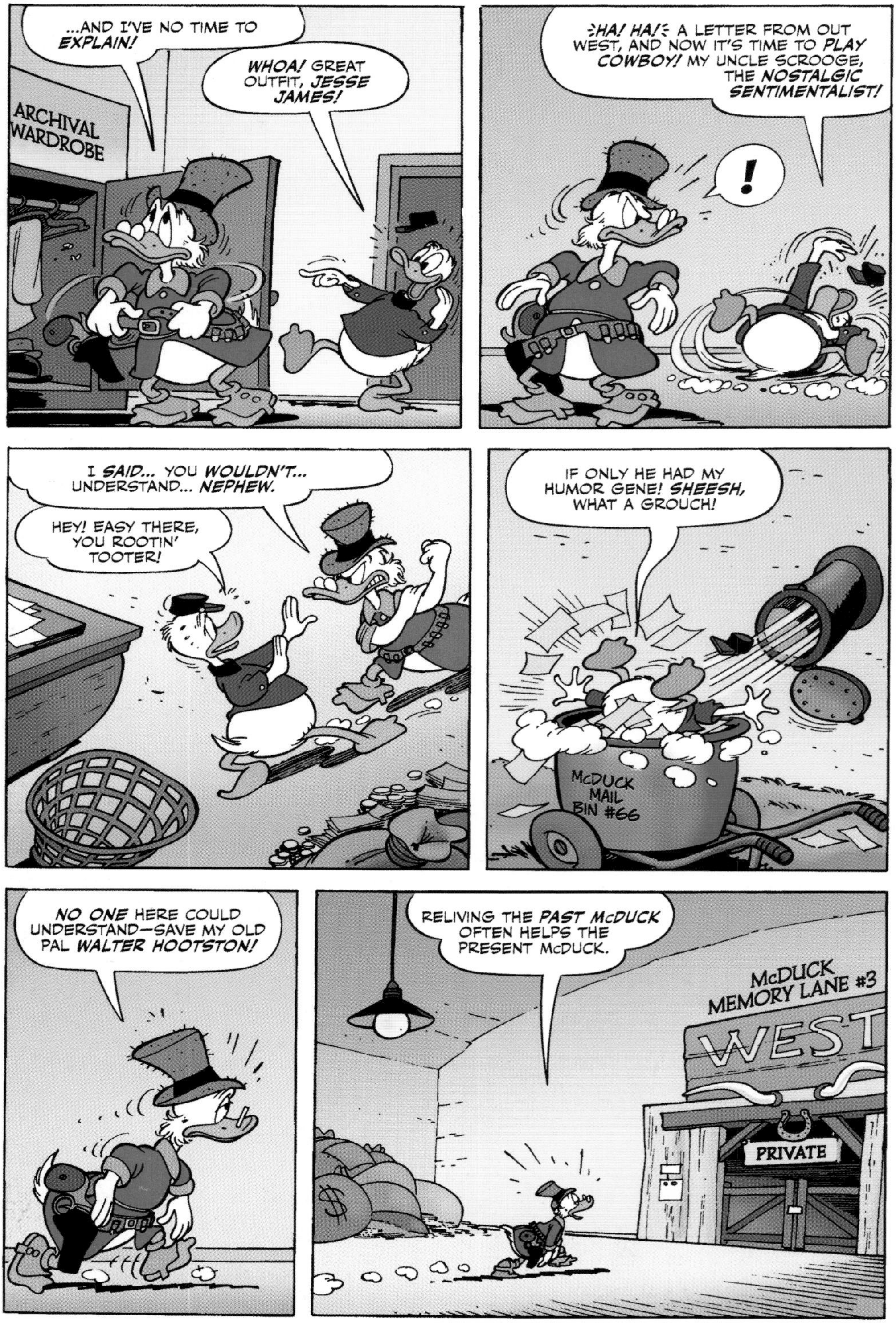
...AND I'VE NO TIME TO EXPLAIN!
ARCHIVAL WARDROBE
WHOA! GREAT OUTFIT, JESSE JAMES!
HA! HA! A LETTER FROM OUT WEST, AND NOW IT'S TIME TO PLAY COWBOY! MY UNCLE SCROOGE, THE NOSTALGIC SENTIMENTALIST!
!
I SAID... YOU WOULDN'T... UNDERSTAND... NEPHEW.
HEY! EASY THERE, YOU ROOTIN' TOOTER!
IF ONLY HE HAD MY HUMOR GENE! SHEESH, WHAT A GROUCH!
McDUCK MAIL BIN #66
NO ONE HERE COULD UNDERSTAND—SAVE MY OLD PAL WALTER HOOTSTON!
RELIVING THE PAST McDUCK OFTEN HELPS THE PRESENT McDUCK.
McDUCK MEMORY LANE #3
WEST
PRIVATE

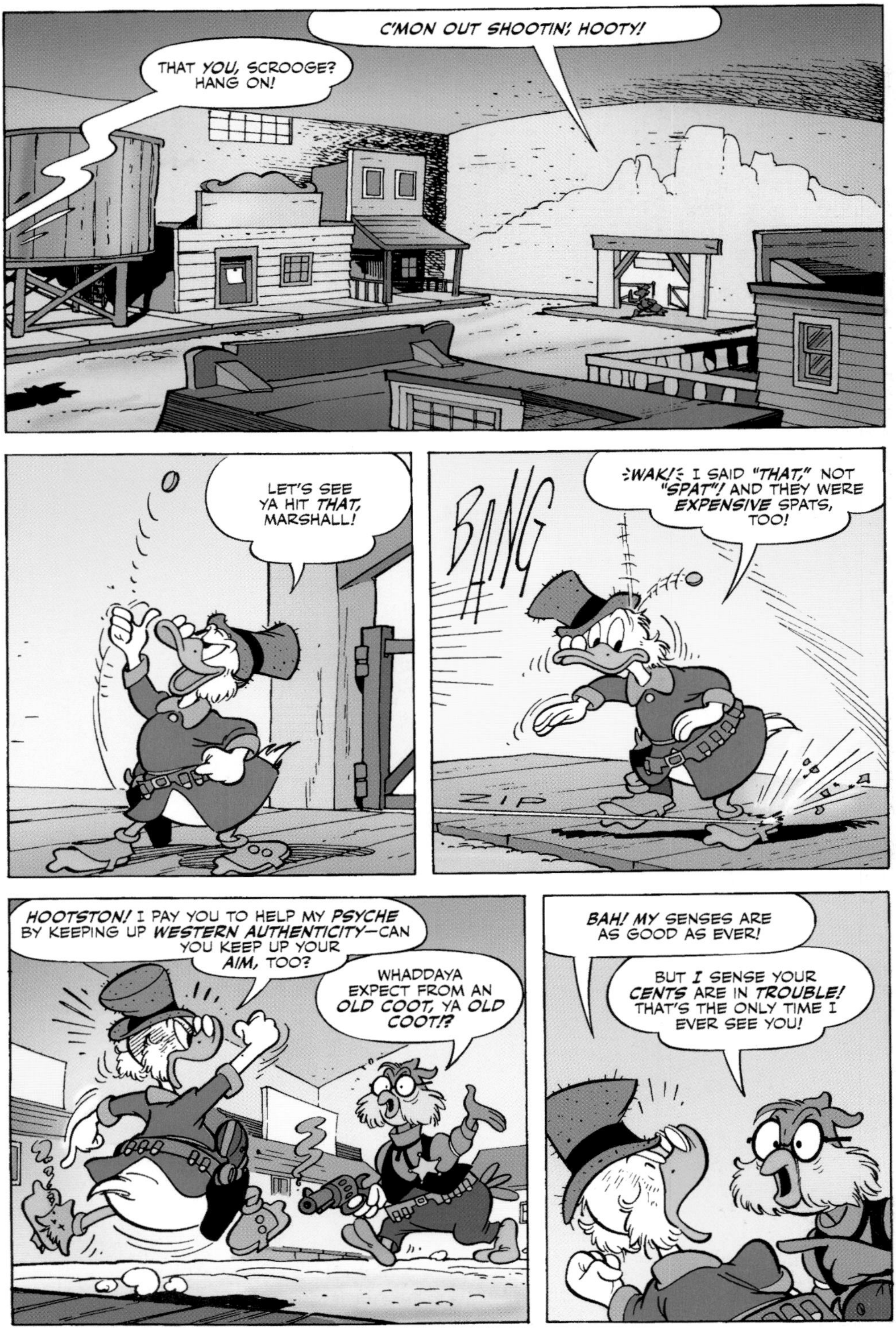
C'MON OUT SHOOTIN', HOOTY!
THAT YOU, SCROOGE? HANG ON!
LET'S SEE YA HIT THAT, MARSHALL!
BANG
ZIP
WAK! I SAID "THAT," NOT "SPAT"! AND THEY WERE EXPENSIVE SPATS, TOO!
HOOTSTON! I PAY YOU TO HELP MY PSYCHE BY KEEPING UP WESTERN AUTHENTICITY—CAN YOU KEEP UP YOUR AIM, TOO?
WHADDAYA EXPECT FROM AN OLD COOT, YA OLD COOT!?
BAH! MY SENSES ARE AS GOOD AS EVER!
BUT I SENSE YOUR CENTS ARE IN TROUBLE! THAT'S THE ONLY TIME I EVER SEE YOU!

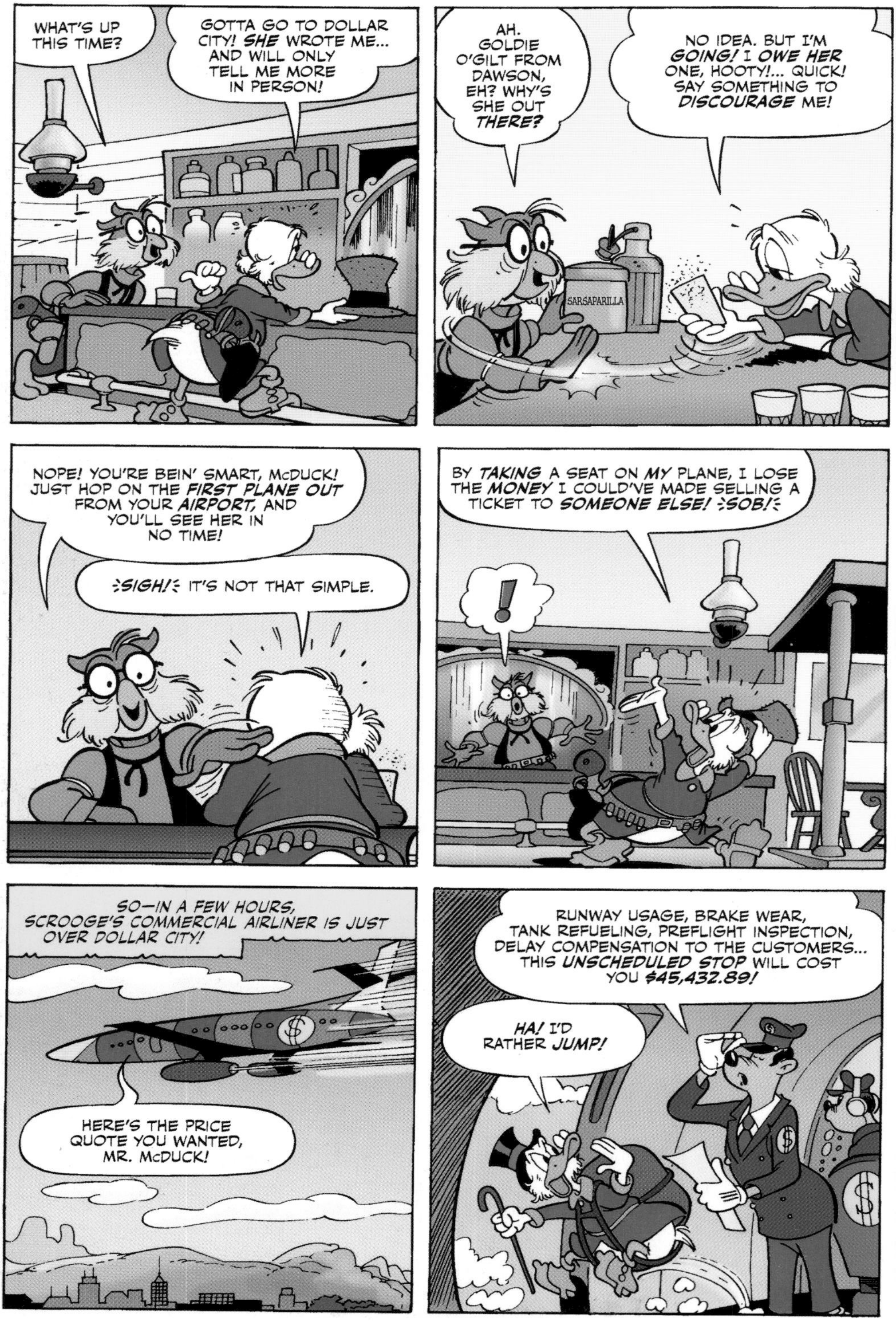
WHAT'S UP THIS TIME?
GOTTA GO TO DOLLAR CITY! SHE WROTE ME... AND WILL ONLY TELL ME MORE IN PERSON!
AH. GOLDIE O'GILT FROM DAWSON, EH? WHY'S SHE OUT THERE?
SARSAPARILLA
NO IDEA. BUT I'M GOING! I OWE HER ONE, HOOTY!... QUICK! SAY SOMETHING TO DISCOURAGE ME!
NOPE! YOU'RE BEIN' SMART, McDUCK! JUST HOP ON THE FIRST PLANE OUT FROM YOUR AIRPORT, AND YOU'LL SEE HER IN NO TIME!
SIGH! IT'S NOT THAT SIMPLE.
BY TAKING A SEAT ON MY PLANE, I LOSE THE MONEY I COULD'VE MADE SELLING A TICKET TO SOMEONE ELSE! SOB!
!
SO—IN A FEW HOURS, SCROOGE'S COMMERCIAL AIRLINER IS JUST OVER DOLLAR CITY!
HERE'S THE PRICE QUOTE YOU WANTED, MR. McDUCK!
RUNWAY USAGE, BRAKE WEAR, TANK REFUELING, PREFLIGHT INSPECTION, DELAY COMPENSATION TO THE CUSTOMERS... THIS UNSCHEDULED STOP WILL COST YOU $45,432.89!
HA! I'D RATHER JUMP!

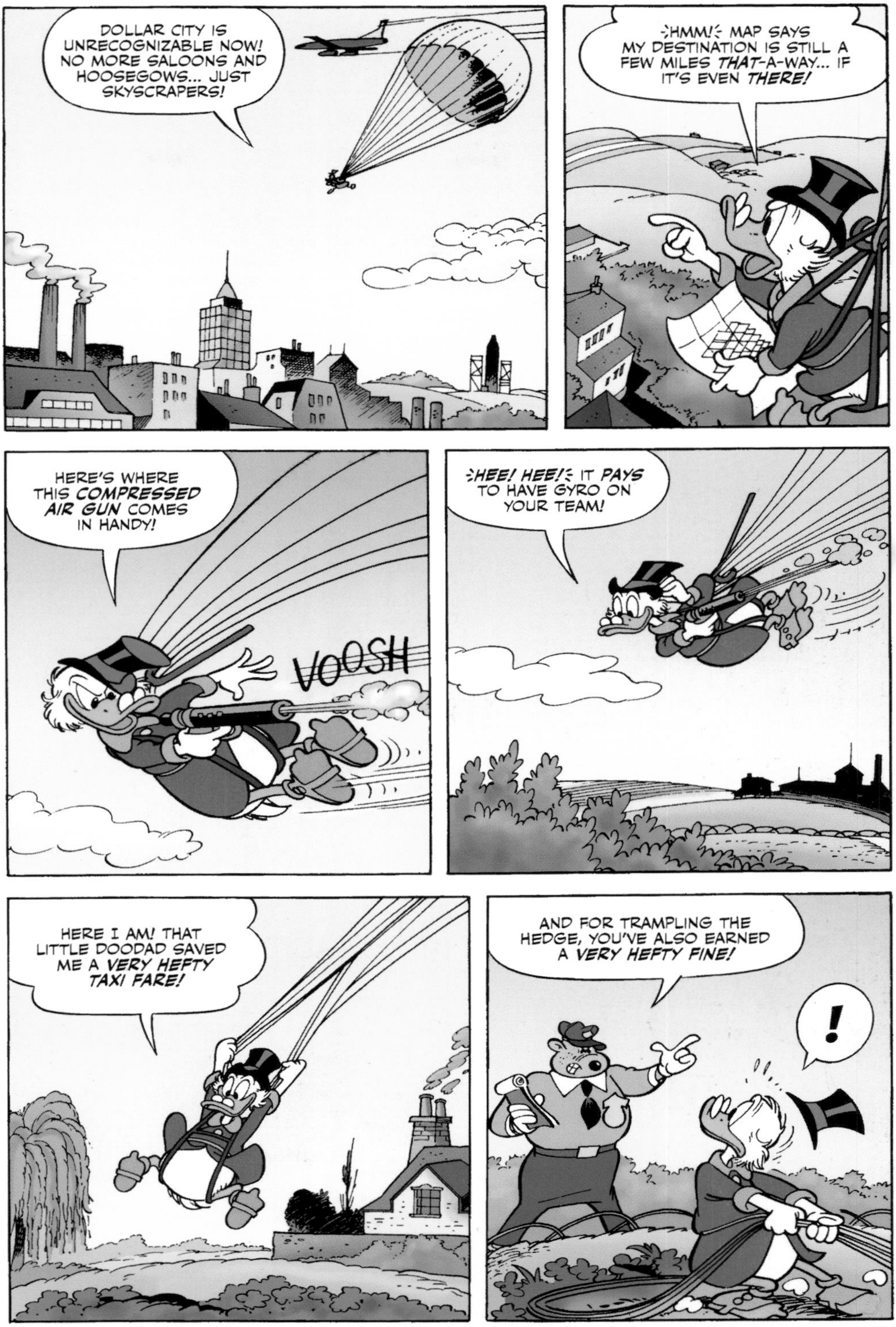
DOLLAR CITY IS UNRECOGNIZABLE NOW! NO MORE SALOONS AND HOOSEGOWS... JUST SKYSCRAPERS!
HMM! MAP SAYS MY DESTINATION IS STILL A FEW MILES THAT-A-WAY... IF IT'S EVEN THERE!
HERE'S WHERE THIS COMPRESSED AIR GUN COMES IN HANDY!
VOOSH
HEE! HEE! IT PAYS TO HAVE GYRO ON YOUR TEAM!
HERE I AM! THAT LITTLE DOODAD SAVED ME A VERY HEFTY TAXI FARE!
AND FOR TRAMPLING THE HEDGE, YOU'VE ALSO EARNED A VERY HEFTY FINE!
!

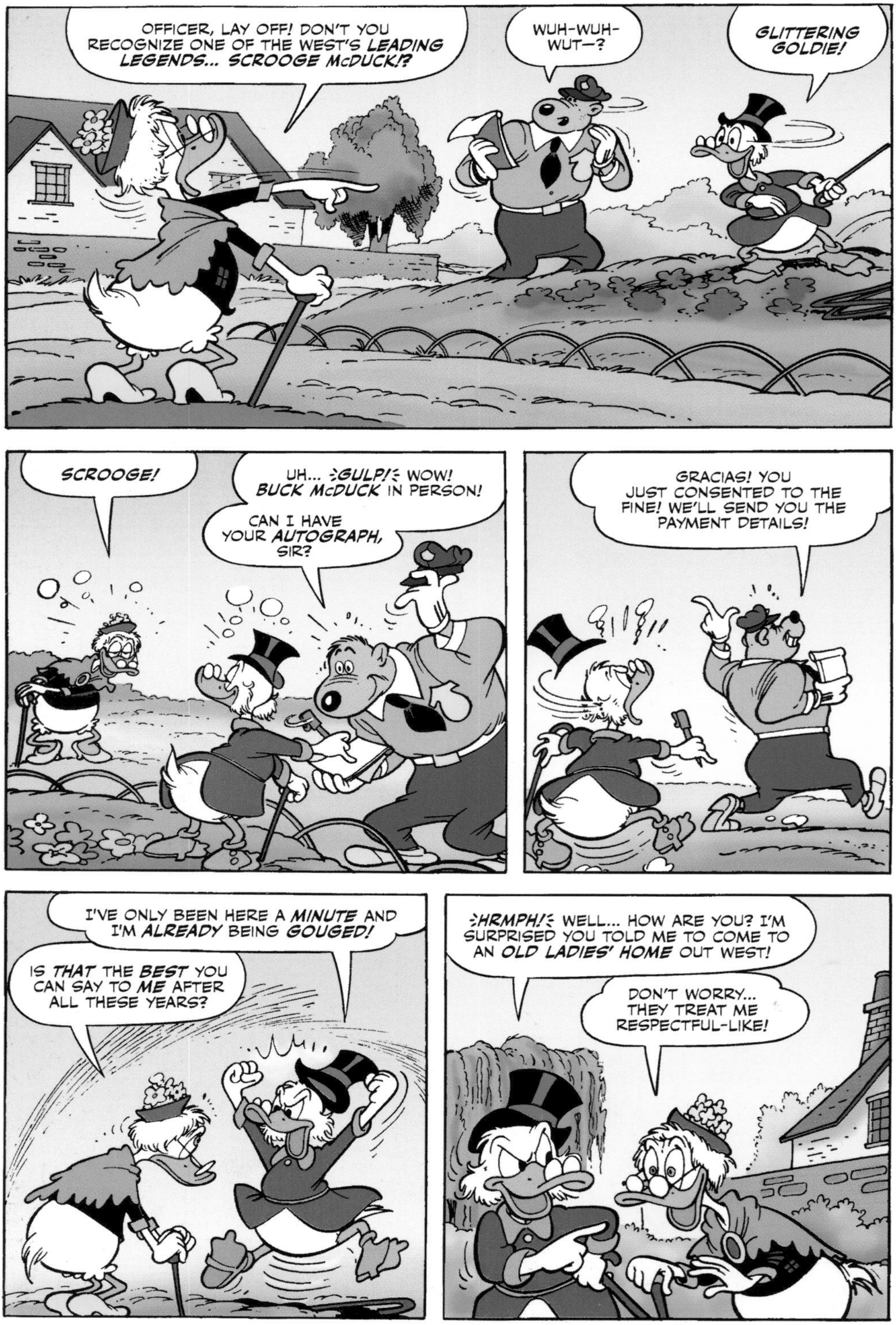
OFFICER, LAY OFF! DON'T YOU RECOGNIZE ONE OF THE WEST'S LEADING LEGENDS... SCROOGE McDUCK!?
WUH-WUH-WUT—?
GLITTERING GOLDIE!
SCROOGE!
UH... GULP! WOW! BUCK McDUCK IN PERSON!
CAN I HAVE YOUR AUTOGRAPH, SIR?
GRACIAS! YOU JUST CONSENTED TO THE FINE! WE'LL SEND YOU THE PAYMENT DETAILS!
I'VE ONLY BEEN HERE A MINUTE AND I'M ALREADY BEING GOUGED!
IS THAT THE BEST YOU CAN SAY TO ME AFTER ALL THESE YEARS?
HRMPH! WELL... HOW ARE YOU? I'M SURPRISED YOU TOLD ME TO COME TO AN OLD LADIES' HOME OUT WEST!
DON'T WORRY... THEY TREAT ME RESPECTFUL-LIKE!

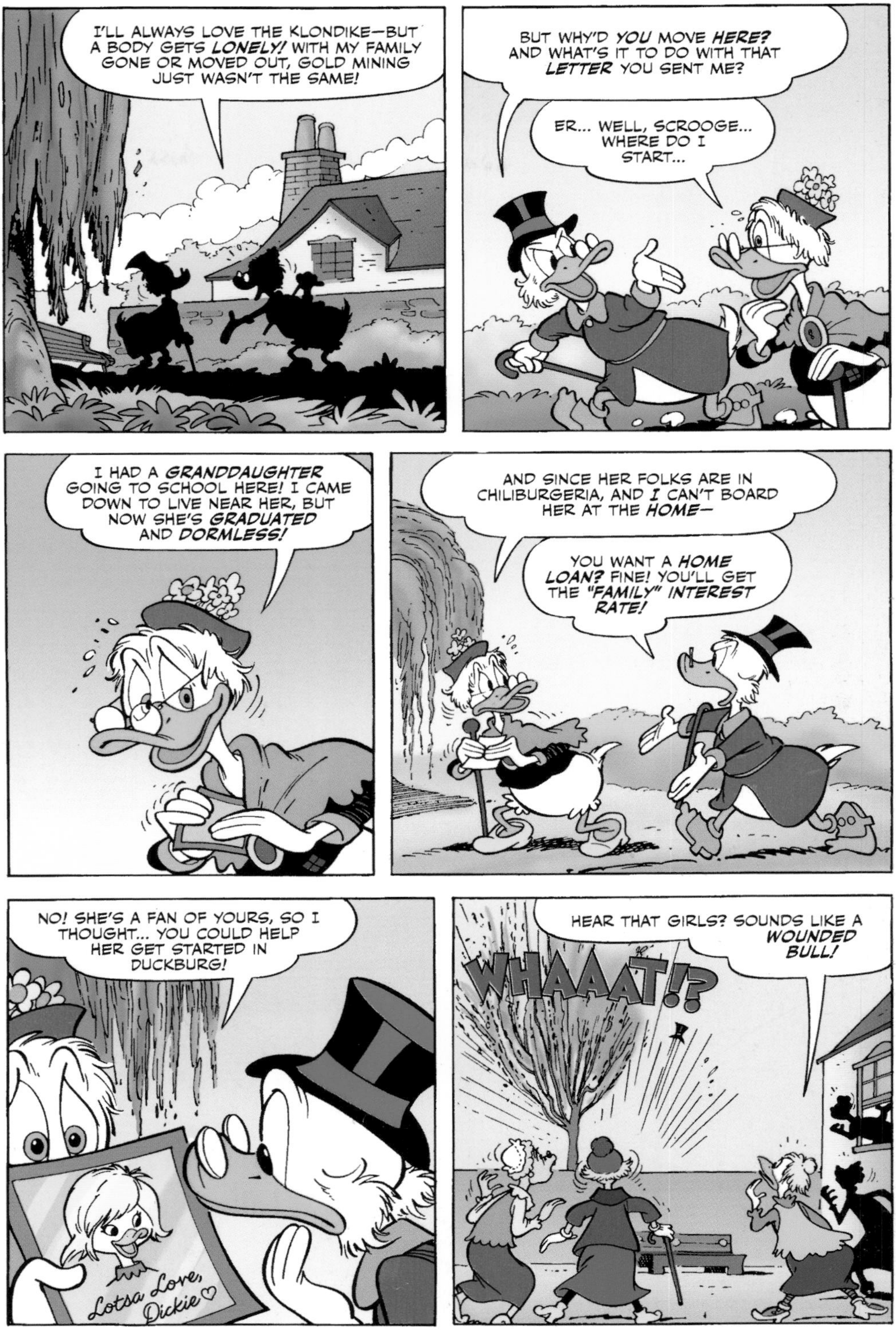
I'LL ALWAYS LOVE THE KLONDIKE—BUT A BODY GETS LONELY! WITH MY FAMILY GONE OR MOVED OUT, GOLD MINING JUST WASN'T THE SAME!
BUT WHY'D YOU MOVE HERE? AND WHAT'S IT TO DO WITH THAT LETTER YOU SENT ME?
ER... WELL, SCROOGE... WHERE DO I START...
I HAD A GRANDDAUGHTER GOING TO SCHOOL HERE! I CAME DOWN TO LIVE NEAR HER, BUT NOW SHE'S GRADUATED AND DORMLESS!
AND SINCE HER FOLKS ARE IN CHILIBURGERIA, AND I CAN'T BOARD HER AT THE HOME—
YOU WANT A HOME LOAN? FINE! YOU'LL GET THE "FAMILY" INTEREST RATE!
NO! SHE'S A FAN OF YOURS, SO I THOUGHT... YOU COULD HELP HER GET STARTED IN DUCKBURG!
Lotsa Love, Dickie
WHAAAT!?
HEAR THAT GIRLS? SOUNDS LIKE A WOUNDED BULL!

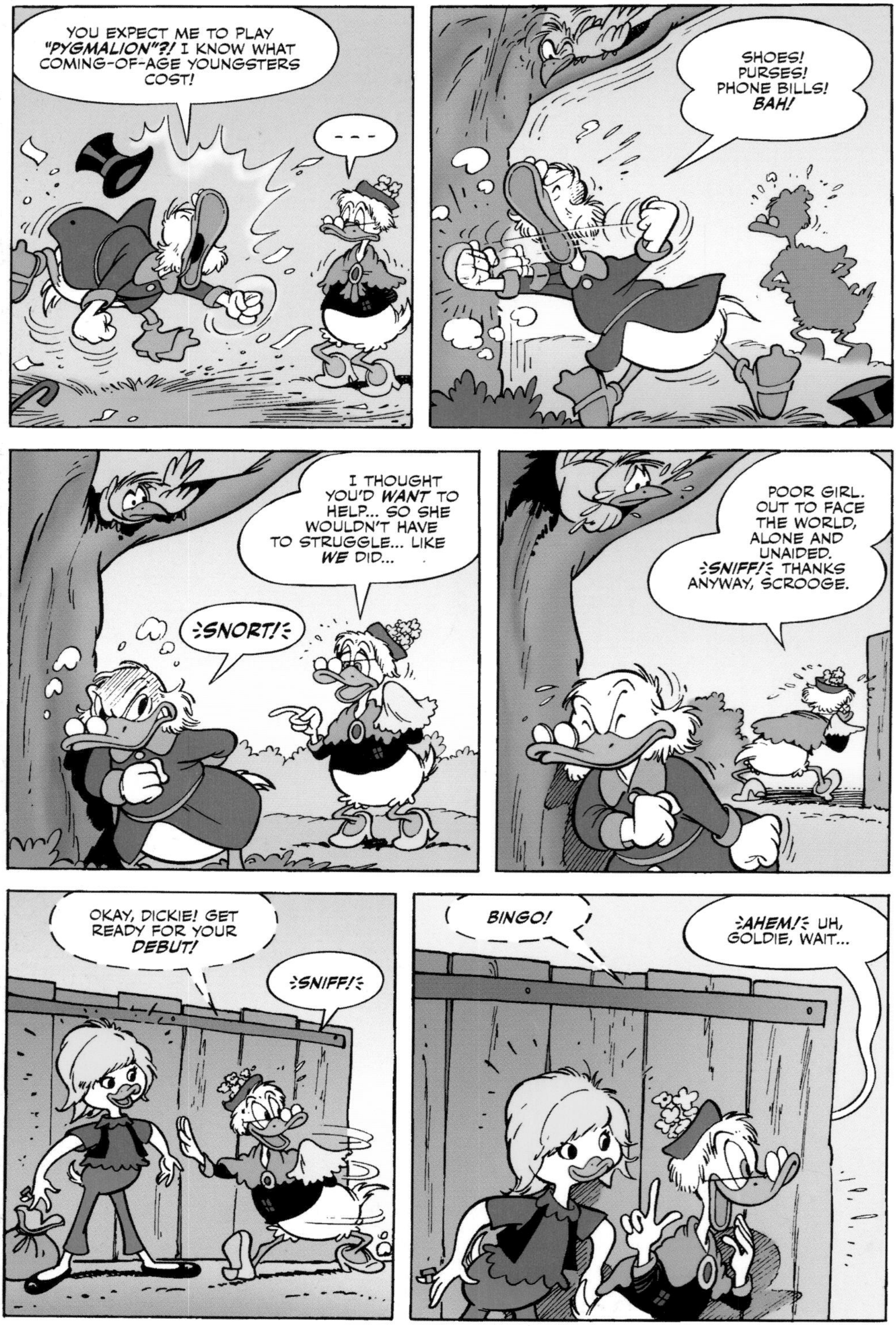
YOU EXPECT ME TO PLAY "PYGMALION"?! I KNOW WHAT COMING-OF-AGE YOUNGSTERS COST!
- - -
SHOES! PURSES! PHONE BILLS! BAH!
I THOUGHT YOU'D WANT TO HELP... SO SHE WOULDN'T HAVE TO STRUGGLE... LIKE WE DID...
SNORT!
POOR GIRL. OUT TO FACE THE WORLD, ALONE AND UNAIDED. SNIFF! THANKS ANYWAY, SCROOGE.
OKAY, DICKIE! GET READY FOR YOUR DEBUT!
SNIFF!
BINGO!
AHEM! UH, GOLDIE, WAIT...

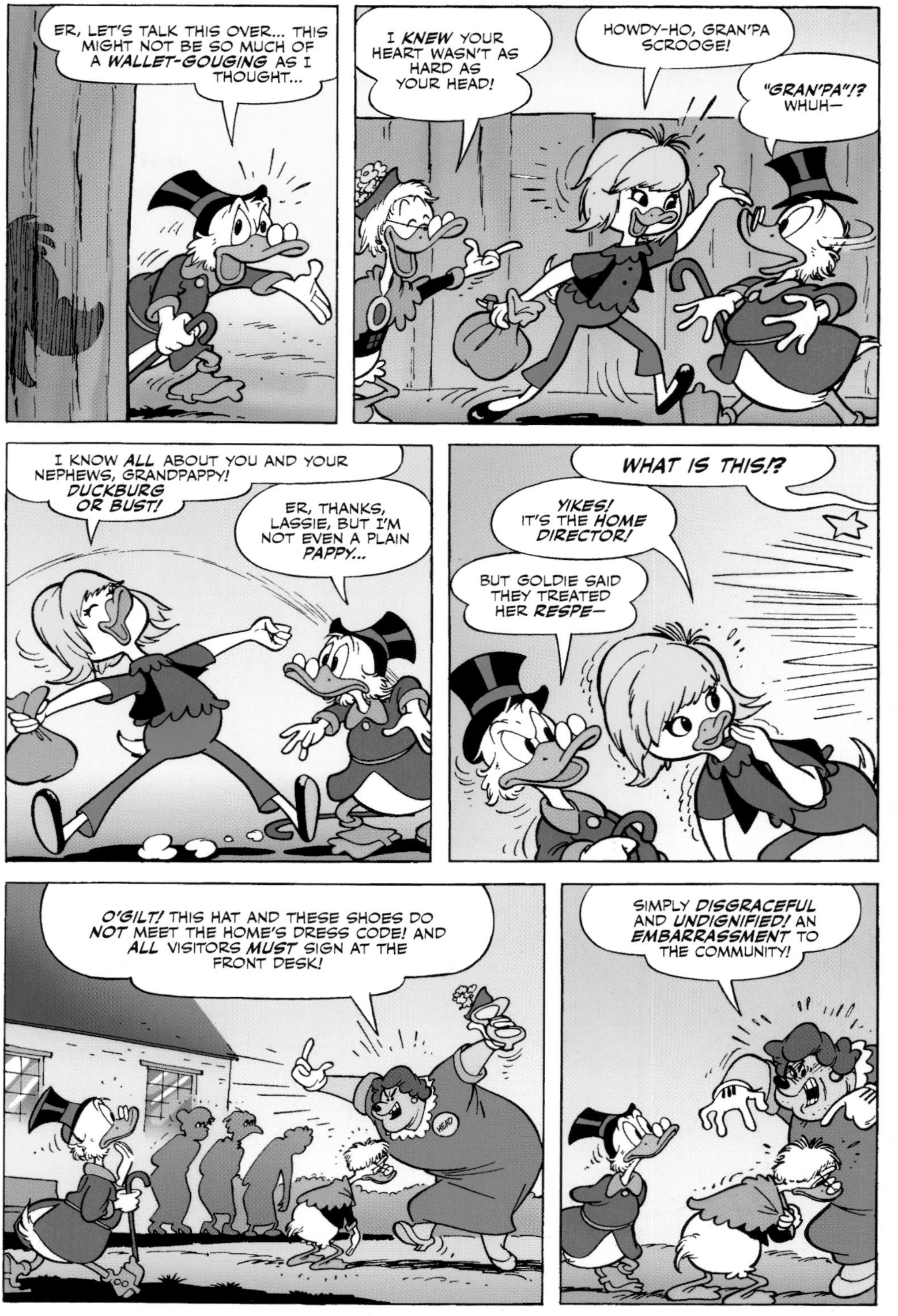
ER, LET'S TALK THIS OVER... THIS MIGHT NOT BE SO MUCH OF A WALLET-GOUGING AS I THOUGHT...
I KNEW YOUR HEART WASN'T AS HARD AS YOUR HEAD!
HOWDY-HO, GRAN'PA SCROOGE!
"GRAN'PA"!? WHUH—
I KNOW ALL ABOUT YOU AND YOUR NEPHEWS, GRANDPAPPY! DUCKBURG OR BUST!
ER, THANKS, LASSIE, BUT I'M NOT EVEN A PLAIN PAPPY...
WHAT IS THIS!?
YIKES! IT'S THE HOME DIRECTOR!
BUT GOLDIE SAID THEY TREATED HER RESPE—
O'GILT! THIS HAT AND THESE SHOES DO NOT MEET THE HOME'S DRESS CODE! AND ALL VISITORS MUST SIGN AT THE FRONT DESK!
HEAD
SIMPLY DISGRACEFUL AND UNDIGNIFIED! AN EMBARRASSMENT TO THE COMMUNITY!

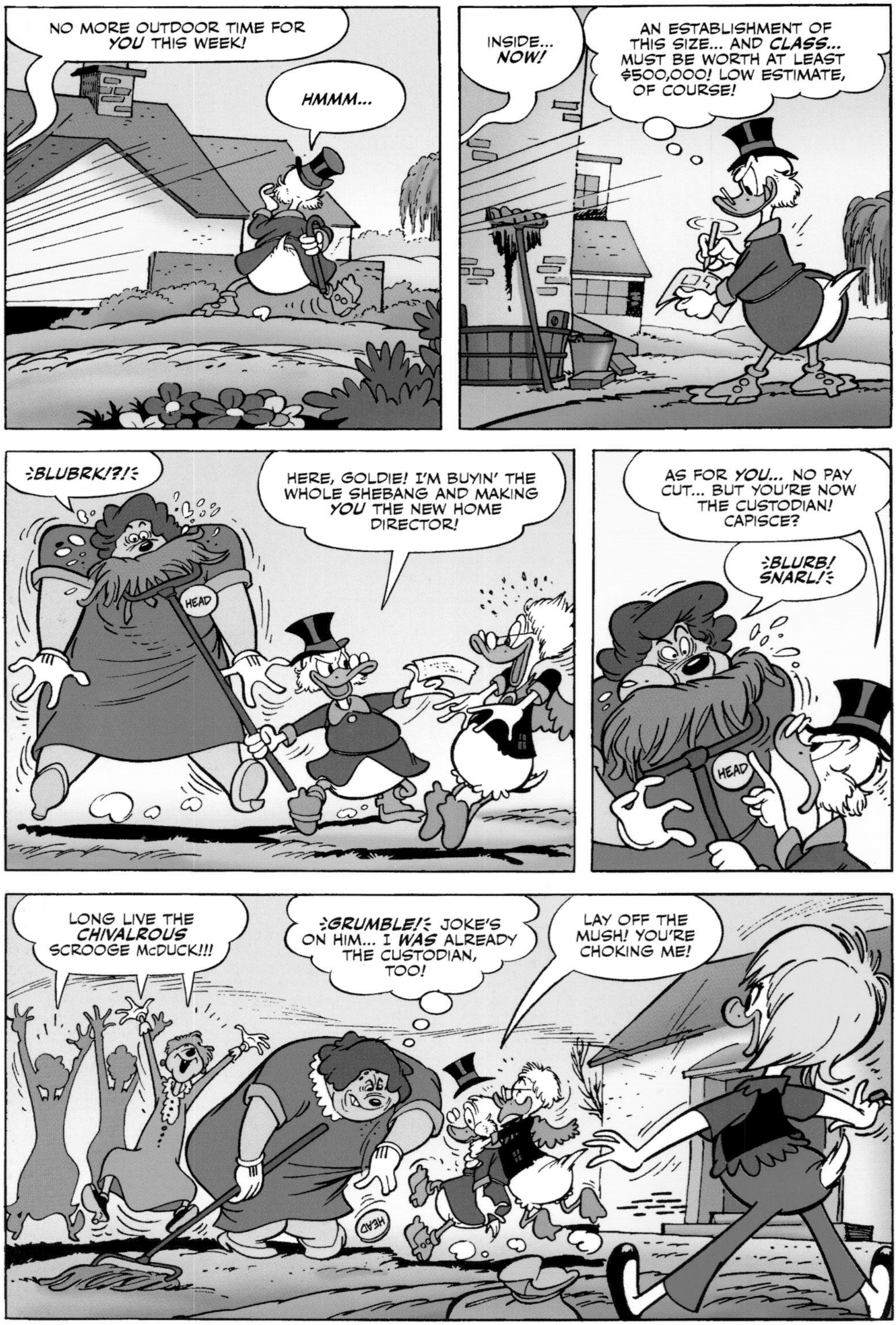
NO MORE OUTDOOR TIME FOR *YOU* THIS WEEK!
HMMM...
INSIDE... *NOW!*
AN ESTABLISHMENT OF THIS SIZE... AND *CLASS...* MUST BE WORTH AT LEAST $500,000! LOW ESTIMATE, OF COURSE!
BLUBRK!?!
HEAD
HERE, GOLDIE! I'M BUYIN' THE WHOLE SHEBANG AND MAKING *YOU* THE NEW HOME DIRECTOR!
AS FOR *YOU...* NO PAY CUT... BUT YOU'RE NOW THE CUSTODIAN! CAPISCE?
BLURB! SNARL!
HEAD
LONG LIVE THE *CHIVALROUS* SCROOGE McDUCK!!!
GRUMBLE! JOKE'S ON HIM... I *WAS* ALREADY THE CUSTODIAN, TOO!
LAY OFF THE MUSH! YOU'RE CHOKING ME!
HEAD

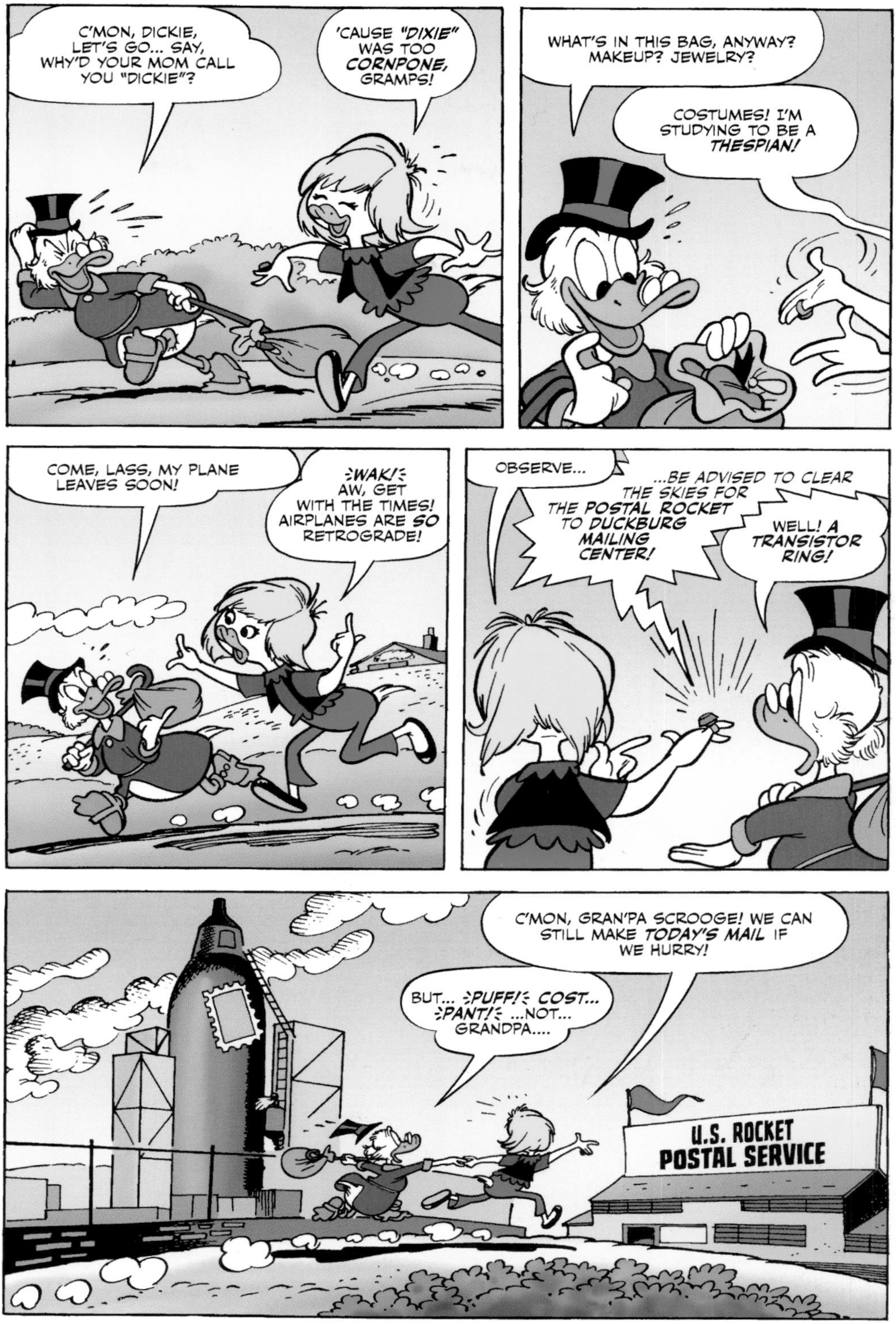

C'MON, DICKIE, LET'S GO... SAY, WHY'D YOUR MOM CALL YOU "DICKIE"?
'CAUSE "DIXIE" WAS TOO CORNPONE, GRAMPS!
WHAT'S IN THIS BAG, ANYWAY? MAKEUP? JEWELRY?
COSTUMES! I'M STUDYING TO BE A THESPIAN!
COME, LASS, MY PLANE LEAVES SOON!
WAK! AW, GET WITH THE TIMES! AIRPLANES ARE SO RETROGRADE!
OBSERVE...
...BE ADVISED TO CLEAR THE SKIES FOR THE POSTAL ROCKET TO DUCKBURG MAILING CENTER!
WELL! A TRANSISTOR RING!
C'MON, GRAN'PA SCROOGE! WE CAN STILL MAKE TODAY'S MAIL IF WE HURRY!
BUT... PUFF! COST... PANT! ...NOT... GRANDPA....
U.S. ROCKET POSTAL SERVICE

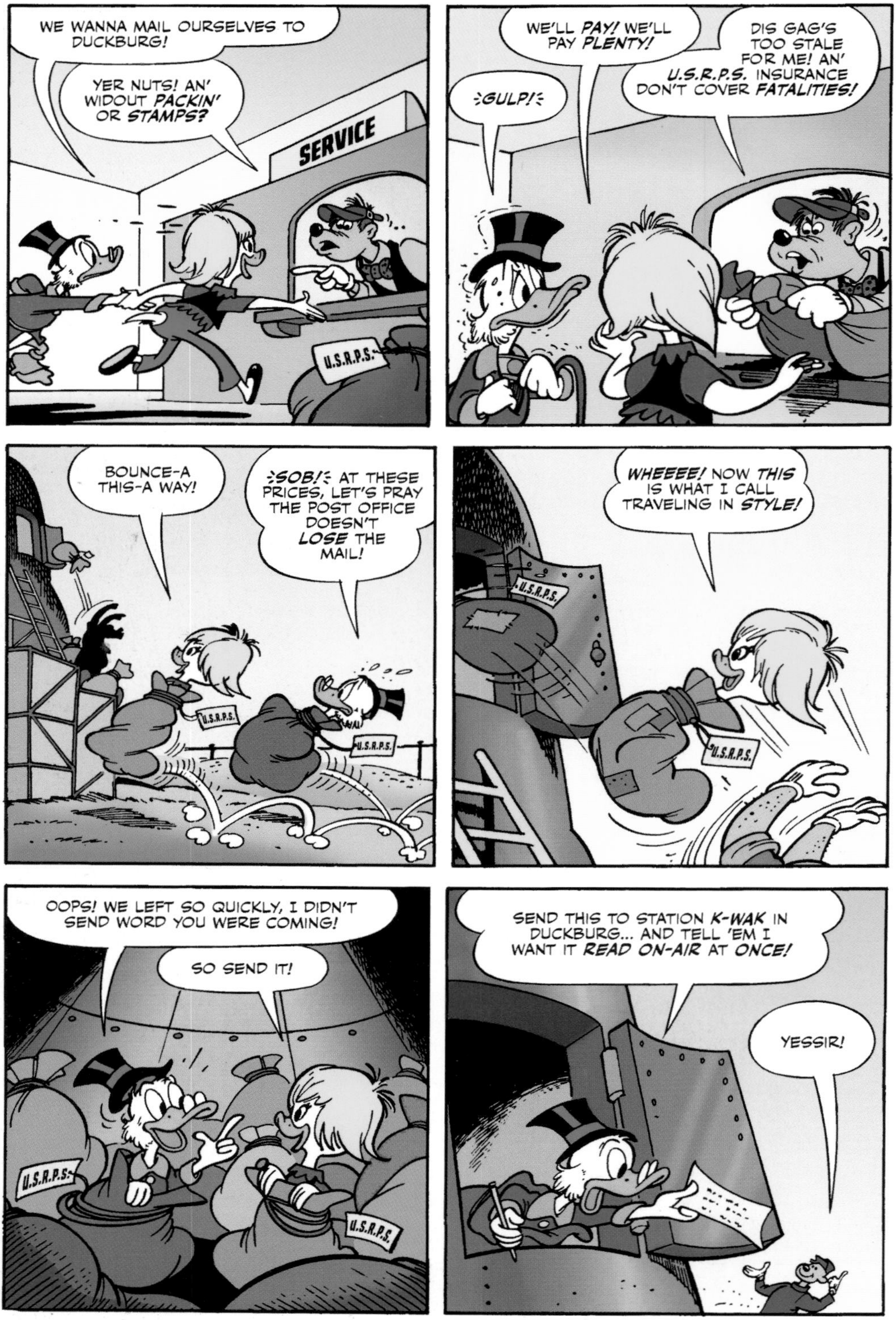

WE WANNA MAIL OURSELVES TO DUCKBURG!
YER NUTS! AN' WIDOUT PACKIN' OR STAMPS?
SERVICE
U.S.R.P.S.
:GULP!:
WE'LL PAY! WE'LL PAY PLENTY!
DIS GAG'S TOO STALE FOR ME! AN' U.S.R.P.S. INSURANCE DON'T COVER FATALITIES!
BOUNCE-A THIS-A WAY!
:SOB!: AT THESE PRICES, LET'S PRAY THE POST OFFICE DOESN'T LOSE THE MAIL!
U.S.R.P.S.
U.S.R.P.S.
WHEEEE! NOW THIS IS WHAT I CALL TRAVELING IN STYLE!
U.S.R.P.S.
U.S.R.P.S.
OOPS! WE LEFT SO QUICKLY, I DIDN'T SEND WORD YOU WERE COMING!
SO SEND IT!
U.S.R.P.S.
U.S.R.P.S.
SEND THIS TO STATION K-WAK IN DUCKBURG... AND TELL 'EM I WANT IT READ ON-AIR AT ONCE!
YESSIR!

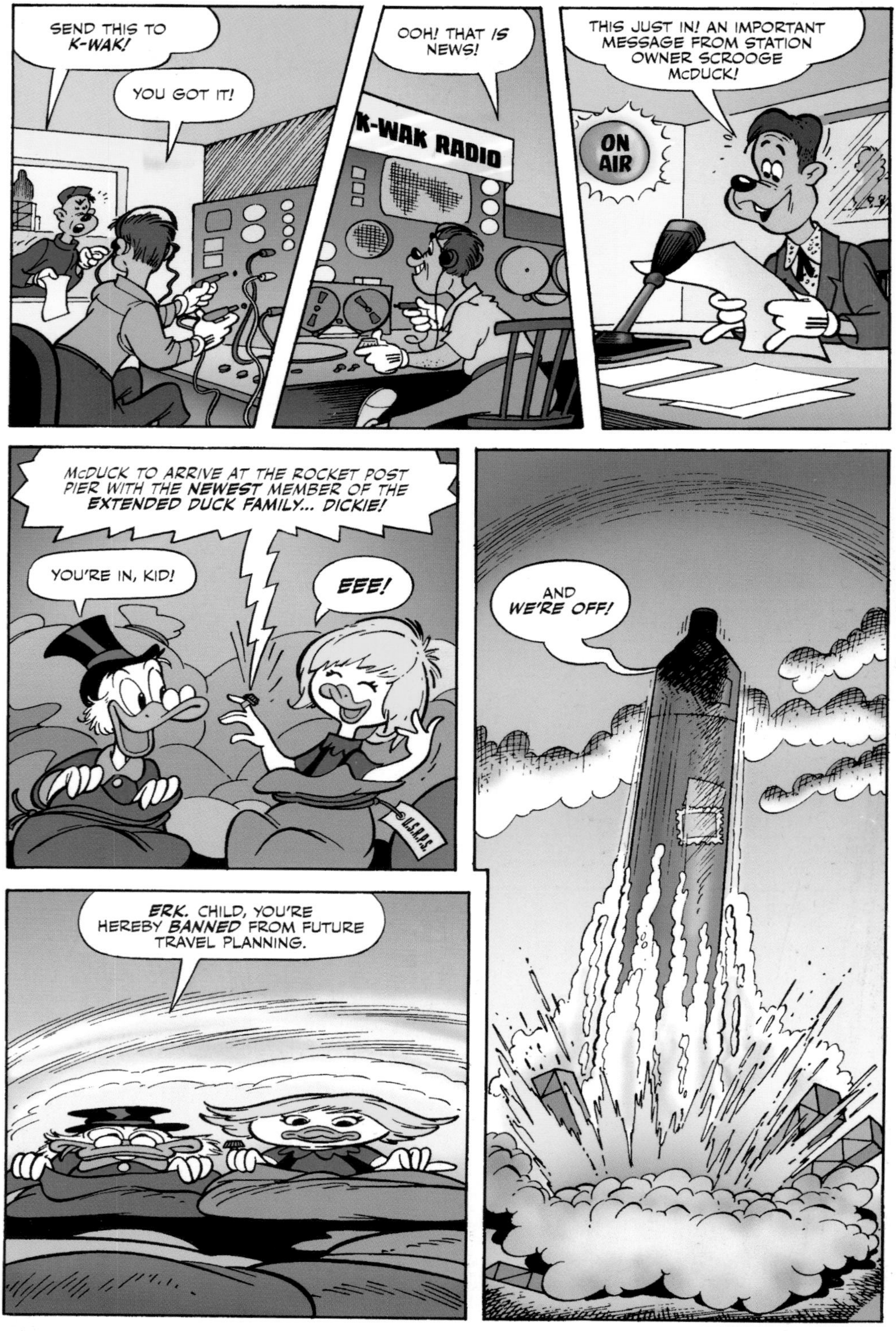
SEND THIS TO K-WAK!
YOU GOT IT!
OOH! THAT IS NEWS!
K-WAK RADIO
THIS JUST IN! AN IMPORTANT MESSAGE FROM STATION OWNER SCROOGE McDUCK!
ON AIR
McDUCK TO ARRIVE AT THE ROCKET POST PIER WITH THE NEWEST MEMBER OF THE EXTENDED DUCK FAMILY... DICKIE!
YOU'RE IN, KID!
EEE!
AND WE'RE OFF!
ERK. CHILD, YOU'RE HEREBY BANNED FROM FUTURE TRAVEL PLANNING.

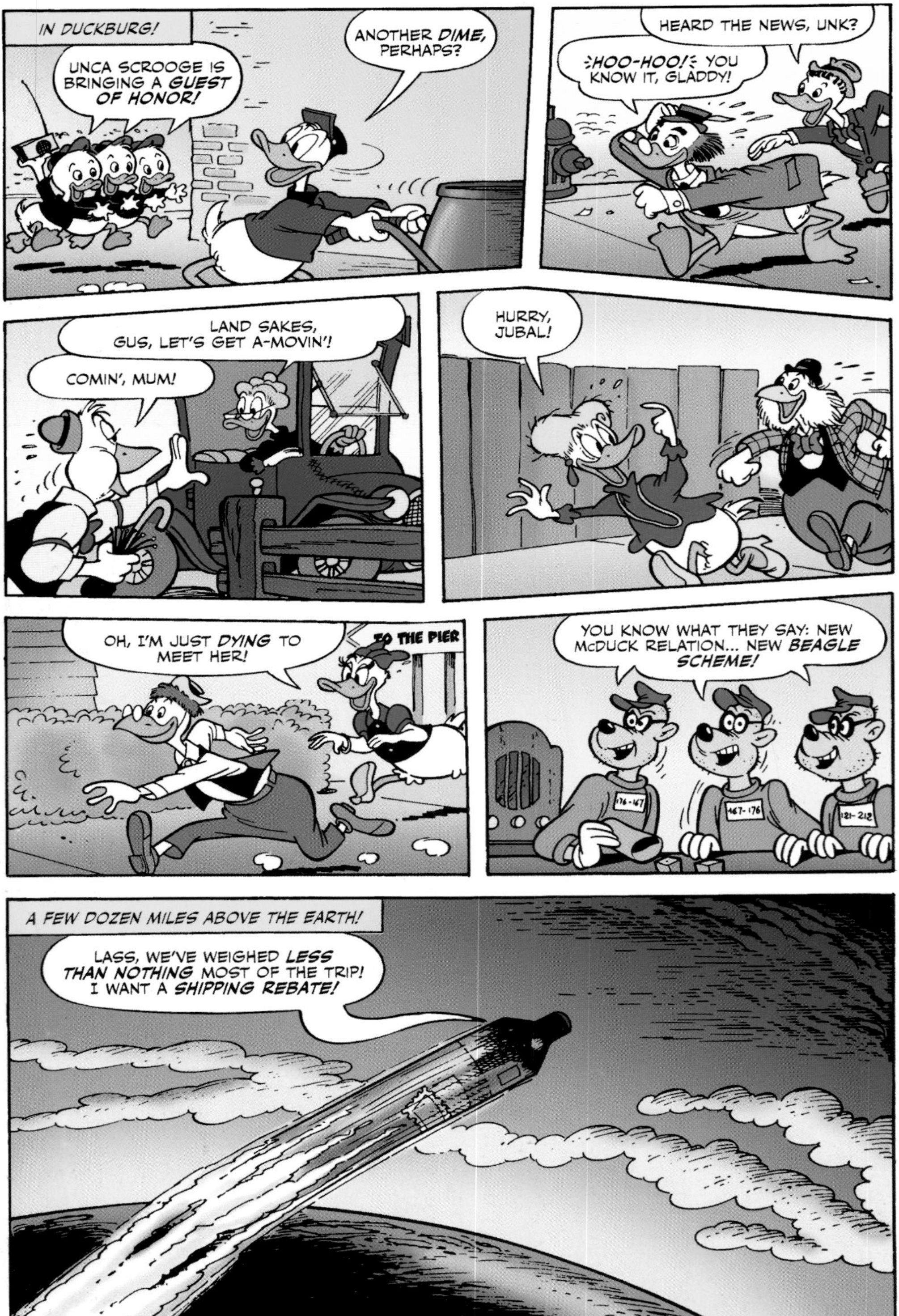
IN DUCKBURG!
UNCA SCROOGE IS BRINGING A GUEST OF HONOR!
ANOTHER DIME, PERHAPS?
HEARD THE NEWS, UNK?
HOO-HOO! YOU KNOW IT, GLADDY!
LAND SAKES, GUS, LET'S GET A-MOVIN'!
COMIN', MUM!
HURRY, JUBAL!
OH, I'M JUST DYING TO MEET HER!
TO THE PIER
YOU KNOW WHAT THEY SAY: NEW McDUCK RELATION... NEW BEAGLE SCHEME!
176-167
467-176
121-212
A FEW DOZEN MILES ABOVE THE EARTH!
LASS, WE'VE WEIGHED LESS THAN NOTHING MOST OF THE TRIP! I WANT A SHIPPING REBATE!

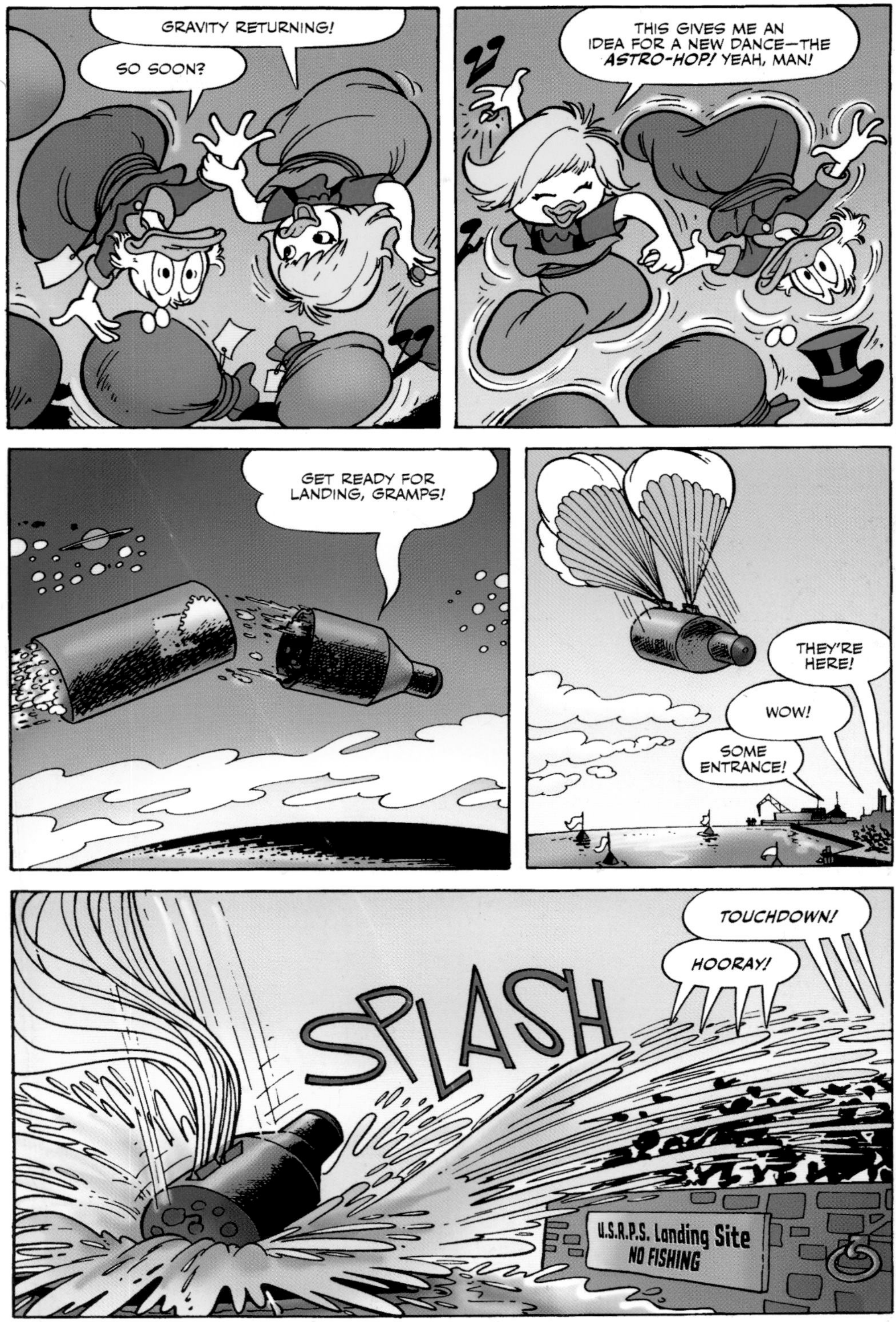
GRAVITY RETURNING!
SO SOON?
THIS GIVES ME AN IDEA FOR A NEW DANCE—THE *ASTRO-HOP!* YEAH, MAN!
GET READY FOR LANDING, GRAMPS!
THEY'RE HERE!
WOW!
SOME ENTRANCE!
TOUCHDOWN!
HOORAY!
SPLASH
U.S.R.P.S. Landing Site
NO FISHING

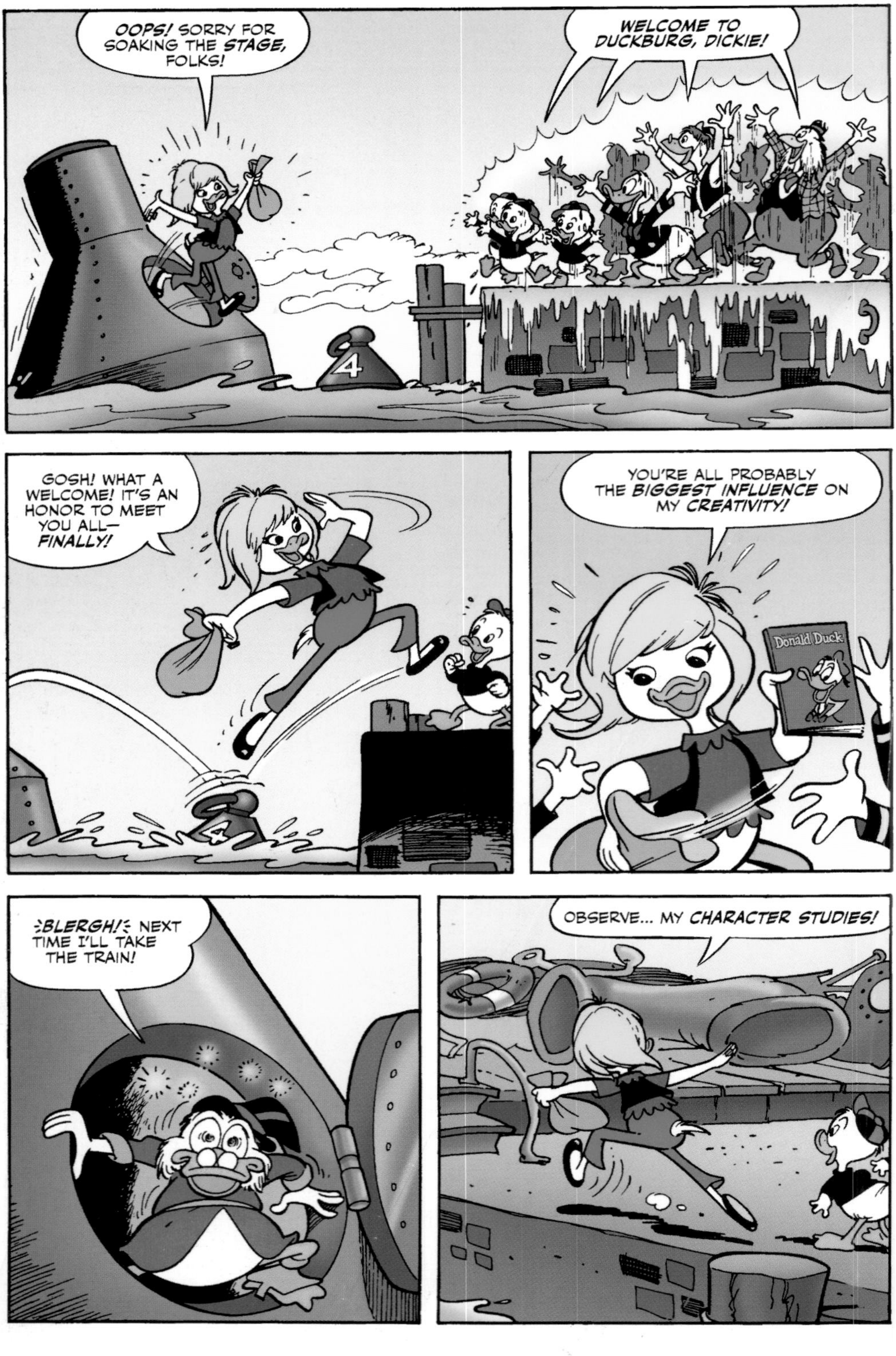
OOPS! SORRY FOR SOAKING THE STAGE, FOLKS!
WELCOME TO DUCKBURG, DICKIE!
GOSH! WHAT A WELCOME! IT'S AN HONOR TO MEET YOU ALL— FINALLY!
YOU'RE ALL PROBABLY THE BIGGEST INFLUENCE ON MY CREATIVITY!
Donald Duck
BLERGH! NEXT TIME I'LL TAKE THE TRAIN!
OBSERVE... MY CHARACTER STUDIES!

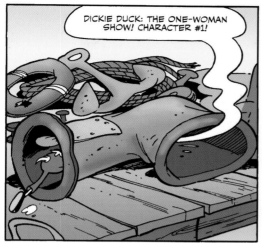

DICKIE DUCK: THE ONE-WOMAN SHOW! CHARACTER #1!

⸽WAK!⸽ PHOOEY! EVERYTHING HAPPENS TO ME! ⸽WAK!⸽

HA HA

HA HA

NOW FOR ANOTHER WELL-KNOWN DUCKBURG CITIZEN... BRIGITTA MACBRIDGE!

CLAP CLAP CLAP CLAP CLAP

♪ LAMMIEKINS! LET'S FILL OUT A JOINT TAX RETURN THIS YEAR! ♫

⸽HEH!⸽ WOW, SHE'S A BORN ENTERTAINER! JUST LIKE HER GRANDMA!

HA HA HA HA

SOME MEN COME RUNNING FOR A FALLEN HANKY... BUT I KNOW "SCROOGIE" BETTER!

CLINK

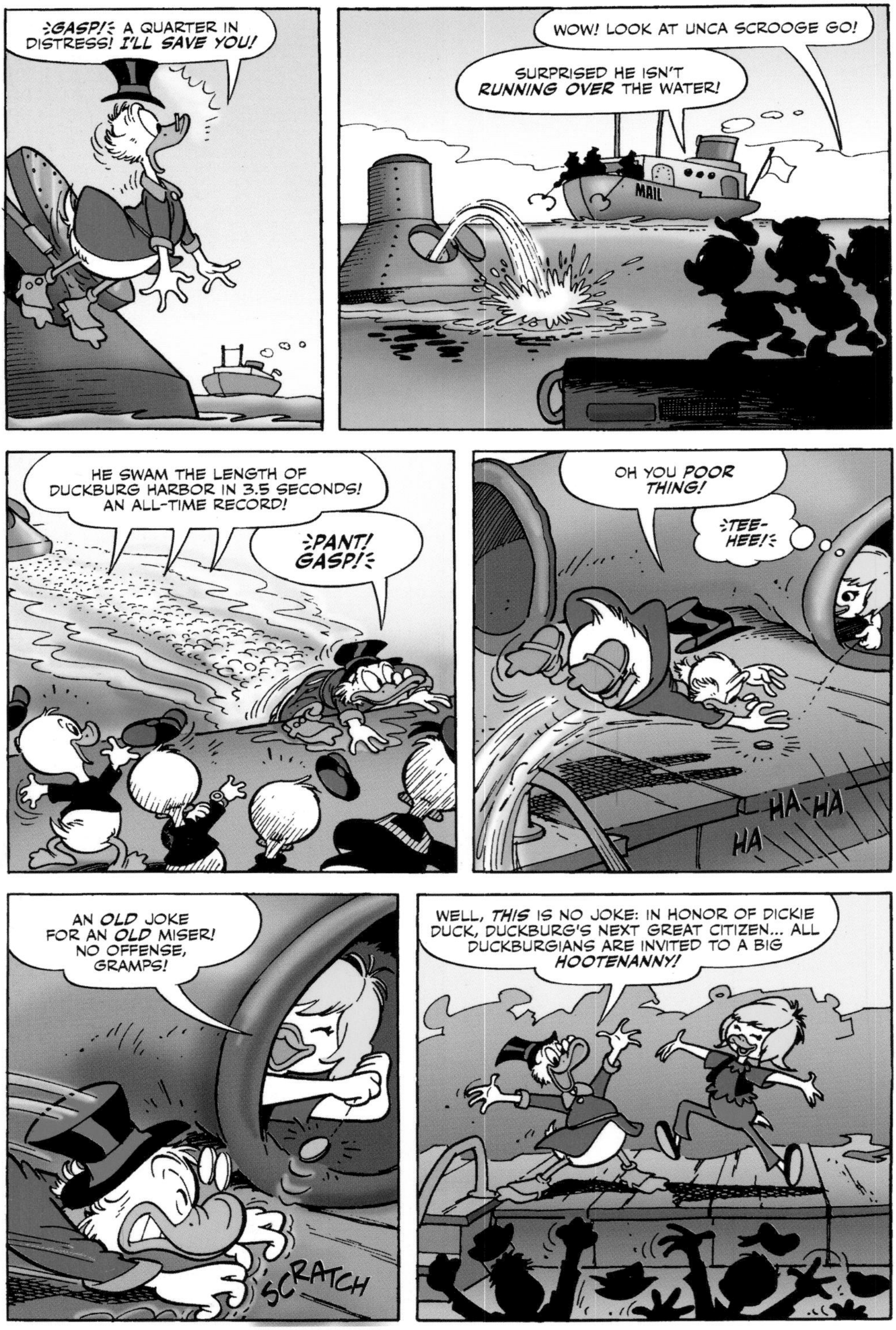
GASP! A QUARTER IN DISTRESS! *I'LL SAVE YOU!*
WOW! LOOK AT UNCA SCROOGE GO!
SURPRISED HE ISN'T *RUNNING OVER* THE WATER!
MAIL
HE SWAM THE LENGTH OF DUCKBURG HARBOR IN 3.5 SECONDS! AN ALL-TIME RECORD!
PANT! GASP!
OH YOU *POOR THING!*
TEE-HEE!
HA HA HA HA
AN *OLD* JOKE FOR AN *OLD* MISER! NO OFFENSE, GRAMPS!
SCRATCH
WELL, *THIS* IS NO JOKE: IN HONOR OF DICKIE DUCK, DUCKBURG'S NEXT GREAT CITIZEN... ALL DUCKBURGIANS ARE INVITED TO A BIG *HOOTENANNY!*

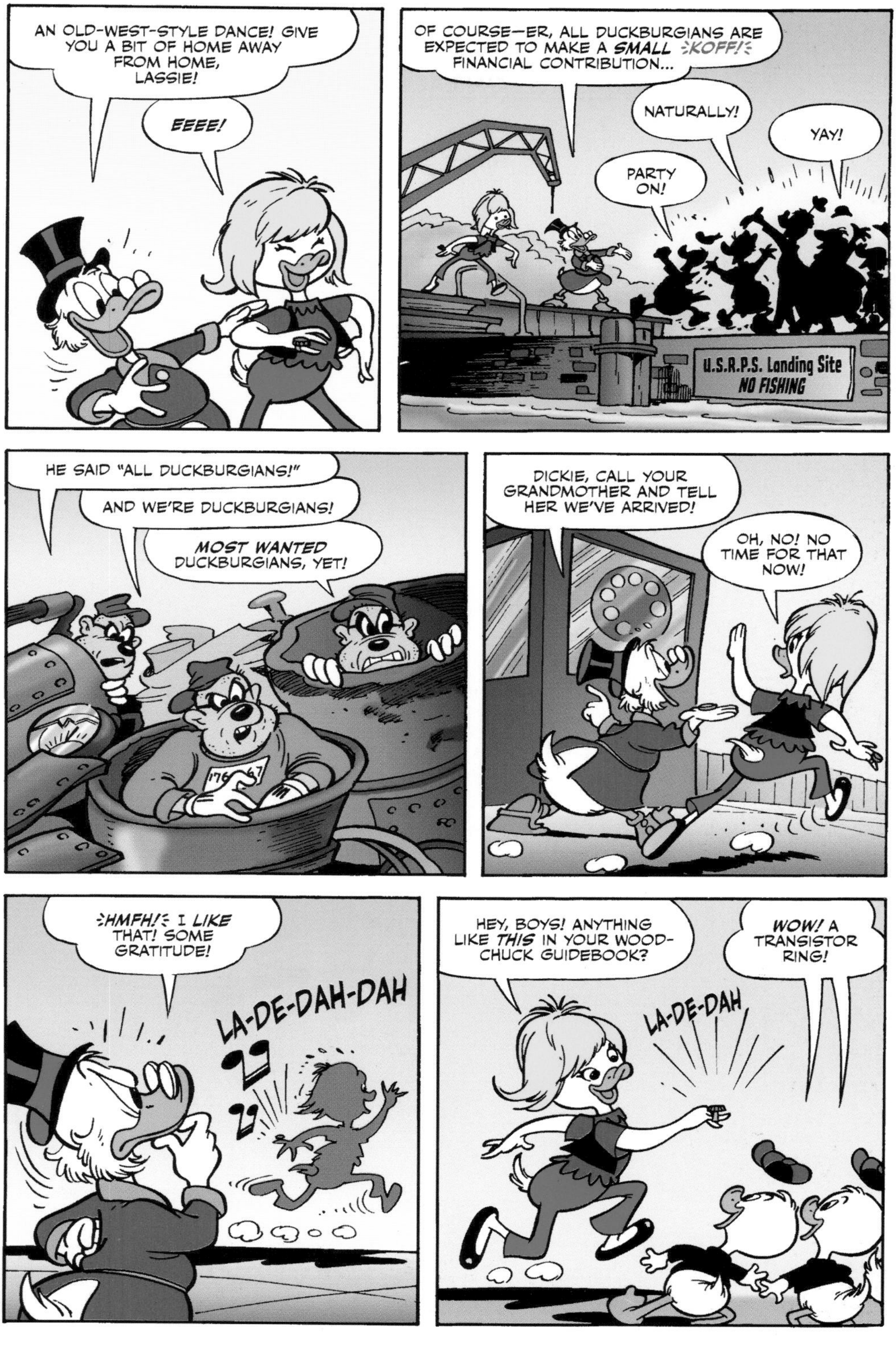
AN OLD-WEST-STYLE DANCE! GIVE YOU A BIT OF HOME AWAY FROM HOME, LASSIE!
EEEE!
OF COURSE—ER, ALL DUCKBURGIANS ARE EXPECTED TO MAKE A SMALL KOFF! FINANCIAL CONTRIBUTION...
NATURALLY!
YAY!
PARTY ON!
U.S.R.P.S. Landing Site
NO FISHING
HE SAID "ALL DUCKBURGIANS!"
AND WE'RE DUCKBURGIANS!
MOST WANTED DUCKBURGIANS, YET!
176-67
DICKIE, CALL YOUR GRANDMOTHER AND TELL HER WE'VE ARRIVED!
OH, NO! NO TIME FOR THAT NOW!
HMFH! I LIKE THAT! SOME GRATITUDE!
LA-DE-DAH-DAH
HEY, BOYS! ANYTHING LIKE THIS IN YOUR WOOD-CHUCK GUIDEBOOK?
WOW! A TRANSISTOR RING!
LA-DE-DAH

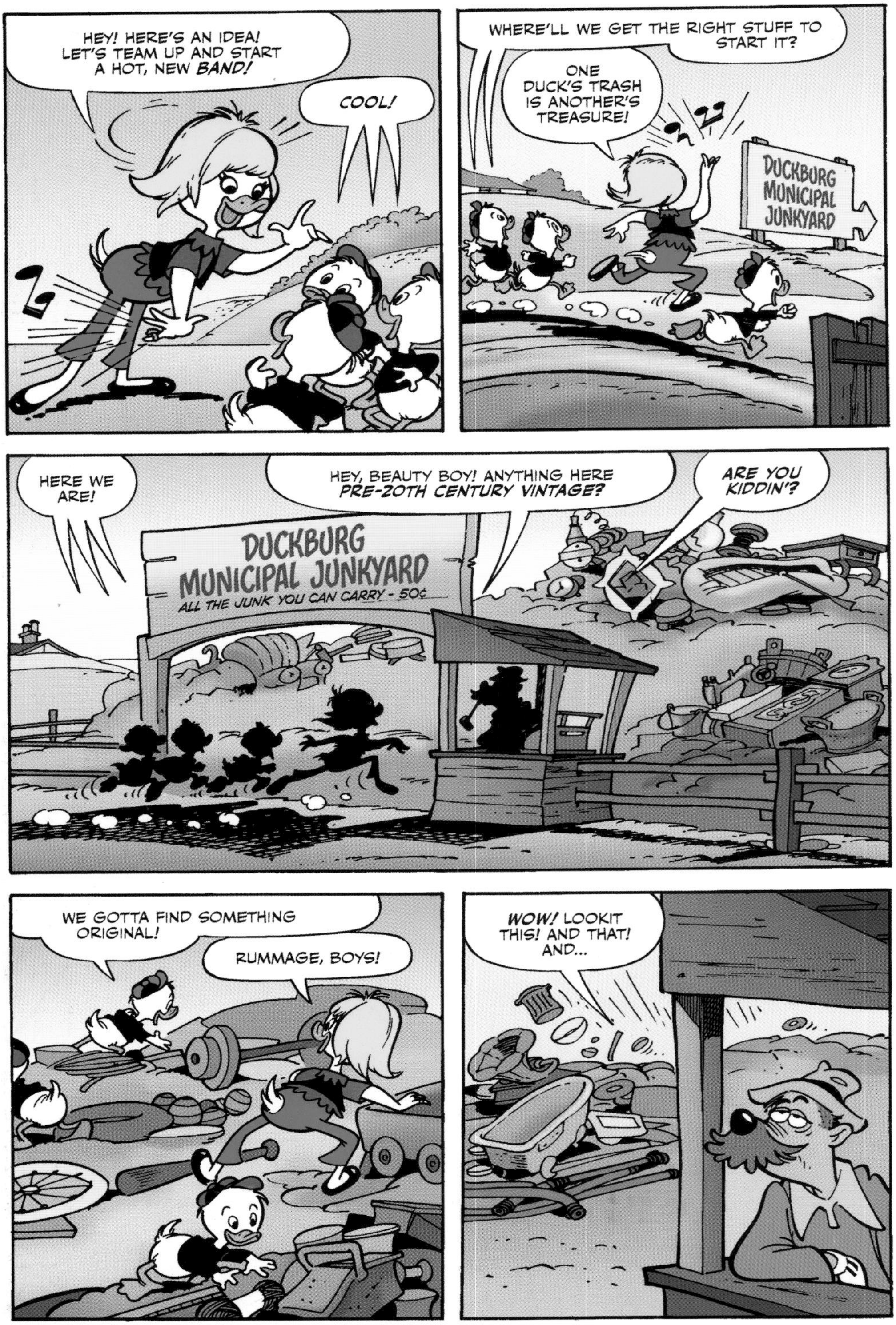

HEY! HERE'S AN IDEA! LET'S TEAM UP AND START A HOT, NEW *BAND!*
COOL!
WHERE'LL WE GET THE RIGHT STUFF TO START IT?
ONE DUCK'S TRASH IS ANOTHER'S TREASURE!
DUCKBURG MUNICIPAL JUNKYARD
HERE WE ARE!
HEY, BEAUTY BOY! ANYTHING HERE *PRE-20TH CENTURY VINTAGE?*
ARE YOU KIDDIN'?
DUCKBURG MUNICIPAL JUNKYARD
ALL THE JUNK YOU CAN CARRY - 50¢
WE GOTTA FIND SOMETHING ORIGINAL!
RUMMAGE, BOYS!
WOW! LOOKIT THIS! AND THAT! AND...

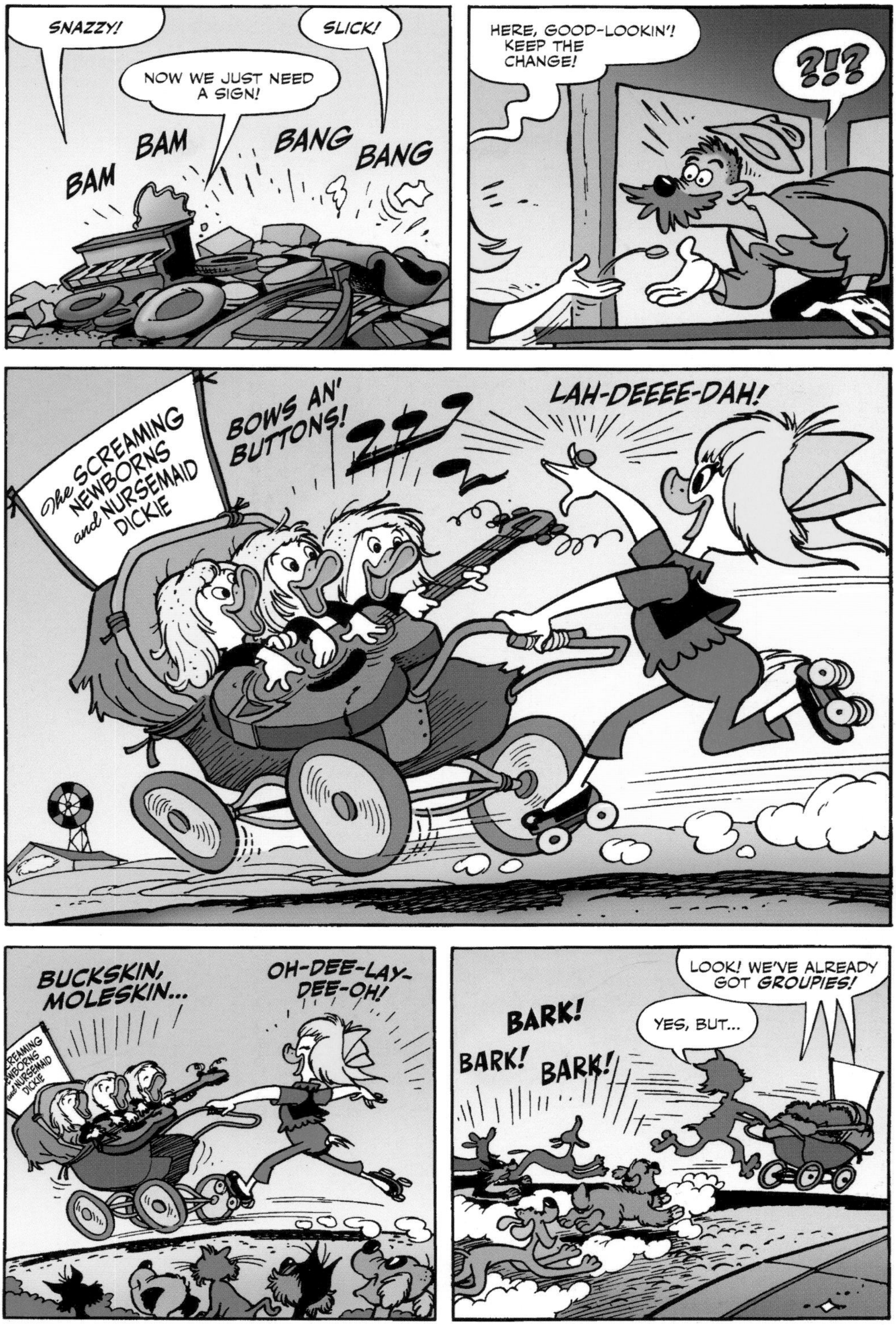
SNAZZY!
NOW WE JUST NEED A SIGN!
SLICK!
BAM
BAM
BANG
BANG
HERE, GOOD-LOOKIN'! KEEP THE CHANGE!
?!?
The SCREAMING NEWBORNS and NURSEMAID DICKIE
BOWS AN' BUTTONS!
LAH-DEEEE-DAH!
BUCKSKIN, MOLESKIN...
OH-DEE-LAY-DEE-OH!
CREAMING NEWBORNS and NURSEMAID DICKIE
LOOK! WE'VE ALREADY GOT GROUPIES!
BARK!
BARK!
BARK!
YES, BUT...

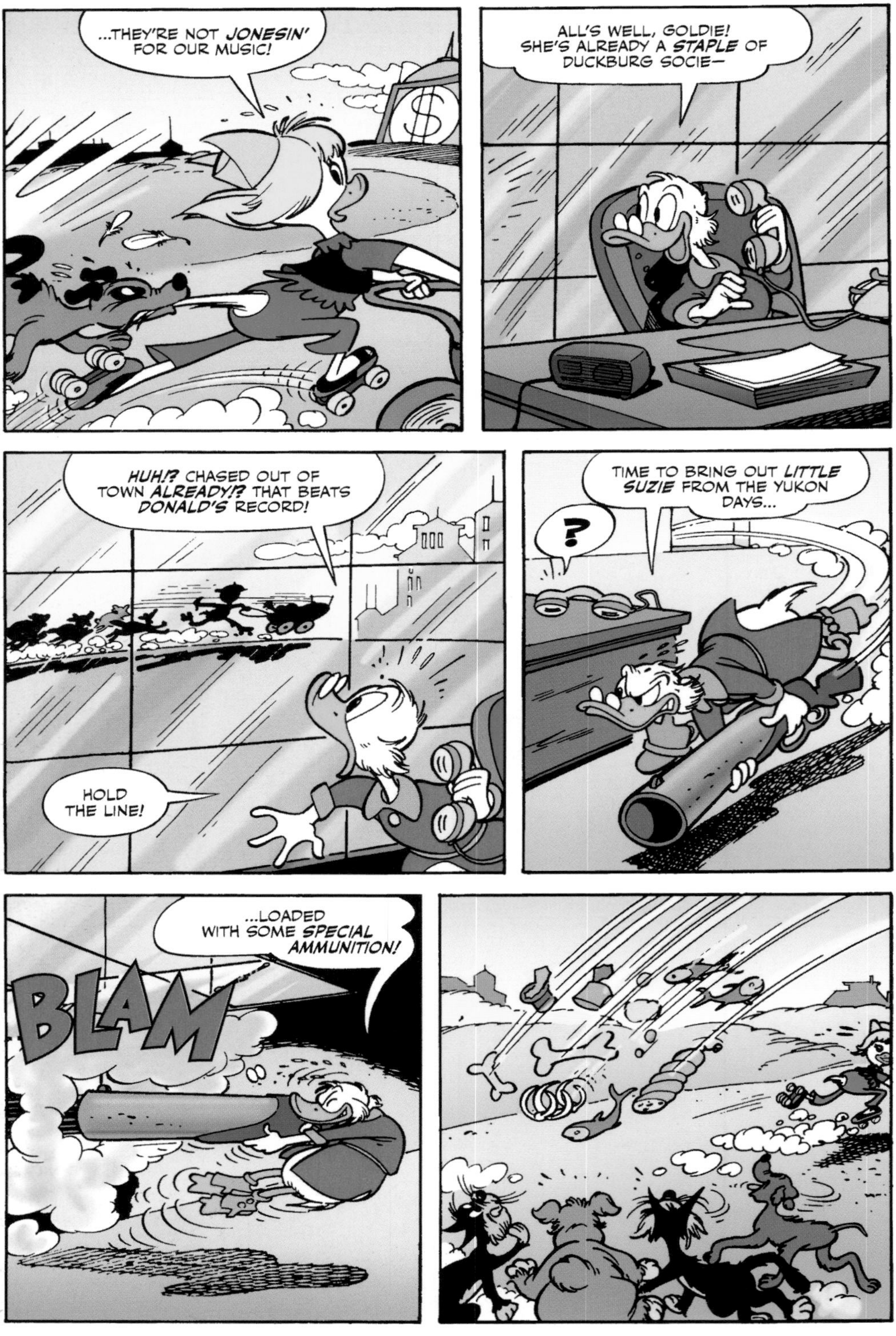
...THEY'RE NOT JONESIN' FOR OUR MUSIC!
ALL'S WELL, GOLDIE! SHE'S ALREADY A STAPLE OF DUCKBURG SOCIE—
HUH!? CHASED OUT OF TOWN ALREADY!? THAT BEATS DONALD'S RECORD!
HOLD THE LINE!
?
TIME TO BRING OUT LITTLE SUZIE FROM THE YUKON DAYS...
...LOADED WITH SOME SPECIAL AMMUNITION!
BLAM

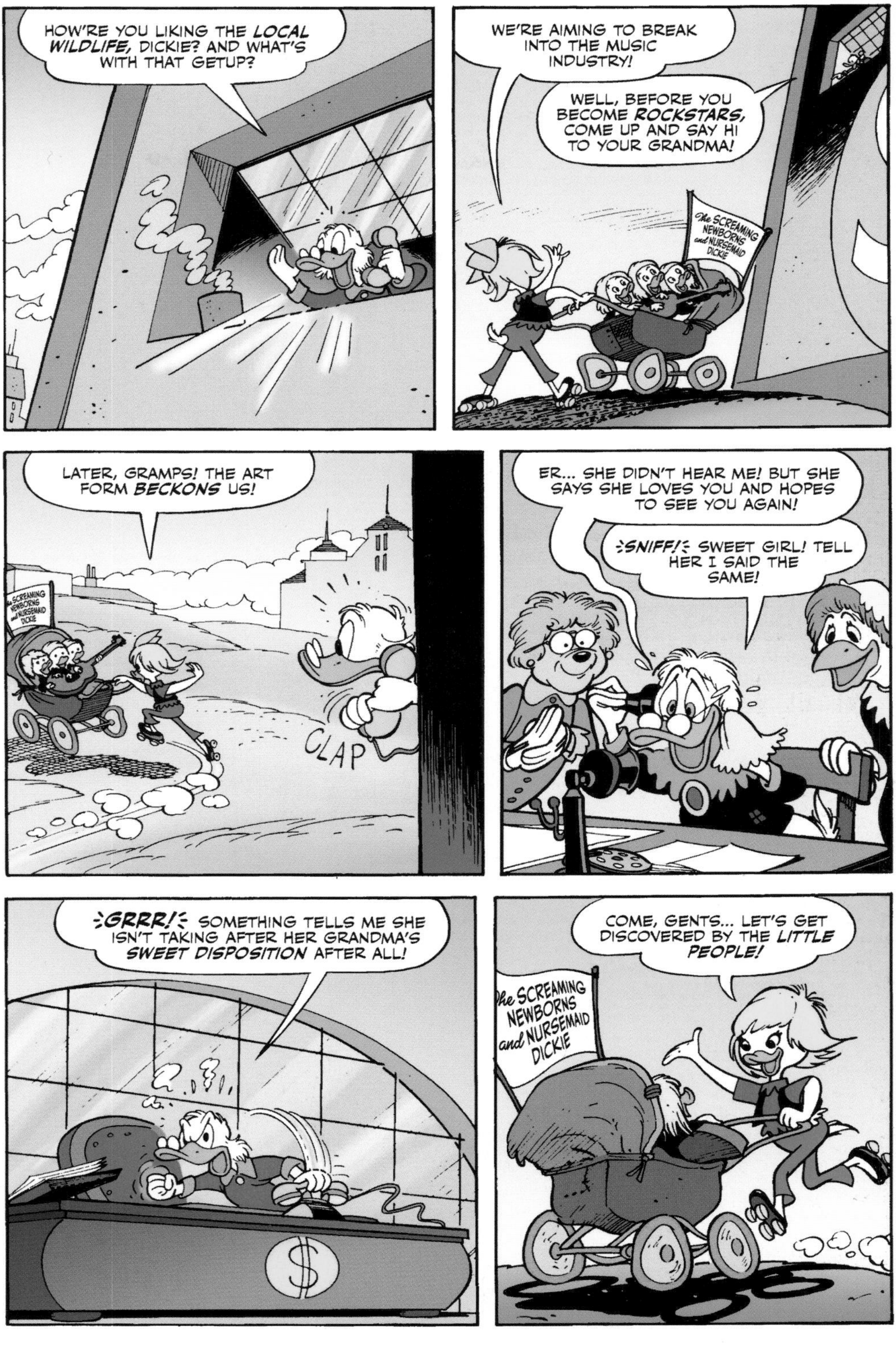
HOW'RE YOU LIKING THE LOCAL WILDLIFE, DICKIE? AND WHAT'S WITH THAT GETUP?
WE'RE AIMING TO BREAK INTO THE MUSIC INDUSTRY!
WELL, BEFORE YOU BECOME ROCKSTARS, COME UP AND SAY HI TO YOUR GRANDMA!
The SCREAMING NEWBORNS and NURSEMAID DICKIE
LATER, GRAMPS! THE ART FORM BECKONS US!
CLAP
ER... SHE DIDN'T HEAR ME! BUT SHE SAYS SHE LOVES YOU AND HOPES TO SEE YOU AGAIN!
SNIFF! SWEET GIRL! TELL HER I SAID THE SAME!
GRRR! SOMETHING TELLS ME SHE ISN'T TAKING AFTER HER GRANDMA'S SWEET DISPOSITION AFTER ALL!
COME, GENTS... LET'S GET DISCOVERED BY THE LITTLE PEOPLE!
The SCREAMING NEWBORNS and NURSEMAID DICKIE

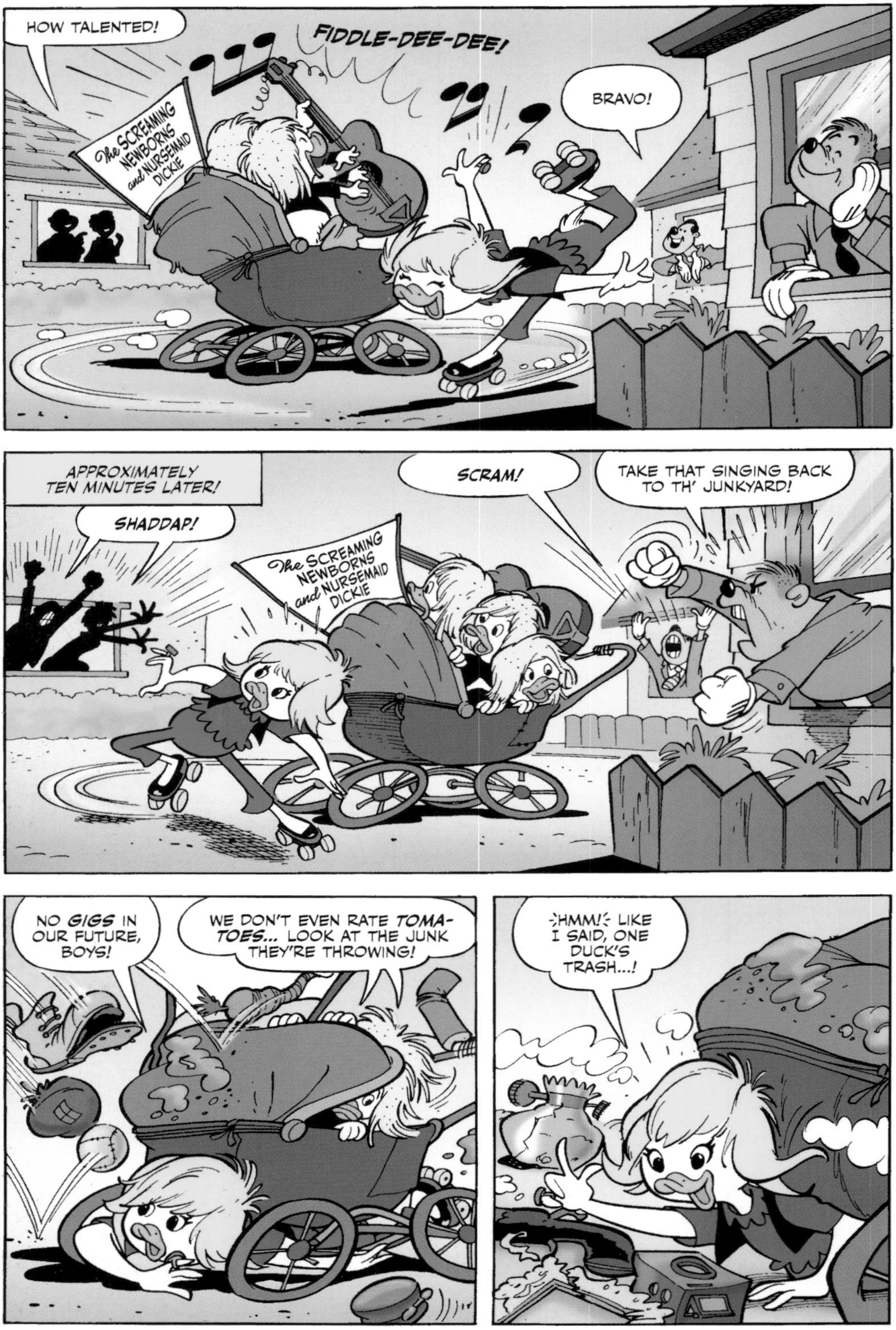
HOW TALENTED!
FIDDLE-DEE-DEE!
The SCREAMING NEWBORNS and NURSEMAID DICKIE
BRAVO!
APPROXIMATELY TEN MINUTES LATER!
SHADDAP!
The SCREAMING NEWBORNS and NURSEMAID DICKIE
SCRAM!
TAKE THAT SINGING BACK TO TH' JUNKYARD!
NO *GIGS* IN OUR FUTURE, BOYS!
WE DON'T EVEN RATE *TOMA-TOES...* LOOK AT THE JUNK THEY'RE THROWING!
HMM! LIKE I SAID, ONE DUCK'S TRASH...!

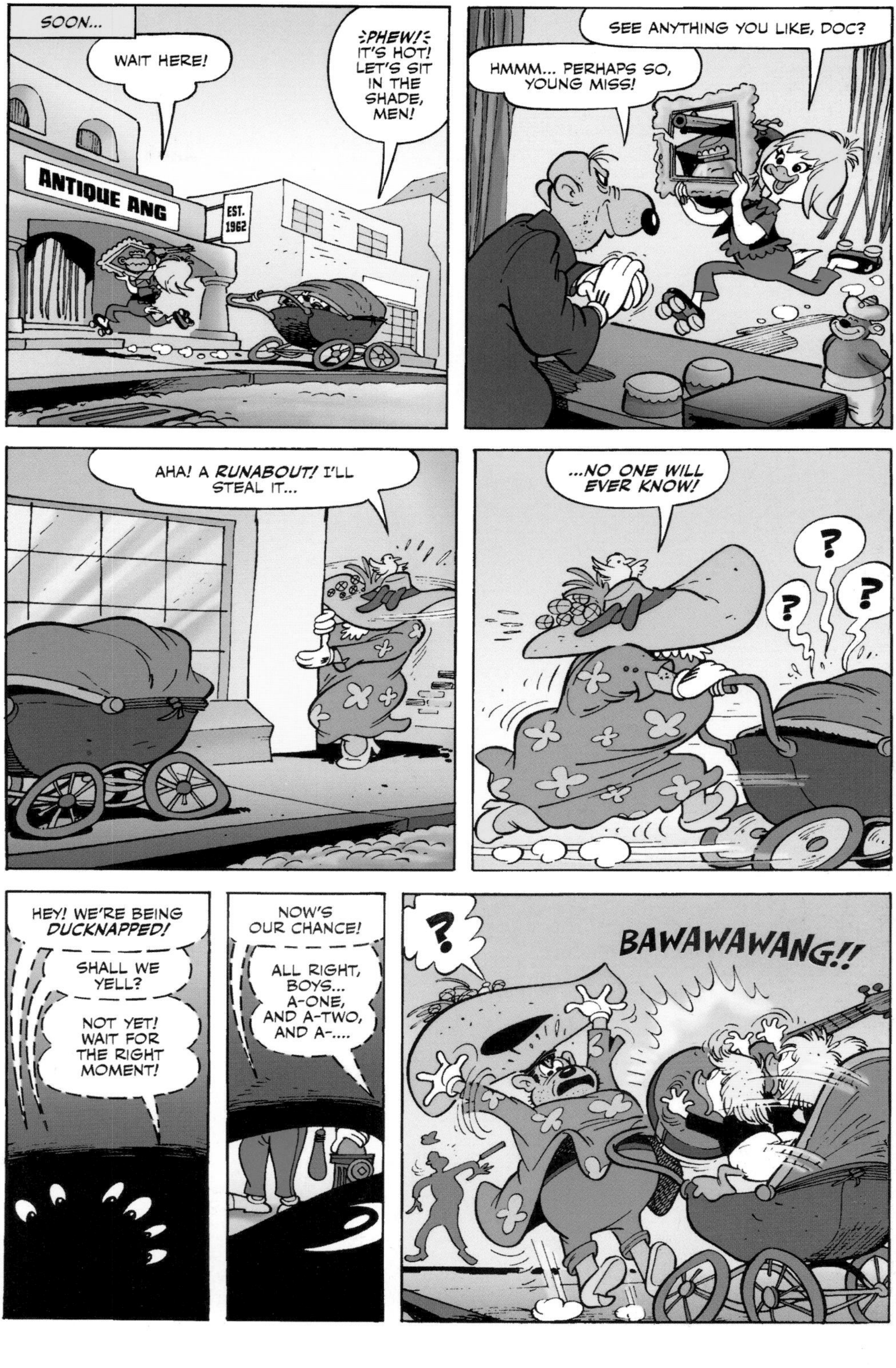
SOON...
WAIT HERE!
ANTIQUE ANG
EST. 1962
PHEW! IT'S HOT! LET'S SIT IN THE SHADE, MEN!
SEE ANYTHING YOU LIKE, DOC?
HMMM... PERHAPS SO, YOUNG MISS!
AHA! A RUNABOUT! I'LL STEAL IT...
...NO ONE WILL EVER KNOW!
?
?
?
HEY! WE'RE BEING DUCKNAPPED!
SHALL WE YELL?
NOT YET! WAIT FOR THE RIGHT MOMENT!
NOW'S OUR CHANCE!
ALL RIGHT, BOYS... A-ONE, AND A-TWO, AND A-....
?
BAWAWAWANG!!

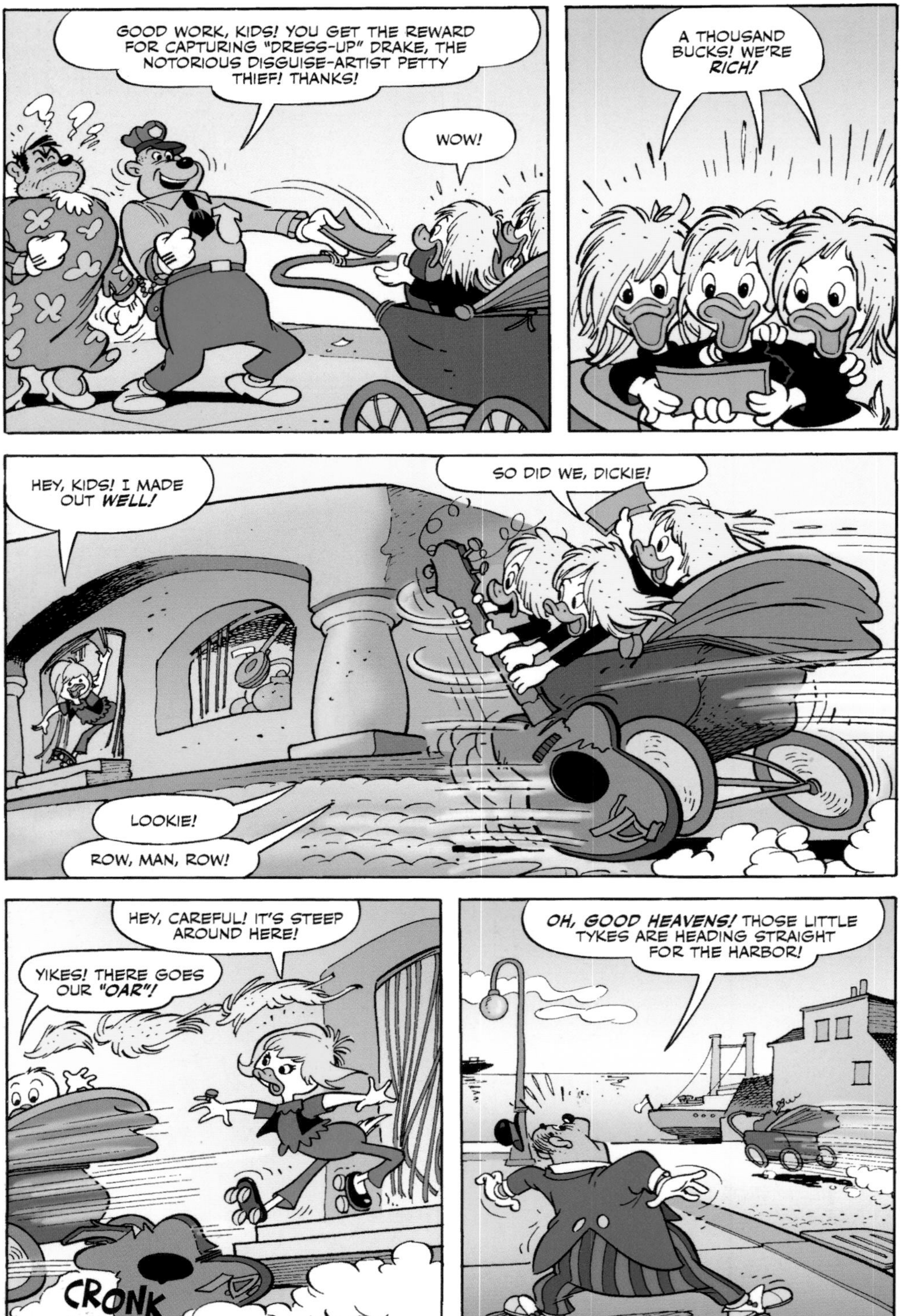
GOOD WORK, KIDS! YOU GET THE REWARD FOR CAPTURING "DRESS-UP" DRAKE, THE NOTORIOUS DISGUISE-ARTIST PETTY THIEF! THANKS!
WOW!
A THOUSAND BUCKS! WE'RE *RICH!*
HEY, KIDS! I MADE OUT ***WELL!***
SO DID WE, DICKIE!
LOOKIE!
ROW, MAN, ROW!
HEY, CAREFUL! IT'S STEEP AROUND HERE!
YIKES! THERE GOES OUR ***"OAR"!***
CRONK
OH, GOOD HEAVENS! THOSE LITTLE TYKES ARE HEADING STRAIGHT FOR THE HARBOR!

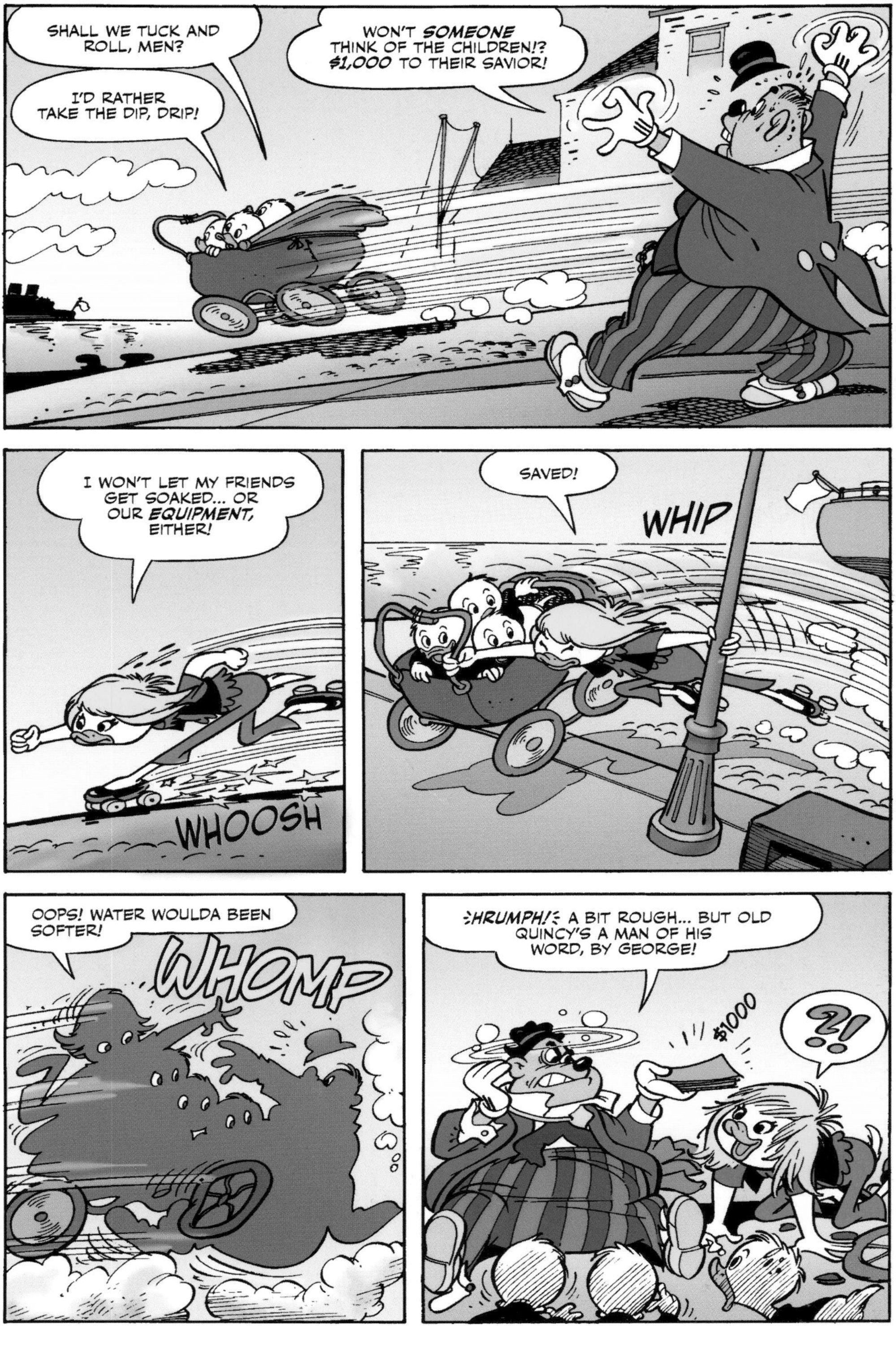
SHALL WE TUCK AND ROLL, MEN?
I'D RATHER TAKE THE DIP, DRIP!
WON'T SOMEONE THINK OF THE CHILDREN!? $1,000 TO THEIR SAVIOR!
I WON'T LET MY FRIENDS GET SOAKED... OR OUR EQUIPMENT, EITHER!
WHOOSH
SAVED!
WHIP
OOPS! WATER WOULDA BEEN SOFTER!
WHOMP
HRUMPH! A BIT ROUGH... BUT OLD QUINCY'S A MAN OF HIS WORD, BY GEORGE!
$1000
?!

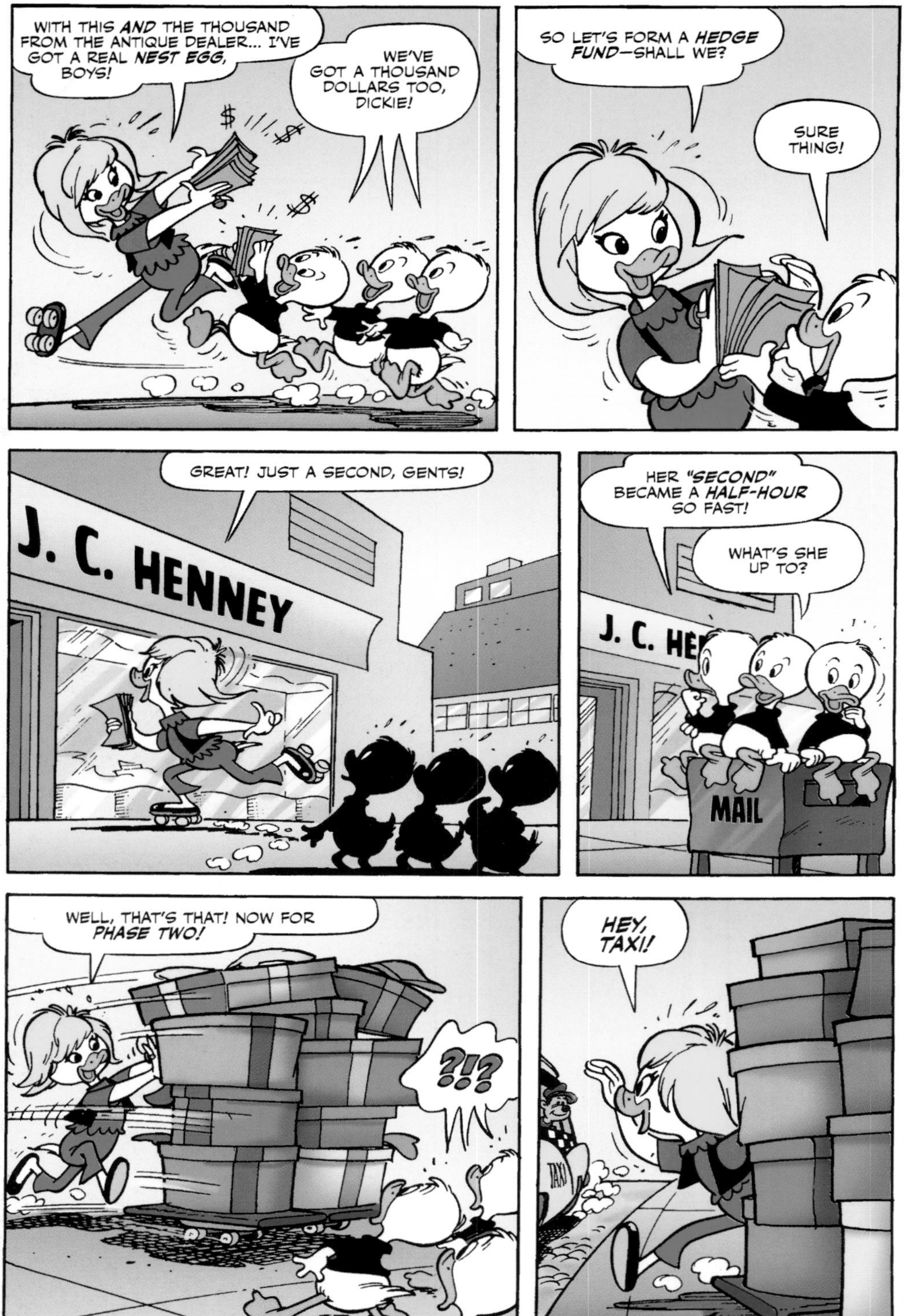
WITH THIS AND THE THOUSAND FROM THE ANTIQUE DEALER... I'VE GOT A REAL NEST EGG, BOYS!
WE'VE GOT A THOUSAND DOLLARS TOO, DICKIE!
SO LET'S FORM A HEDGE FUND—SHALL WE?
SURE THING!
GREAT! JUST A SECOND, GENTS!
J. C. HENNEY
HER "SECOND" BECAME A HALF-HOUR SO FAST!
WHAT'S SHE UP TO?
J. C. HE
MAIL
WELL, THAT'S THAT! NOW FOR PHASE TWO!
?!?
HEY, TAXI!
TAXI

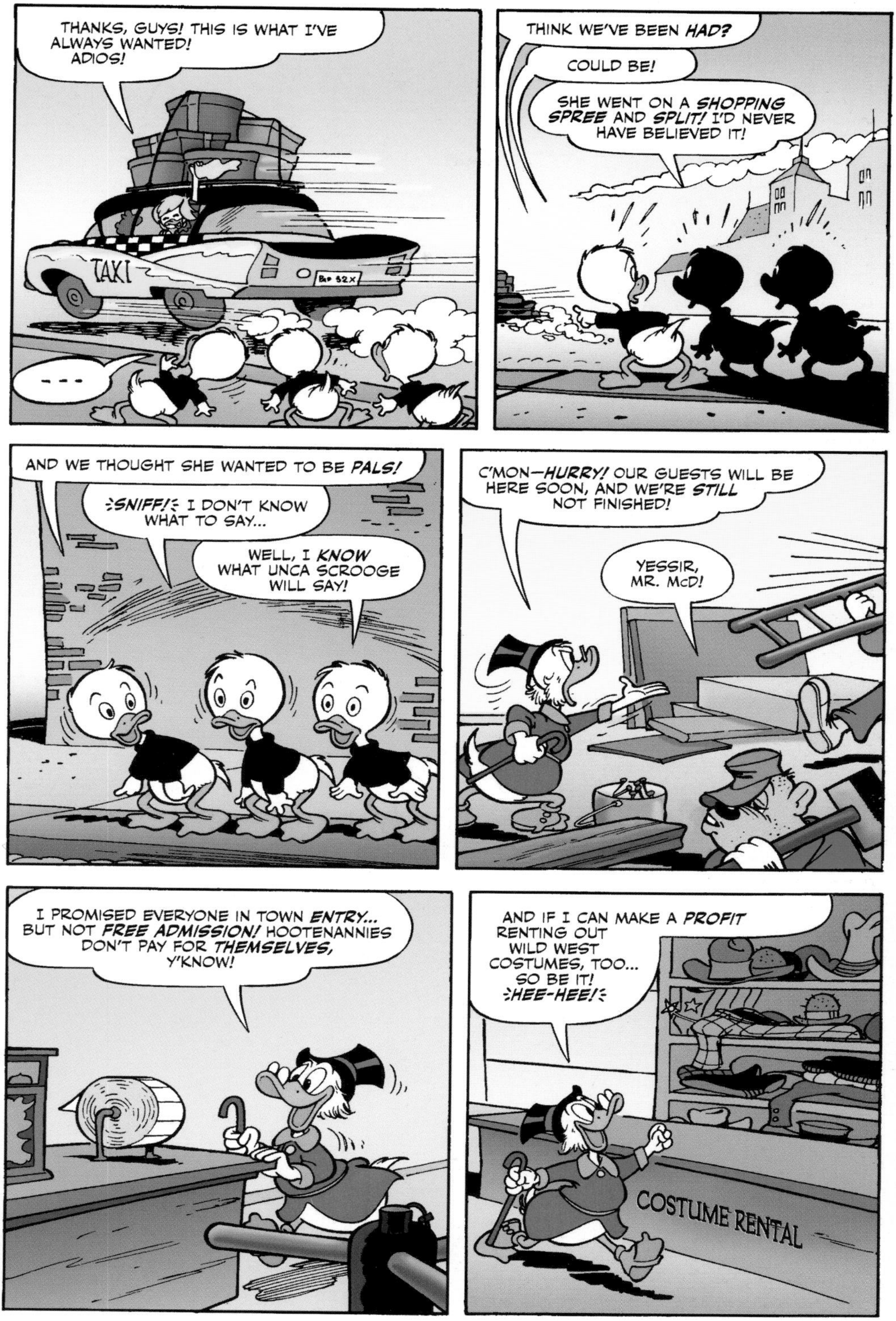
THANKS, GUYS! THIS IS WHAT I'VE ALWAYS WANTED! ADIOS!
TAXI
...
THINK WE'VE BEEN *HAD?*
COULD BE!
SHE WENT ON A *SHOPPING SPREE* AND *SPLIT!* I'D NEVER HAVE BELIEVED IT!
AND WE THOUGHT SHE WANTED TO BE *PALS!*
SNIFF! I DON'T KNOW WHAT TO SAY...
WELL, I *KNOW* WHAT UNCA SCROOGE WILL SAY!
C'MON—*HURRY!* OUR GUESTS WILL BE HERE SOON, AND WE'RE *STILL* NOT FINISHED!
YESSIR, MR. McD!
I PROMISED EVERYONE IN TOWN *ENTRY...* BUT NOT *FREE ADMISSION!* HOOTENANNIES DON'T PAY FOR *THEMSELVES,* Y'KNOW!
AND IF I CAN MAKE A *PROFIT* RENTING OUT WILD WEST COSTUMES, TOO... SO BE IT! *HEE-HEE!*
COSTUME RENTAL

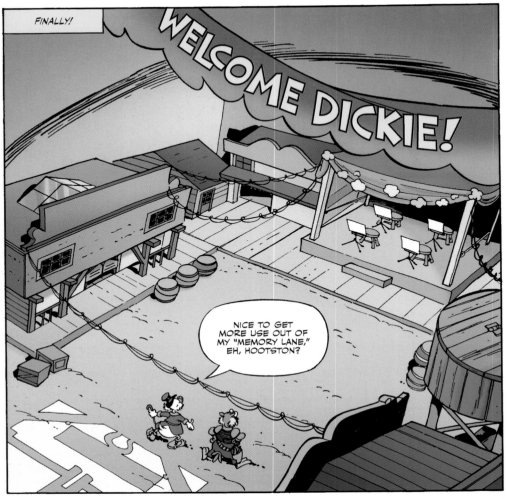

FINALLY!

WELCOME DICKIE!

NICE TO GET MORE USE OUT OF MY "MEMORY LANE," EH, HOOTSTON?

{HEH!} BY GUM, IT'S A SIGHT TO SEE YA SO *RADIANT* ABOUT THIS, SCROOGE!

GOLDIE'S KIN DESERVES IT! YESSIR, IT'S A *GREAT FEELING!*

{...AND IT DOESN'T HURT IF YOU CAN *MAKE MONEY* FEELIN' IT!}

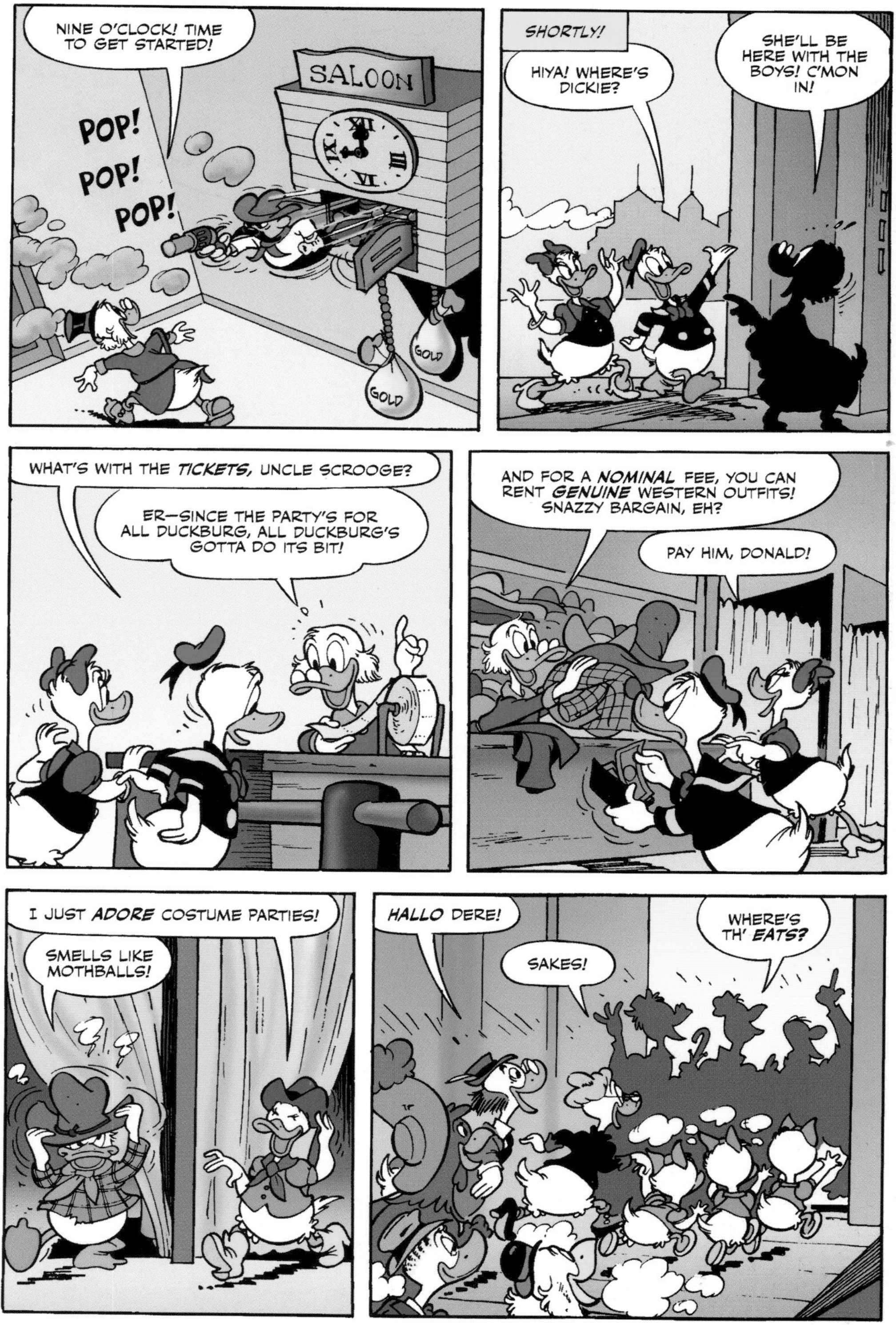
NINE O'CLOCK! TIME TO GET STARTED!
SALOON
POP!
POP!
POP!
GOLD
GOLD
SHORTLY!
HIYA! WHERE'S DICKIE?
SHE'LL BE HERE WITH THE BOYS! C'MON IN!
WHAT'S WITH THE *TICKETS,* UNCLE SCROOGE?
ER—SINCE THE PARTY'S FOR ALL DUCKBURG, ALL DUCKBURG'S GOTTA DO ITS BIT!
AND FOR A *NOMINAL* FEE, YOU CAN RENT *GENUINE* WESTERN OUTFITS! SNAZZY BARGAIN, EH?
PAY HIM, DONALD!
I JUST *ADORE* COSTUME PARTIES!
SMELLS LIKE MOTHBALLS!
HALLO DERE!
SAKES!
WHERE'S TH' *EATS?*

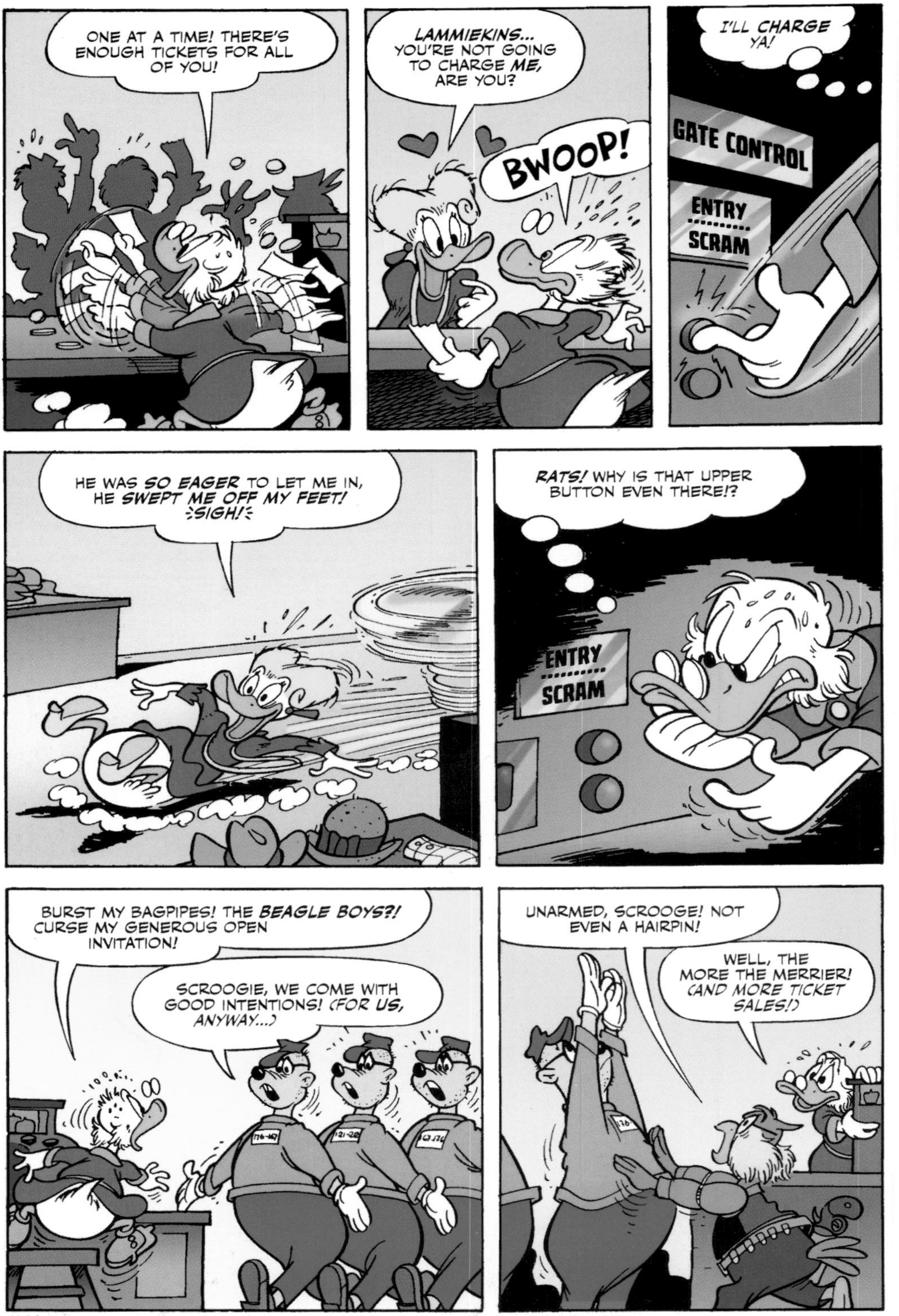
ONE AT A TIME! THERE'S ENOUGH TICKETS FOR ALL OF YOU!
LAMMIEKINS... YOU'RE NOT GOING TO CHARGE ME, ARE YOU?
BWOOP!
I'LL CHARGE YA!
GATE CONTROL
ENTRY
SCRAM
HE WAS SO EAGER TO LET ME IN, HE SWEPT ME OFF MY FEET! SIGH!
RATS! WHY IS THAT UPPER BUTTON EVEN THERE!?
ENTRY
SCRAM
BURST MY BAGPIPES! THE BEAGLE BOYS?! CURSE MY GENEROUS OPEN INVITATION!
SCROOGIE, WE COME WITH GOOD INTENTIONS! (FOR US, ANYWAY...)
UNARMED, SCROOGE! NOT EVEN A HAIRPIN!
WELL, THE MORE THE MERRIER! (AND MORE TICKET SALES!)

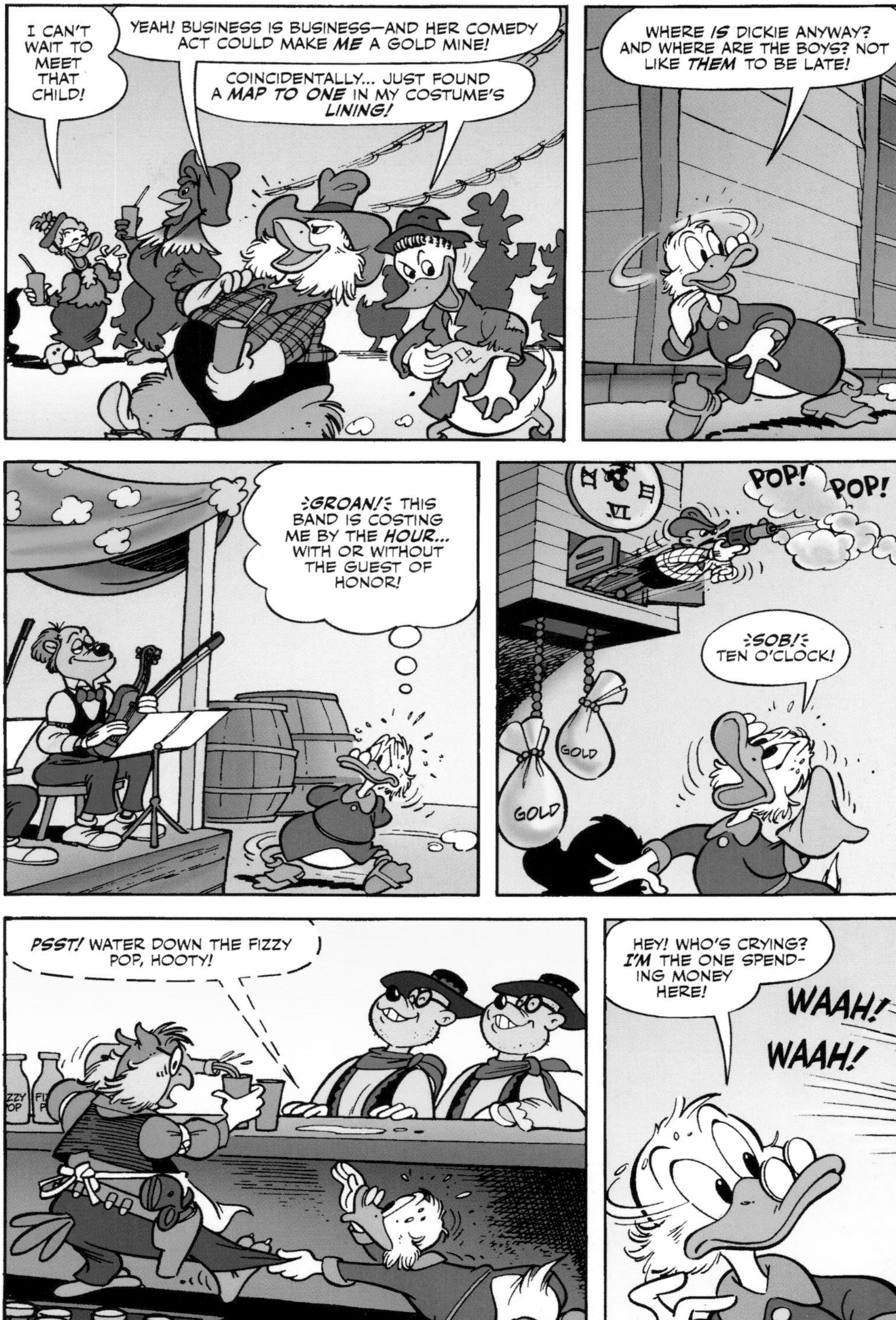
I CAN'T WAIT TO MEET THAT CHILD!
YEAH! BUSINESS IS BUSINESS—AND HER COMEDY ACT COULD MAKE ME A GOLD MINE!
COINCIDENTALLY... JUST FOUND A MAP TO ONE IN MY COSTUME'S LINING!
WHERE IS DICKIE ANYWAY? AND WHERE ARE THE BOYS? NOT LIKE THEM TO BE LATE!
GROAN! THIS BAND IS COSTING ME BY THE HOUR... WITH OR WITHOUT THE GUEST OF HONOR!
POP! POP!
SOB! TEN O'CLOCK!
GOLD
GOLD
PSST! WATER DOWN THE FIZZY POP, HOOTY!
HEY! WHO'S CRYING? I'M THE ONE SPENDING MONEY HERE!
WAAH!
WAAH!

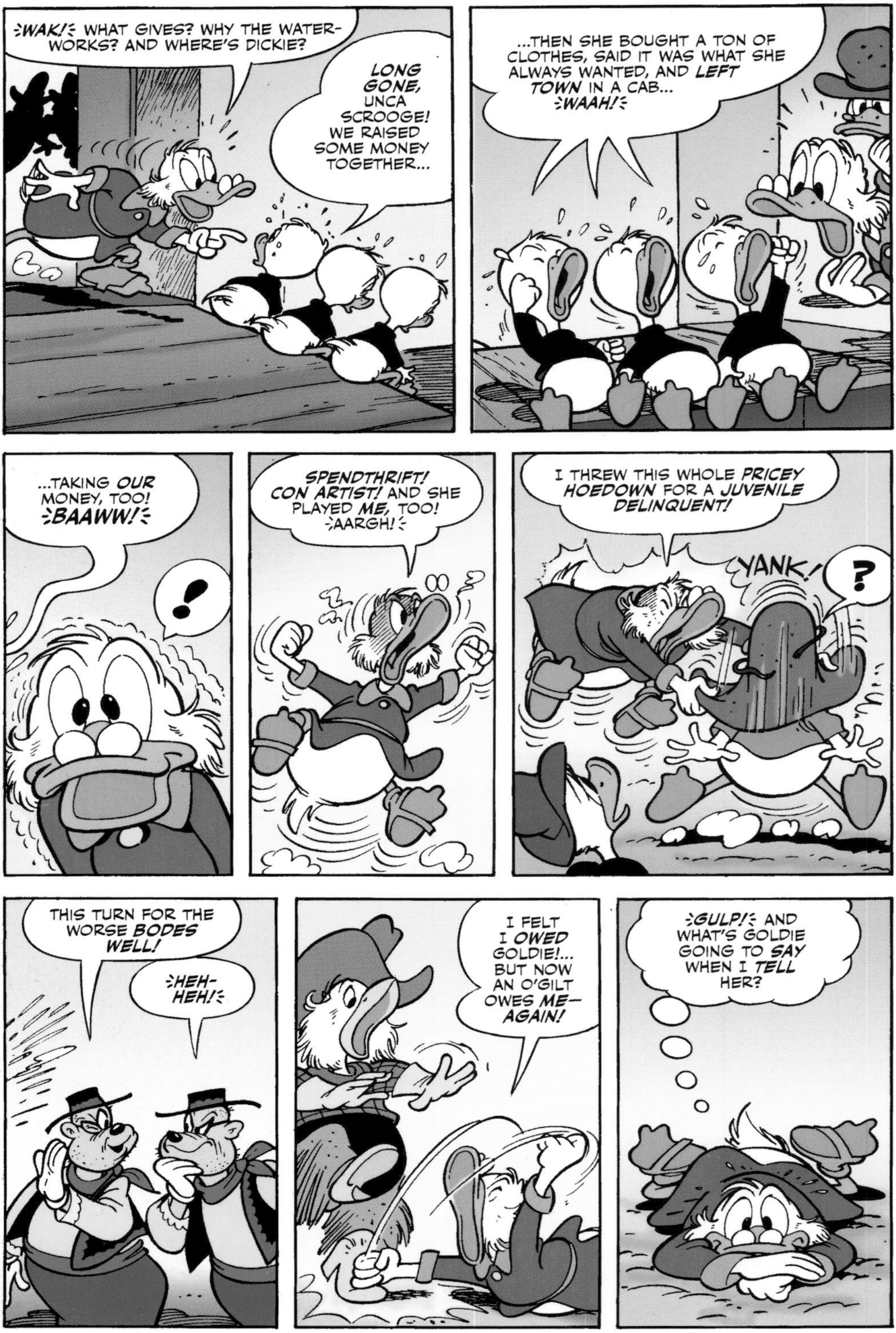

WAK! WHAT GIVES? WHY THE WATERWORKS? AND WHERE'S DICKIE?
LONG GONE, UNCA SCROOGE! WE RAISED SOME MONEY TOGETHER...
...THEN SHE BOUGHT A TON OF CLOTHES, SAID IT WAS WHAT SHE ALWAYS WANTED, AND LEFT TOWN IN A CAB... WAAH!
...TAKING OUR MONEY, TOO! BAAWW!
!
SPENDTHRIFT! CON ARTIST! AND SHE PLAYED ME, TOO! AARGH!
I THREW THIS WHOLE PRICEY HOEDOWN FOR A JUVENILE DELINQUENT!
YANK!
?
THIS TURN FOR THE WORSE BODES WELL!
HEH-HEH!
I FELT I OWED GOLDIE!... BUT NOW AN O'GILT OWES ME—AGAIN!
GULP! AND WHAT'S GOLDIE GOING TO SAY WHEN I TELL HER?

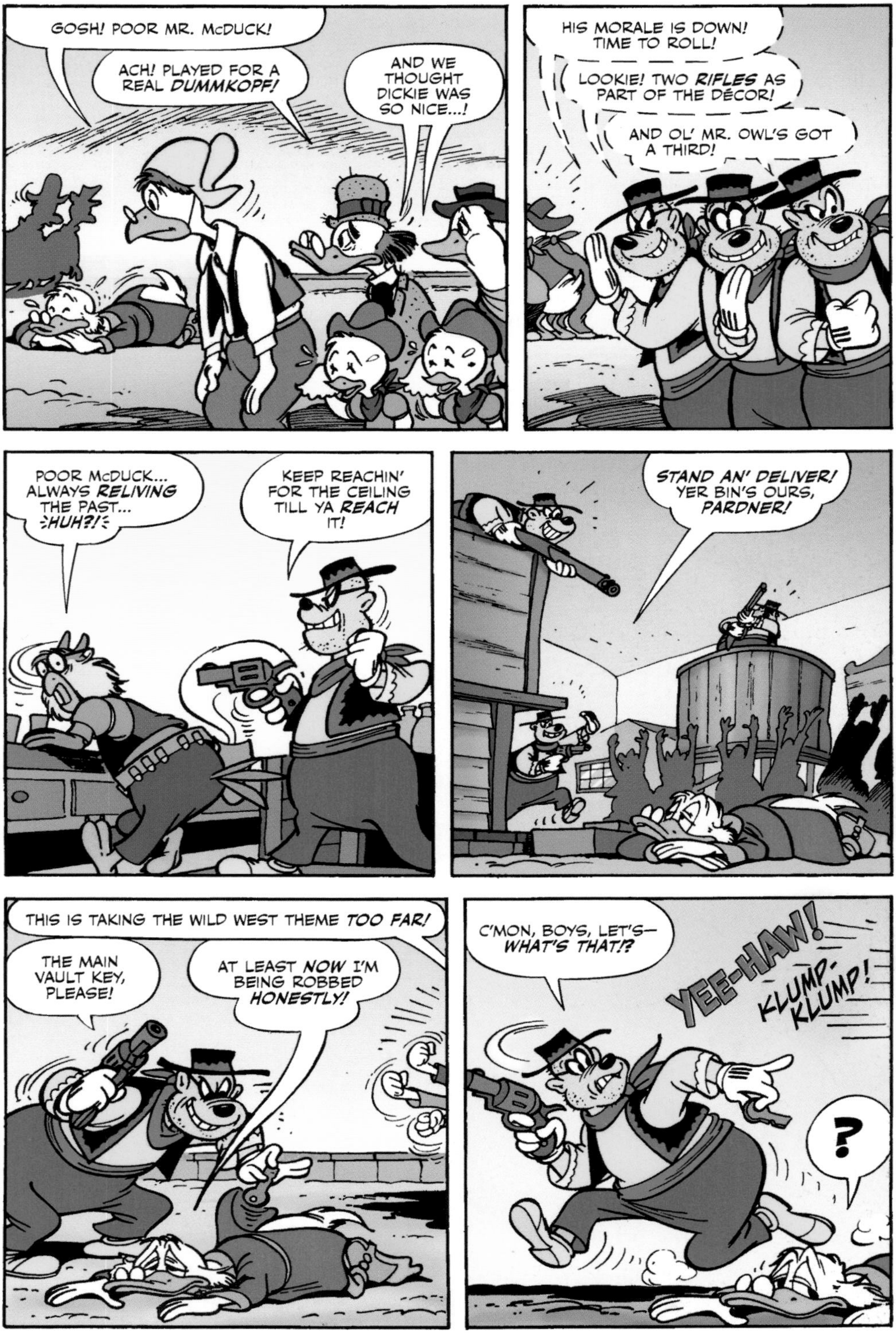
GOSH! POOR MR. McDUCK!
ACH! PLAYED FOR A REAL DUMMKOPF!
AND WE THOUGHT DICKIE WAS SO NICE...!
HIS MORALE IS DOWN! TIME TO ROLL!
LOOKIE! TWO RIFLES AS PART OF THE DÉCOR!
AND OL' MR. OWL'S GOT A THIRD!
POOR McDUCK... ALWAYS RELIVING THE PAST... HUH?!
KEEP REACHIN' FOR THE CEILING TILL YA REACH IT!
STAND AN' DELIVER! YER BIN'S OURS, PARDNER!
THIS IS TAKING THE WILD WEST THEME TOO FAR!
THE MAIN VAULT KEY, PLEASE!
AT LEAST NOW I'M BEING ROBBED HONESTLY!
C'MON, BOYS, LET'S— WHAT'S THAT!?
YEE-HAW!
KLUMP-KLUMP!
?

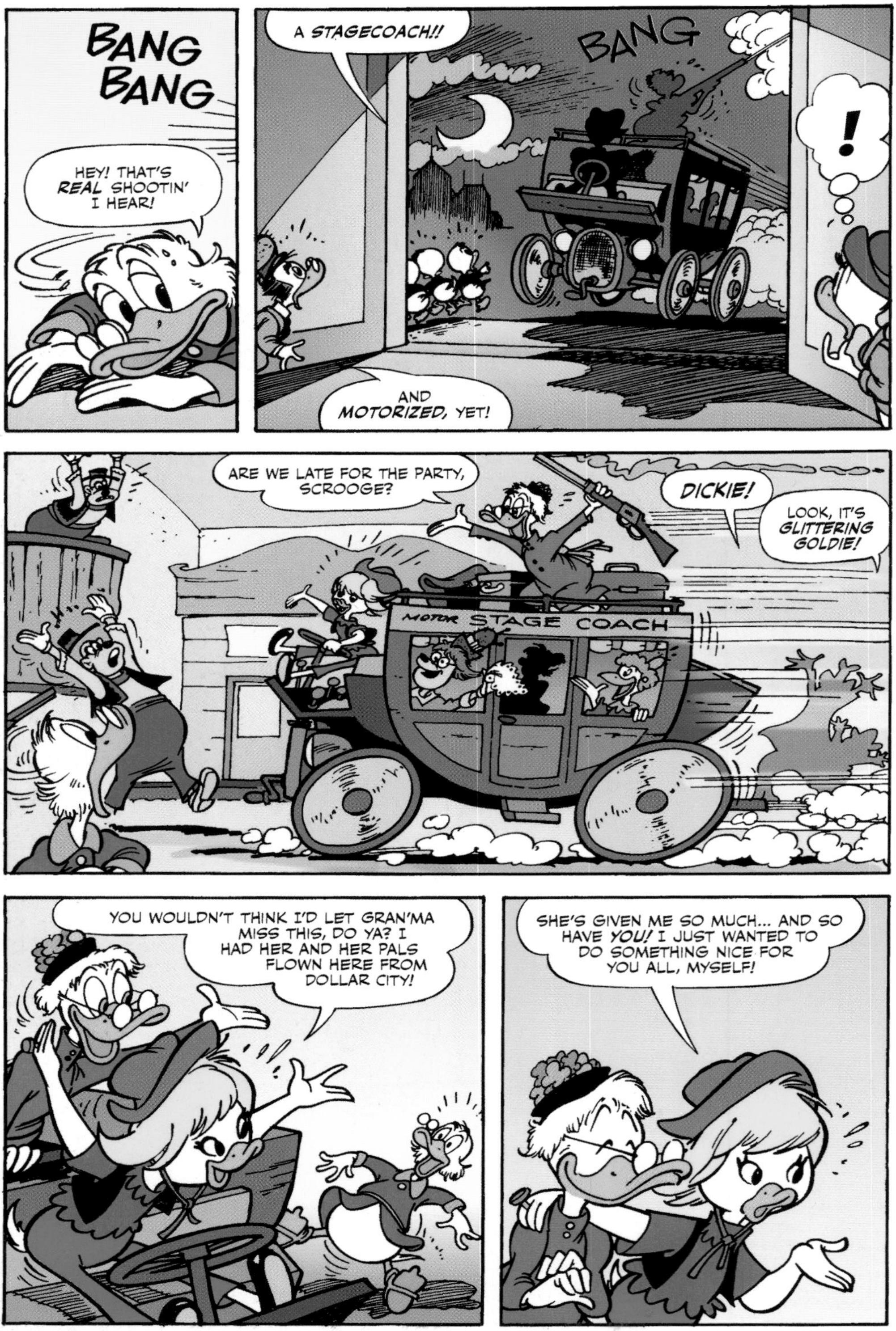
BANG BANG
HEY! THAT'S REAL SHOOTIN' I HEAR!
A STAGECOACH!!
BANG
!
AND MOTORIZED, YET!
ARE WE LATE FOR THE PARTY, SCROOGE?
DICKIE!
LOOK, IT'S GLITTERING GOLDIE!
MOTOR STAGE COACH
YOU WOULDN'T THINK I'D LET GRAN'MA MISS THIS, DO YA? I HAD HER AND HER PALS FLOWN HERE FROM DOLLAR CITY!
SHE'S GIVEN ME SO MUCH... AND SO HAVE YOU! I JUST WANTED TO DO SOMETHING NICE FOR YOU ALL, MYSELF!

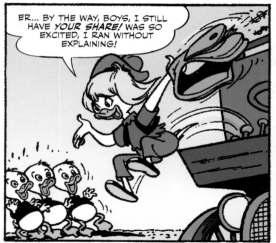

ER... BY THE WAY, BOYS, I STILL HAVE *YOUR SHARE!* WAS SO EXCITED, I RAN WITHOUT EXPLAINING!

A REAL SWEETIE, ISN'T SHE, SCROOGE?

I'LL SAY IT TWICE, GOLDIE! WHO KNEW?

LET'S HEAR IT FOR DICKIE DUCK!

AND THE "HEARTS OF THE YUKON," TOO! ≿*HOO-HOO!*≾

GOSH, SCROOGIE! YOU WAS SAD... AND WE JUST WANTED TO *LIVEN UP* THE PARTY, WESTERN-STYLE!

LET'S KEEP IT *LIVE* WITH THE *CROOKS* GOIN' TO *JAIL!*

ER...

SO YOU'RE BRIGITTA, EH? I KNOW WHAT YOU'RE THINKING... BUT I'M FROM SCROOGE'S PAST... *YOU'RE* HIS PRESENT!

SO TAKE IT FROM A GAL WITH *REAL* McDUCK EXPERIENCE! IF YOU WANT TO WOO SCROOGE... HE'S GOT TO KNOW YOU LOVE HIS *THRIFT* AS MUCH AS *HIM!* GET ME? ≿*HEH!*≾

OH! THANKS, MS. O'GILT!

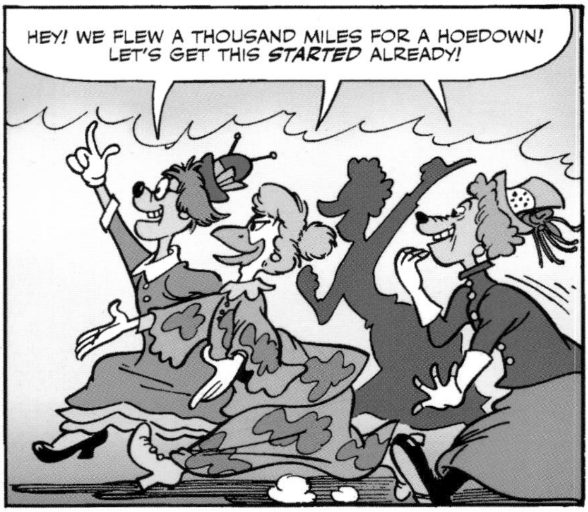
HEY! WE FLEW A THOUSAND MILES FOR A HOEDOWN! LET'S GET THIS STARTED ALREADY!

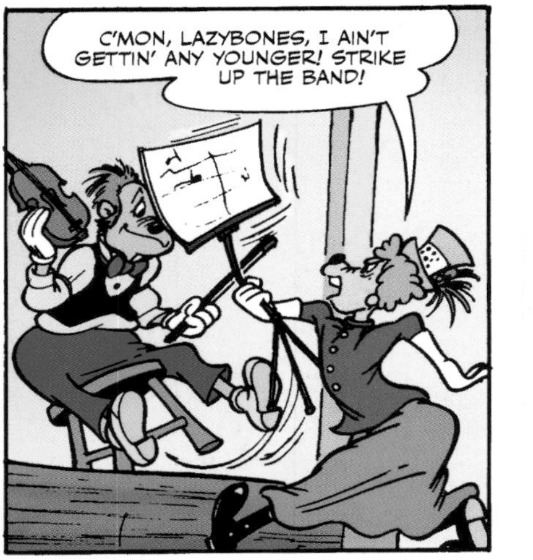
C'MON, LAZYBONES, I AIN'T GETTIN' ANY YOUNGER! STRIKE UP THE BAND!

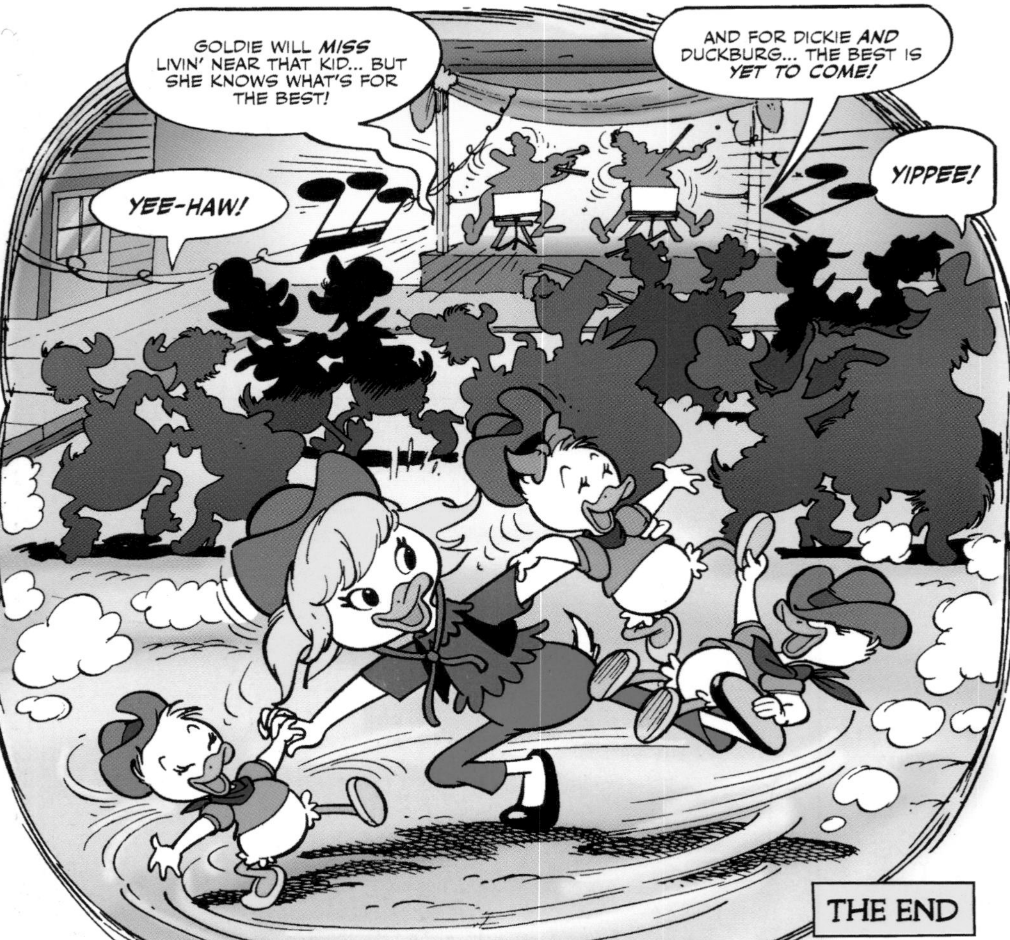
GOLDIE WILL MISS LIVIN' NEAR THAT KID... BUT SHE KNOWS WHAT'S FOR THE BEST!
AND FOR DICKIE AND DUCKBURG... THE BEST IS YET TO COME!
YEE-HAW!
YIPPEE!
THE END

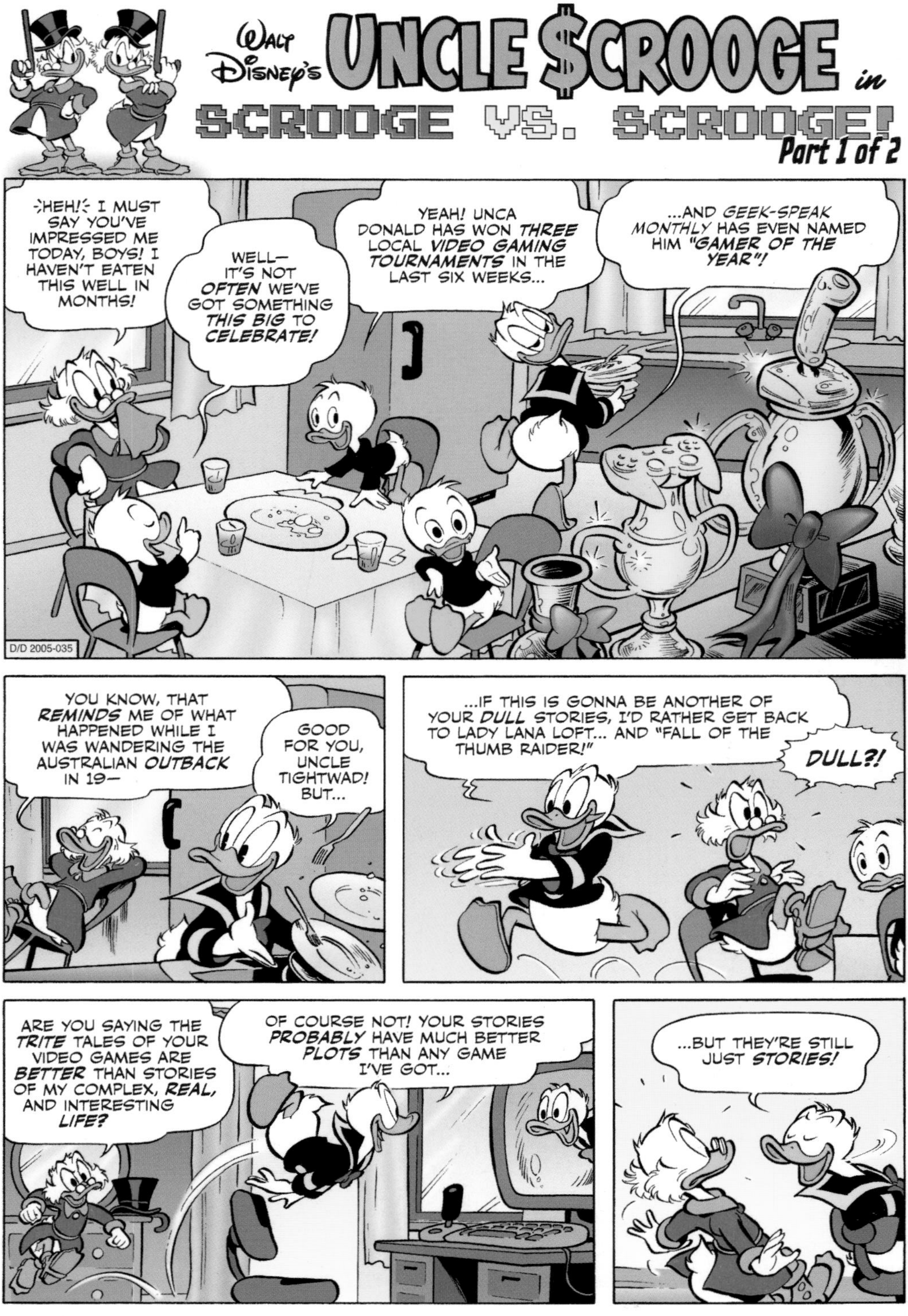
WALT DISNEY'S UNCLE $CROOGE in
SCROOGE VS. SCROOGE!
Part 1 of 2
✧HEH!✧ I MUST SAY YOU'VE IMPRESSED ME TODAY, BOYS! I HAVEN'T EATEN THIS WELL IN MONTHS!
WELL— IT'S NOT OFTEN WE'VE GOT SOMETHING THIS BIG TO CELEBRATE!
YEAH! UNCA DONALD HAS WON THREE LOCAL VIDEO GAMING TOURNAMENTS IN THE LAST SIX WEEKS...
...AND GEEK-SPEAK MONTHLY HAS EVEN NAMED HIM "GAMER OF THE YEAR"!
D/D 2005-035
YOU KNOW, THAT REMINDS ME OF WHAT HAPPENED WHILE I WAS WANDERING THE AUSTRALIAN OUTBACK IN 19—
GOOD FOR YOU, UNCLE TIGHTWAD! BUT...
...IF THIS IS GONNA BE ANOTHER OF YOUR DULL STORIES, I'D RATHER GET BACK TO LADY LANA LOFT... AND "FALL OF THE THUMB RAIDER!"
DULL?!
ARE YOU SAYING THE TRITE TALES OF YOUR VIDEO GAMES ARE BETTER THAN STORIES OF MY COMPLEX, REAL, AND INTERESTING LIFE?
OF COURSE NOT! YOUR STORIES PROBABLY HAVE MUCH BETTER PLOTS THAN ANY GAME I'VE GOT...
...BUT THEY'RE STILL JUST STORIES!

Originally published in *Kaczor Donald* #36/2009 (Poland, 2009)

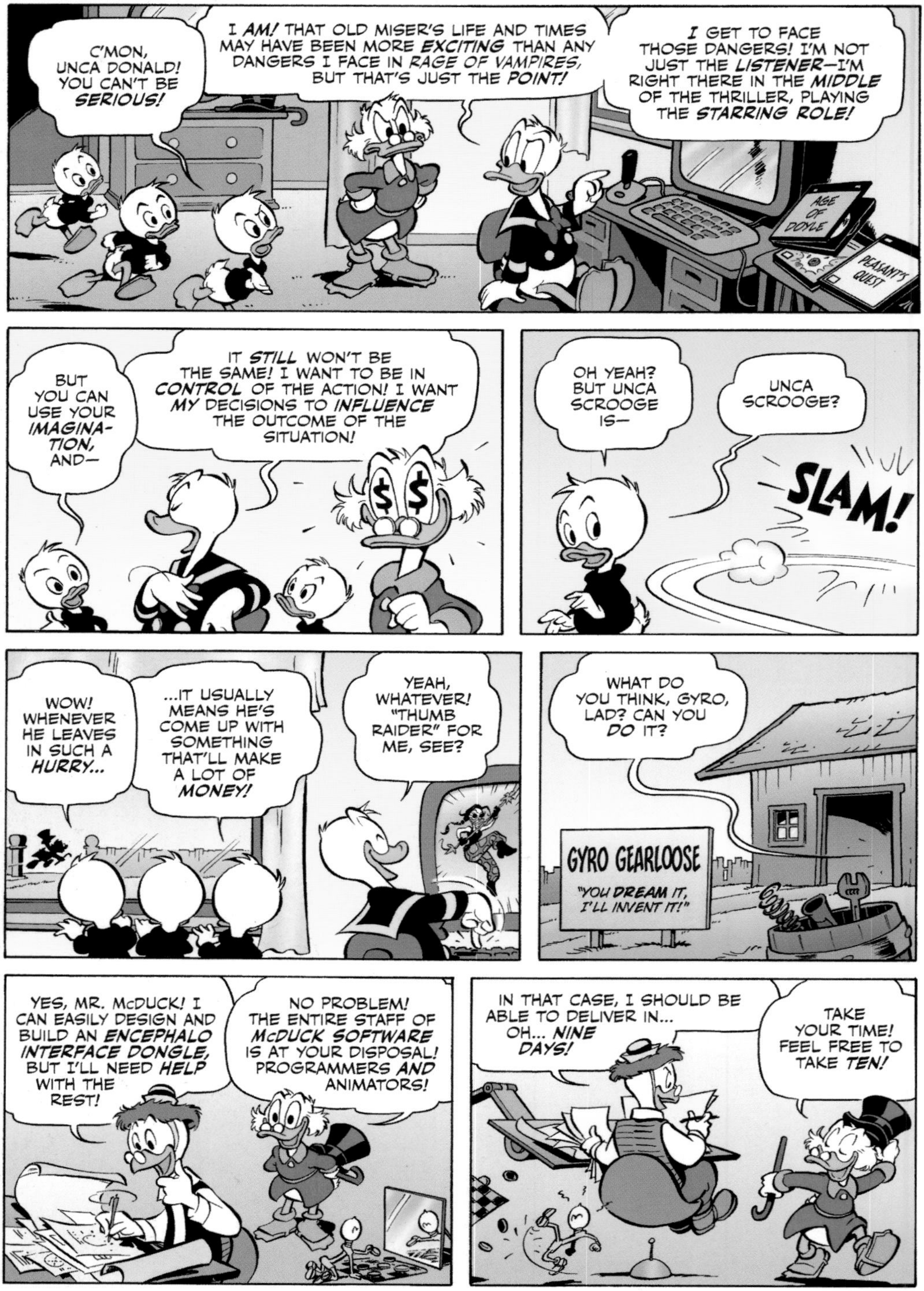
C'MON, UNCA DONALD! YOU CAN'T BE SERIOUS!
I AM! THAT OLD MISER'S LIFE AND TIMES MAY HAVE BEEN MORE EXCITING THAN ANY DANGERS I FACE IN RAGE OF VAMPIRES, BUT THAT'S JUST THE POINT!
I GET TO FACE THOSE DANGERS! I'M NOT JUST THE LISTENER—I'M RIGHT THERE IN THE MIDDLE OF THE THRILLER, PLAYING THE STARRING ROLE!
AGE OF DOYLE
PEASANT'S QUEST
BUT YOU CAN USE YOUR IMAGINATION, AND—
IT STILL WON'T BE THE SAME! I WANT TO BE IN CONTROL OF THE ACTION! I WANT MY DECISIONS TO INFLUENCE THE OUTCOME OF THE SITUATION!
OH YEAH? BUT UNCA SCROOGE IS—
UNCA SCROOGE?
SLAM!
WOW! WHENEVER HE LEAVES IN SUCH A HURRY...
...IT USUALLY MEANS HE'S COME UP WITH SOMETHING THAT'LL MAKE A LOT OF MONEY!
YEAH, WHATEVER! "THUMB RAIDER" FOR ME, SEE?
WHAT DO YOU THINK, GYRO, LAD? CAN YOU DO IT?
GYRO GEARLOOSE
"YOU DREAM IT, I'LL INVENT IT!"
YES, MR. McDUCK! I CAN EASILY DESIGN AND BUILD AN ENCEPHALO INTERFACE DONGLE, BUT I'LL NEED HELP WITH THE REST!
NO PROBLEM! THE ENTIRE STAFF OF McDUCK SOFTWARE IS AT YOUR DISPOSAL! PROGRAMMERS AND ANIMATORS!
IN THAT CASE, I SHOULD BE ABLE TO DELIVER IN... OH... NINE DAYS!
TAKE YOUR TIME! FEEL FREE TO TAKE TEN!

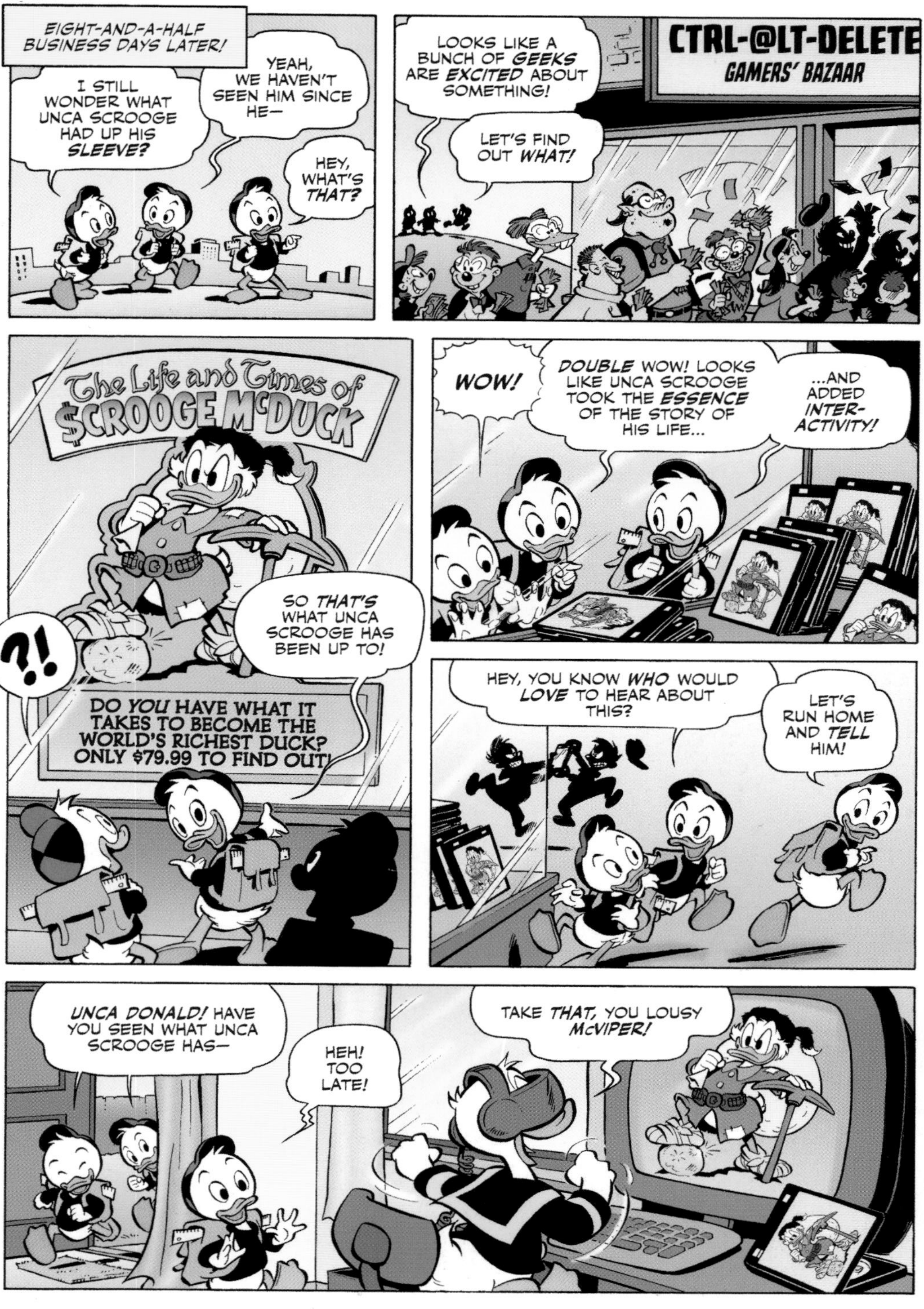
EIGHT-AND-A-HALF BUSINESS DAYS LATER!
I STILL WONDER WHAT UNCA SCROOGE HAD UP HIS SLEEVE?
YEAH, WE HAVEN'T SEEN HIM SINCE HE—
HEY, WHAT'S THAT?
LOOKS LIKE A BUNCH OF GEEKS ARE EXCITED ABOUT SOMETHING!
CTRL-@LT-DELETE
GAMERS' BAZAAR
LET'S FIND OUT WHAT!
The Life and Times of $CROOGE McDUCK
?!
SO THAT'S WHAT UNCA SCROOGE HAS BEEN UP TO!
DO YOU HAVE WHAT IT TAKES TO BECOME THE WORLD'S RICHEST DUCK? ONLY $79.99 TO FIND OUT!
WOW!
DOUBLE WOW! LOOKS LIKE UNCA SCROOGE TOOK THE ESSENCE OF THE STORY OF HIS LIFE...
...AND ADDED INTER-ACTIVITY!
HEY, YOU KNOW WHO WOULD LOVE TO HEAR ABOUT THIS?
LET'S RUN HOME AND TELL HIM!
UNCA DONALD! HAVE YOU SEEN WHAT UNCA SCROOGE HAS—
HEH! TOO LATE!
TAKE THAT, YOU LOUSY McVIPER!

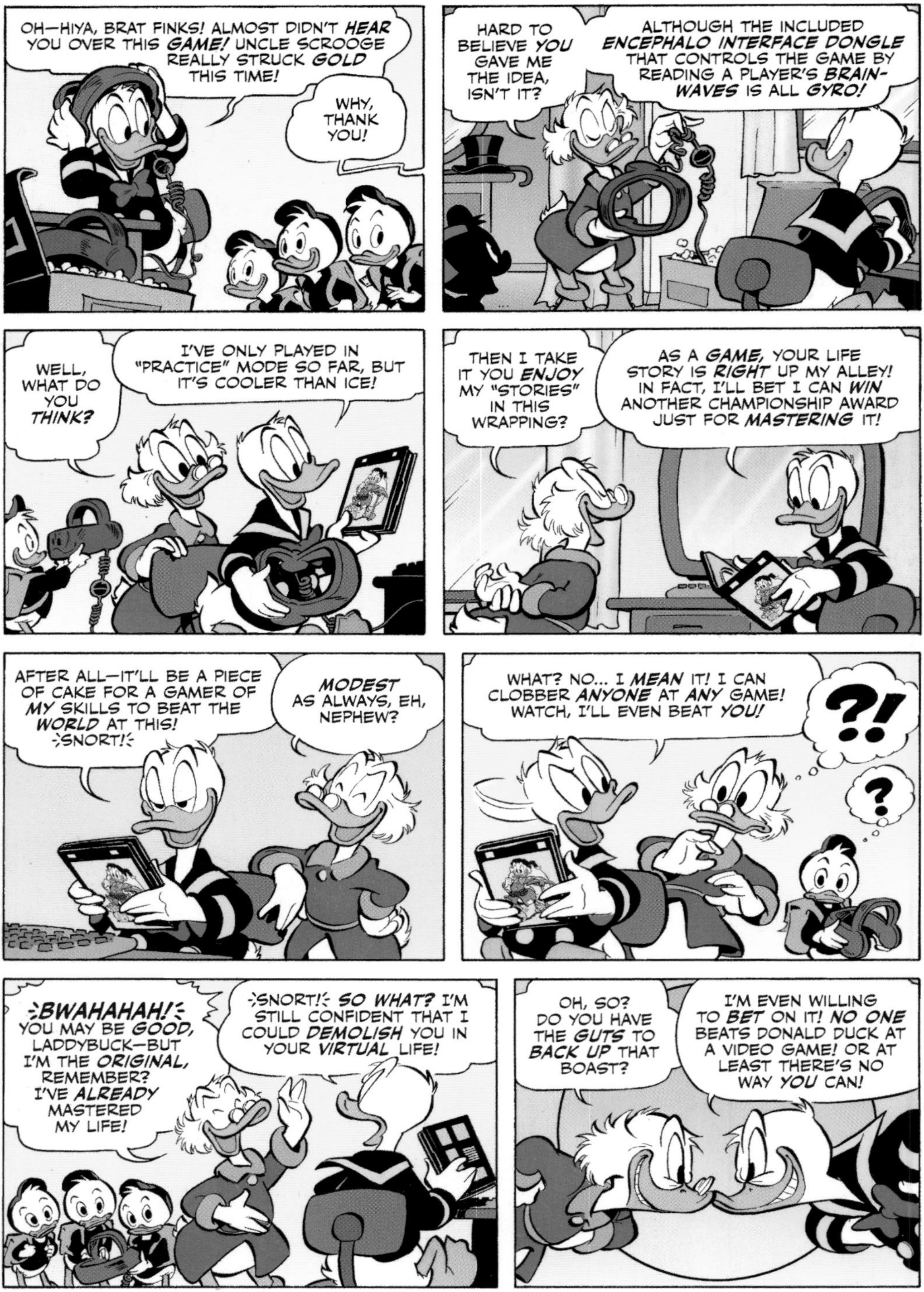
OH—HIYA, BRAT FINKS! ALMOST DIDN'T HEAR YOU OVER THIS GAME! UNCLE SCROOGE REALLY STRUCK GOLD THIS TIME!
WHY, THANK YOU!
HARD TO BELIEVE YOU GAVE ME THE IDEA, ISN'T IT?
ALTHOUGH THE INCLUDED ENCEPHALO INTERFACE DONGLE THAT CONTROLS THE GAME BY READING A PLAYER'S BRAIN-WAVES IS ALL GYRO!
WELL, WHAT DO YOU THINK?
I'VE ONLY PLAYED IN "PRACTICE" MODE SO FAR, BUT IT'S COOLER THAN ICE!
THEN I TAKE IT YOU ENJOY MY "STORIES" IN THIS WRAPPING?
AS A GAME, YOUR LIFE STORY IS RIGHT UP MY ALLEY! IN FACT, I'LL BET I CAN WIN ANOTHER CHAMPIONSHIP AWARD JUST FOR MASTERING IT!
AFTER ALL—IT'LL BE A PIECE OF CAKE FOR A GAMER OF MY SKILLS TO BEAT THE WORLD AT THIS! -SNORT!-
MODEST AS ALWAYS, EH, NEPHEW?
WHAT? NO... I MEAN IT! I CAN CLOBBER ANYONE AT ANY GAME! WATCH, I'LL EVEN BEAT YOU!
?!
?
-BWAHAHAH!- YOU MAY BE GOOD, LADDYBUCK—BUT I'M THE ORIGINAL, REMEMBER? I'VE ALREADY MASTERED MY LIFE!
-SNORT!- SO WHAT? I'M STILL CONFIDENT THAT I COULD DEMOLISH YOU IN YOUR VIRTUAL LIFE!
OH, SO? DO YOU HAVE THE GUTS TO BACK UP THAT BOAST?
I'M EVEN WILLING TO BET ON IT! NO ONE BEATS DONALD DUCK AT A VIDEO GAME! OR AT LEAST THERE'S NO WAY YOU CAN!

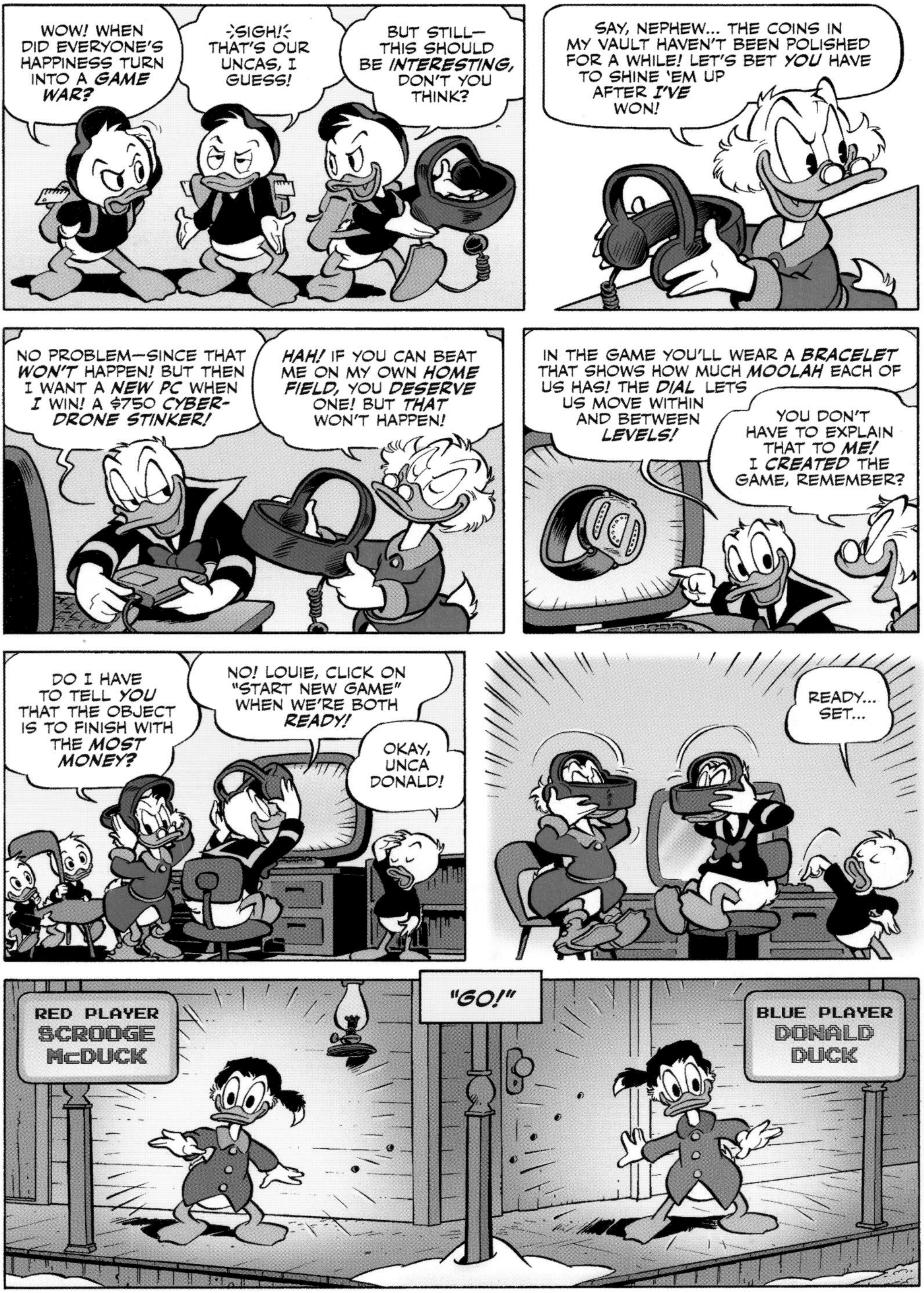
WOW! WHEN DID EVERYONE'S HAPPINESS TURN INTO A GAME WAR?
SIGH! THAT'S OUR UNCAS, I GUESS!
BUT STILL— THIS SHOULD BE INTERESTING, DON'T YOU THINK?
SAY, NEPHEW... THE COINS IN MY VAULT HAVEN'T BEEN POLISHED FOR A WHILE! LET'S BET YOU HAVE TO SHINE 'EM UP AFTER I'VE WON!
NO PROBLEM—SINCE THAT WON'T HAPPEN! BUT THEN I WANT A NEW PC WHEN I WIN! A $750 CYBER-DRONE STINKER!
HAH! IF YOU CAN BEAT ME ON MY OWN HOME FIELD, YOU DESERVE ONE! BUT THAT WON'T HAPPEN!
IN THE GAME YOU'LL WEAR A BRACELET THAT SHOWS HOW MUCH MOOLAH EACH OF US HAS! THE DIAL LETS US MOVE WITHIN AND BETWEEN LEVELS!
YOU DON'T HAVE TO EXPLAIN THAT TO ME! I CREATED THE GAME, REMEMBER?
DO I HAVE TO TELL YOU THAT THE OBJECT IS TO FINISH WITH THE MOST MONEY?
NO! LOUIE, CLICK ON "START NEW GAME" WHEN WE'RE BOTH READY!
OKAY, UNCA DONALD!
READY... SET...
"GO!"
RED PLAYER
SCROOGE McDUCK
BLUE PLAYER
DONALD DUCK

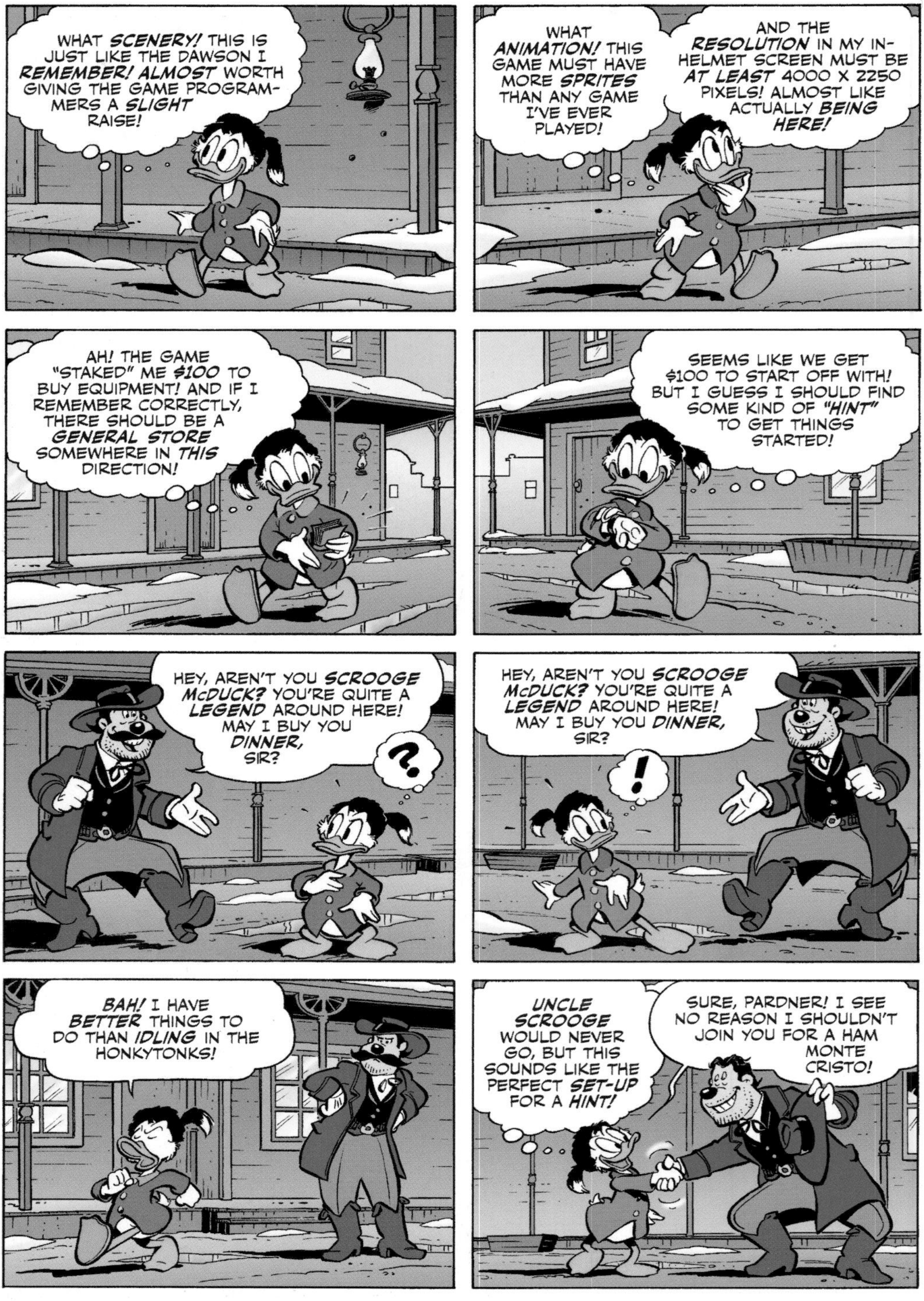
WHAT SCENERY! THIS IS JUST LIKE THE DAWSON I REMEMBER! ALMOST WORTH GIVING THE GAME PROGRAMMERS A SLIGHT RAISE!
WHAT ANIMATION! THIS GAME MUST HAVE MORE SPRITES THAN ANY GAME I'VE EVER PLAYED!
AND THE RESOLUTION IN MY IN-HELMET SCREEN MUST BE AT LEAST 4000 X 2250 PIXELS! ALMOST LIKE ACTUALLY BEING HERE!
AH! THE GAME "STAKED" ME $100 TO BUY EQUIPMENT! AND IF I REMEMBER CORRECTLY, THERE SHOULD BE A GENERAL STORE SOMEWHERE IN THIS DIRECTION!
SEEMS LIKE WE GET $100 TO START OFF WITH! BUT I GUESS I SHOULD FIND SOME KIND OF "HINT" TO GET THINGS STARTED!
HEY, AREN'T YOU SCROOGE McDUCK? YOU'RE QUITE A LEGEND AROUND HERE! MAY I BUY YOU DINNER, SIR?
?
HEY, AREN'T YOU SCROOGE McDUCK? YOU'RE QUITE A LEGEND AROUND HERE! MAY I BUY YOU DINNER, SIR?
!
BAH! I HAVE BETTER THINGS TO DO THAN IDLING IN THE HONKYTONKS!
UNCLE SCROOGE WOULD NEVER GO, BUT THIS SOUNDS LIKE THE PERFECT SET-UP FOR A HINT!
SURE, PARDNER! I SEE NO REASON I SHOULDN'T JOIN YOU FOR A HAM MONTE CRISTO!

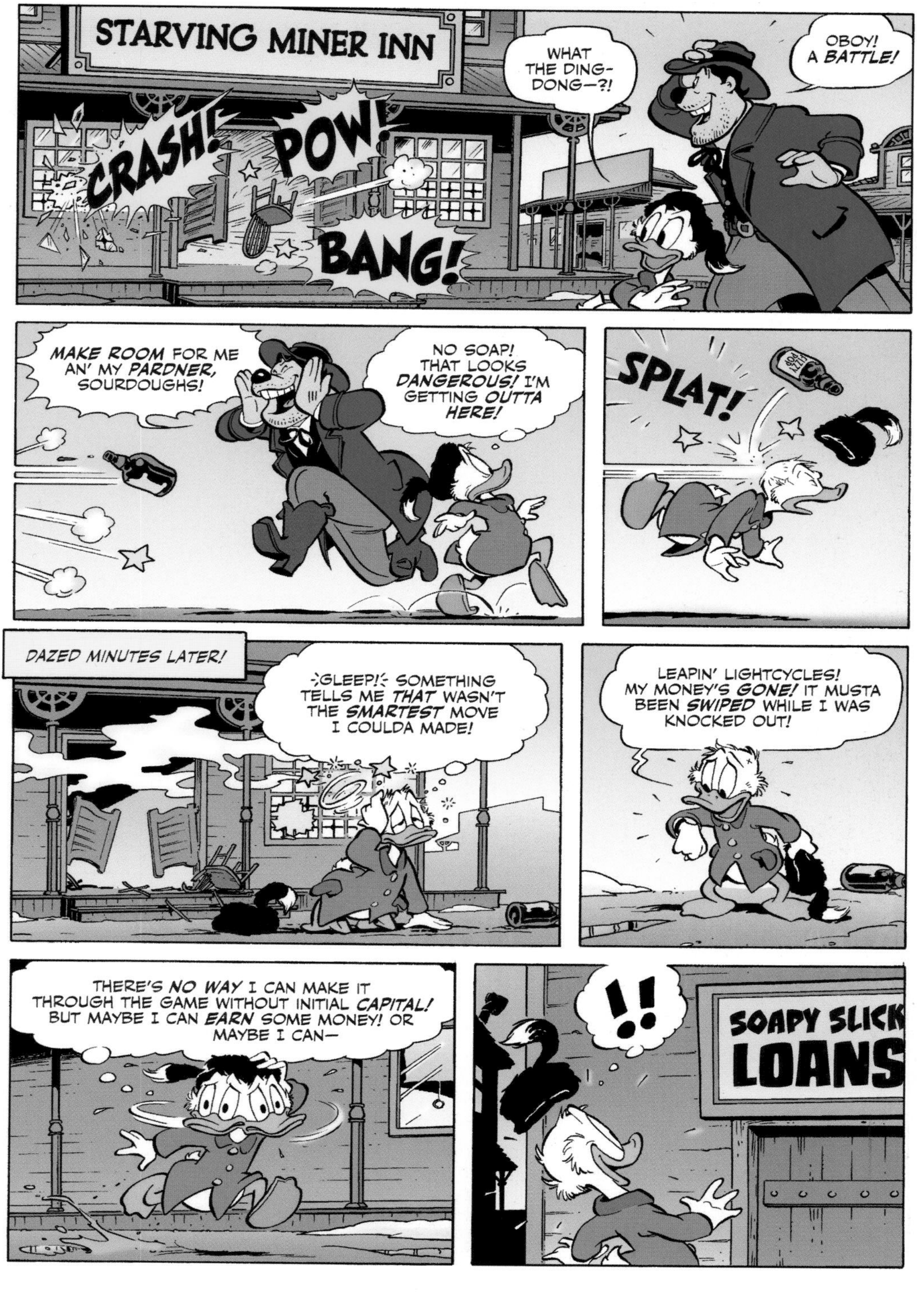
STARVING MINER INN
CRASH!
POW!
BANG!
WHAT THE DING-DONG—?!
OBOY! A BATTLE!
MAKE ROOM FOR ME AN' MY PARDNER, SOURDOUGHS!
NO SOAP! THAT LOOKS DANGEROUS! I'M GETTING OUTTA HERE!
SPLAT!
DAZED MINUTES LATER!
-GLEEP!- SOMETHING TELLS ME THAT WASN'T THE SMARTEST MOVE I COULDA MADE!
LEAPIN' LIGHTCYCLES! MY MONEY'S GONE! IT MUSTA BEEN SWIPED WHILE I WAS KNOCKED OUT!
THERE'S NO WAY I CAN MAKE IT THROUGH THE GAME WITHOUT INITIAL CAPITAL! BUT MAYBE I CAN EARN SOME MONEY! OR MAYBE I CAN—
!!
SOAPY SLICK
LOANS

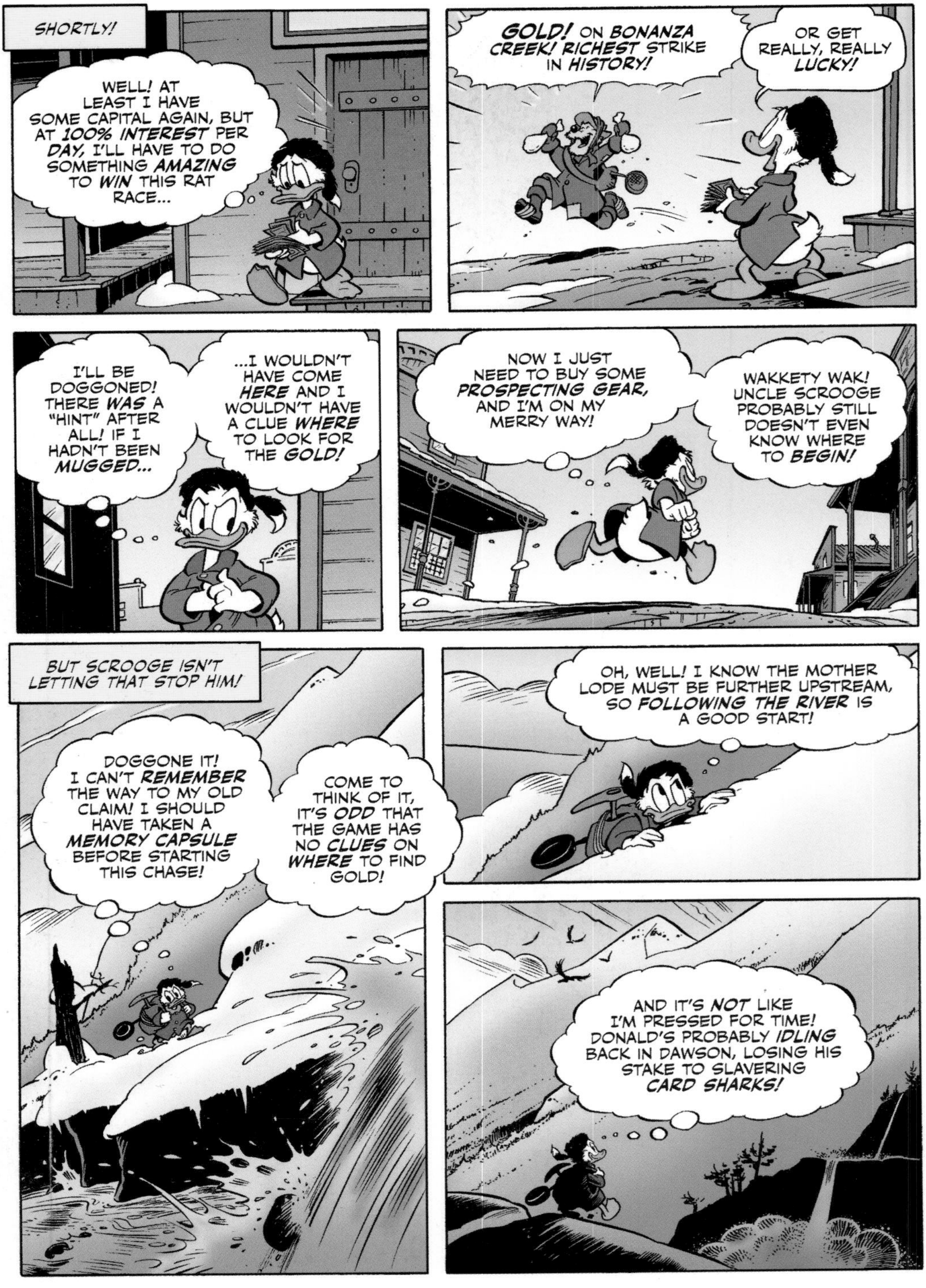
SHORTLY!
WELL! AT LEAST I HAVE SOME CAPITAL AGAIN, BUT AT 100% INTEREST PER DAY, I'LL HAVE TO DO SOMETHING AMAZING TO WIN THIS RAT RACE...
GOLD! ON BONANZA CREEK! RICHEST STRIKE IN HISTORY!
OR GET REALLY, REALLY LUCKY!
I'LL BE DOGGONED! THERE WAS A "HINT" AFTER ALL! IF I HADN'T BEEN MUGGED...
...I WOULDN'T HAVE COME HERE AND I WOULDN'T HAVE A CLUE WHERE TO LOOK FOR THE GOLD!
NOW I JUST NEED TO BUY SOME PROSPECTING GEAR, AND I'M ON MY MERRY WAY!
WAKKETY WAK! UNCLE SCROOGE PROBABLY STILL DOESN'T EVEN KNOW WHERE TO BEGIN!
BUT SCROOGE ISN'T LETTING THAT STOP HIM!
DOGGONE IT! I CAN'T REMEMBER THE WAY TO MY OLD CLAIM! I SHOULD HAVE TAKEN A MEMORY CAPSULE BEFORE STARTING THIS CHASE!
COME TO THINK OF IT, IT'S ODD THAT THE GAME HAS NO CLUES ON WHERE TO FIND GOLD!
OH, WELL! I KNOW THE MOTHER LODE MUST BE FURTHER UPSTREAM, SO FOLLOWING THE RIVER IS A GOOD START!
AND IT'S NOT LIKE I'M PRESSED FOR TIME! DONALD'S PROBABLY IDLING BACK IN DAWSON, LOSING HIS STAKE TO SLAVERING CARD SHARKS!

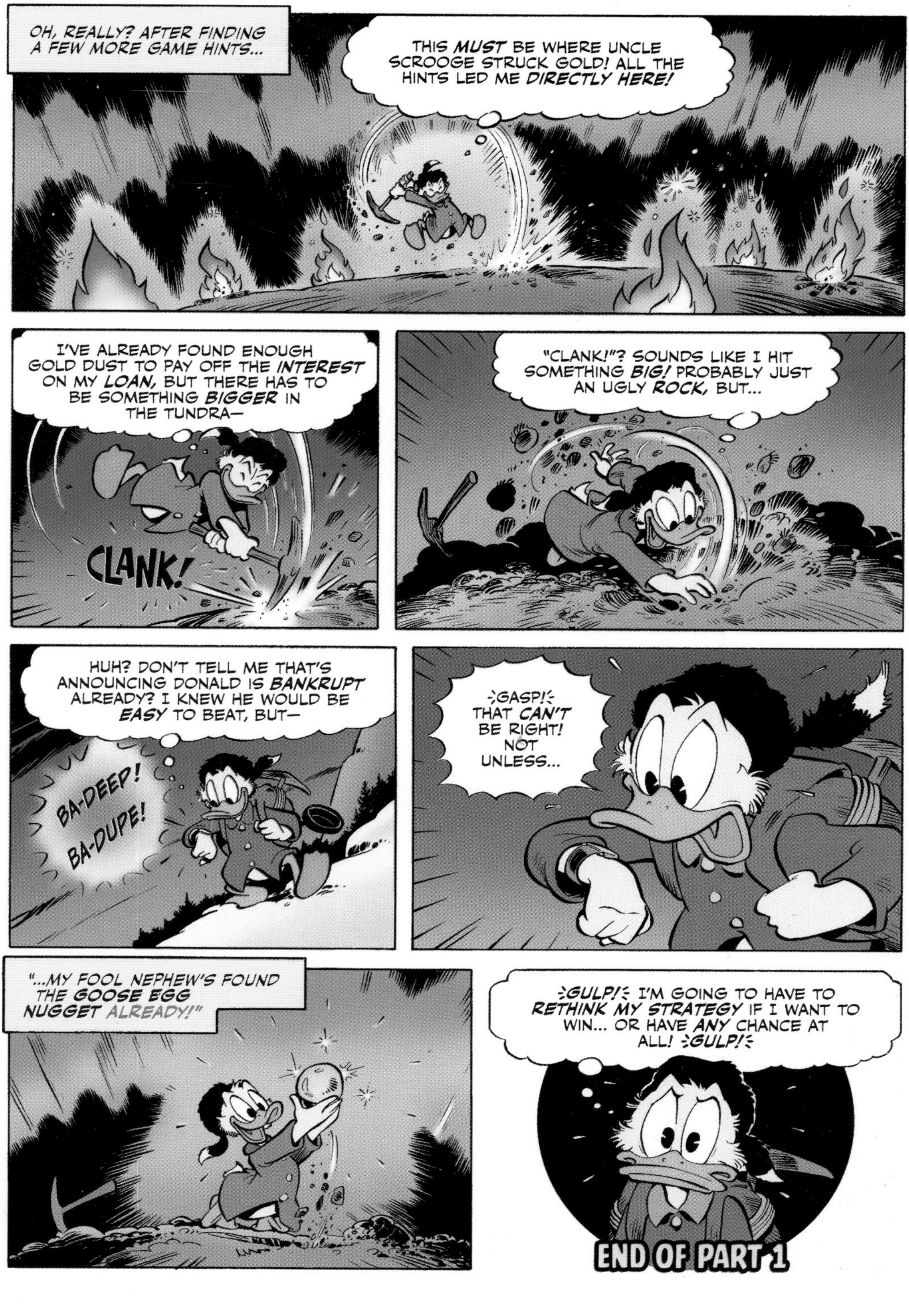
OH, REALLY? AFTER FINDING A FEW MORE GAME HINTS...
THIS MUST BE WHERE UNCLE SCROOGE STRUCK GOLD! ALL THE HINTS LED ME DIRECTLY HERE!
I'VE ALREADY FOUND ENOUGH GOLD DUST TO PAY OFF THE INTEREST ON MY LOAN, BUT THERE HAS TO BE SOMETHING BIGGER IN THE TUNDRA—
CLANK!
"CLANK!"? SOUNDS LIKE I HIT SOMETHING BIG! PROBABLY JUST AN UGLY ROCK, BUT...
HUH? DON'T TELL ME THAT'S ANNOUNCING DONALD IS BANKRUPT ALREADY? I KNEW HE WOULD BE EASY TO BEAT, BUT—
BA-DEEP! BA-DUPE!
GASP! THAT CAN'T BE RIGHT! NOT UNLESS...
"...MY FOOL NEPHEW'S FOUND THE GOOSE EGG NUGGET ALREADY!"
GULP! I'M GOING TO HAVE TO RETHINK MY STRATEGY IF I WANT TO WIN... OR HAVE ANY CHANCE AT ALL! GULP!
END OF PART 1

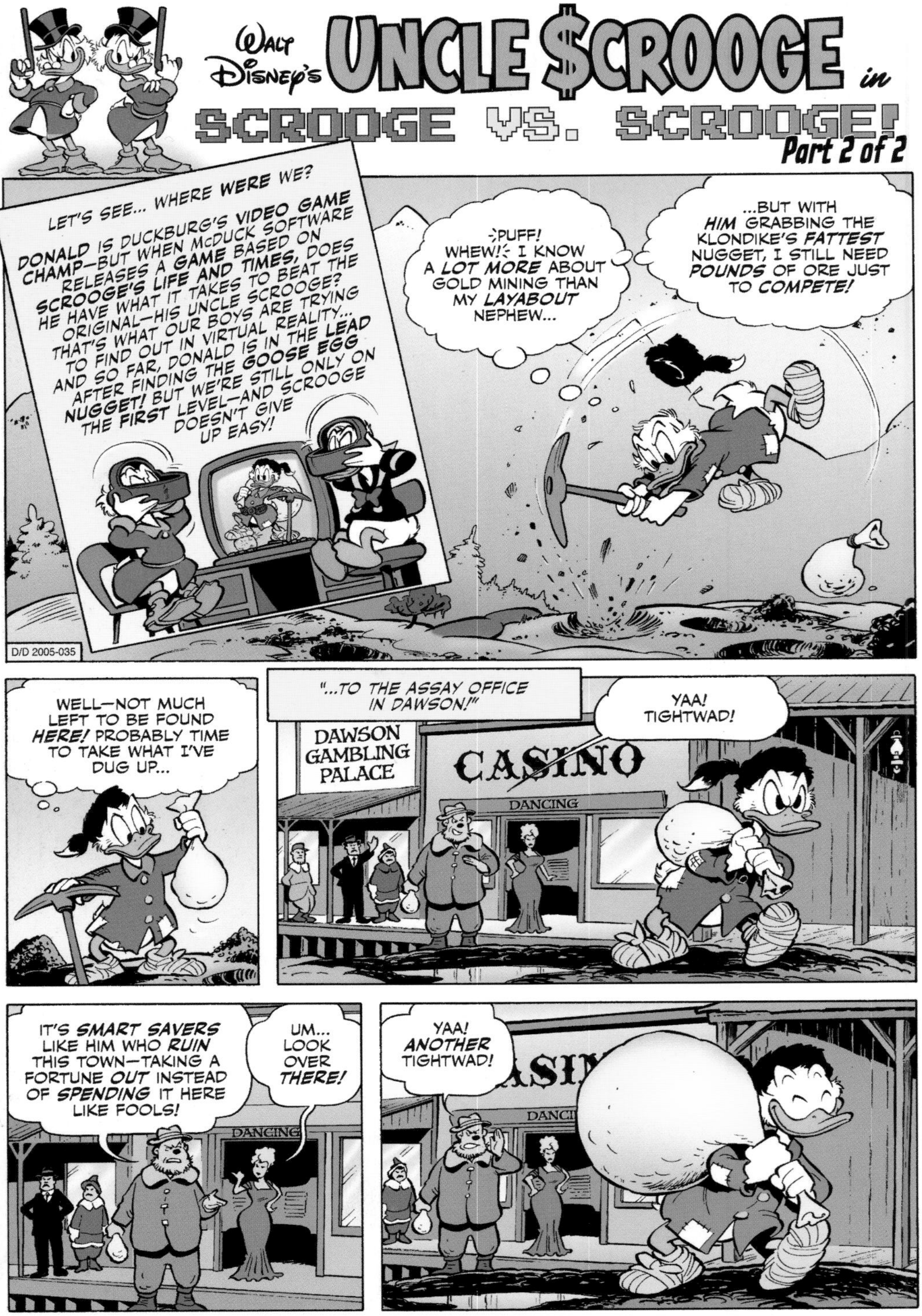
WALT DISNEY'S UNCLE $CROOGE in
SCROOGE VS. SCROOGE!
Part 2 of 2
LET'S SEE... WHERE WERE WE?
DONALD IS DUCKBURG'S VIDEO GAME CHAMP—BUT WHEN McDUCK SOFTWARE RELEASES A GAME BASED ON SCROOGE'S LIFE AND TIMES, DOES HE HAVE WHAT IT TAKES TO BEAT THE ORIGINAL—HIS UNCLE SCROOGE? THAT'S WHAT OUR BOYS ARE TRYING TO FIND OUT IN VIRTUAL REALITY... AND SO FAR, DONALD IS IN THE LEAD AFTER FINDING THE GOOSE EGG NUGGET! BUT WE'RE STILL ONLY ON THE FIRST LEVEL—AND SCROOGE DOESN'T GIVE UP EASY!
PUFF! WHEW! I KNOW A LOT MORE ABOUT GOLD MINING THAN MY LAYABOUT NEPHEW...
...BUT WITH HIM GRABBING THE KLONDIKE'S FATTEST NUGGET, I STILL NEED POUNDS OF ORE JUST TO COMPETE!
D/D 2005-035
WELL—NOT MUCH LEFT TO BE FOUND HERE! PROBABLY TIME TO TAKE WHAT I'VE DUG UP...
"...TO THE ASSAY OFFICE IN DAWSON!"
DAWSON GAMBLING PALACE
CASINO
DANCING
YAA! TIGHTWAD!
IT'S SMART SAVERS LIKE HIM WHO RUIN THIS TOWN—TAKING A FORTUNE OUT INSTEAD OF SPENDING IT HERE LIKE FOOLS!
UM... LOOK OVER THERE!
DANCING
YAA! ANOTHER TIGHTWAD!

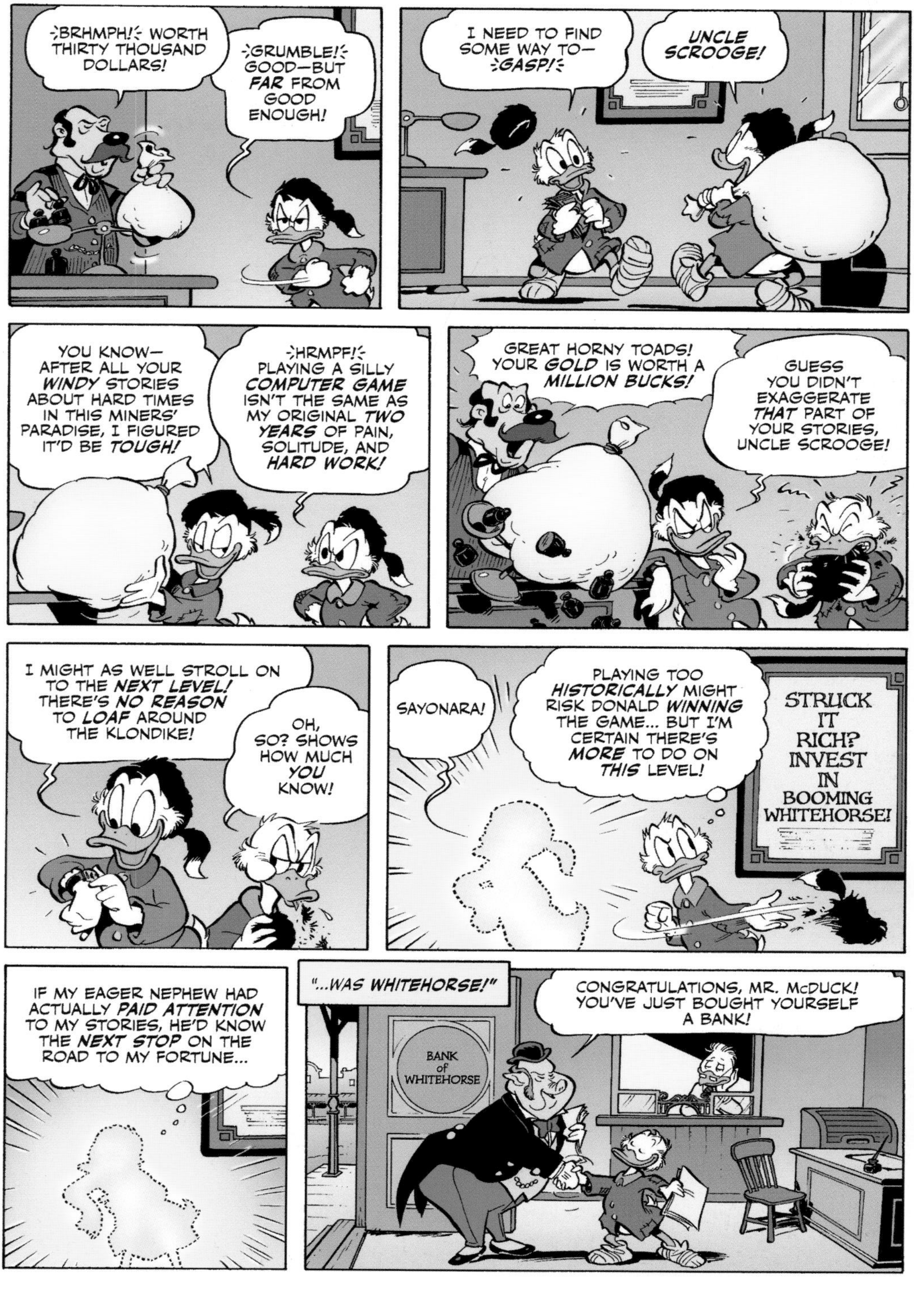

-BRHMPH!- WORTH THIRTY THOUSAND DOLLARS!
-GRUMBLE!- GOOD—BUT FAR FROM GOOD ENOUGH!
I NEED TO FIND SOME WAY TO— -GASP!-
UNCLE SCROOGE!
YOU KNOW— AFTER ALL YOUR WINDY STORIES ABOUT HARD TIMES IN THIS MINERS' PARADISE, I FIGURED IT'D BE TOUGH!
-HRMPF!- PLAYING A SILLY COMPUTER GAME ISN'T THE SAME AS MY ORIGINAL TWO YEARS OF PAIN, SOLITUDE, AND HARD WORK!
GREAT HORNY TOADS! YOUR GOLD IS WORTH A MILLION BUCKS!
GUESS YOU DIDN'T EXAGGERATE THAT PART OF YOUR STORIES, UNCLE SCROOGE!
I MIGHT AS WELL STROLL ON TO THE NEXT LEVEL! THERE'S NO REASON TO LOAF AROUND THE KLONDIKE!
OH, SO? SHOWS HOW MUCH YOU KNOW!
SAYONARA!
PLAYING TOO HISTORICALLY MIGHT RISK DONALD WINNING THE GAME... BUT I'M CERTAIN THERE'S MORE TO DO ON THIS LEVEL!
STRUCK IT RICH? INVEST IN BOOMING WHITEHORSE!
IF MY EAGER NEPHEW HAD ACTUALLY PAID ATTENTION TO MY STORIES, HE'D KNOW THE NEXT STOP ON THE ROAD TO MY FORTUNE...
"...WAS WHITEHORSE!"
BANK of WHITEHORSE
CONGRATULATIONS, MR. McDUCK! YOU'VE JUST BOUGHT YOURSELF A BANK!

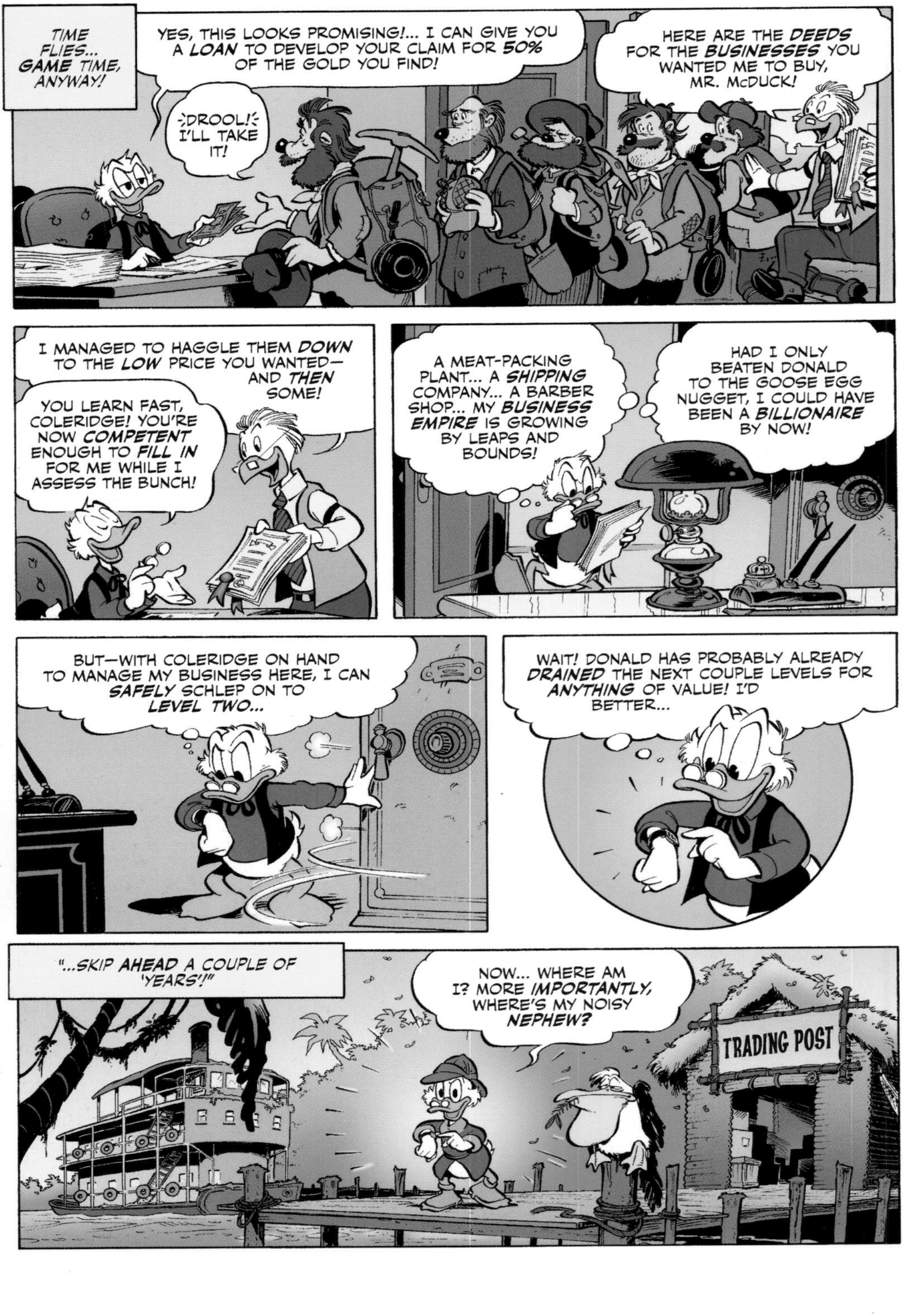
TIME FLIES... GAME TIME, ANYWAY!
YES, THIS LOOKS PROMISING!... I CAN GIVE YOU A LOAN TO DEVELOP YOUR CLAIM FOR 50% OF THE GOLD YOU FIND!
DROOL! I'LL TAKE IT!
HERE ARE THE DEEDS FOR THE BUSINESSES YOU WANTED ME TO BUY, MR. McDUCK!
I MANAGED TO HAGGLE THEM DOWN TO THE LOW PRICE YOU WANTED— AND THEN SOME!
YOU LEARN FAST, COLERIDGE! YOU'RE NOW COMPETENT ENOUGH TO FILL IN FOR ME WHILE I ASSESS THE BUNCH!
A MEAT-PACKING PLANT... A SHIPPING COMPANY... A BARBER SHOP... MY BUSINESS EMPIRE IS GROWING BY LEAPS AND BOUNDS!
HAD I ONLY BEATEN DONALD TO THE GOOSE EGG NUGGET, I COULD HAVE BEEN A BILLIONAIRE BY NOW!
BUT—WITH COLERIDGE ON HAND TO MANAGE MY BUSINESS HERE, I CAN SAFELY SCHLEP ON TO LEVEL TWO...
WAIT! DONALD HAS PROBABLY ALREADY DRAINED THE NEXT COUPLE LEVELS FOR ANYTHING OF VALUE! I'D BETTER...
"...SKIP AHEAD A COUPLE OF 'YEARS'!"
NOW... WHERE AM I? MORE IMPORTANTLY, WHERE'S MY NOISY NEPHEW?
TRADING POST

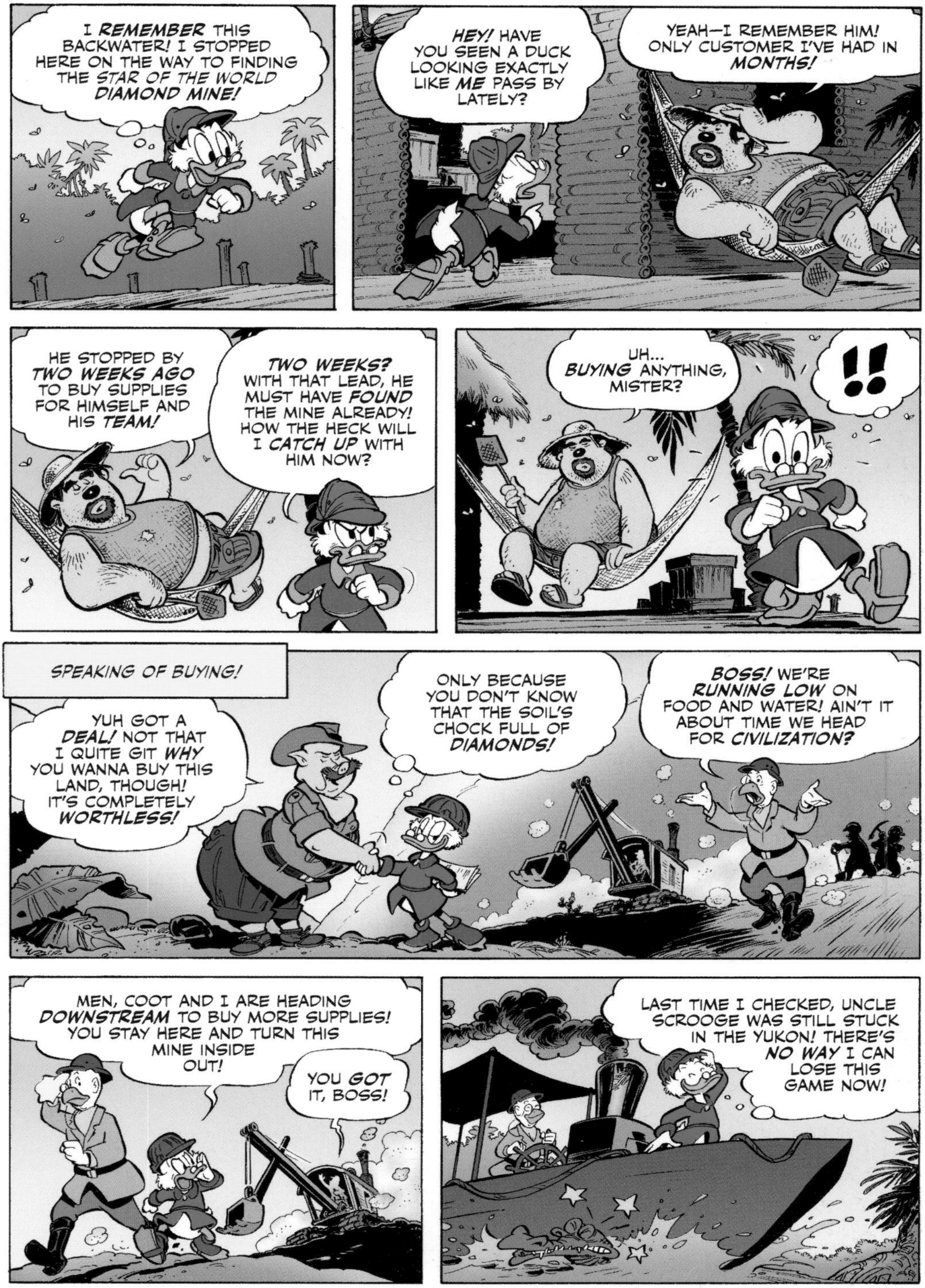

I REMEMBER THIS BACKWATER! I STOPPED HERE ON THE WAY TO FINDING THE STAR OF THE WORLD DIAMOND MINE!
HEY! HAVE YOU SEEN A DUCK LOOKING EXACTLY LIKE ME PASS BY LATELY?
YEAH—I REMEMBER HIM! ONLY CUSTOMER I'VE HAD IN MONTHS!
HE STOPPED BY TWO WEEKS AGO TO BUY SUPPLIES FOR HIMSELF AND HIS TEAM!
TWO WEEKS? WITH THAT LEAD, HE MUST HAVE FOUND THE MINE ALREADY! HOW THE HECK WILL I CATCH UP WITH HIM NOW?
UH... BUYING ANYTHING, MISTER?
!!
SPEAKING OF BUYING!
YUH GOT A DEAL! NOT THAT I QUITE GIT WHY YOU WANNA BUY THIS LAND, THOUGH! IT'S COMPLETELY WORTHLESS!
ONLY BECAUSE YOU DON'T KNOW THAT THE SOIL'S CHOCK FULL OF DIAMONDS!
BOSS! WE'RE RUNNING LOW ON FOOD AND WATER! AIN'T IT ABOUT TIME WE HEAD FOR CIVILIZATION?
MEN, COOT AND I ARE HEADING DOWNSTREAM TO BUY MORE SUPPLIES! YOU STAY HERE AND TURN THIS MINE INSIDE OUT!
YOU GOT IT, BOSS!
LAST TIME I CHECKED, UNCLE SCROOGE WAS STILL STUCK IN THE YUKON! THERE'S NO WAY I CAN LOSE THIS GAME NOW!

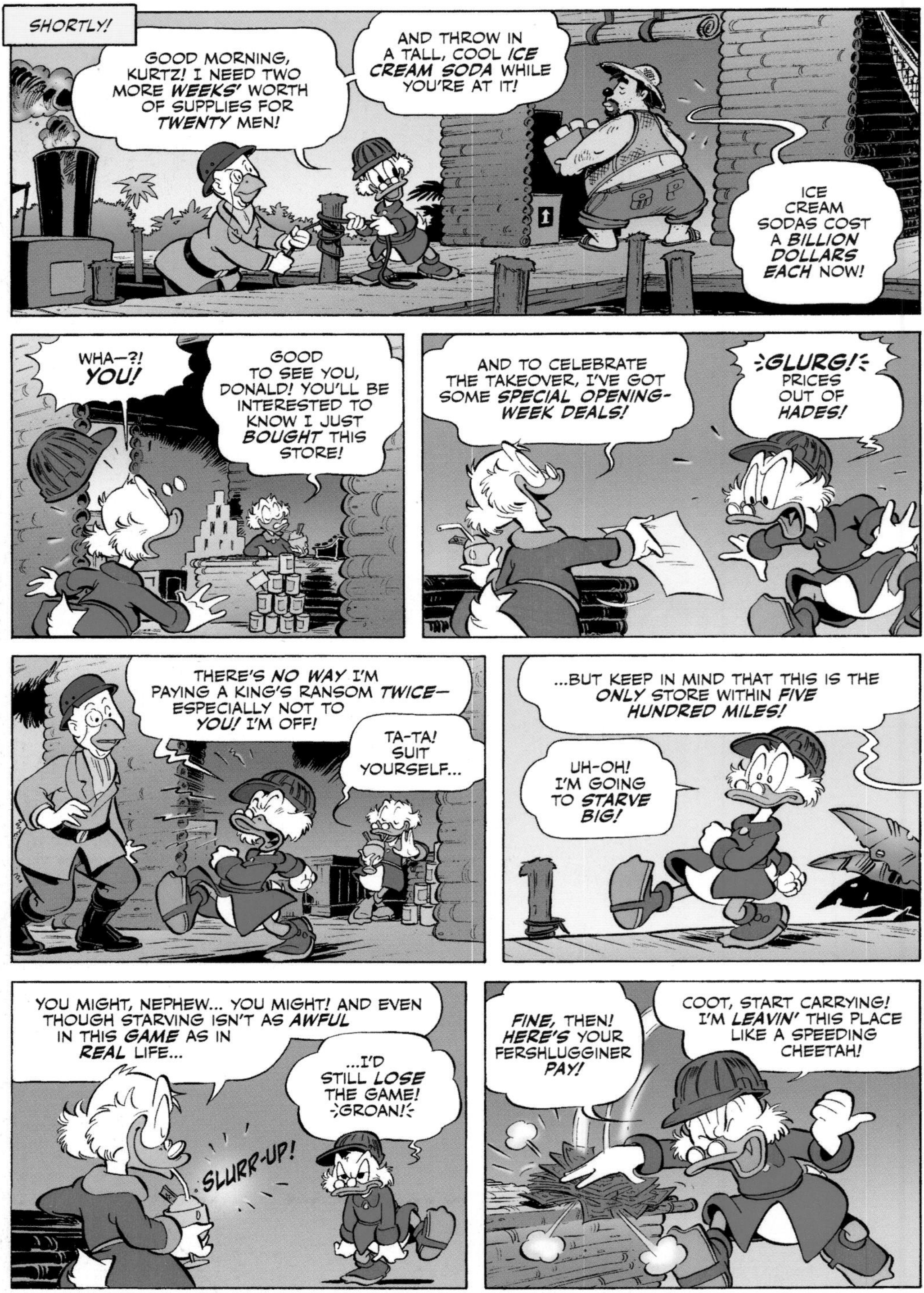
SHORTLY!
GOOD MORNING, KURTZ! I NEED TWO MORE WEEKS' WORTH OF SUPPLIES FOR TWENTY MEN!
AND THROW IN A TALL, COOL ICE CREAM SODA WHILE YOU'RE AT IT!
ICE CREAM SODAS COST A BILLION DOLLARS EACH NOW!
WHA—?! YOU!
GOOD TO SEE YOU, DONALD! YOU'LL BE INTERESTED TO KNOW I JUST BOUGHT THIS STORE!
AND TO CELEBRATE THE TAKEOVER, I'VE GOT SOME SPECIAL OPENING-WEEK DEALS!
GLURG! PRICES OUT OF HADES!
THERE'S NO WAY I'M PAYING A KING'S RANSOM TWICE—ESPECIALLY NOT TO YOU! I'M OFF!
TA-TA! SUIT YOURSELF...
...BUT KEEP IN MIND THAT THIS IS THE ONLY STORE WITHIN FIVE HUNDRED MILES!
UH-OH! I'M GOING TO STARVE BIG!
YOU MIGHT, NEPHEW... YOU MIGHT! AND EVEN THOUGH STARVING ISN'T AS AWFUL IN THIS GAME AS IN REAL LIFE...
...I'D STILL LOSE THE GAME! GROAN!
SLURR-UP!
FINE, THEN! HERE'S YOUR FERSHLUGGINER PAY!
COOT, START CARRYING! I'M LEAVIN' THIS PLACE LIKE A SPEEDING CHEETAH!

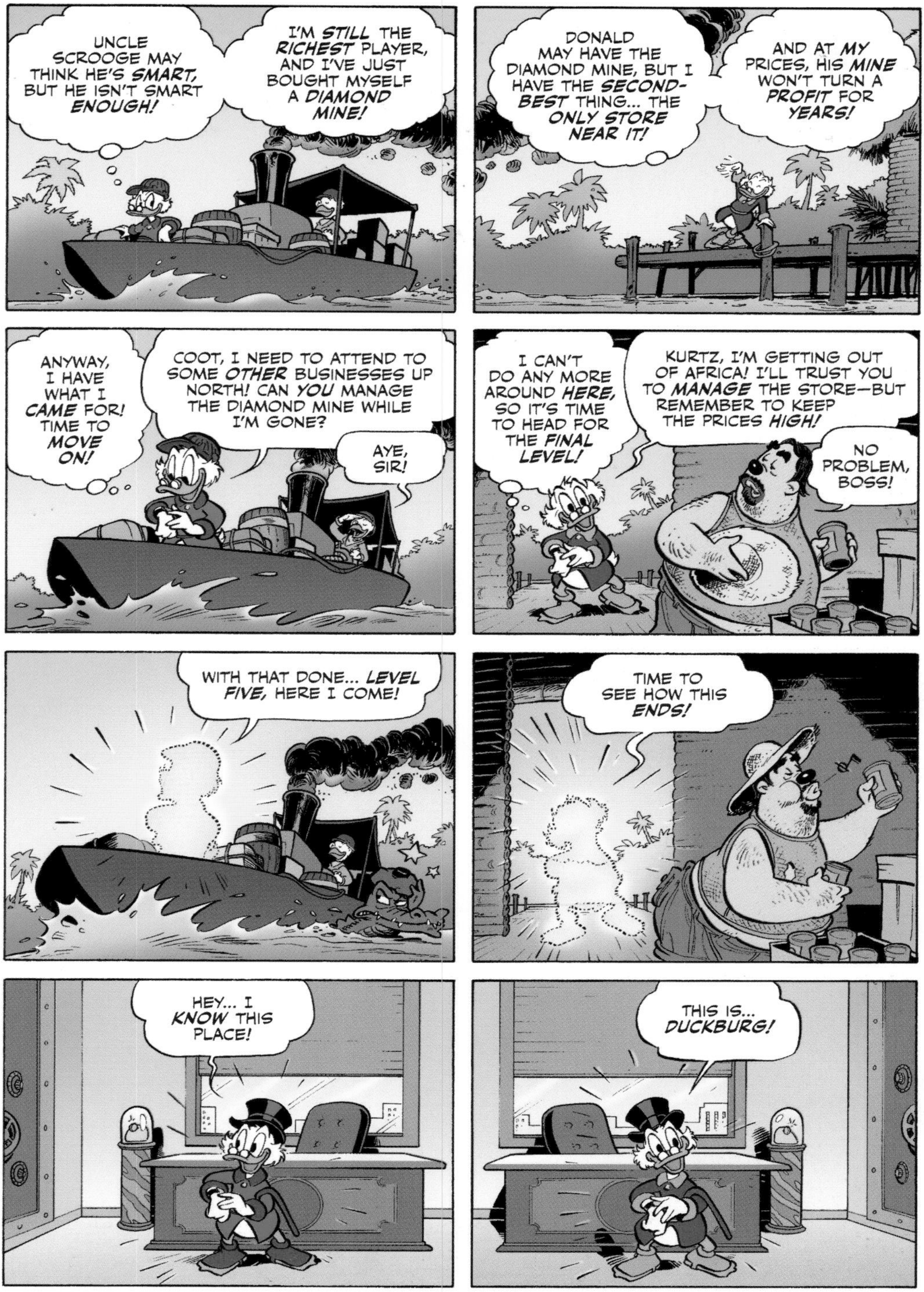
UNCLE SCROOGE MAY THINK HE'S SMART, BUT HE ISN'T SMART ENOUGH!
I'M STILL THE RICHEST PLAYER, AND I'VE JUST BOUGHT MYSELF A DIAMOND MINE!
DONALD MAY HAVE THE DIAMOND MINE, BUT I HAVE THE SECOND-BEST THING... THE ONLY STORE NEAR IT!
AND AT MY PRICES, HIS MINE WON'T TURN A PROFIT FOR YEARS!
ANYWAY, I HAVE WHAT I CAME FOR! TIME TO MOVE ON!
COOT, I NEED TO ATTEND TO SOME OTHER BUSINESSES UP NORTH! CAN YOU MANAGE THE DIAMOND MINE WHILE I'M GONE?
AYE, SIR!
I CAN'T DO ANY MORE AROUND HERE, SO IT'S TIME TO HEAD FOR THE FINAL LEVEL!
KURTZ, I'M GETTING OUT OF AFRICA! I'LL TRUST YOU TO MANAGE THE STORE—BUT REMEMBER TO KEEP THE PRICES HIGH!
NO PROBLEM, BOSS!
WITH THAT DONE... LEVEL FIVE, HERE I COME!
TIME TO SEE HOW THIS ENDS!
HEY... I KNOW THIS PLACE!
THIS IS... DUCKBURG!

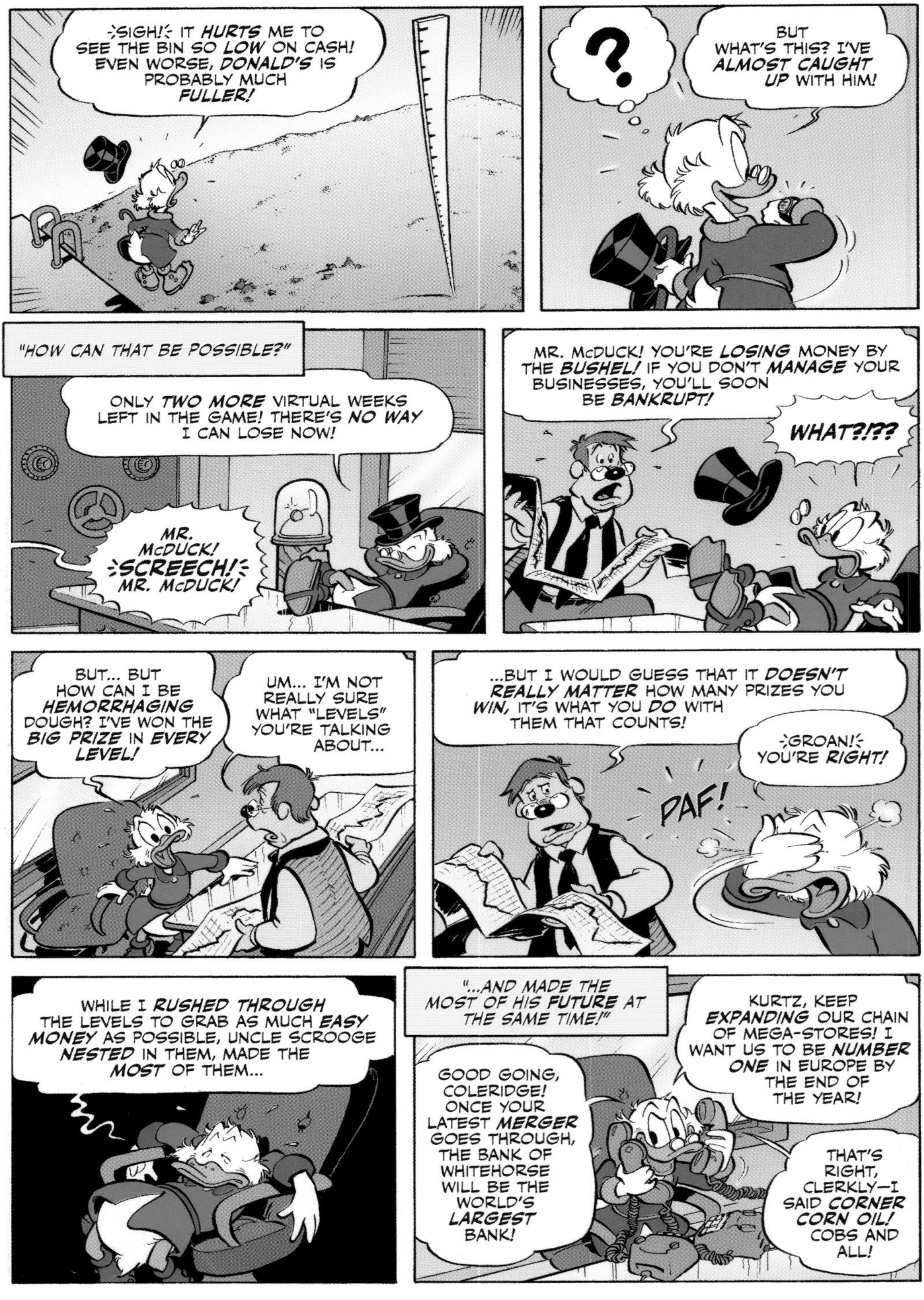
-SIGH!- IT HURTS ME TO SEE THE BIN SO LOW ON CASH! EVEN WORSE, DONALD'S IS PROBABLY MUCH FULLER!
?
BUT WHAT'S THIS? I'VE ALMOST CAUGHT UP WITH HIM!
"HOW CAN THAT BE POSSIBLE?"
ONLY TWO MORE VIRTUAL WEEKS LEFT IN THE GAME! THERE'S NO WAY I CAN LOSE NOW!
MR. McDUCK! -SCREECH!- MR. McDUCK!
MR. McDUCK! YOU'RE LOSING MONEY BY THE BUSHEL! IF YOU DON'T MANAGE YOUR BUSINESSES, YOU'LL SOON BE BANKRUPT!
WHAT?!??
BUT... BUT HOW CAN I BE HEMORRHAGING DOUGH? I'VE WON THE BIG PRIZE IN EVERY LEVEL!
UM... I'M NOT REALLY SURE WHAT "LEVELS" YOU'RE TALKING ABOUT...
...BUT I WOULD GUESS THAT IT DOESN'T REALLY MATTER HOW MANY PRIZES YOU WIN, IT'S WHAT YOU DO WITH THEM THAT COUNTS!
-GROAN!- YOU'RE RIGHT!
PAF!
WHILE I RUSHED THROUGH THE LEVELS TO GRAB AS MUCH EASY MONEY AS POSSIBLE, UNCLE SCROOGE NESTED IN THEM, MADE THE MOST OF THEM...
"...AND MADE THE MOST OF HIS FUTURE AT THE SAME TIME!"
KURTZ, KEEP EXPANDING OUR CHAIN OF MEGA-STORES! I WANT US TO BE NUMBER ONE IN EUROPE BY THE END OF THE YEAR!
GOOD GOING, COLERIDGE! ONCE YOUR LATEST MERGER GOES THROUGH, THE BANK OF WHITEHORSE WILL BE THE WORLD'S LARGEST BANK!
THAT'S RIGHT, CLERKLY—I SAID CORNER CORN OIL! COBS AND ALL!

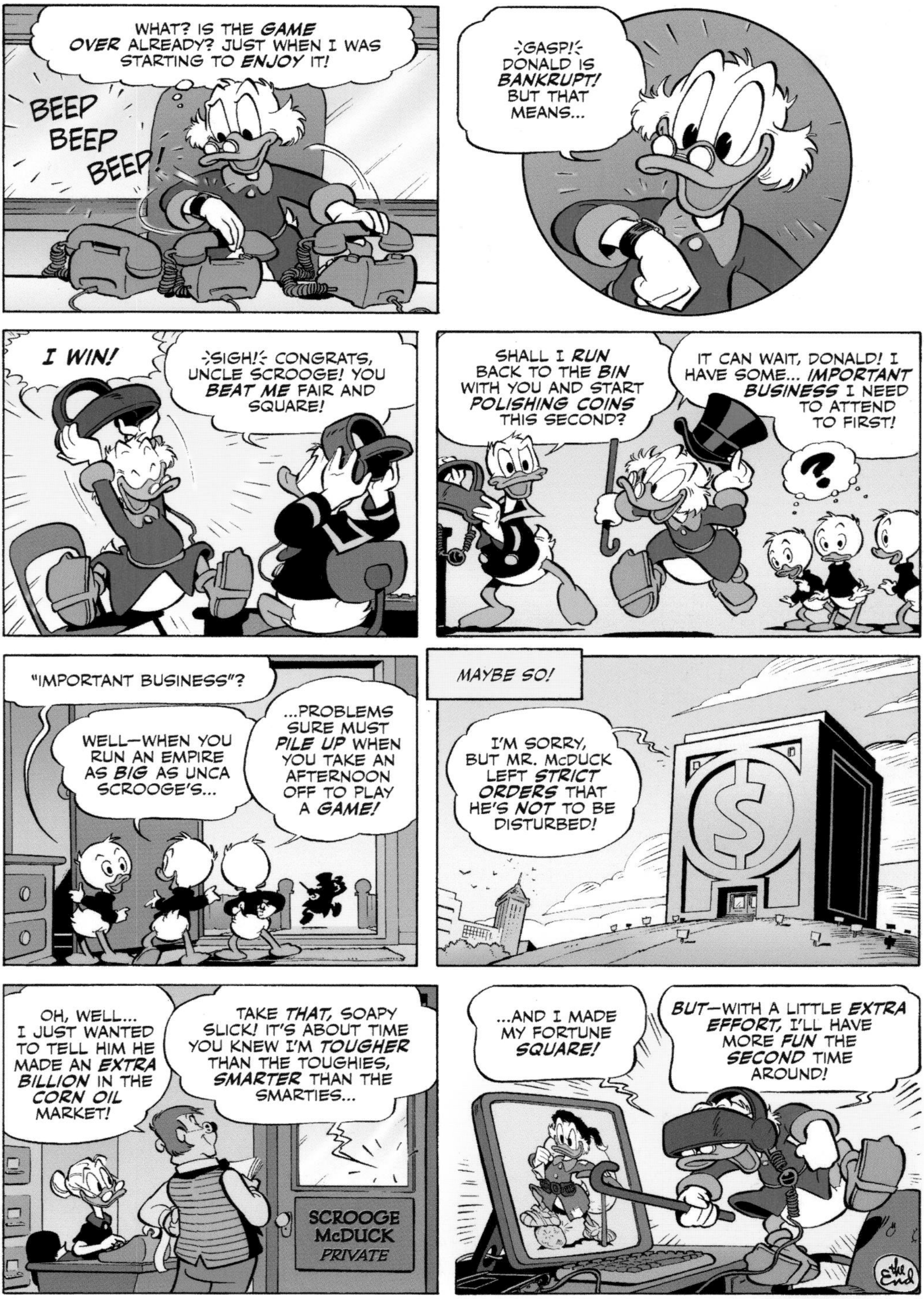
WHAT? IS THE GAME OVER ALREADY? JUST WHEN I WAS STARTING TO ENJOY IT!
BEEP BEEP BEEP!
-GASP!- DONALD IS BANKRUPT! BUT THAT MEANS...
I WIN!
-SIGH!- CONGRATS, UNCLE SCROOGE! YOU BEAT ME FAIR AND SQUARE!
SHALL I RUN BACK TO THE BIN WITH YOU AND START POLISHING COINS THIS SECOND?
IT CAN WAIT, DONALD! I HAVE SOME... IMPORTANT BUSINESS I NEED TO ATTEND TO FIRST!
?
"IMPORTANT BUSINESS"?
WELL—WHEN YOU RUN AN EMPIRE AS BIG AS UNCA SCROOGE'S...
...PROBLEMS SURE MUST PILE UP WHEN YOU TAKE AN AFTERNOON OFF TO PLAY A GAME!
MAYBE SO!
I'M SORRY, BUT MR. McDUCK LEFT STRICT ORDERS THAT HE'S NOT TO BE DISTURBED!
OH, WELL... I JUST WANTED TO TELL HIM HE MADE AN EXTRA BILLION IN THE CORN OIL MARKET!
TAKE THAT, SOAPY SLICK! IT'S ABOUT TIME YOU KNEW I'M TOUGHER THAN THE TOUGHIES, SMARTER THAN THE SMARTIES...
SCROOGE McDUCK PRIVATE
...AND I MADE MY FORTUNE SQUARE!
BUT—WITH A LITTLE EXTRA EFFORT, I'LL HAVE MORE FUN THE SECOND TIME AROUND!
the End

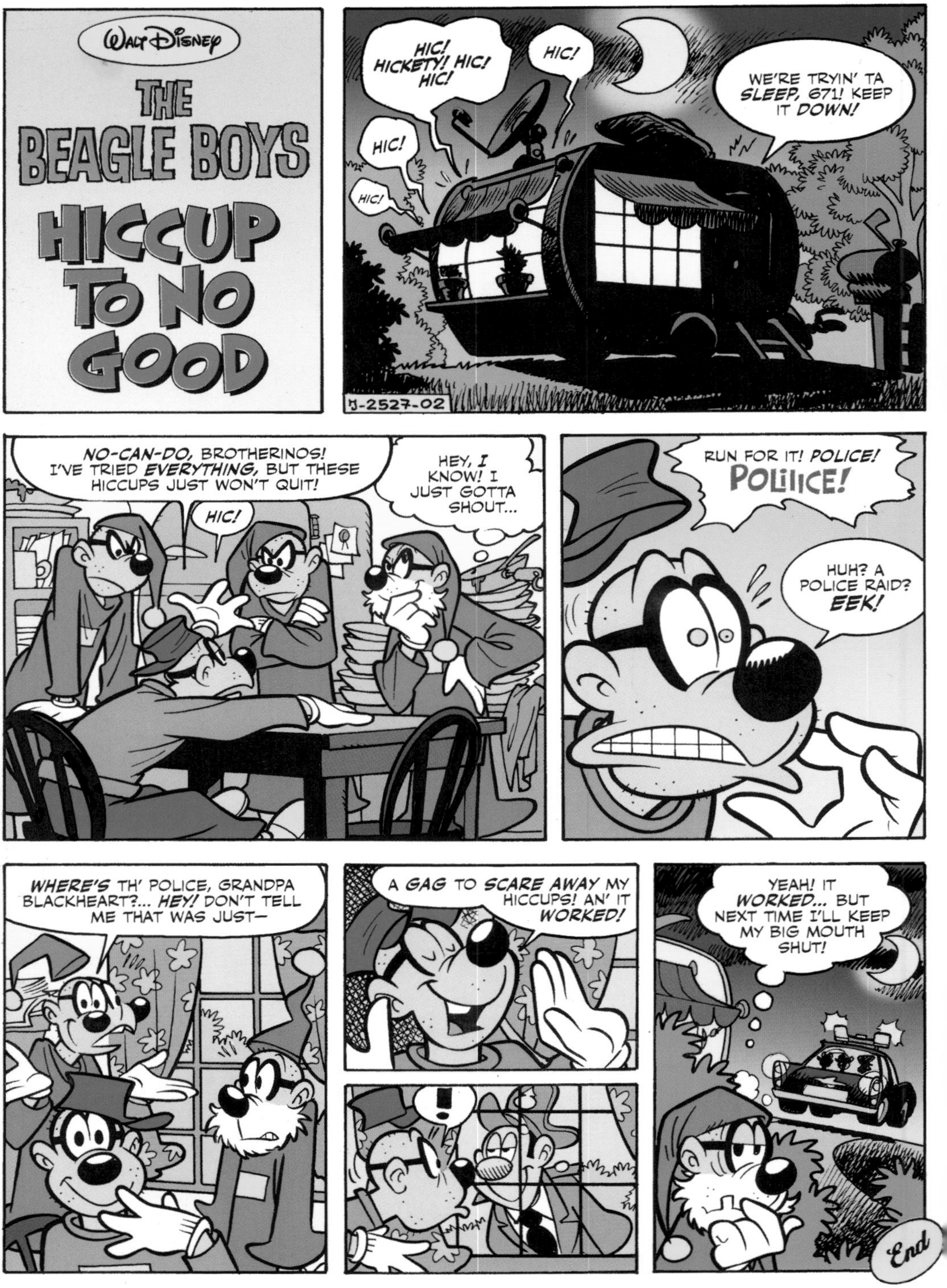
WALT DISNEY
THE BEAGLE BOYS
HICCUP TO NO GOOD
HIC! HICKETY! HIC! HIC!
HIC!
HIC!
HIC!
WE'RE TRYIN' TA SLEEP, 671! KEEP IT DOWN!
MJ-2527-02
NO-CAN-DO, BROTHERINOS! I'VE TRIED EVERYTHING, BUT THESE HICCUPS JUST WON'T QUIT!
HIC!
HEY, I KNOW! I JUST GOTTA SHOUT...
RUN FOR IT! POLICE! POLIIICE!
HUH? A POLICE RAID? EEK!
WHERE'S TH' POLICE, GRANDPA BLACKHEART?... HEY! DON'T TELL ME THAT WAS JUST—
A GAG TO SCARE AWAY MY HICCUPS! AN' IT WORKED!
!
YEAH! IT WORKED... BUT NEXT TIME I'LL KEEP MY BIG MOUTH SHUT!
End

Originally published in *Topolino* #2527 (Italy, 2004)

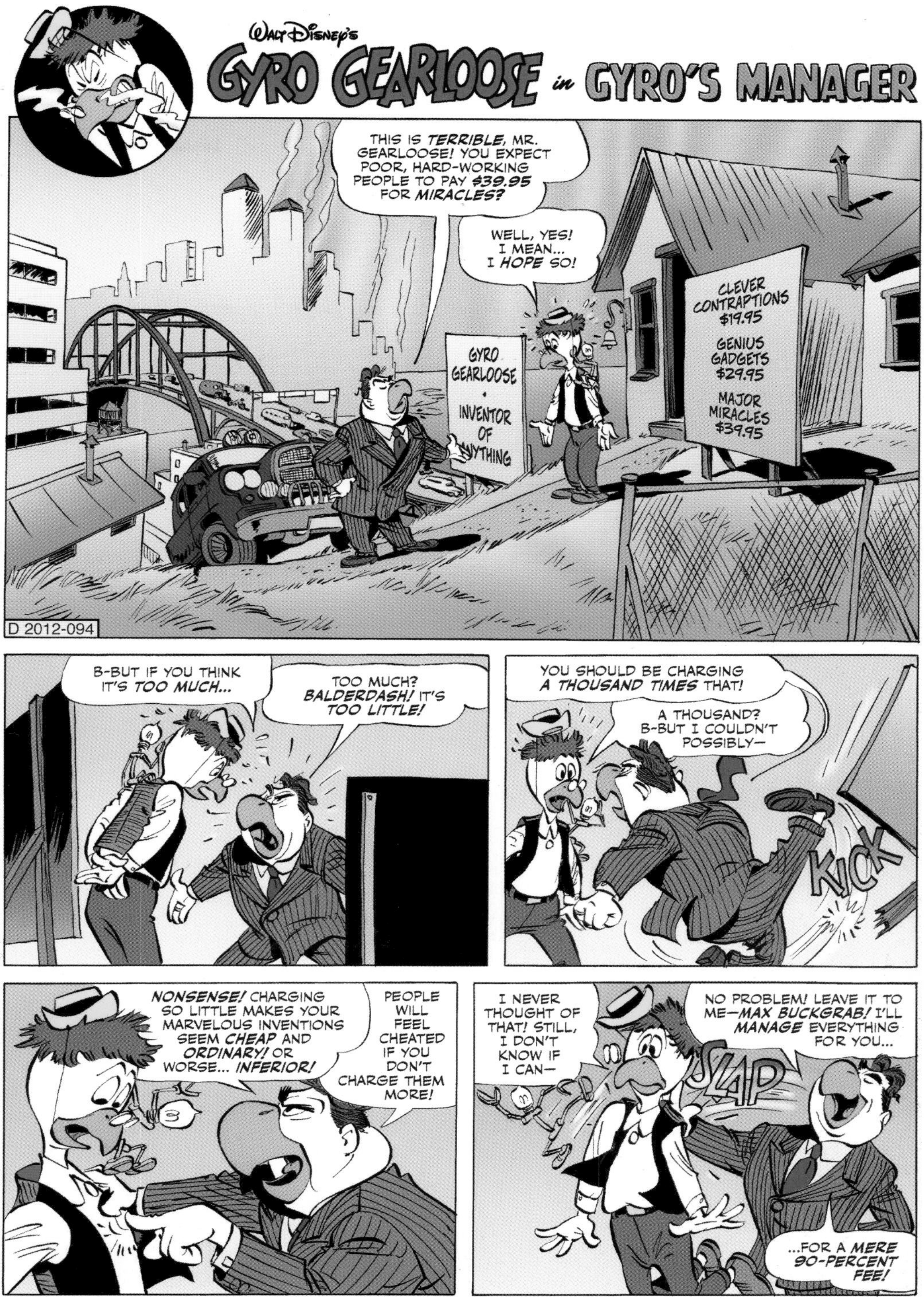
WALT DISNEY'S
GYRO GEARLOOSE in GYRO'S MANAGER
THIS IS TERRIBLE, MR. GEARLOOSE! YOU EXPECT POOR, HARD-WORKING PEOPLE TO PAY $39.95 FOR MIRACLES?
WELL, YES! I MEAN... I HOPE SO!
GYRO GEARLOOSE • INVENTOR OF ANYTHING
CLEVER CONTRAPTIONS $19.95
GENIUS GADGETS $29.95
MAJOR MIRACLES $39.95
D 2012-094
B-BUT IF YOU THINK IT'S TOO MUCH...
TOO MUCH? BALDERDASH! IT'S TOO LITTLE!
YOU SHOULD BE CHARGING A THOUSAND TIMES THAT!
A THOUSAND? B-BUT I COULDN'T POSSIBLY—
KICK
NONSENSE! CHARGING SO LITTLE MAKES YOUR MARVELOUS INVENTIONS SEEM CHEAP AND ORDINARY! OR WORSE... INFERIOR!
PEOPLE WILL FEEL CHEATED IF YOU DON'T CHARGE THEM MORE!
I NEVER THOUGHT OF THAT! STILL, I DON'T KNOW IF I CAN—
NO PROBLEM! LEAVE IT TO ME—MAX BUCKGRAB! I'LL MANAGE EVERYTHING FOR YOU...
SLAP
...FOR A MERE 90-PERCENT FEE!

Originally published in *Kalle Anka & C:o* #50/2014 (Sweden, 2014)

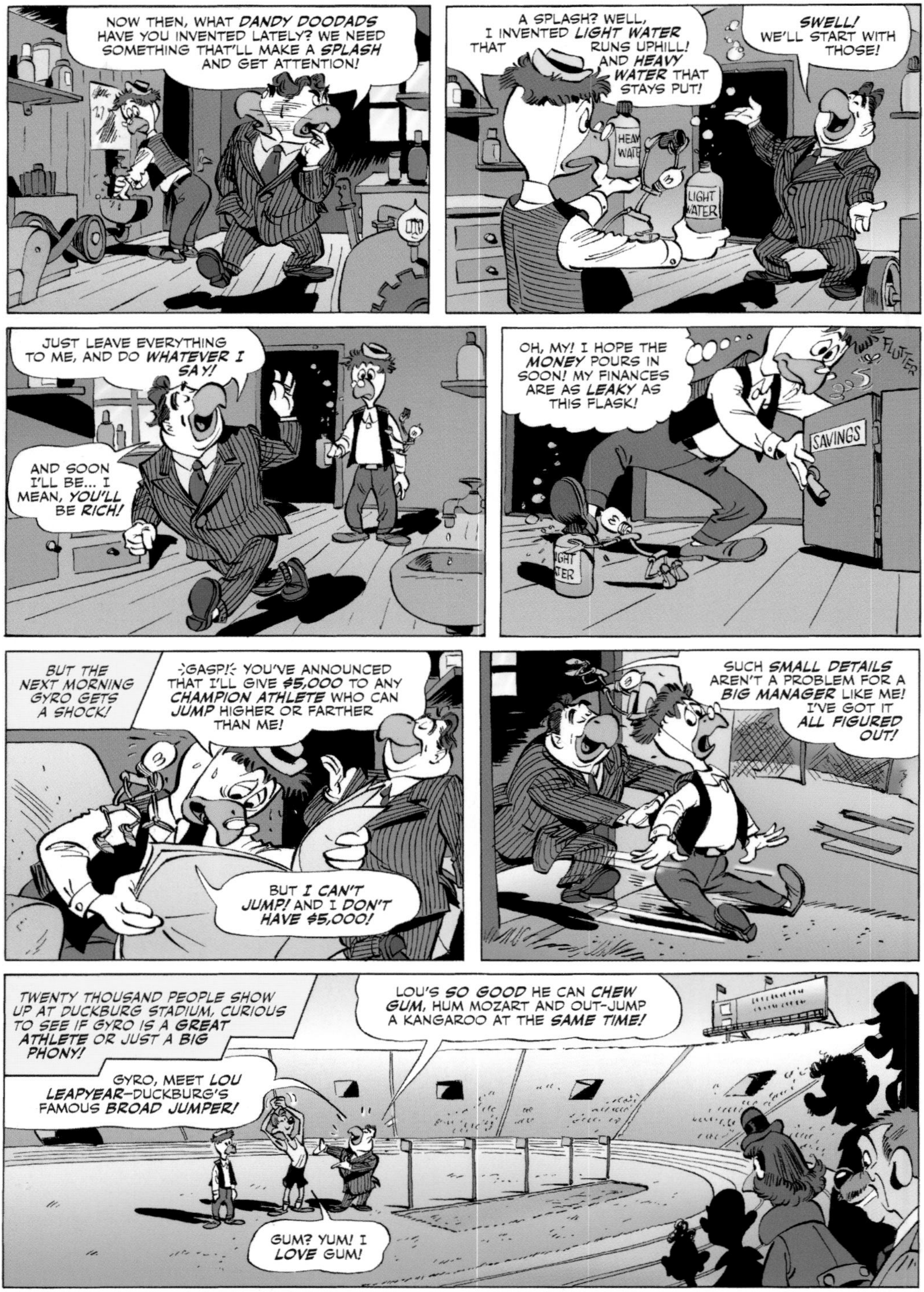
NOW THEN, WHAT DANDY DOODADS HAVE YOU INVENTED LATELY? WE NEED SOMETHING THAT'LL MAKE A SPLASH AND GET ATTENTION!
A SPLASH? WELL, I INVENTED LIGHT WATER THAT RUNS UPHILL! AND HEAVY WATER THAT STAYS PUT!
HEAVY WATER
LIGHT WATER
SWELL! WE'LL START WITH THOSE!
JUST LEAVE EVERYTHING TO ME, AND DO WHATEVER I SAY!
AND SOON I'LL BE... I MEAN, YOU'LL BE RICH!
OH, MY! I HOPE THE MONEY POURS IN SOON! MY FINANCES ARE AS LEAKY AS THIS FLASK!
FLUTTER
SAVINGS
BUT THE NEXT MORNING GYRO GETS A SHOCK!
-GASP!- YOU'VE ANNOUNCED THAT I'LL GIVE $5,000 TO ANY CHAMPION ATHLETE WHO CAN JUMP HIGHER OR FARTHER THAN ME!
BUT I CAN'T JUMP! AND I DON'T HAVE $5,000!
SUCH SMALL DETAILS AREN'T A PROBLEM FOR A BIG MANAGER LIKE ME! I'VE GOT IT ALL FIGURED OUT!
TWENTY THOUSAND PEOPLE SHOW UP AT DUCKBURG STADIUM, CURIOUS TO SEE IF GYRO IS A GREAT ATHLETE OR JUST A BIG PHONY!
GYRO, MEET LOU LEAPYEAR—DUCKBURG'S FAMOUS BROAD JUMPER!
LOU'S SO GOOD HE CAN CHEW GUM, HUM MOZART AND OUT-JUMP A KANGAROO AT THE SAME TIME!
GUM? YUM! I LOVE GUM!

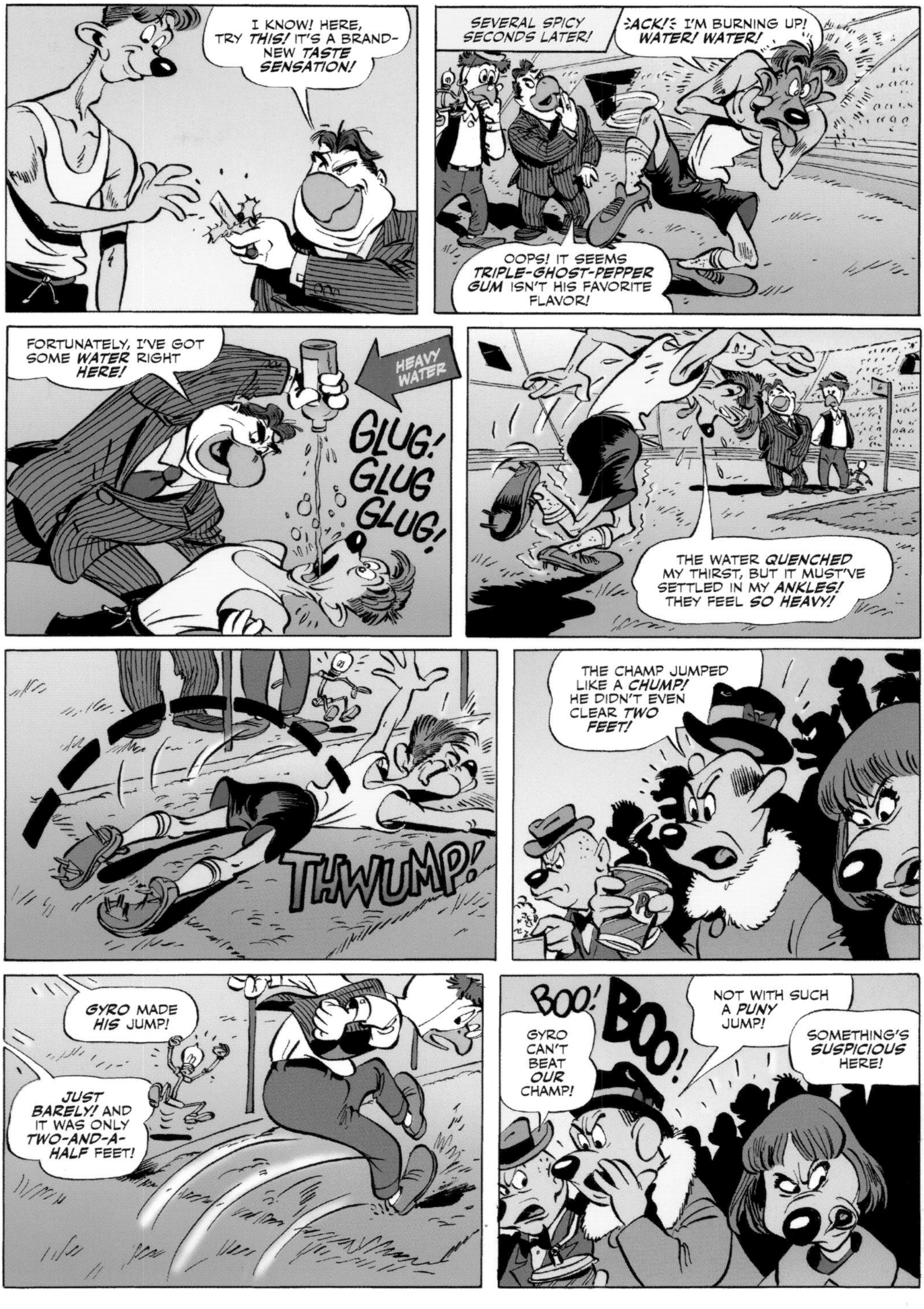
I KNOW! HERE, TRY THIS! IT'S A BRAND-NEW TASTE SENSATION!
SEVERAL SPICY SECONDS LATER!
ACK! I'M BURNING UP! WATER! WATER!
OOPS! IT SEEMS TRIPLE-GHOST-PEPPER GUM ISN'T HIS FAVORITE FLAVOR!
FORTUNATELY, I'VE GOT SOME WATER RIGHT HERE!
HEAVY WATER
GLUG! GLUG GLUG!
THE WATER QUENCHED MY THIRST, BUT IT MUST'VE SETTLED IN MY ANKLES! THEY FEEL SO HEAVY!
THWUMP!
THE CHAMP JUMPED LIKE A CHUMP! HE DIDN'T EVEN CLEAR TWO FEET!
GYRO MADE HIS JUMP!
JUST BARELY! AND IT WAS ONLY TWO-AND-A-HALF FEET!
BOO! BOO!
GYRO CAN'T BEAT OUR CHAMP!
NOT WITH SUCH A PUNY JUMP!
SOMETHING'S SUSPICIOUS HERE!

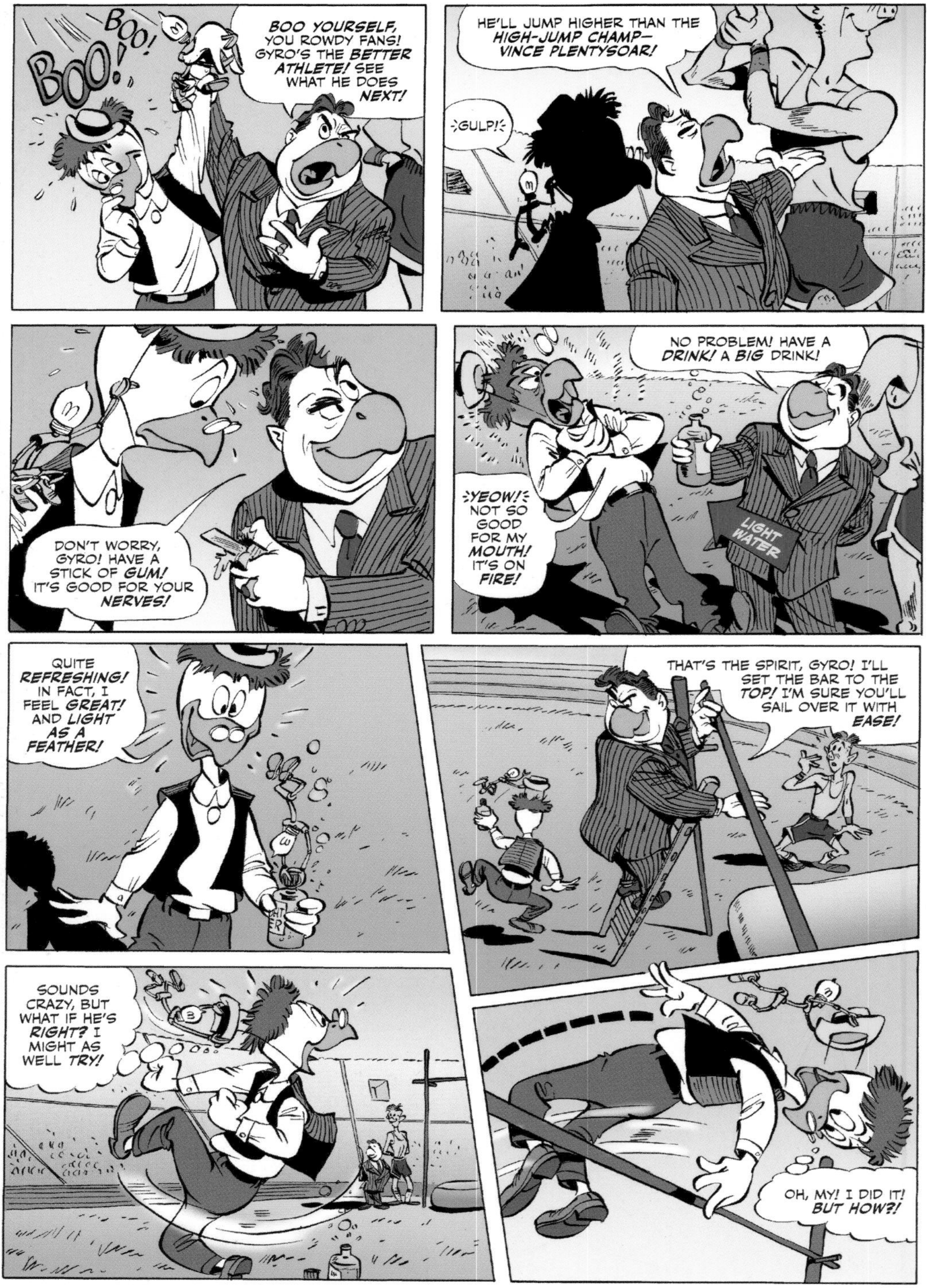
BOO! BOO!
BOO YOURSELF, YOU ROWDY FANS! GYRO'S THE BETTER ATHLETE! SEE WHAT HE DOES NEXT!
HE'LL JUMP HIGHER THAN THE HIGH-JUMP CHAMP— VINCE PLENTYSOAR!
GULP!
DON'T WORRY, GYRO! HAVE A STICK OF GUM! IT'S GOOD FOR YOUR NERVES!
NO PROBLEM! HAVE A DRINK! A BIG DRINK!
YEOW! NOT SO GOOD FOR MY MOUTH! IT'S ON FIRE!
LIGHT WATER
QUITE REFRESHING! IN FACT, I FEEL GREAT! AND LIGHT AS A FEATHER!
THAT'S THE SPIRIT, GYRO! I'LL SET THE BAR TO THE TOP! I'M SURE YOU'LL SAIL OVER IT WITH EASE!
SOUNDS CRAZY, BUT WHAT IF HE'S RIGHT? I MIGHT AS WELL TRY!
OH, MY! I DID IT! BUT HOW?!

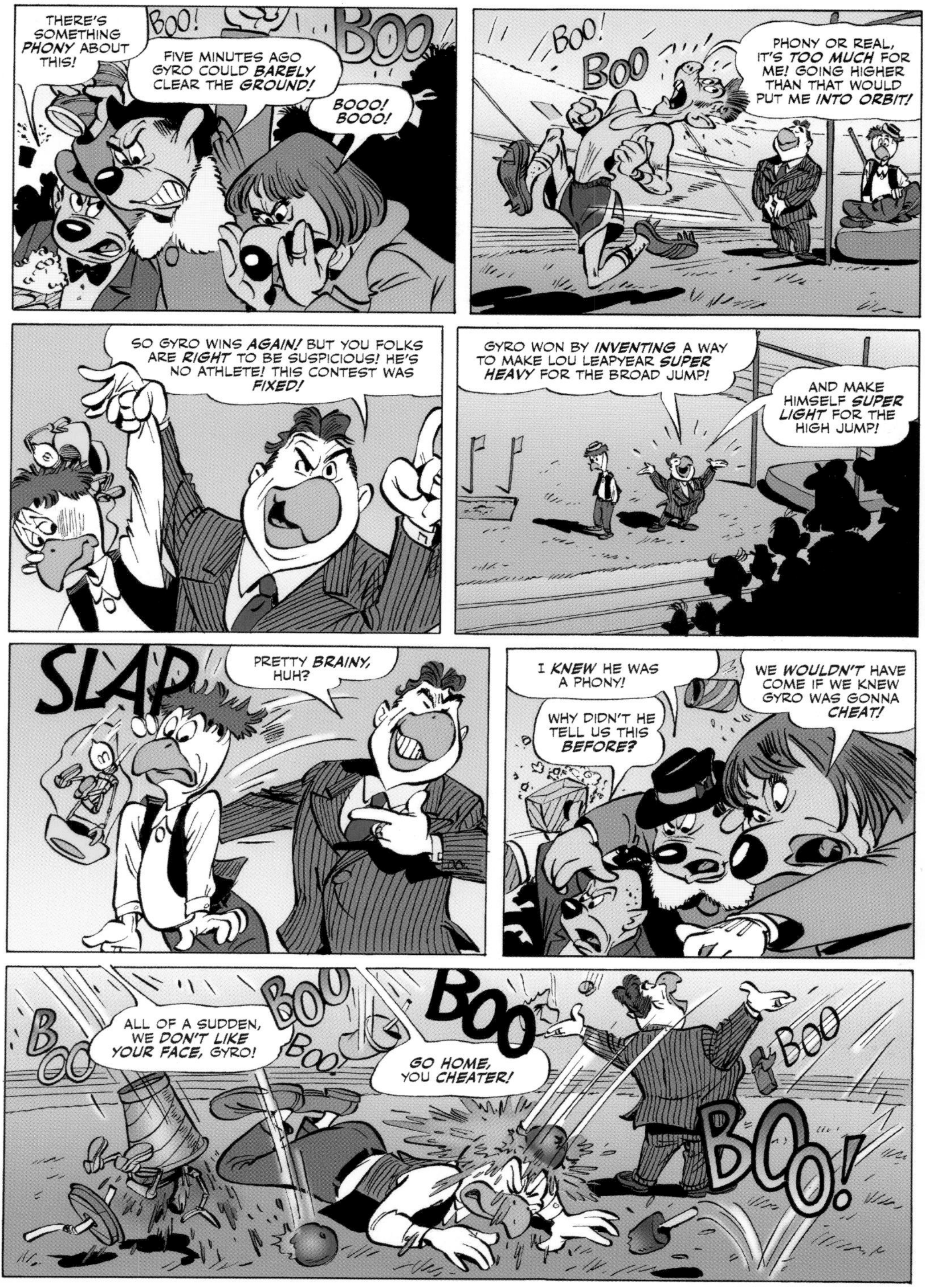

THERE'S SOMETHING PHONY ABOUT THIS!
FIVE MINUTES AGO GYRO COULD BARELY CLEAR THE GROUND!
BOO!
BOO
BOOO! BOOO!
BOO!
BOO
PHONY OR REAL, IT'S TOO MUCH FOR ME! GOING HIGHER THAN THAT WOULD PUT ME INTO ORBIT!
SO GYRO WINS AGAIN! BUT YOU FOLKS ARE RIGHT TO BE SUSPICIOUS! HE'S NO ATHLETE! THIS CONTEST WAS FIXED!
GYRO WON BY INVENTING A WAY TO MAKE LOU LEAPYEAR SUPER HEAVY FOR THE BROAD JUMP!
AND MAKE HIMSELF SUPER LIGHT FOR THE HIGH JUMP!
SLAP
PRETTY BRAINY, HUH?
I KNEW HE WAS A PHONY!
WHY DIDN'T HE TELL US THIS BEFORE?
WE WOULDN'T HAVE COME IF WE KNEW GYRO WAS GONNA CHEAT!
BOO
ALL OF A SUDDEN, WE DON'T LIKE YOUR FACE, GYRO!
BOO
BOO!
BOO
GO HOME, YOU CHEATER!
BOO
BOO!

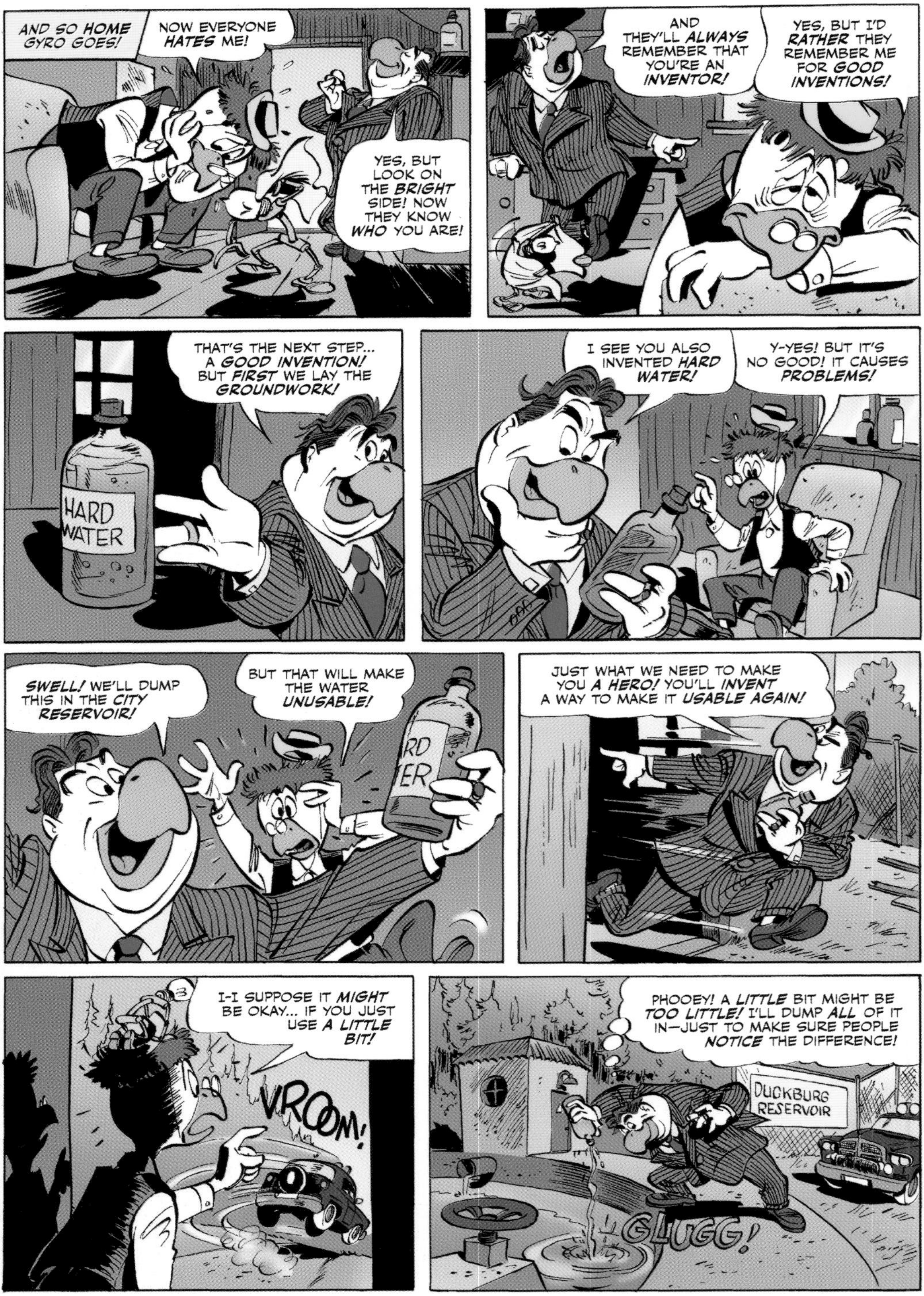
AND SO HOME GYRO GOES!
NOW EVERYONE HATES ME!
YES, BUT LOOK ON THE BRIGHT SIDE! NOW THEY KNOW WHO YOU ARE!
AND THEY'LL ALWAYS REMEMBER THAT YOU'RE AN INVENTOR!
YES, BUT I'D RATHER THEY REMEMBER ME FOR GOOD INVENTIONS!
THAT'S THE NEXT STEP... A GOOD INVENTION! BUT FIRST WE LAY THE GROUNDWORK!
HARD WATER
I SEE YOU ALSO INVENTED HARD WATER!
Y-YES! BUT IT'S NO GOOD! IT CAUSES PROBLEMS!
SWELL! WE'LL DUMP THIS IN THE CITY RESERVOIR!
BUT THAT WILL MAKE THE WATER UNUSABLE!
JUST WHAT WE NEED TO MAKE YOU A HERO! YOU'LL INVENT A WAY TO MAKE IT USABLE AGAIN!
I-I SUPPOSE IT MIGHT BE OKAY... IF YOU JUST USE A LITTLE BIT!
VROOM!
PHOOEY! A LITTLE BIT MIGHT BE TOO LITTLE! I'LL DUMP ALL OF IT IN—JUST TO MAKE SURE PEOPLE NOTICE THE DIFFERENCE!
DUCKBURG RESERVOIR
GLUGG!

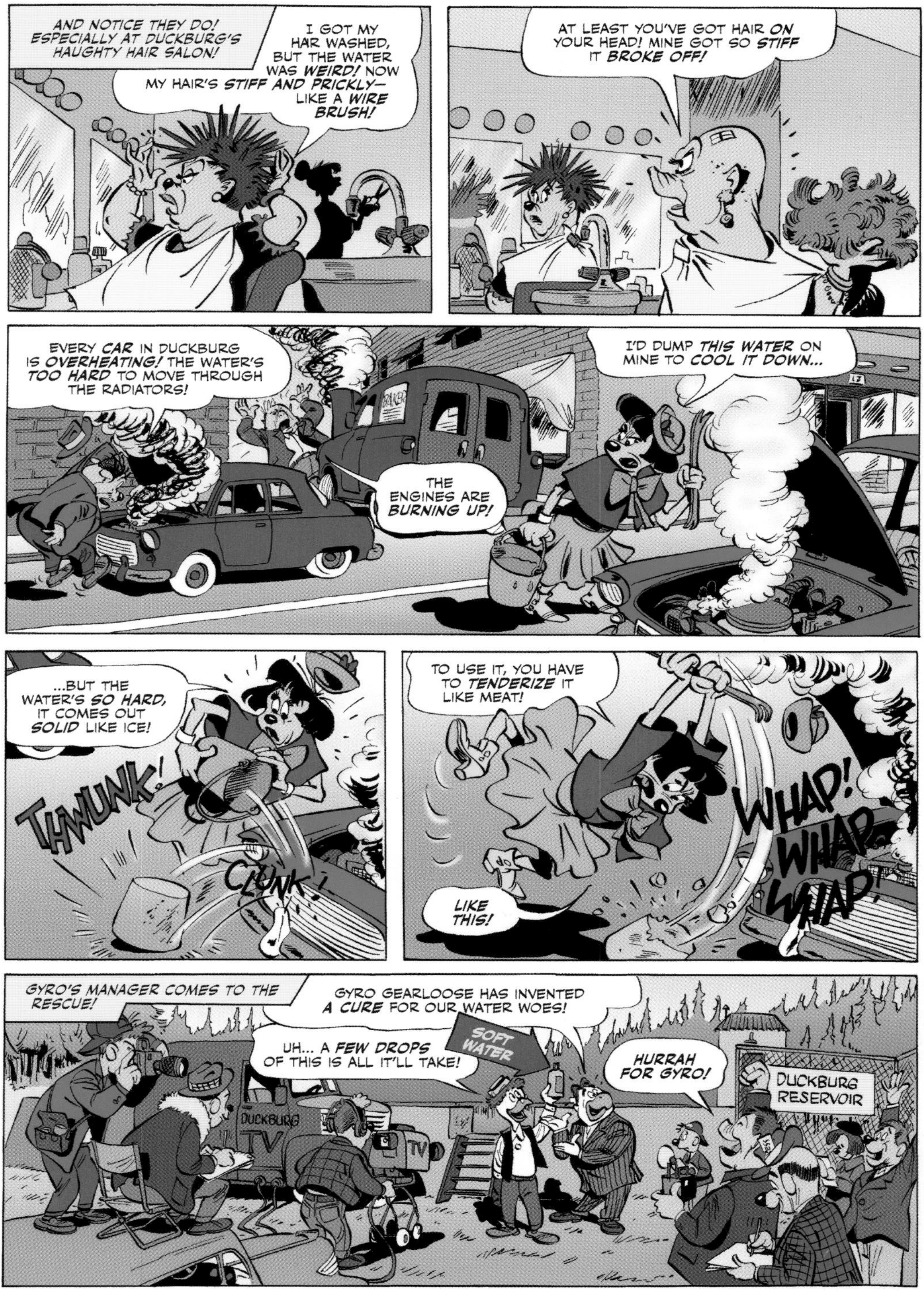
AND NOTICE THEY DO! ESPECIALLY AT DUCKBURG'S HAUGHTY HAIR SALON!
I GOT MY HAIR WASHED, BUT THE WATER WAS WEIRD! NOW MY HAIR'S STIFF AND PRICKLY— LIKE A WIRE BRUSH!
AT LEAST YOU'VE GOT HAIR ON YOUR HEAD! MINE GOT SO STIFF IT BROKE OFF!
EVERY CAR IN DUCKBURG IS OVERHEATING! THE WATER'S TOO HARD TO MOVE THROUGH THE RADIATORS!
BAKER
THE ENGINES ARE BURNING UP!
I'D DUMP THIS WATER ON MINE TO COOL IT DOWN...
...BUT THE WATER'S SO HARD, IT COMES OUT SOLID LIKE ICE!
THWUNK!
CLUNK!
TO USE IT, YOU HAVE TO TENDERIZE IT LIKE MEAT!
WHAP! WHAP! WHAP!
LIKE THIS!
GYRO'S MANAGER COMES TO THE RESCUE!
GYRO GEARLOOSE HAS INVENTED A CURE FOR OUR WATER WOES!
UH... A FEW DROPS OF THIS IS ALL IT'LL TAKE!
SOFT WATER
HURRAH FOR GYRO!
DUCKBURG TV
DUCKBURG RESERVOIR

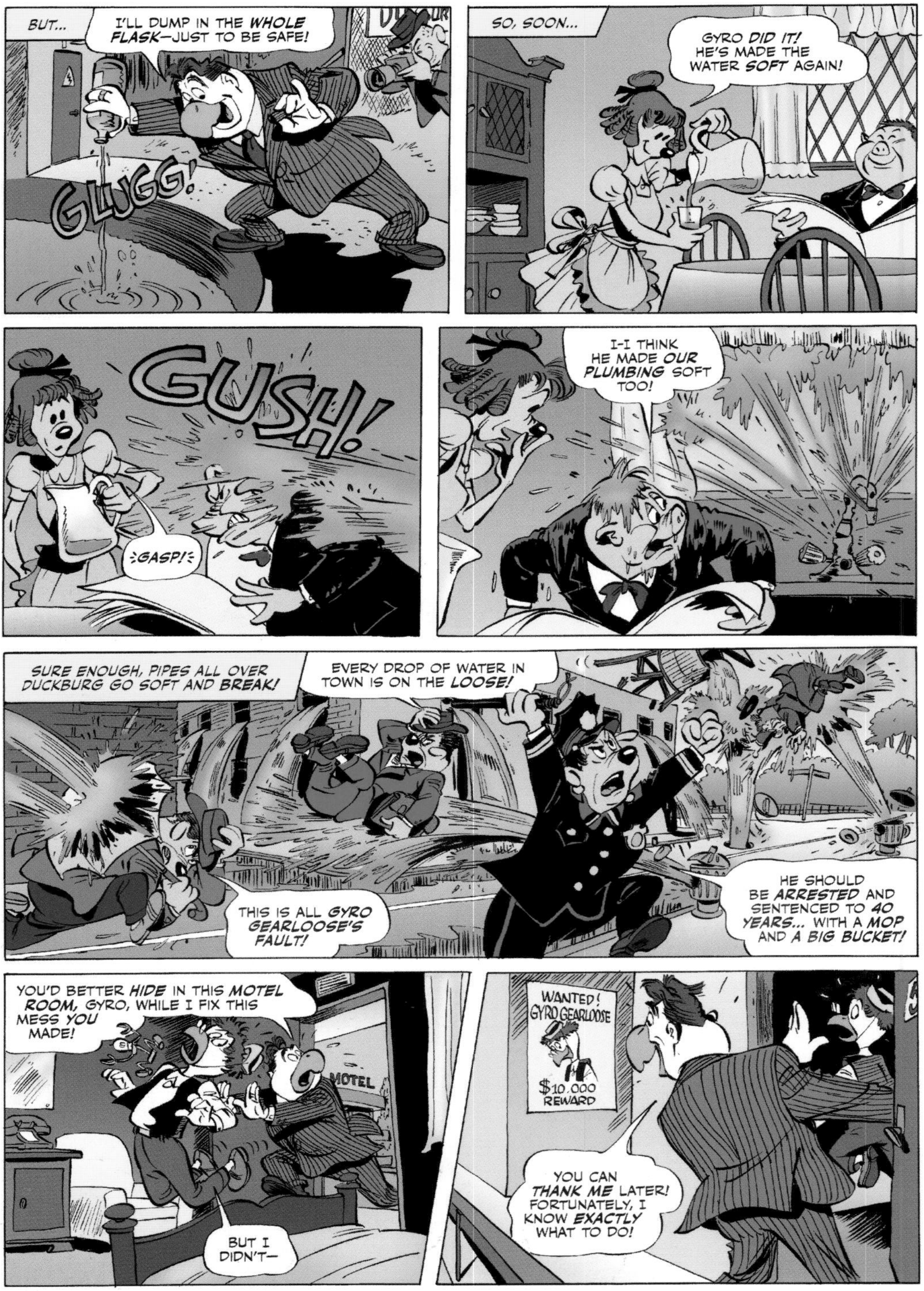
BUT...
I'LL DUMP IN THE WHOLE FLASK—JUST TO BE SAFE!
GLUGG!
SO, SOON...
GYRO DID IT! HE'S MADE THE WATER SOFT AGAIN!
GUSH!
GASP!
I-I THINK HE MADE OUR PLUMBING SOFT TOO!
SURE ENOUGH, PIPES ALL OVER DUCKBURG GO SOFT AND BREAK!
EVERY DROP OF WATER IN TOWN IS ON THE LOOSE!
THIS IS ALL GYRO GEARLOOSE'S FAULT!
HE SHOULD BE ARRESTED AND SENTENCED TO 40 YEARS... WITH A MOP AND A BIG BUCKET!
YOU'D BETTER HIDE IN THIS MOTEL ROOM, GYRO, WHILE I FIX THIS MESS YOU MADE!
MOTEL
BUT I DIDN'T—
WANTED! GYRO GEARLOOSE
$10.000 REWARD
YOU CAN THANK ME LATER! FORTUNATELY, I KNOW EXACTLY WHAT TO DO!

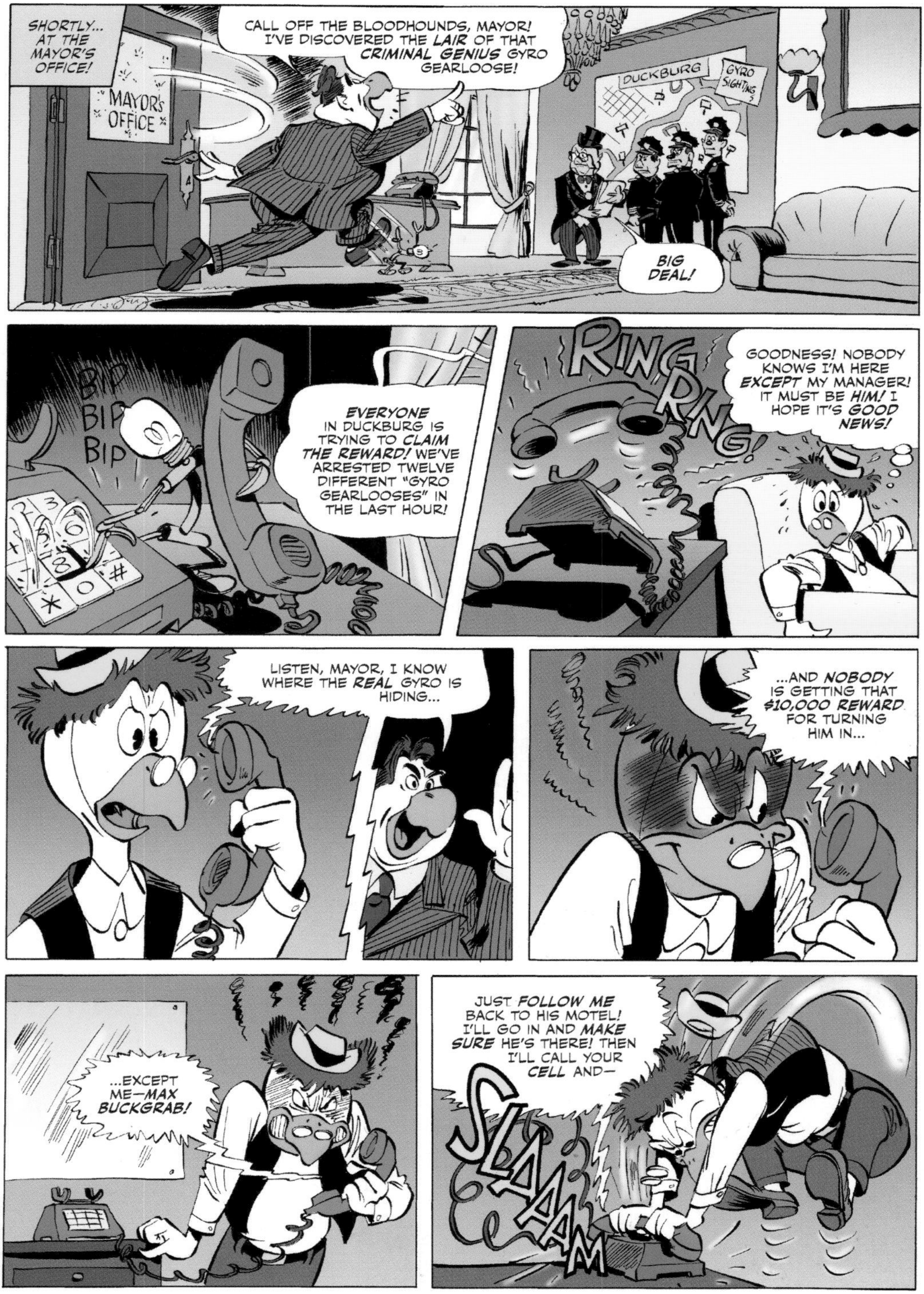

SHORTLY... AT THE MAYOR'S OFFICE!
MAYOR'S OFFICE
CALL OFF THE BLOODHOUNDS, MAYOR! I'VE DISCOVERED THE LAIR OF THAT CRIMINAL GENIUS GYRO GEARLOOSE!
DUCKBURG
GYRO SIGHTINGS
BIG DEAL!
BIP BIP BIP
EVERYONE IN DUCKBURG IS TRYING TO CLAIM THE REWARD! WE'VE ARRESTED TWELVE DIFFERENT "GYRO GEARLOOSES" IN THE LAST HOUR!
RING RING!
GOODNESS! NOBODY KNOWS I'M HERE EXCEPT MY MANAGER! IT MUST BE HIM! I HOPE IT'S GOOD NEWS!
LISTEN, MAYOR, I KNOW WHERE THE REAL GYRO IS HIDING...
...AND NOBODY IS GETTING THAT $10,000 REWARD FOR TURNING HIM IN...
...EXCEPT ME—MAX BUCKGRAB!
JUST FOLLOW ME BACK TO HIS MOTEL! I'LL GO IN AND MAKE SURE HE'S THERE! THEN I'LL CALL YOUR CELL AND—
SLAAAM

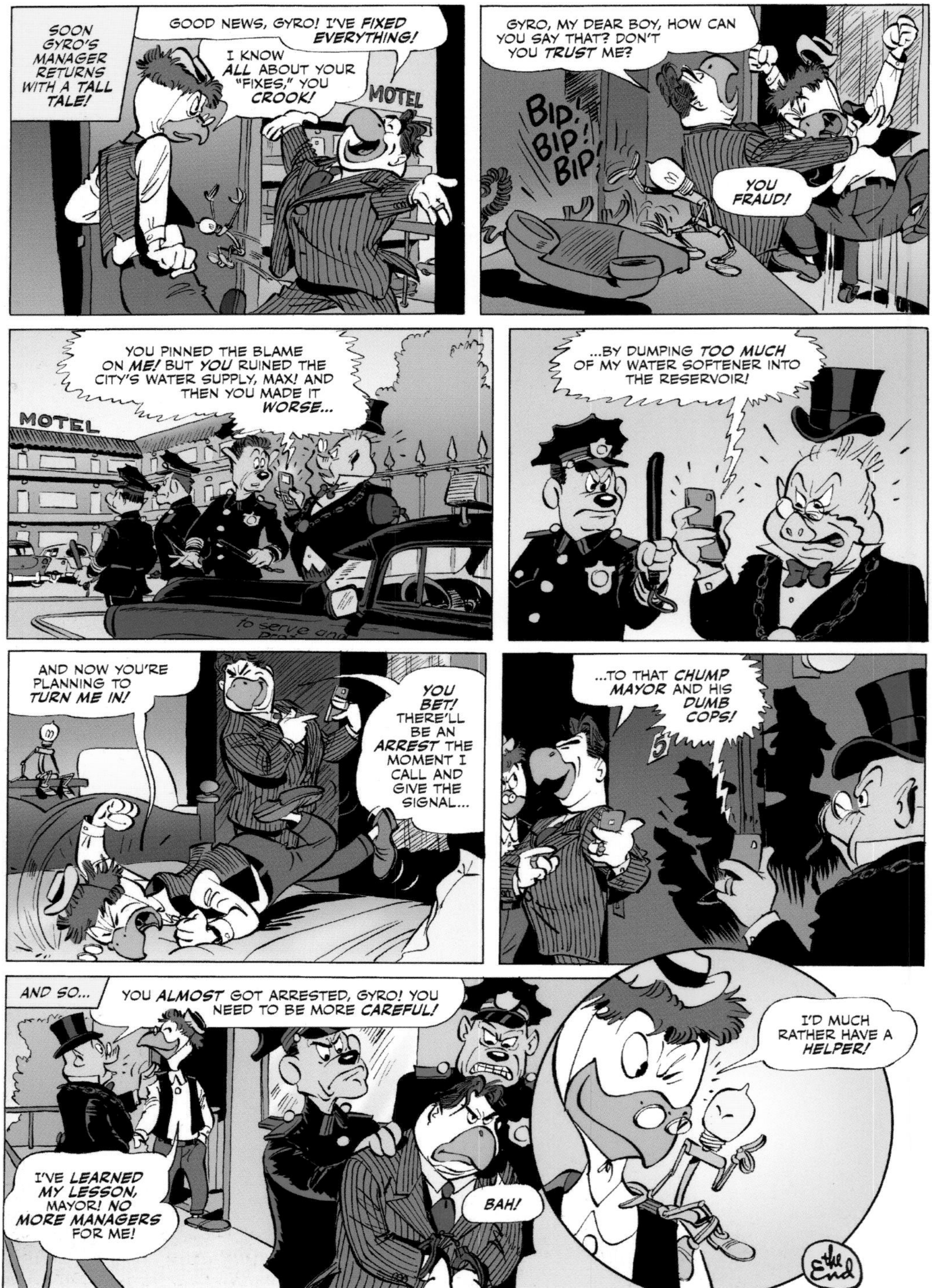
SOON GYRO'S MANAGER RETURNS WITH A TALL TALE!
GOOD NEWS, GYRO! I'VE FIXED EVERYTHING!
I KNOW ALL ABOUT YOUR "FIXES," YOU CROOK!
MOTEL
GYRO, MY DEAR BOY, HOW CAN YOU SAY THAT? DON'T YOU TRUST ME?
BIP! BIP! BIP!
YOU FRAUD!
YOU PINNED THE BLAME ON ME! BUT YOU RUINED THE CITY'S WATER SUPPLY, MAX! AND THEN YOU MADE IT WORSE...
MOTEL
...BY DUMPING TOO MUCH OF MY WATER SOFTENER INTO THE RESERVOIR!
AND NOW YOU'RE PLANNING TO TURN ME IN!
YOU BET! THERE'LL BE AN ARREST THE MOMENT I CALL AND GIVE THE SIGNAL...
...TO THAT CHUMP MAYOR AND HIS DUMB COPS!
AND SO...
YOU ALMOST GOT ARRESTED, GYRO! YOU NEED TO BE MORE CAREFUL!
I'VE LEARNED MY LESSON, MAYOR! NO MORE MANAGERS FOR ME!
BAH!
I'D MUCH RATHER HAVE A HELPER!
the End

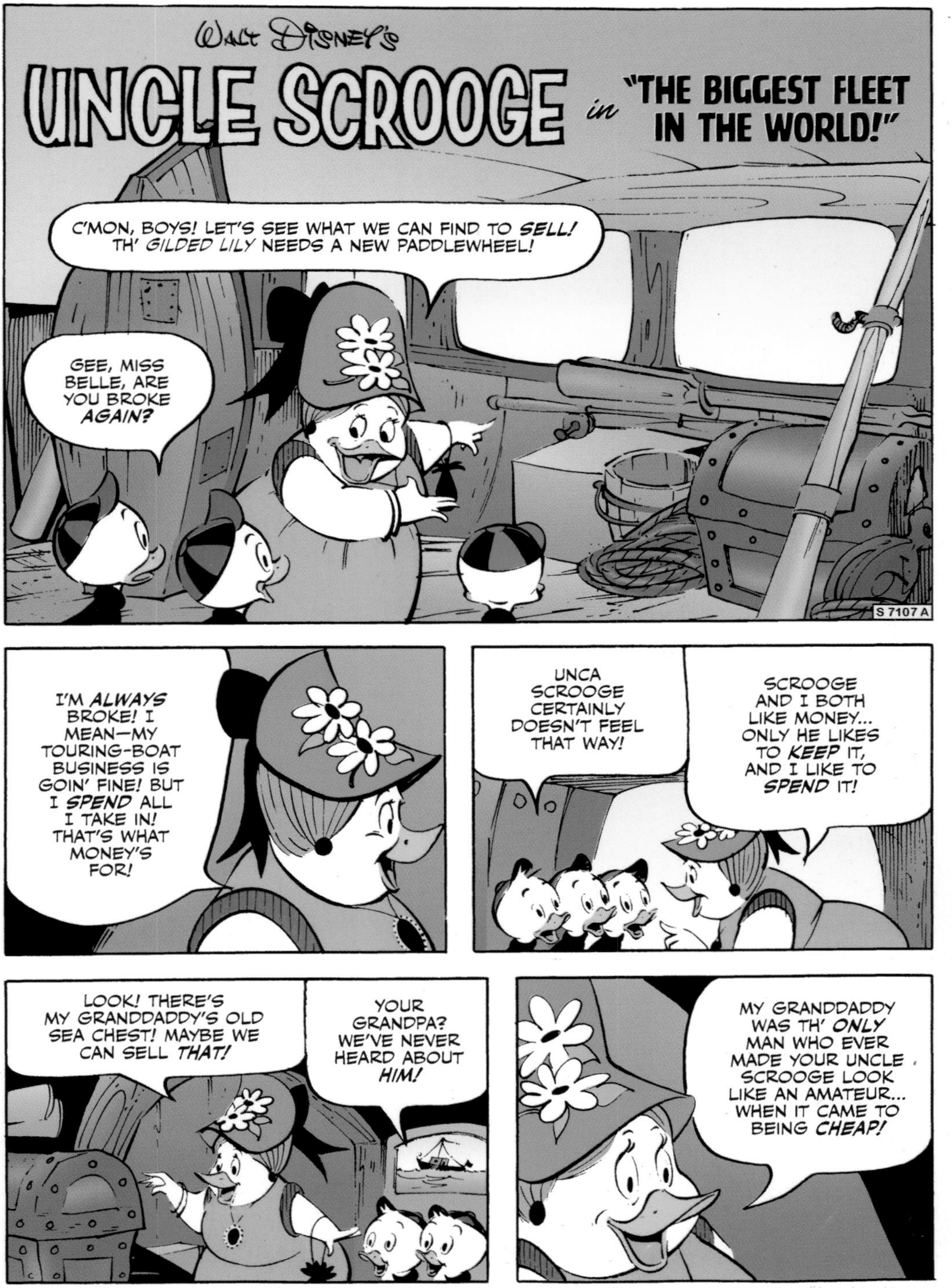
WALT DISNEY'S
UNCLE SCROOGE in "THE BIGGEST FLEET IN THE WORLD!"
C'MON, BOYS! LET'S SEE WHAT WE CAN FIND TO SELL! TH' GILDED LILY NEEDS A NEW PADDLEWHEEL!
GEE, MISS BELLE, ARE YOU BROKE AGAIN?
S 7107 A
I'M ALWAYS BROKE! I MEAN—MY TOURING-BOAT BUSINESS IS GOIN' FINE! BUT I SPEND ALL I TAKE IN! THAT'S WHAT MONEY'S FOR!
UNCA SCROOGE CERTAINLY DOESN'T FEEL THAT WAY!
SCROOGE AND I BOTH LIKE MONEY... ONLY HE LIKES TO KEEP IT, AND I LIKE TO SPEND IT!
LOOK! THERE'S MY GRANDDADDY'S OLD SEA CHEST! MAYBE WE CAN SELL THAT!
YOUR GRANDPA? WE'VE NEVER HEARD ABOUT HIM!
MY GRANDDADDY WAS TH' ONLY MAN WHO EVER MADE YOUR UNCLE SCROOGE LOOK LIKE AN AMATEUR... WHEN IT CAME TO BEING CHEAP!

Originally published in *Topolino* #734 (Italy, 1969)

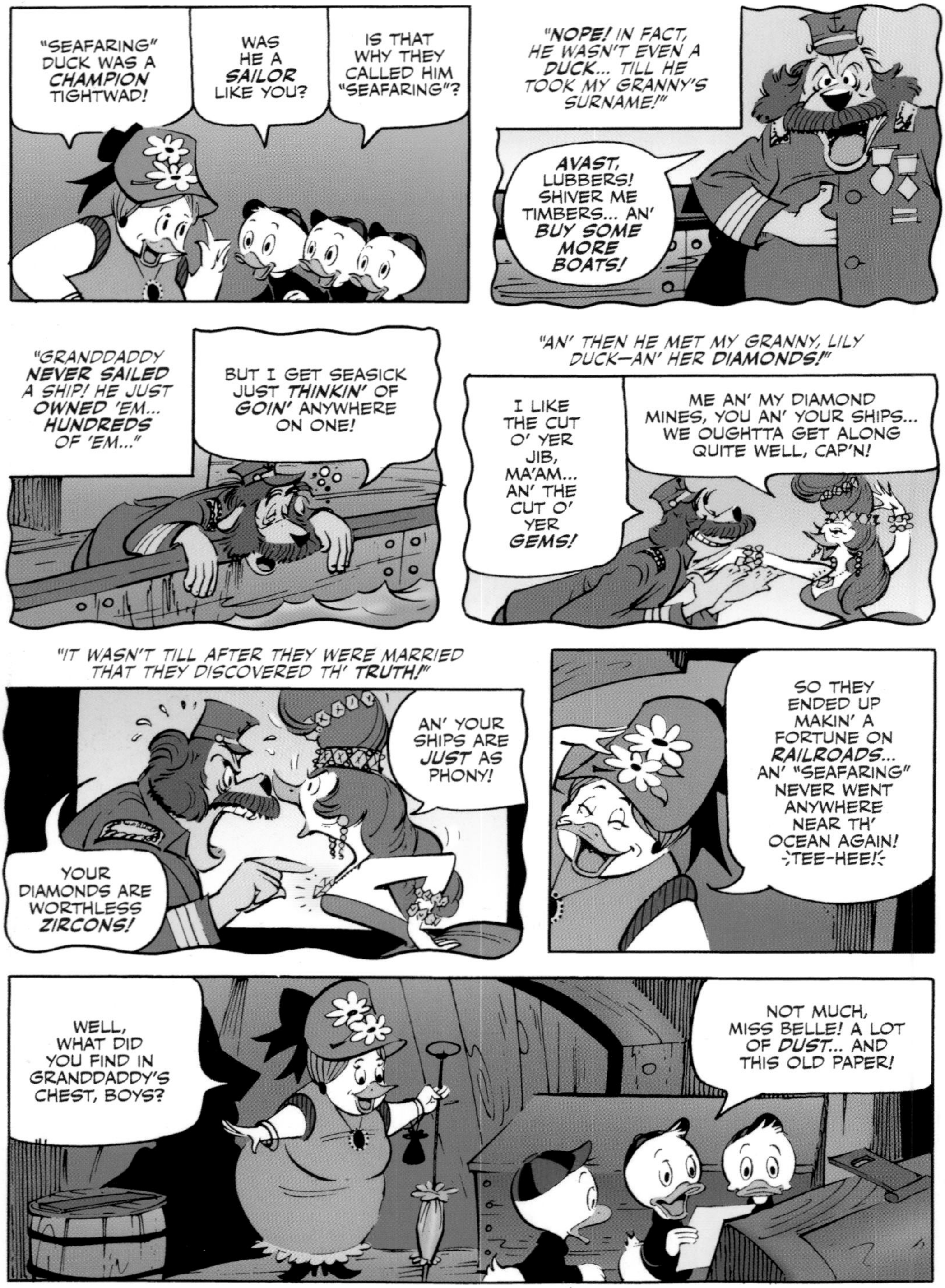
"SEAFARING" DUCK WAS A CHAMPION TIGHTWAD!
WAS HE A SAILOR LIKE YOU?
IS THAT WHY THEY CALLED HIM "SEAFARING"?
"NOPE! IN FACT, HE WASN'T EVEN A DUCK... TILL HE TOOK MY GRANNY'S SURNAME!"
AVAST, LUBBERS! SHIVER ME TIMBERS... AN' BUY SOME MORE BOATS!
"GRANDDADDY NEVER SAILED A SHIP! HE JUST OWNED 'EM... HUNDREDS OF 'EM..."
BUT I GET SEASICK JUST THINKIN' OF GOIN' ANYWHERE ON ONE!
"AN' THEN HE MET MY GRANNY, LILY DUCK—AN' HER DIAMONDS!"
I LIKE THE CUT O' YER JIB, MA'AM... AN' THE CUT O' YER GEMS!
ME AN' MY DIAMOND MINES, YOU AN' YOUR SHIPS... WE OUGHTTA GET ALONG QUITE WELL, CAP'N!
"IT WASN'T TILL AFTER THEY WERE MARRIED THAT THEY DISCOVERED TH' TRUTH!"
YOUR DIAMONDS ARE WORTHLESS ZIRCONS!
AN' YOUR SHIPS ARE JUST AS PHONY!
SO THEY ENDED UP MAKIN' A FORTUNE ON RAILROADS... AN' "SEAFARING" NEVER WENT ANYWHERE NEAR TH' OCEAN AGAIN! TEE-HEE!
WELL, WHAT DID YOU FIND IN GRANDDADDY'S CHEST, BOYS?
NOT MUCH, MISS BELLE! A LOT OF DUST... AND THIS OLD PAPER!

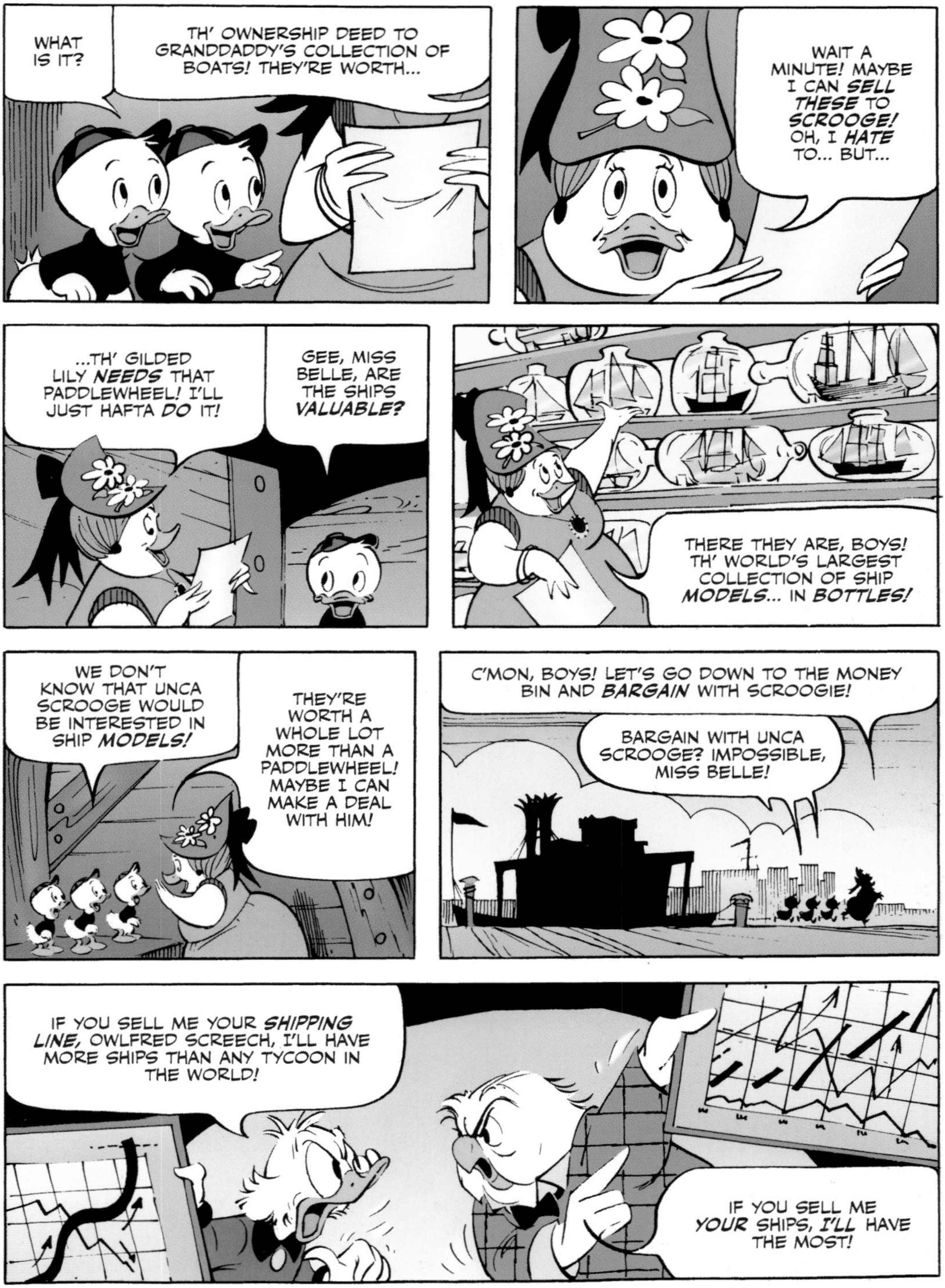

WHAT IS IT?
TH' OWNERSHIP DEED TO GRANDDADDY'S COLLECTION OF BOATS! THEY'RE WORTH...
WAIT A MINUTE! MAYBE I CAN SELL THESE TO SCROOGE! OH, I HATE TO... BUT...
...TH' GILDED LILY NEEDS THAT PADDLEWHEEL! I'LL JUST HAFTA DO IT!
GEE, MISS BELLE, ARE THE SHIPS VALUABLE?
THERE THEY ARE, BOYS! TH' WORLD'S LARGEST COLLECTION OF SHIP MODELS... IN BOTTLES!
WE DON'T KNOW THAT UNCA SCROOGE WOULD BE INTERESTED IN SHIP MODELS!
THEY'RE WORTH A WHOLE LOT MORE THAN A PADDLEWHEEL! MAYBE I CAN MAKE A DEAL WITH HIM!
C'MON, BOYS! LET'S GO DOWN TO THE MONEY BIN AND BARGAIN WITH SCROOGIE!
BARGAIN WITH UNCA SCROOGE? IMPOSSIBLE, MISS BELLE!
IF YOU SELL ME YOUR SHIPPING LINE, OWLFRED SCREECH, I'LL HAVE MORE SHIPS THAN ANY TYCOON IN THE WORLD!
IF YOU SELL ME YOUR SHIPS, I'LL HAVE THE MOST!

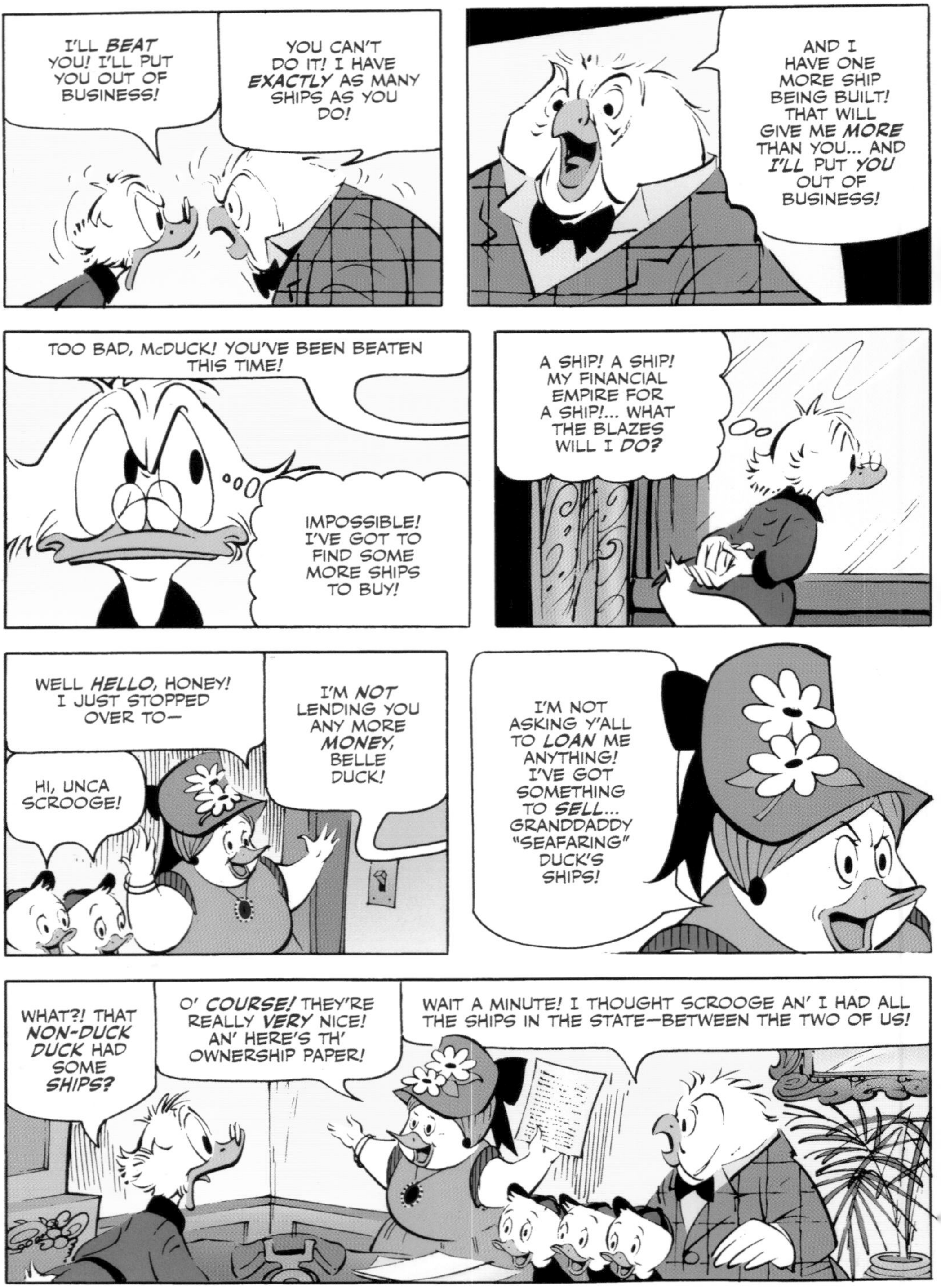
I'LL BEAT YOU! I'LL PUT YOU OUT OF BUSINESS!
YOU CAN'T DO IT! I HAVE EXACTLY AS MANY SHIPS AS YOU DO!
AND I HAVE ONE MORE SHIP BEING BUILT! THAT WILL GIVE ME MORE THAN YOU... AND I'LL PUT YOU OUT OF BUSINESS!
TOO BAD, McDUCK! YOU'VE BEEN BEATEN THIS TIME!
IMPOSSIBLE! I'VE GOT TO FIND SOME MORE SHIPS TO BUY!
A SHIP! A SHIP! MY FINANCIAL EMPIRE FOR A SHIP!... WHAT THE BLAZES WILL I DO?
WELL HELLO, HONEY! I JUST STOPPED OVER TO—
HI, UNCA SCROOGE!
I'M NOT LENDING YOU ANY MORE MONEY, BELLE DUCK!
I'M NOT ASKING Y'ALL TO LOAN ME ANYTHING! I'VE GOT SOMETHING TO SELL... GRANDDADDY "SEAFARING" DUCK'S SHIPS!
WHAT?! THAT NON-DUCK DUCK HAD SOME SHIPS?
O' COURSE! THEY'RE REALLY VERY NICE! AN' HERE'S TH' OWNERSHIP PAPER!
WAIT A MINUTE! I THOUGHT SCROOGE AN' I HAD ALL THE SHIPS IN THE STATE—BETWEEN THE TWO OF US!

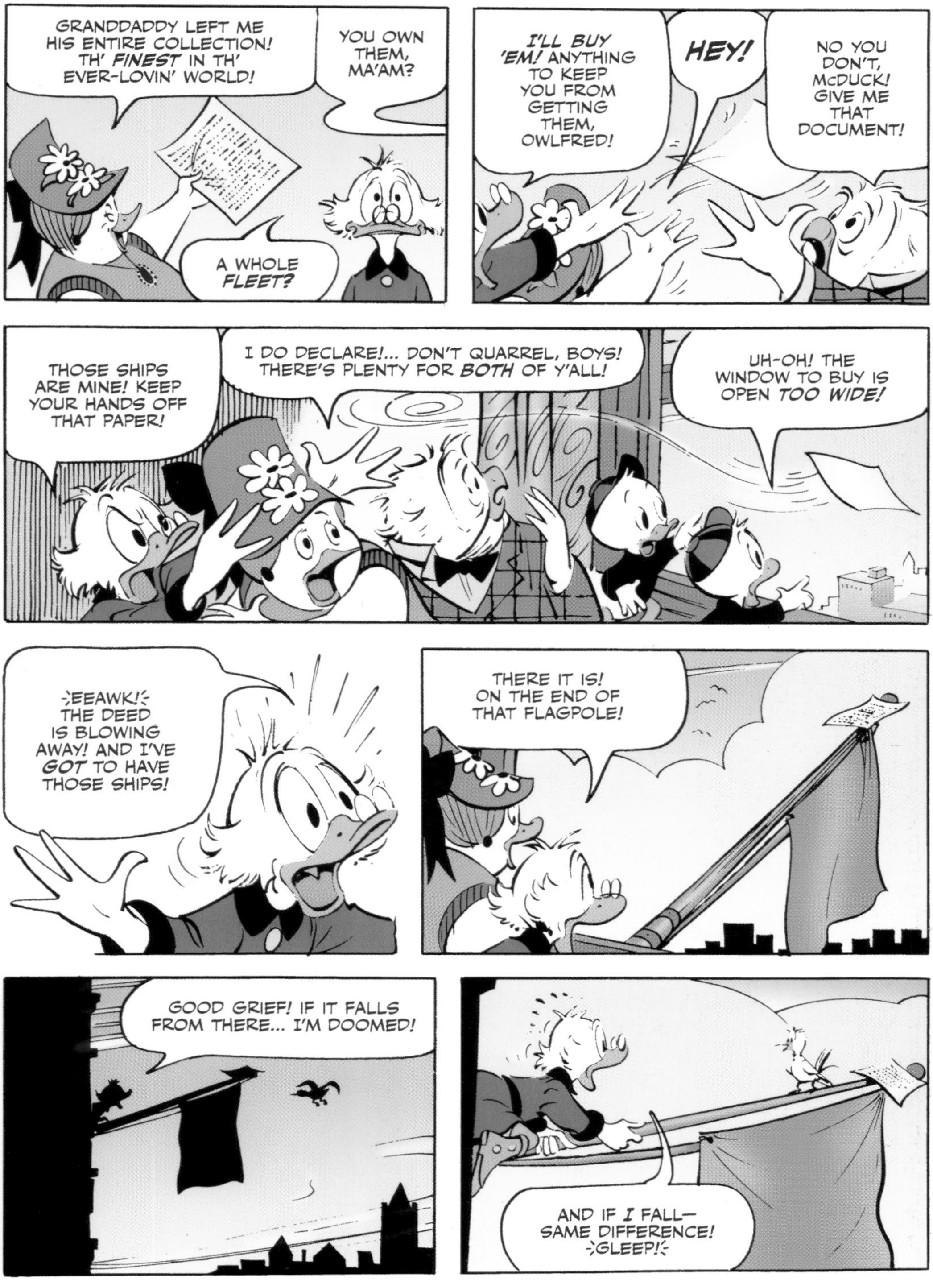
GRANDDADDY LEFT ME HIS ENTIRE COLLECTION! TH' *FINEST* IN TH' EVER-LOVIN' WORLD!
YOU OWN THEM, MA'AM?
A WHOLE *FLEET?*
I'LL BUY 'EM! ANYTHING TO KEEP YOU FROM GETTING THEM, OWLFRED!
HEY!
NO YOU DON'T, McDUCK! GIVE ME THAT DOCUMENT!
THOSE SHIPS ARE MINE! KEEP YOUR HANDS OFF THAT PAPER!
I DO DECLARE!... DON'T QUARREL, BOYS! THERE'S PLENTY FOR *BOTH* OF Y'ALL!
UH-OH! THE WINDOW TO BUY IS OPEN *TOO WIDE!*
EEAWK! THE DEED IS BLOWING AWAY! AND I'VE *GOT* TO HAVE THOSE SHIPS!
THERE IT IS! ON THE END OF THAT FLAGPOLE!
GOOD GRIEF! IF IT FALLS FROM THERE... I'M DOOMED!
AND IF *I* FALL— SAME DIFFERENCE! GLEEP!

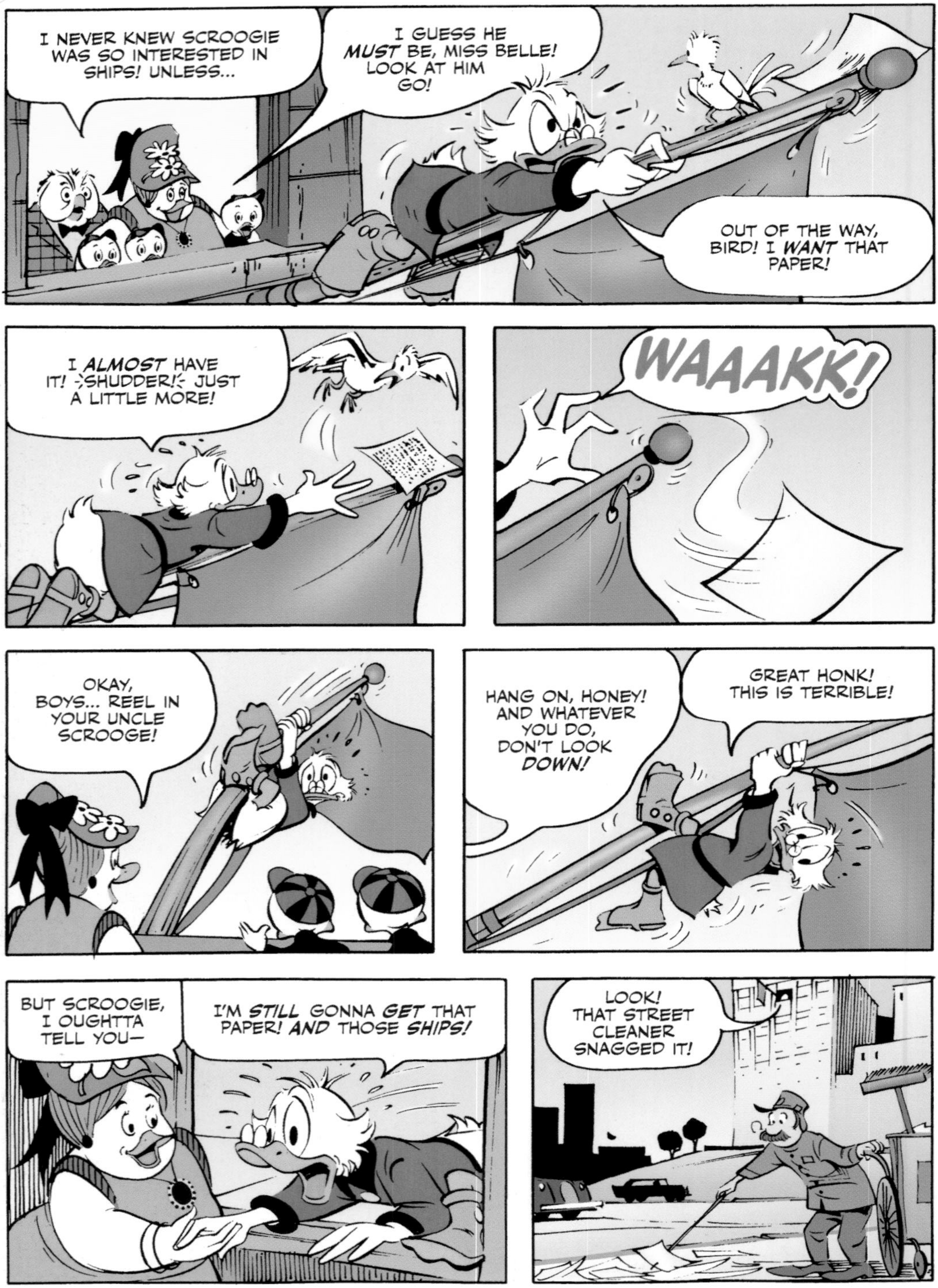

I NEVER KNEW SCROOGIE WAS SO INTERESTED IN SHIPS! UNLESS...
I GUESS HE *MUST* BE, MISS BELLE! LOOK AT HIM GO!
OUT OF THE WAY, BIRD! I *WANT* THAT PAPER!
I *ALMOST* HAVE IT! *SHUDDER!* JUST A LITTLE MORE!
WAAAKK!
OKAY, BOYS... REEL IN YOUR UNCLE SCROOGE!
HANG ON, HONEY! AND WHATEVER YOU DO, DON'T LOOK *DOWN!*
GREAT HONK! THIS IS TERRIBLE!
BUT SCROOGIE, I OUGHTTA TELL YOU—
I'M *STILL* GONNA *GET* THAT PAPER! *AND* THOSE *SHIPS!*
LOOK! THAT STREET CLEANER SNAGGED IT!

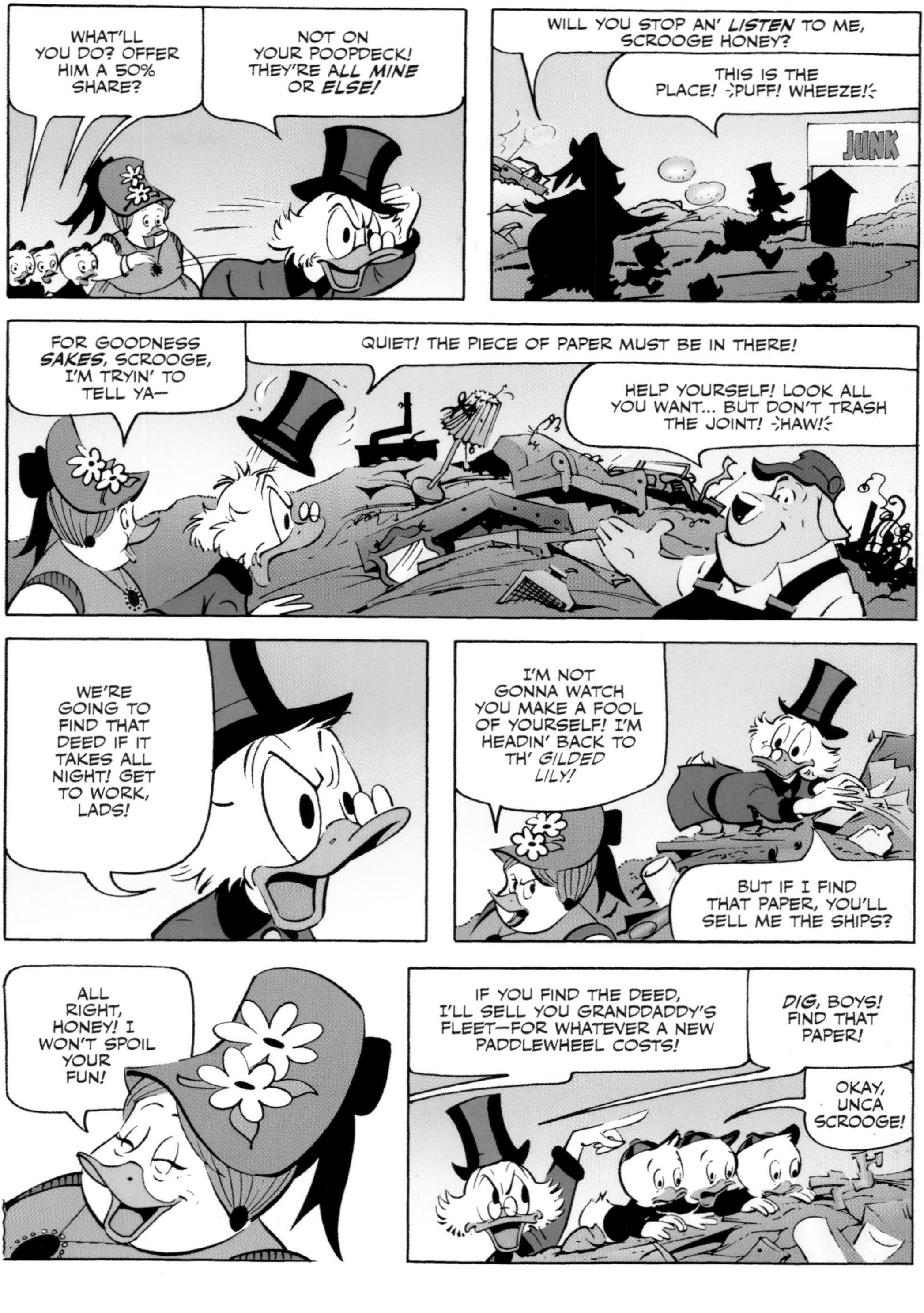
WHAT'LL YOU DO? OFFER HIM A 50% SHARE?
NOT ON YOUR POOPDECK! THEY'RE ALL *MINE* OR *ELSE!*
WILL YOU STOP AN' *LISTEN* TO ME, SCROOGE HONEY?
THIS IS THE PLACE! -PUFF! WHEEZE!-
JUNK
FOR GOODNESS *SAKES*, SCROOGE, I'M TRYIN' TO TELL YA—
QUIET! THE PIECE OF PAPER MUST BE IN THERE!
HELP YOURSELF! LOOK ALL YOU WANT... BUT DON'T TRASH THE JOINT! -HAW!-
WE'RE GOING TO FIND THAT DEED IF IT TAKES ALL NIGHT! GET TO WORK, LADS!
I'M NOT GONNA WATCH YOU MAKE A FOOL OF YOURSELF! I'M HEADIN' BACK TO TH' *GILDED LILY!*
BUT IF I FIND THAT PAPER, YOU'LL SELL ME THE SHIPS?
ALL RIGHT, HONEY! I WON'T SPOIL YOUR FUN!
IF YOU FIND THE DEED, I'LL SELL YOU GRANDDADDY'S FLEET—FOR WHATEVER A NEW PADDLEWHEEL COSTS!
DIG, BOYS! FIND THAT PAPER!
OKAY, UNCA SCROOGE!

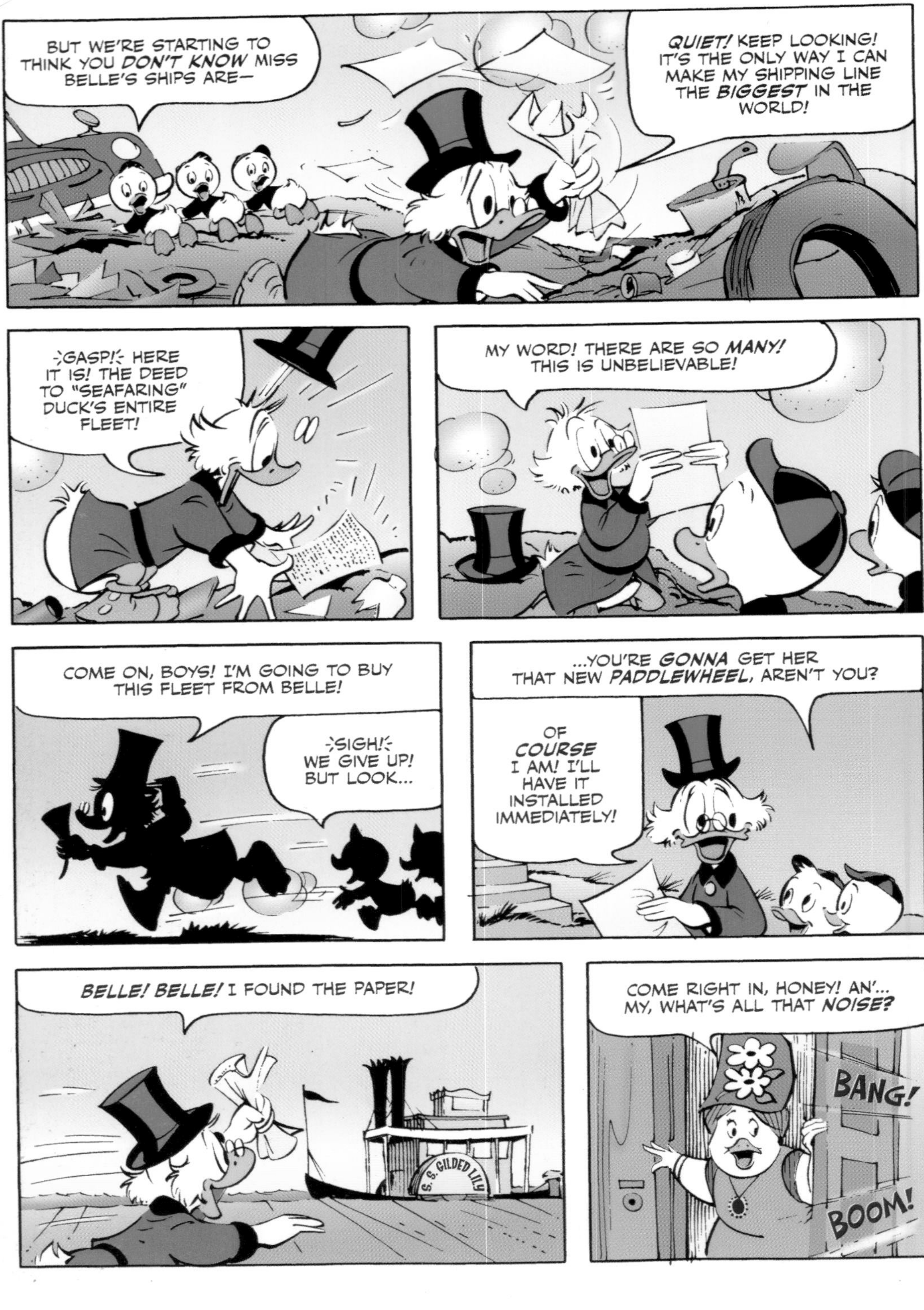

BUT WE'RE STARTING TO THINK YOU DON'T KNOW MISS BELLE'S SHIPS ARE—
QUIET! KEEP LOOKING! IT'S THE ONLY WAY I CAN MAKE MY SHIPPING LINE THE BIGGEST IN THE WORLD!
GASP! HERE IT IS! THE DEED TO "SEAFARING" DUCK'S ENTIRE FLEET!
MY WORD! THERE ARE SO MANY! THIS IS UNBELIEVABLE!
COME ON, BOYS! I'M GOING TO BUY THIS FLEET FROM BELLE!
SIGH! WE GIVE UP! BUT LOOK...
...YOU'RE GONNA GET HER THAT NEW PADDLEWHEEL, AREN'T YOU?
OF COURSE I AM! I'LL HAVE IT INSTALLED IMMEDIATELY!
BELLE! BELLE! I FOUND THE PAPER!
S. S. GILDED LILY
COME RIGHT IN, HONEY! AN'... MY, WHAT'S ALL THAT NOISE?
BANG!
BOOM!

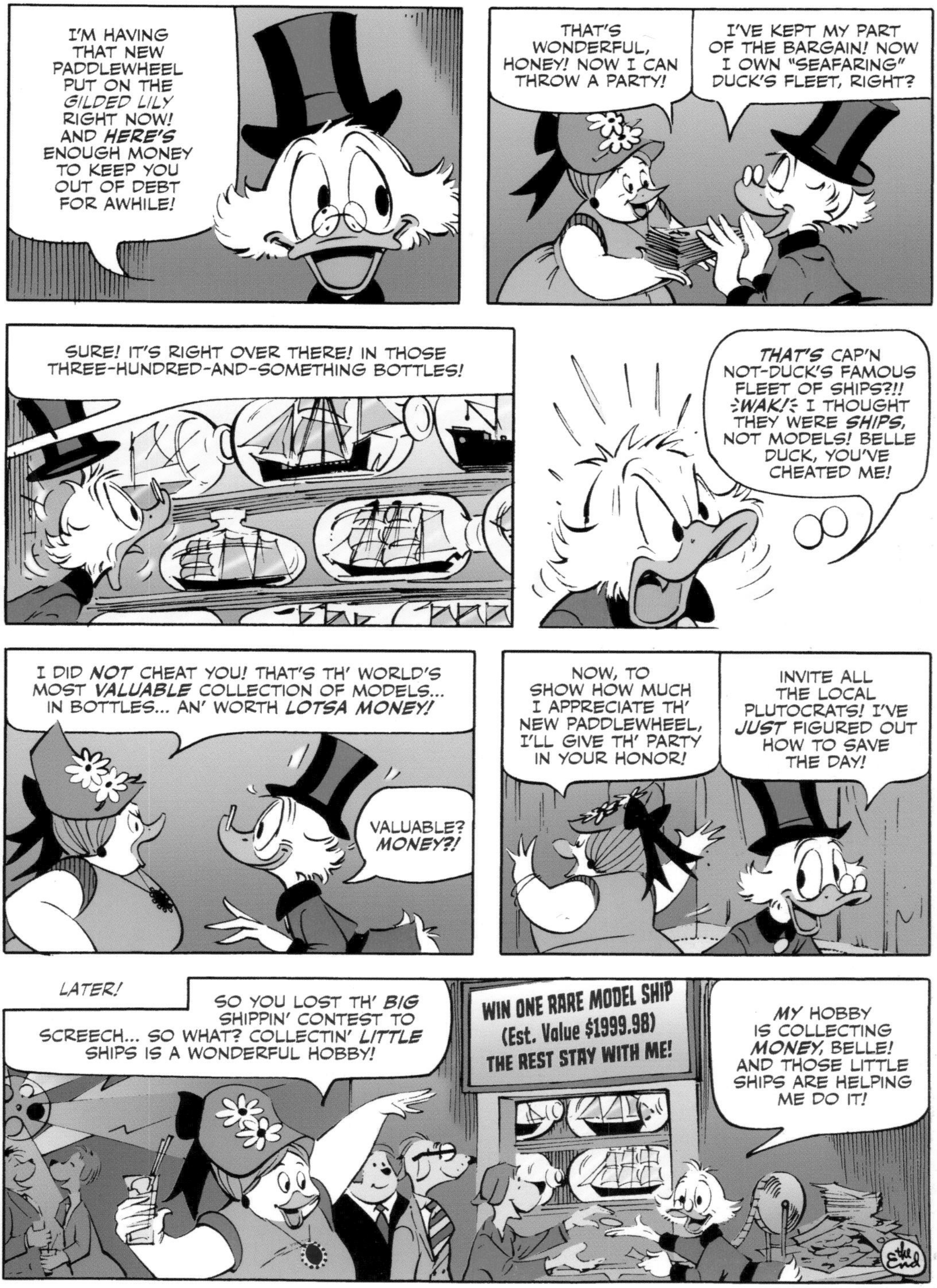
I'M HAVING THAT NEW PADDLEWHEEL PUT ON THE GILDED LILY RIGHT NOW! AND HERE'S ENOUGH MONEY TO KEEP YOU OUT OF DEBT FOR AWHILE!
THAT'S WONDERFUL, HONEY! NOW I CAN THROW A PARTY!
I'VE KEPT MY PART OF THE BARGAIN! NOW I OWN "SEAFARING" DUCK'S FLEET, RIGHT?
SURE! IT'S RIGHT OVER THERE! IN THOSE THREE-HUNDRED-AND-SOMETHING BOTTLES!
THAT'S CAP'N NOT-DUCK'S FAMOUS FLEET OF SHIPS?!! WAK! I THOUGHT THEY WERE SHIPS, NOT MODELS! BELLE DUCK, YOU'VE CHEATED ME!
I DID NOT CHEAT YOU! THAT'S TH' WORLD'S MOST VALUABLE COLLECTION OF MODELS... IN BOTTLES... AN' WORTH LOTSA MONEY!
VALUABLE? MONEY?!
NOW, TO SHOW HOW MUCH I APPRECIATE TH' NEW PADDLEWHEEL, I'LL GIVE TH' PARTY IN YOUR HONOR!
INVITE ALL THE LOCAL PLUTOCRATS! I'VE JUST FIGURED OUT HOW TO SAVE THE DAY!
LATER!
SO YOU LOST TH' BIG SHIPPIN' CONTEST TO SCREECH... SO WHAT? COLLECTIN' LITTLE SHIPS IS A WONDERFUL HOBBY!
WIN ONE RARE MODEL SHIP (Est. Value $1999.98) THE REST STAY WITH ME!
MY HOBBY IS COLLECTING MONEY, BELLE! AND THOSE LITTLE SHIPS ARE HELPING ME DO IT!
the End

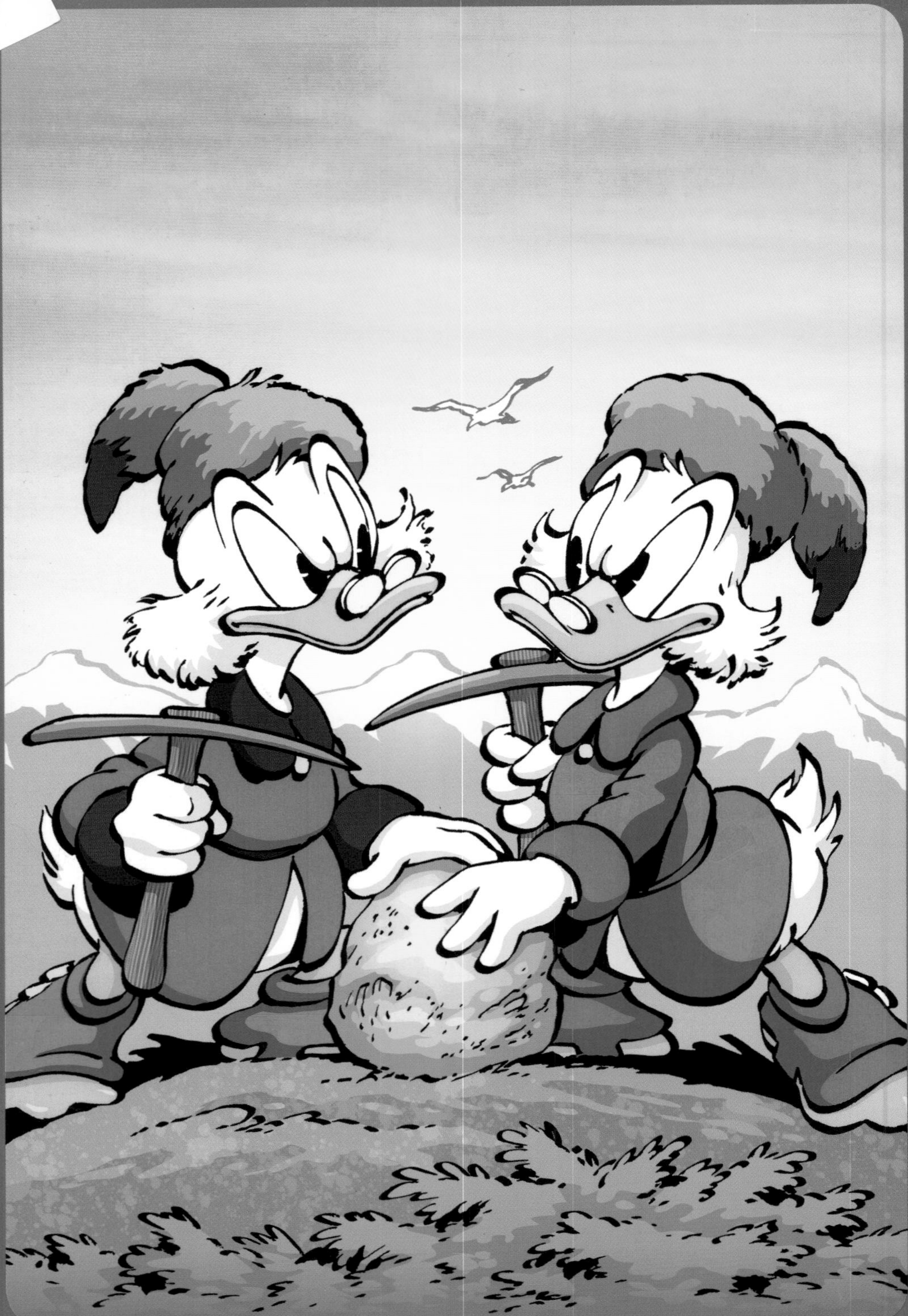

Art by Marco Rota, Colors by Ronda Pattison

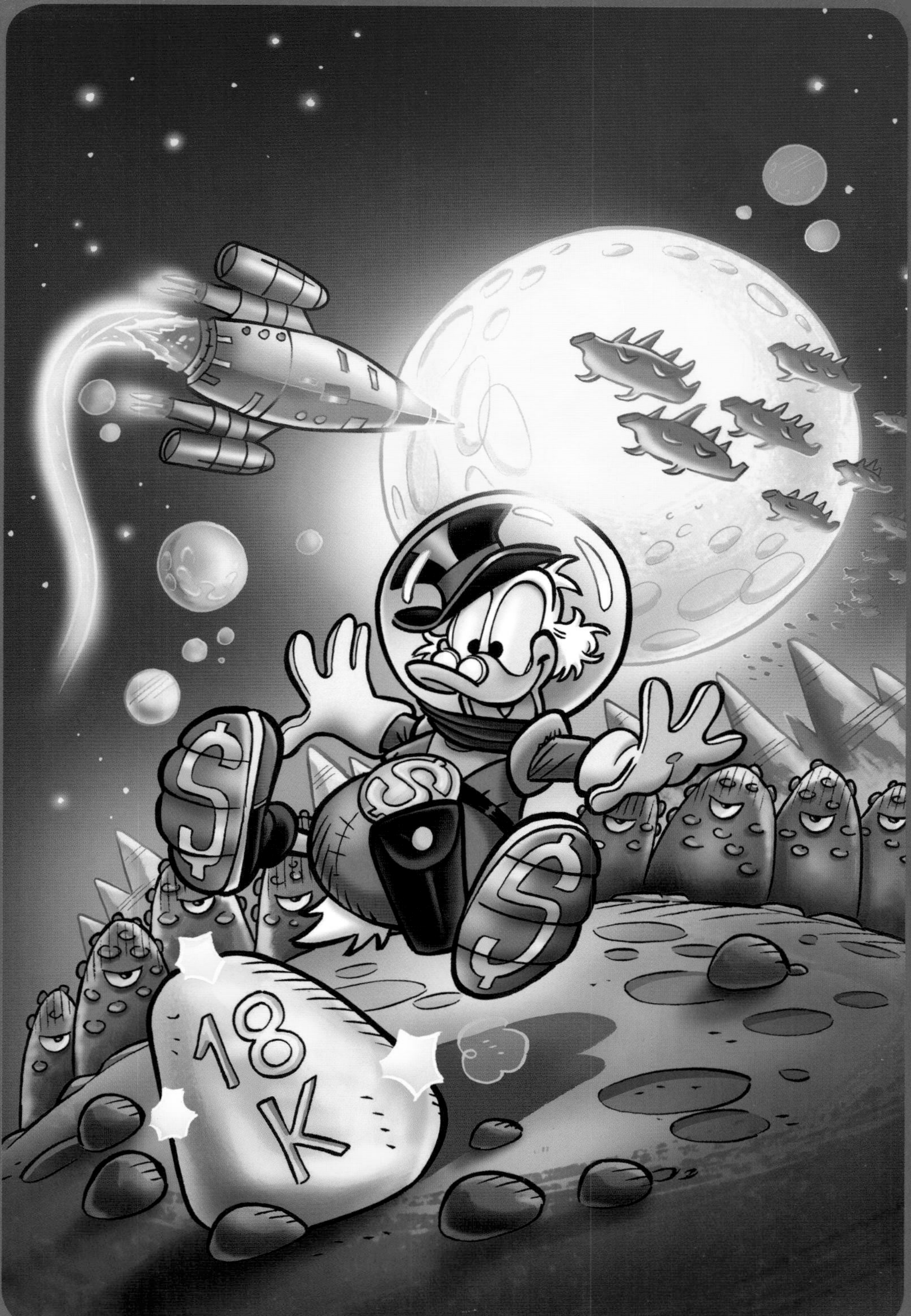
18
K

Art by Marco Gervasio, Colors by Marco Colletti

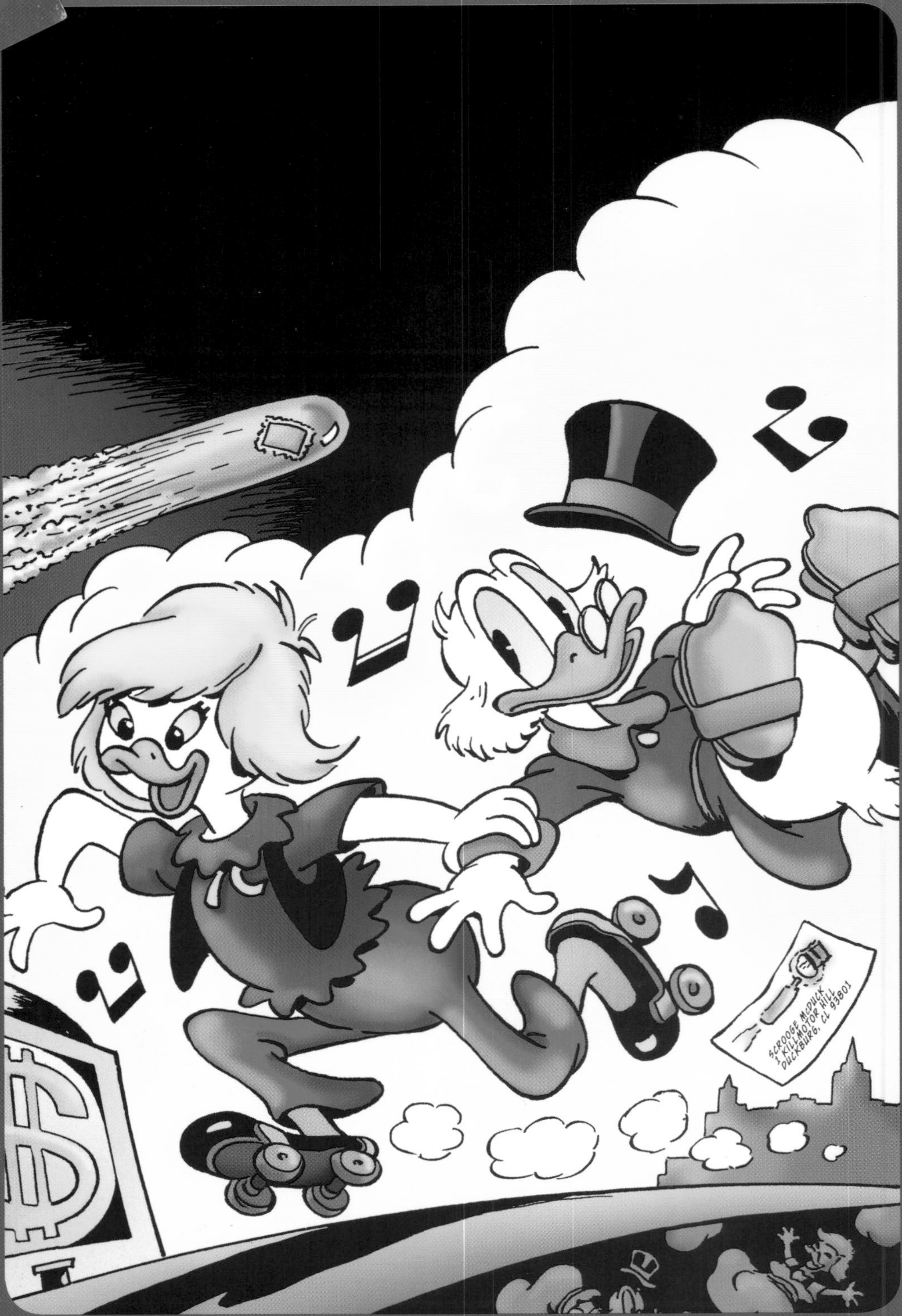
SCROOGE McDUCK
1 KILLMOTOR HILL
DUCKBURG, CL 93801

Art by Marco Rota, Colors by Disney Italia with David Gerstein

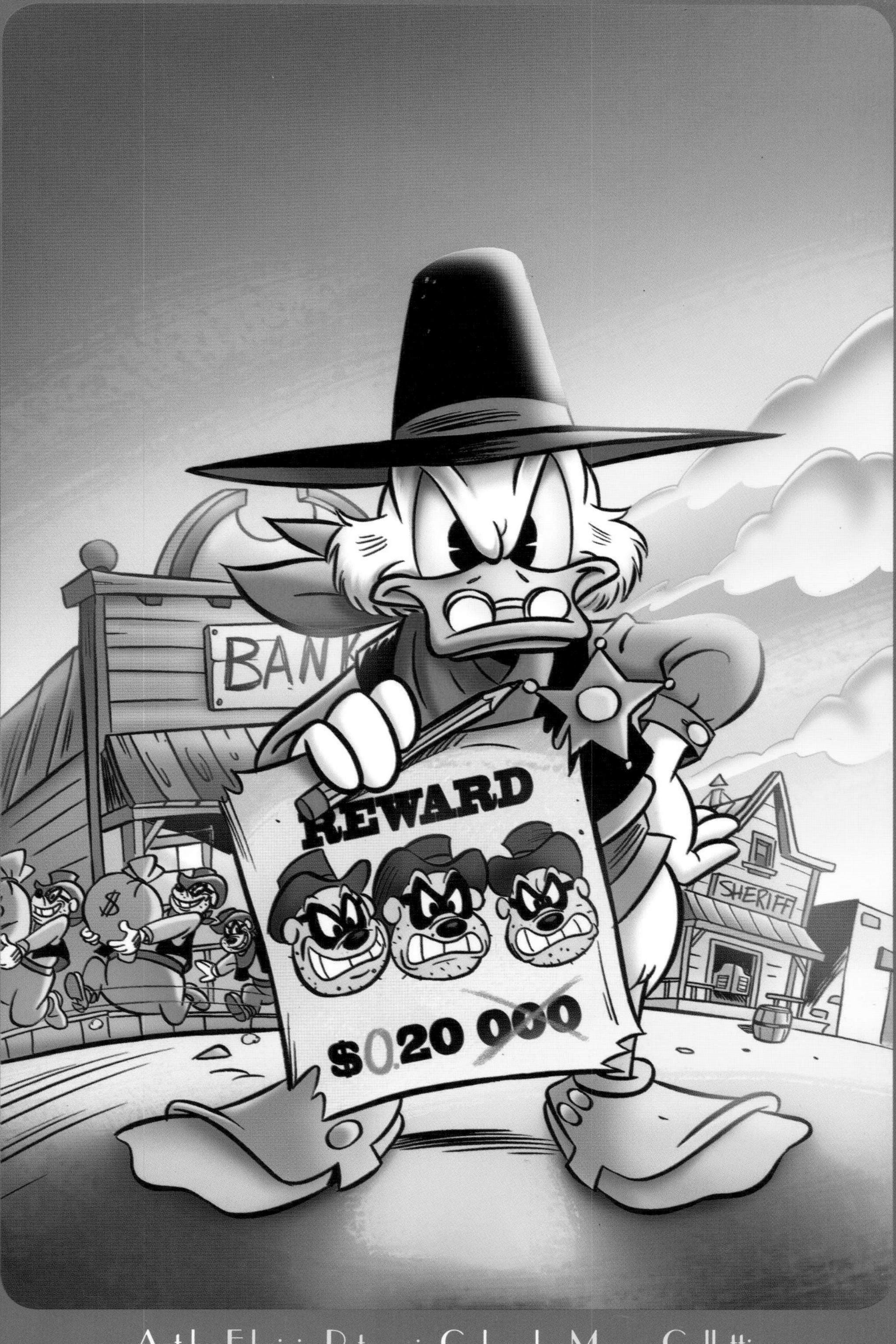
BANK
REWARD
SHERIFF
$0.20 000

Art by Fabrizio Petrossi, Colors by Marco Colletti

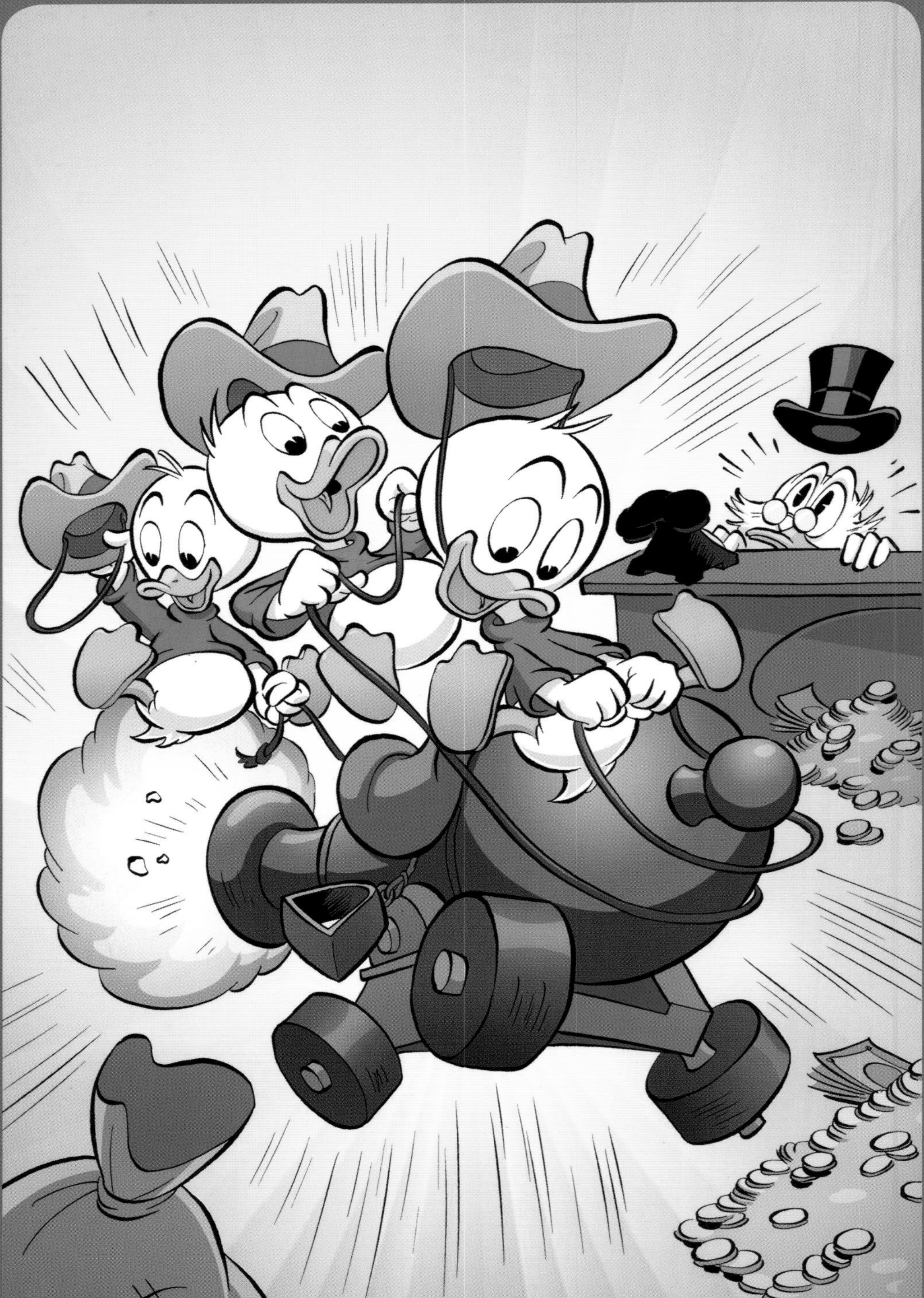

By Gaute Moe (concept) and Ulrich Schroeder (art), Colors by Ronda Pattison

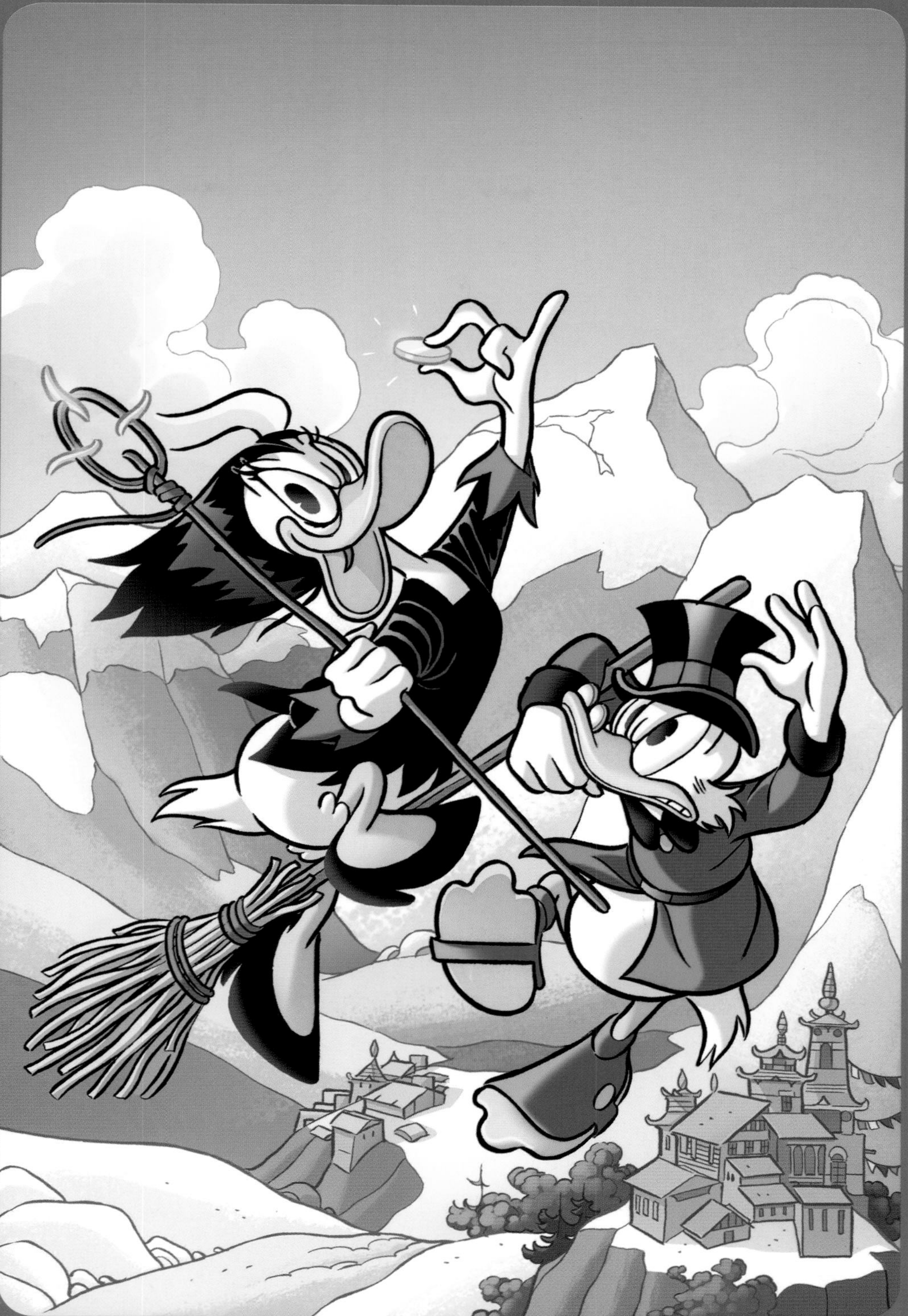

Art by Andrea Freccero, Colors by Mario Perrotta

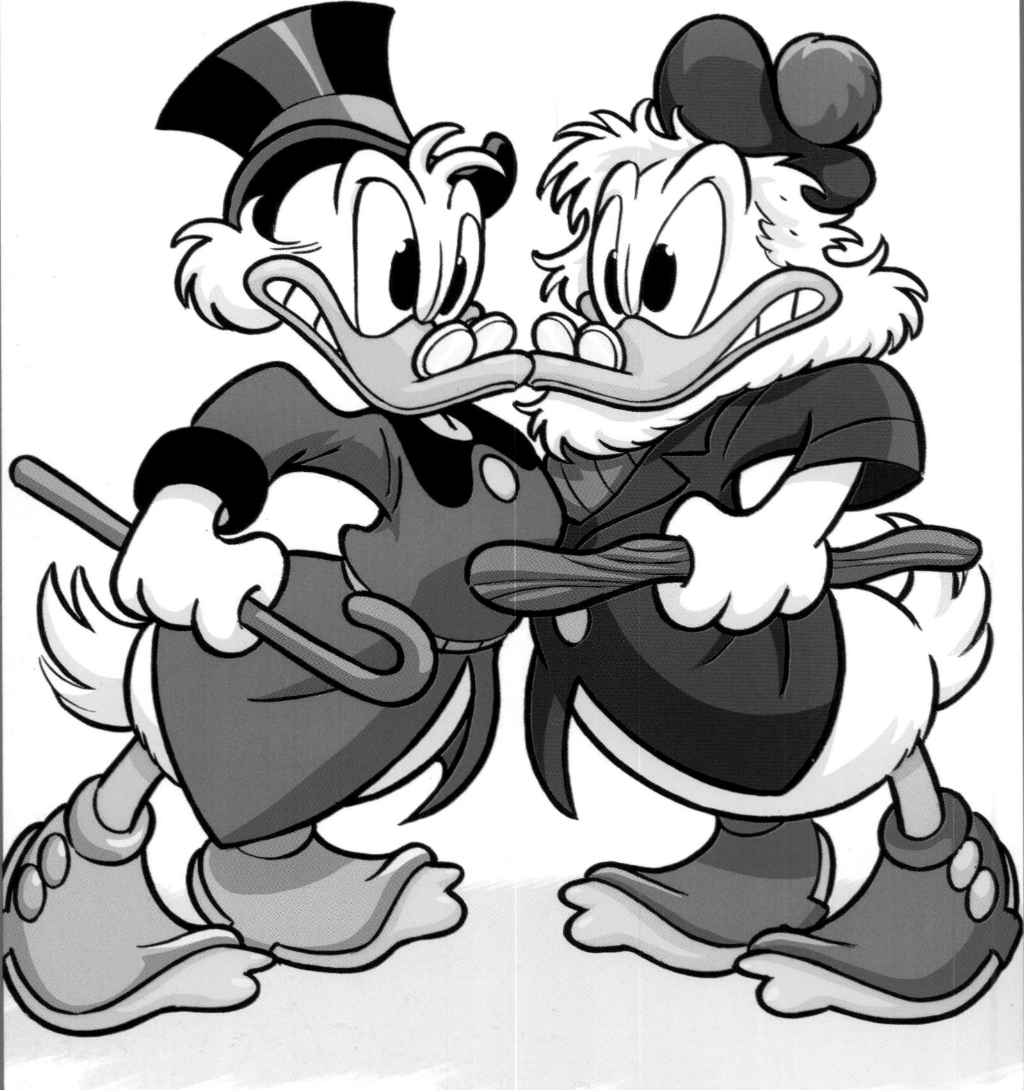
Art by Andrea Freccero, Colors by Ronda Pattison

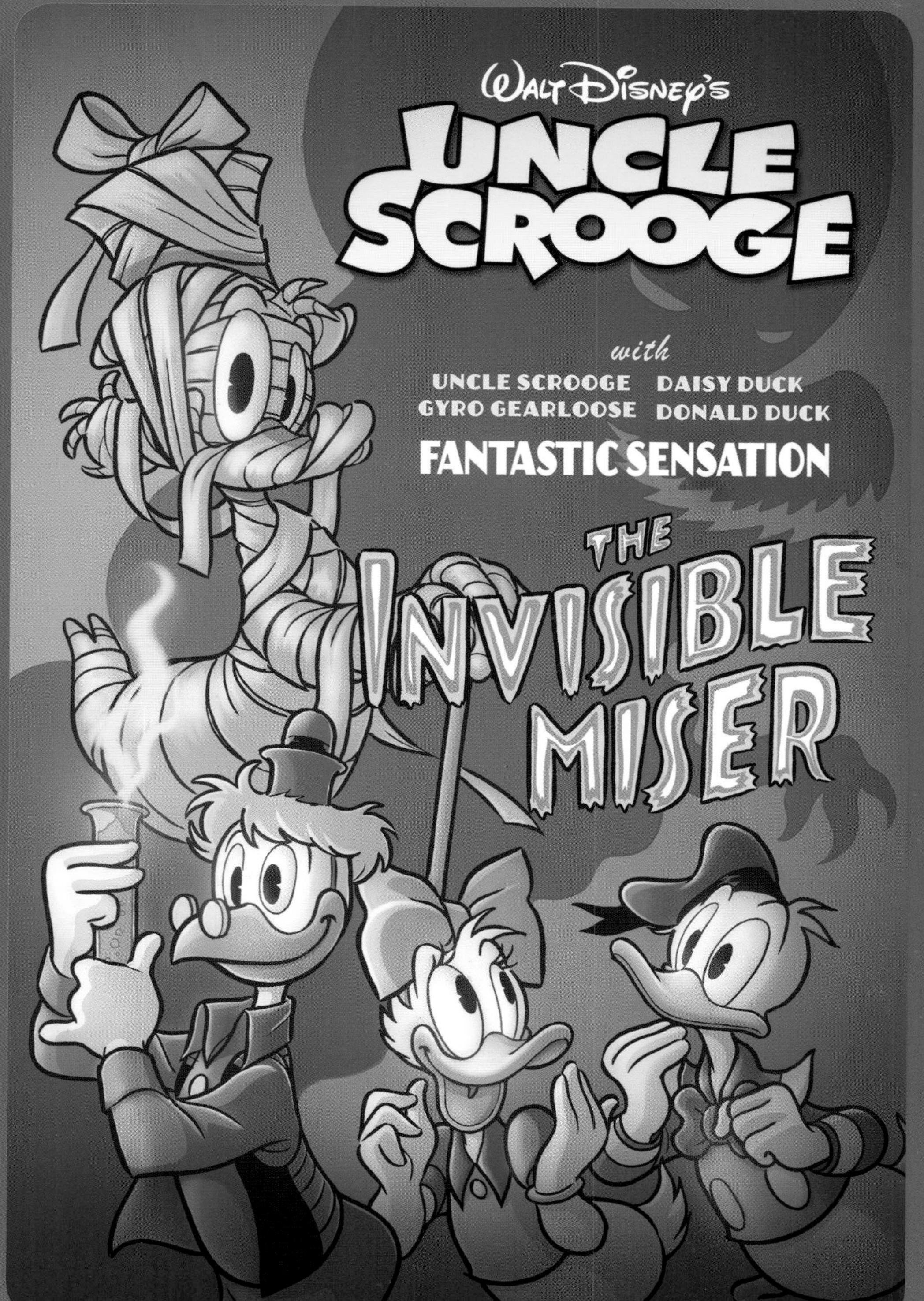
Walt Disney's
UNCLE SCROOGE
with
UNCLE SCROOGE
DAISY DUCK
GYRO GEARLOOSE
DONALD DUCK
FANTASTIC SENSATION
THE INVISIBLE MISER

Art by Andrea Freccero, Colors by Fabio LoMonaco